Rambling Rose

"Bold and candid.
A memorable reading experience."
Chicago Sun-Times

"An exact evocation of the old South . . .
Funny and moving—
Quite a novel"
Herman Wouk

"One of the most hilarious novels
of the year!"
New York Daily News

"*Rambling Rose* is magnificent!"
Christopher Isherwood

"A love-offering,
a valentine to a towheaded country girl
with cornflower-blue eyes"
The New York Times

"His best novel yet!"
Cosmopolitan

CALDER
WILLINGHAM

AVON BOOKS NEW YORK

Portions of the lyrics of the song "Ramblin' Rose" used by permission of ATV-Kirshner for Sweco Music Corporation. The line on page v is from the poem "Nevertheless" from *The Collected Poems of Marianne Moore,* copyright 1944 by Marianne Moore. Renewed 1972 by Marianne Moore. Reprinted by permission of the publisher, The Macmillan Company.

AVON BOOKS
A division of
The Hearst Corporation
1350 Avenue of the Americas
New York, New York 10019

Published by arrangement with the author
Library of Congress Catalog Card Number: 72-83351
ISBN: 0-380-76683-3

First Avon Books Printing: October 1991

Printed in the U.S.A.

RA 10 9 8 7 6 5 4 3 2 1

"What sap went through that little thread
to make the cherry red!"

MARIANNE MOORE

For D.B. and W.

In apology for the feebleness of memory, in greater apology for a sad dearth here of the unlimited creative power of life, as M. might say, and in even greater apology for the pure sheer mischief of it all, which will be fully recognized and deplored by D., this work—

—a compound of above-said memory, imagination and pure sheer mischief intended to reveal what *might* have happened if a girl like R. had ever come to our house in 1935 with dusty shoes, runs in her stockings and cornflower eyes—

—is hereby dedicated and inscribed, with love and continuing affection and bittersweet nostalgia for days long ago, to D.B. and W., my sister and my brother, in the firm hope that whatever this work's pitiful errors, they will reject merely the inconsequential scribble itself and never turn their backs,

and look away from

C.W.

A Necessary Note to the Reader

I hate notes to the reader, especially necessary notes. But as can readily be perceived from the dedication of this book and no doubt also from its contents, this novel is unlike others I have written. I cannot say this story is made up of wholly imaginary characters and that any resemblance to living or real persons is entirely coincidental. That would be a lie, and to tell a lie is a sin. The major characters of this book—the boy, his father, his mother, his sister and brother—are intended to be based on real people who lived in this world. But may I hasten to make one exception? I hope so; it would seem necessary from an ethical standpoint if from no other.

Therefore, let me say unequivocally and even humbly that the girls who worked for my family in the Great Depression were of excellent moral character and bore no resemblance whatsoever to the title character of this novel.

CALDER WILLINGHAM

Shingle Camp Hill
April 1, 1972

Contents

1

Rose comes to our house

I WILL CALL her Rose. On a broiling August afternoon in 1935 when I was close to thirteen years of age, a big tow-haired country girl came to our house with dusty shoes, runs in her stockings and a twinkle in her cornflower eyes. For a considerable period of time, she created in our family, and elsewhere, in the words of my father: "One hell of a damnable commotion." It was not her intention, I am sure, to cause any such commotion; as my mother often said, there was no trace of harm in her, a kinder or more good-hearted girl never lived. Unfortunately, however, she had one fault, one failing: Rose rambled.

In earlier years, like most middle-class families of the Deep South, we had hired black help to do household work. My mother, however, was a rather curious and unusual woman and she had a theory it was a criminal exploitation to hire anyone to do such work, and especially criminal to hire any black person. "Why, it's a remnant of slavery days," she said. "It's disgusting and criminal to exploit those girls and women like that. One of these days the South will pay a bitter price, a price of blood and pain, mark my words."

Nevertheless, since my mother at that time was engaged in writing the thesis for a master's degree she'd almost earned some years before, it was necessary to have some help around the house. It was also necessary because my mother, to be very candid about it, was a bit of a screwball, a trifle out of touch with the cruel world out there, from time to time *non compos mentis*, isolated by deafness, hypersensitivity and other afflictions.

Mother decided therefore to find some homeless and unfortunate white girl and take her into the house not merely as a servant but as a companion to herself and the entire family. The girl would eat with us and be treated as a friend, as a guest in our home. In this way, Mother figured, she would not be exploiting the girl criminally.

The girl would of course do cooking and housework and help take care of me and my younger sister and little brother, in exchange for her room and board and twenty-five dollars a month, which was fair pay in the Great Depression—but that, according to Mother, was merely a swap and not criminal exploitation. Simply hiring a girl was immoral, but taking her into your home and heart was moral. Such was Mother's reasoning. As I said, she was a rather curious and unusual woman.

To find an appropriate homeless and unfortunate girl in 1935 was hardly a great challenge. My father had thought of taking an ad in the paper, but before he could do so he heard from a traveling man of a good-natured and cheerful and highly unfortunate girl who was working for a farm family down near Gadsden, Alabama, not too many miles from Glenville, and this girl seemed suitable. Not only was she unfortunate, she was soon to be homeless, because the farmer for whom she was working could not afford her, the price of cotton was way down and she was one more mouth to feed and had to go.

But she had nowhere to go, nowhere on earth to go, except back to Birmingham where some scoundrel man had tried to induce her to become a prostitute. This I believe was the aspect of her story that impressed my father. The girl had showed up on the doorstep of the Gadsden farmer with a battered suitcase one day. She had once lived, she said, on a poor tenant farm not far off, but all her folks now were dead. She begged for a job, any kind of job, she would work hard for no pay because they were trying in Birmingham to make her do something she couldn't do, they had threatened to beat her and even disfigure her. The Gadsden farmer, who was modestly well-to-do, did remember the girl's father. The man was a drunken, bitterly poor tenant farmer with one mule and several motherless wretched little children, one of whom must have been this girl herself.

The traveling salesman who told my father this story was a first cousin of the Gadsden farmer and he had seen and met this girl. Her name was Rose and she was a big blonde buxom girl of about nineteen years with a cheerful disposition, a hard worker, affectionate to children. She knew a little about cooking and housework and would be very grateful to any family that would take her in and protect her and give her a home. The girl really needed protection, she was a perfect victim of predatory men—she was very naïve, had almost no education whatever, and although a big strapping country girl she was very attractive, with an excellent figure and pretty blonde hair and blue eyes.

I did a great amount of eavesdropping at thirteen and I overheard my father decide in a conference with my mother to hire this girl recommended by the traveling man, who was one of the guests in Mother's hotel which Daddy managed. "Of course, now," he said, "the girl comes from the worst possible type of dirt farm and God knows what kind of childhood she had, probably a childhood of pure sheer hell. Charlie says she's completely ignorant, can barely write her name. But he says her basic intelligence is good, she can cook a little, works hard, has a happy, cheerful nature and likes children. And I admire the fact she wouldn't be a whore. I never could stand a whore, somehow or other. Just can't stand them, they rub me the wrong way, whores. I think I'll call up that farmer in Gadsden long distance and offer the unfortunate, homeless creature a job and save her from those scoundrels in Birmingham, unless you have some objections."

My mother had no objections, she too liked what she'd heard of the girl, and thus Rose was hired sight unseen by a long-distance call. It seemed reasonable enough; a trip down to Gadsden was inconvenient and Daddy had had a firsthand report on her. However, before he made it final my father did express certain doubts about this unknown girl and he did investigate her a little, or, as he put it, sniffed around a little to smell out the facts. At supper one night he said to us all:

"Well, she sounds fine and dandy, this Miss Rosebud.

However, a girl brought up on a tenant farm in dire poverty might not have the same *outlook* we ourselves have. I will probably hire her, but before I do I want to do a bit of sniffing around to smell out the facts and get a firm grasp of the situation. Definitely. Oh yes, definitely. I'll put it as a bald, stark proposition to this farmer and I'll find a polite way to put it to the girl herself. After all, we don't want some kind of hotcha character coming up here and ruffling the waters. Life is too short for that type of whoopee, much too short for it. I'll put it to them as a bald, stark proposition, I'll lay it before them frankly and candidly."

Therefore, when Daddy called the Gadsden farmer on the phone, he asked: "And what, sir, is this girl's moral character?"

Excellent! said the farmer. Perfect! Irreproachable! She was one of the most virtuous and well-behaved girls he'd ever encountered and his wife would say the same thing. She was almost saintly in her restraint insofar as the opposite sex was concerned, she seemed to have no interest at all in boys or men, or practically none. She was a moral jewel, no less.

"Um-*hmmm,*" said Daddy pensively. Later, he said: "The son of a bitch was trying to get rid of her, damn him!" But at this time he said pensively: "Um-*hmmm.* Put the young lady on. I'd like a word with her."

When Daddy got Rose herself on the phone he said: "All right, honey, now I am Mr. Hillyer and I am thinking of offering you a job. What? Speak up, honey, I can't hear you. Speak up, you don't have to be afraid of me . . . now wait a minute, wait a minute, don't start crying! Now *wait* a minute, hold the phone, control yourself, there's nothing to cry about, I just want to ask you one question! And it's very simple, very very simple. Are you all right? Can you hear me? Good. Good, dear, fine, fine. Now you understand we have three immature children here and don't be offended, but the question frankly and candidly is this: do you run around in the dark of the moon, are you a wild hotcha character or do you behave yourself? Now don't misunderstand me, honey, I don't mind your going out on dates on your days off, that is only natural. What I want to know is are you a wild hotcha character or not, because we don't want a hotcha character around here, we can't afford it, dear. Now just give me a straight answer and calm down. Now. Now, now, dear. Quit crying because I'm almost certainly going to hire you anyhow, almost totally certainly. Now quit crying, dear, you don't have to tell me anything at all, forget that I asked it . . . just calm yourself, dear, all is well, the little crab apples are everywhere and they are happy, and you should be happy, too, because you are coming up to Glenville on a bus real soon if you'll just give me a dim assurance you're not a hotcha type character . . . you know we do have three small innocent children here. . . .''

I could not of course hear what was said on the other end of the wire, but I was told Rose assured Daddy she was not a hotcha type character—far from it, miles from it, in fact she didn't even want to go out at all, she'd be perfectly happy just to stay at home.

Later, much later, Daddy said: ''I had doubts, that tenant farm, that awful horrible tenant farm the depths of which are beyond human reckoning, and what was she doing in Birmingham in the first place, if she was totally innocent how did those scoundrels get after her? But if there is one thing in this world I can't fight it's a woman's tears. I can't fight a crying woman and what is more that damned farmer deceived me with the greatest weapon of them all, the truth. That's what the son of a bitch did, he deceived me with the truth.''

It was a fact Rose had fought off one or more scoundrels in Birmingham who wanted to force her into a house of ill repute. It was a fact she walked miles on bleeding feet and hitchhiked rides on wagons to get away from them. It was a fact she'd had nothing to eat for two days when she reached the farmer's house and a fact that she fainted from hunger on his porch. It was a fact she was not and never could possibly be a whore. All of that was the truth, but a lot else the farmer said was less than wholly accurate.

So it was that a number of unfortunate, homeless girls arrived at our house in the Great Depression, and so it was that this particular one whom I call Rose arrived on a hot August afternoon in 1935 with a broken cardboard suitcase tied with a string. The understanding was she was supposed to go from the bus station to the hotel and Daddy would drive her in the Ford out to the house. But for some reason she didn't do this; instead she walked in the broiling heat two and a half miles all the way out to our house on the Summerton Road, carrying her battered suitcase and getting dust on her worn-out shoes.

I saw her through the screen door of the front porch coming up the driveway very slowly, suitcase in hand and her blonde hair almost white in the shade of the big oaks. This was the new girl, the unfortunate and homeless girl who had come to be a companion to Mother and a friend to us all. Little did I know what a friend she would be!

Arms folded with dignity like Daddy, lacking only his straw hat tilted backward and a little bit to the side, I stood on the porch and watched her slowly climb the steps in the burning sunshine. She was sweaty, exhausted, pale. She was also badly frightened; the prospect of going to live and work in the home of what she believed to be "rich folks" had her in a state of trembling anxiety. Halfway up the steps she hesitated, brushed perspiration with the back of her hand from her forehead and the bridge of her nose, which had a faint and not unattractive sprinkling of freckles, put her hand on her hip and gave me a tentative, unsure smile. Nervous as she was, the gesture, the hand on her hip and the way she held back her shoulders despite her tiredness and the heat, had a certain style. I was old enough at thirteen to notice it, and I was also old enough to notice her full breasts strained against the material of her cheap, tacky little dress—although, to be sure, I did not think of them as breasts but rather as "titties," since the word "breast" in my vocabulary then was used only to describe a cut of fried chicken. This new girl had great titties and I already had plans to peep on her in the bathroom and get a better look at them, but as it happened I never did.

"Hello," she said in a shaking voice. "I'm Rose, and I've come to live with you and your fam'ly. What's your name? What do they call you?"

"Lots of things," I replied. "Mostly, Buddy."

Her smile became less tentative, less unsure. "Buddy. Well, now, that's a nice name, Buddy. I like it." As she continued up the porch steps her face turned briefly solemn, ceremonial, and she held out her hand. "I am real pleased to meet you, Buddy. And I am real pleased to be here, too, you bet, because my feet *sure* do hurt. Hey look, do you think you got a drink of cold ice water somewhere?''

''Sure,'' I said. ''Let me take your suitcase.''

''You're sweet,'' she answered, with a smile that was not tentative or unsure at all, and as she smiled a little twinkle came into her blue eyes. Despite myself I liked her immediately. At thirteen, I was an insufferably precocious, mean, hostile and for the most part treacherous child, but I liked her immediately and very much. It surprised me then; later I took it for granted. If there was one thing Rose could do, it was establish swift rapport with almost any boy or man.

I might say parenthetically that ''my feet *sure* do hurt'' was one of her classic gambits, one of the great icebreakers she used many times to devastating effect: ''Well, now, Buddy, I just sidle up alongside 'em, and give out a deep little kind of groan and say, 'Ohhh-hh, my feet *sure* do hurt,' and next thing we're in a big conversation, and before you know it we're the best of friends. How about that?''

If there was another thing she could do, it was establish physical contact with the innocence of a child. Rose touched people. As we went across the porch she put an arm across my shoulders with a total unselfconsciousness and said: ''Is your Momma around? I was supposed to go to that hotel, but I didn't. Where's your Daddy, is he at that hotel?''

''Mother's taking a nap,'' I said, ''but I'll wake her up.''

''Oh, no, no, no—don't wake her up! Where's your Daddy?''

She was afraid of Daddy, very afraid of him, that was why she'd walked all the way out to the house rather than go to the hotel as she'd been supposed to do. I took her back to the kitchen and she told me all about her bus trip from Gadsden, a thrilling experience, and she drank three glasses of ice water and said she'd never been so thirsty in her life.

So it was the girl I call Rose, a name which suits and fits her better than her own, came to our house in 1935 long, long ago in the midst of the Great Depression with dusty shoes, runs in her stockings and a mysterious twinkle full of life in her cornflower eyes.

2

Rose falls madly in love with Daddy

AFTER ROSE FINISHED her third glass of ice water, I went to Mother's bedroom-sitting room at the front of the house and told her the new girl had arrived. Mother was already awake from her nap; she sat in her "study" armchair drinking one of her three daily Coca-Colas and smoking one of her seven daily cigarettes. She held the cigarette in a bobby pin in order to smoke it down to a tiny stub and as she smoked she leaned her head back and peered off through narrowed eyes into eternity, relishing the combined sensuality of Coca-Cola and Philip Morris.

"Wonderful," she said, sitting forward. "What's she like, Brother? What is your impression of her?"

"She talks a great deal," I said. "But she's very pretty, I like her. I don't think she's nineteen, she looks about seventeen to me. Maybe she's nineteen though, sometimes blondes look younger than they are. She's very towhaired and has the bluest eyes you ever saw, and very white teeth. She smiles all the time. I like her."

"Hmm," said Mother. "That's very interesting. What other impressions do you have?"

"Well, she has a *real* good figure. She's big, about five nine and must weigh a hundred and thirty or more. She is very strong, she could almost beat up Daddy if she wanted to. But she wouldn't, she's very girlish or womanish, if you know what I mean. She wouldn't hurt anybody, this girl. She couldn't."

"Your impression is *very* reassuring, Brother. I sensed

that this was what the girl was like already, but I am glad to have it reconfirmed."

"You mean confirmed, Mother. I didn't confirm it before. I would have had to confirm it previously, in order for it to be reconfirmed."

"All right, all right," said Mother. "Doll and Waski are upstairs taking their nap, you go get them and bring them down to the living room. Where is the girl?"

"In the kitchen drinking all the ice water in Glenville. She walked out here, she didn't go by the hotel."

"*Walked,* in that heat? It's a wonder she hasn't got sunstroke. I'll telephone Daddy and ask him to come right out. Now you hurry up and get Doll Baby and Waski."

In the living room, Mother "introduced" us all to Rose while we waited for Daddy. She began with my little brother, who was very small, about five years of age.

"Rose, this is Waski. His real name is Warren but we call him Waski. He doesn't like it much and I suppose someday we'll have to stop calling him that."

"You can stop it right now," said Waski. "I sure don't like it much, and I don't like being called that 'Wa-Wa' either, that's worse."

"When he was a baby we called him 'Wa-Wa,' a baby name, you know. You will find him a very good boy. His brother can be bad and so can his sister, but Waski is a very good boy. And as you can see he's beautiful."

"Oh, Mother," said Waski, "cut it out."

"There are plenty of girls who would give thousands of dollars to have your auburn hair," said Mother. "It's even prettier than Brother's hair, almost. Beauty is beauty and that's all there is to it. Beauty is *there* and we have to recognize it. Now Rose, the little girl sitting across from you with the blue eyes is Doll Baby. She looks like an angel and she *is* an angel, but she can be a bad angel sometimes, a naughty angel, though her father won't believe it. He spoils her because he adores her too much, I have to fight that and help the child, because actually she has some wonderful qualities. Her real name is Frances, but we call her Dolly or Doll."

"I don't like it either," said Doll, "it's worse than Waski. I want to be called Fran."

"Daddy wouldn't hear of that," said Mother. "Now the red-haired boy you see sitting there, of course you have met him, he is my oldest son and my most brilliant child. Of course all children have great creative powers, but this one has practically no limits, he is very remarkable. But I don't want to rattle on and brag too much about my children, they say I brag too much about them, especially about Brother. Of course I only tell the truth, but am I boring you, Rose?"

Rose was staring at Mother with her lips apart and her blue eyes slightly popped. "Oh, no, Ma'am," she said in a feeble voice.

"Well, it's rather interesting about Brother, actually," said Mother. "I realized the remarkable thing he had when he was six weeks old. He looked at me and understood me, he knew exactly who I was. I know it sounds crazy but it's true. There's no doubt about it, he's very remarkable, he was born for the ministry and could move millions, but he doesn't know that yet. Mr. Hillyer and I call him Brother, but the children call him Buddy. I have to warn you about him, he can be very dangerous, there is an evil streak in him, a streak of pure sheer meanness that I can't understand. But at heart Brother is saintly and that is why he was born for the ministry even if he doesn't know it."

Rose hadn't caught on to Mother yet and she didn't know what on earth to make of her. She sat moistening her lips and swallowing nervously, her eyes a bit popped with apprehension as she gazed in awe at Mother. For once Rose had no words. She nodded speechlessly as Mother wandered on, covering the field of her remarkable and beautiful children. One thing Mother couldn't be accused of was modesty on behalf of the fruit of her womb.

As I have said, my mother was not fully in touch with the cruel world out there and from time to time she did tend to go off into what my father called "the fourth dimension." One of the ways she did this was by means of such mental or spiritual feats as imagining that a six-week-old baby could look at her and understand her. If that was possible, then it was very simple to ascribe all kinds of incredible qualities to that child and to her other children as well. The first child upon whom she focussed the burning rays of faith and belief would of course get the biggest dose of it. And fortunately and unfortunately that first child happened to be *me*. To be burdened all your life by the expectations of a cuckoo lady is no picnic, but then on the other hand I wonder if I would have ever left the South or written books if she hadn't told me I looked at her at six weeks of age and understood her. She was a curiosity, my mother—as Daddy would say, "A curiosity, son. That woman is a curiosity."

No, Mother was not fully in touch with the cruel world out there, and in a different way neither was Rose herself. Rose wasn't a brilliant screwball like Mother, she wasn't cuckoo in the same way, but she wasn't in touch with the cruel world and later it was a thing she and Mother had beautifully in common. Despite everything that had happened to Rose as a child and afterward—incest with a drunken father at eleven, a runaway at fourteen sick with both gonorrhea and, surprisingly, tuberculosis, a near-victim of a sadistic and murderous pimp at nineteen—despite all of that and more, it wasn't a cruel world in Rose's eyes. Like Mother, she refused to see the cruelty. Perhaps it was there, but she wouldn't look at it. Her answer to the pain, ugliness and terror of life was invariable. I often would say some outrageous, horrible thing to her to elicit the familiar response: "I don't hear you. I don't listen to such things and I don't pay them any mind, I just turn my back and look away." It was Mother's own philosophy and I am sure this shared world view was one of the basic reasons she and Rose later became so very close. Mother, beyond doubt, loved Rose more than any of us, as I think this narrative in time will fully reveal.

However, Rose didn't know what on earth to make of Mother that afternoon she arrived, and she sat popeyed with fright on the sofa as she waited for the dreaded Daddy to come stalking in, which he did after about fifteen minutes.

"Well, well, well," said Daddy. "So Miss Rosebud has arrived. Um-hmm. And you're all assembled here. Yes, indeed. Um-hmm."

Daddy stood in the doorway of the living room, straw hat on the back of his head and tilted a little bit to the side, a Glenville *News-Tribune* rolled tight in his hand and his hand on his hip, his mouth a thin line beneath his clipped moustache and his eyes a trifle red and glary. Pink lips apart, Rose starred at him in popeyed terror, her hands trembling on her lap and her knees quivering beneath her cheap and tacky little dress. His style over the telephone had thrown her completely, she'd never encountered anything like Daddy and she later told me she was so scared sitting there on the sofa she was sure she would wet her pants. However, she was soon to lose all her fear of him, every bit of it.

"Well, Rosebud," said Daddy, "now you are here, darling, and I swear to God graceful as the capital letter S. You will adorn our house, Rosebud, you will give a glow and shine to these old walls. If there's one thing I like to have around, it's a frizzy-haired blonde. Now, I assume Mrs. Hillyer and the children have introduced themselves and made your acquaintance, and so forth and so on?"

Rose could barely answer; her eyes were fixed on Daddy in utter rapt fascination. Finally, she whispered: "Yes, sir."

"All right. Now as head of this household I have a couple of remarks to make. It is my dear wife's belief, which I accept although I do not totally grasp it, that to hire a person to do household work is a criminal practice. Therefore, you are not here as a servant, you are here as a friend, as a guest and hopefully as a member of this family. You will eat your meals with us, you will share life itself with us—in love and harmony, dear Rosebud, in love and harmony. Now I want to say in formal language we are glad to welcome you to our home and I hope you find a safe haven here, I know you've had some troubles in your life. All we ask of you is that you do some cooking and housework as a sort of contribution to the family welfare, that you assist Mrs. Hillyer with the children as much as you can, that you be reasonably kind to the children even though you will find them very aggravating at times, especially the oldest boy. We also hope for a cheerful countenance, a little sunshine in the gloom, a happy cricket chirp out of you once in a while. Otherwise, your life is your own and neither Mrs. Hillyer nor I propose to live it for you. You'll have Thursdays off from noon till midnight and you are free on Sundays after you've helped prepare our Sunday dinner, which we eat at one o'clock. We welcome you to our home, Rosebud, we all welcome you from the heart and hope you are happy here."

As she listened to my father's little speech, which was the way he talked and fairly routine and normal for him, Rose's mouth dropped open and her blue eyes widened in wonder; then her mouth closed, she bit her lips together and the blue eyes filled with tears. Daddy didn't know it but Daddy had made a grave error. No one had ever told Rose she was graceful as the capital letter S, no one had ever called her Rosebud and asked for a happy cricket chirp out of her. And perhaps no one had ever welcomed her to a real home with kindness, either. Rose was mesmerized, enchanted, she sat there with her eyes swimming with tears, unable to speak.

Daddy had made a grave error. It didn't take much to win Rose's heart, and in that brief speech he won it totally. As she confessed to me later, she fell madly in love with him when he called her Rosebud.

3

Rose attacks Daddy at Thermopylae

THE SICKNESS OF love that hit Rose was acute, her fever was high, her pain was great. Long before she "casually" confessed it to Doll and me, it was apparent to us both she was madly in love with Daddy and we wondered with a fascinated interest what would come of this. Even my little brother seemed aware of Rose's pitiful condition, but Mother somehow hadn't noticed a thing, which no doubt was fortunate. Oddly enough, Daddy himself didn't catch on until the morning he jokingly told Rose she was the light of his life and she fled the kitchen in tears.

About three weeks after Rose came to live with us, Doll and I and Waski were in the kitchen having corn flakes for breakfast when Daddy stopped by for a half-a-cup of coffee. As was his habit, he'd gotten up much earlier and gone to the hotel; Daddy had insomnia in reverse and seldom slept past six in the morning. He often was up as early as four-thirty or five, and sometimes to his dismay was wide awake even earlier than that. It drove him stark raving mad, this reverse insomnia.

Rose was in the kitchen with us, but Mother wasn't there, she'd already had breakfast and was studying. As Daddy drank his half-a-cup of coffee, he began joking around and teasing Rose. He enjoyed teasing her and she enjoyed being teased by him; in fact, she delighted in being teased by him, she loved and adored being teased by him. His nicknames for her had grown, proliferated in all directions. "Rosebud," which had won her heart, soon became "Rosebird," and then "Rosebaby Blossom," and "Peachbud," "Peach-bird," "Plum Blossom," "Blossom Girl," and many others.

On this morning the reverse insomnia hadn't been too bad and Daddy was in a good mood, he was carrying on in an even more extravagant manner than usual, calling Rose various names, teasing her with seeming cruelty, whacking her on the rear with his rolled up copy of the Glenville *News-Tribune*, putting an arm around her as she poured his half-a-cup of coffee, and so on and so forth. Rose was blushing and laughing at everything he said, but then Daddy told some joke or other and wound it up by declaring: "Rosebird Baby, you are the light of my life, darling, you . . . are . . . the light of my life! How did we *ever* get by without you?"

That did it. Rose gazed at him for a moment with a stricken expression, then turned her head away, made a little choking sound and fled from the kitchen with a hand across her eyes. The silence she left behind her was deafening. In consternation, Daddy stared after her, then rattled his cup noisily in the saucer, banged the spoon in the saucer, cleared his throat loudly several times, muttered something to the effect it must be the *non compos mentis* time of the month for Rose, rattled his cup nosily again, gave up on it and got up and stomped out of the kitchen. We heard the tires of the Ford spinning gravel as he went down the driveway.

Rose returned to the kitchen a few minutes later and sat down at the table with us and acted as if nothing had happened. However, after talking for a while about this and that, she cleared her throat and said in a "casual" manner: "Ahem-m, I have a little headache this morning and I hope I didn't seem rude to your Daddy leaving the kitchen like that. I had to get an aspirin. Did he say anything about it?"

"He thinks you have your period," I replied.

"Oh, no," said Rose, "it's just a little headache. Well, I'm glad he didn't think it was rude, I wouldn't want him to think that, because I really love your Daddy a lot. He's the funniest man in the world, and the kindest, the best, the most wonderful man, too. I'll never forget what he said to me when I came here. I love him, I really do, I love him a lot, and I wouldn't want him to think I was rude."

As I have said, it was not news to me and Doll that Rose

loved Daddy "a lot." We already knew it perfectly well and it was not much of a surprise in the first place. Daddy had a great appeal for the fair sex, Rose wasn't the only girl or woman ever smitten by him, not by a long shot. As a young man he had been very handsome, a dashing figure with a personality and a style that had a strange catnip effect on women—and "catnip" is the word; he made them dizzy, he turned their heads giddy, made them fall all over themselves in confusion. I often heard from Mother stories of his many conquests before he married; she liked to talk about it for some reason. "Why, he broke their hearts right and left," she said. "It was pitiful, those poor girls."

No, it didn't surprise me Rose would get a crush on Daddy, and looking back on it now it seems to me inevitable something like it would have had to happen. Although I thought at that time Daddy was rather old, he was only forty-five the summer Rose came to our house and he was a youthful and vigorous forty-five and still a handsome man. And he still had in abundance his catnip thing, his strange giddying effect on girls and women.

I've never seen anything quite like Daddy's catnip thing and it's a mystery to me how he pulled it off, even though I saw him do it countless times, to waitresses in restaurants and girls and women everywhere. It was amazing, in two minutes he'd have them giddy. He could say the most outrageous things, take personal liberties, slap them on the behind, pinch them on the leg, insult them and even yell at them—and they'd just giggle and stare at him in fascination.

Where the catnip came from was a mystery to me, but Mother had a theory about it. "Daddy has *'it,'* and I'll tell you why," she said. "I'll tell you exactly why. He's an extremely sexy man, but he's also a gentleman. *That's* how he charms all those girls, a combination like that is fatal to almost any girl or woman. You see, a gentleman is something more than just a snobbish idea; what I am talking about is an inner attitude. Those girls know he doesn't mean the things he says, that he wouldn't hurt a hair of their heads, he's a gentleman. And his extreme sexiness on top of it all knocks them off their feet, it dazzles them. Girls don't run into many men like him and when they do it dazzles them, and that is what his catnip is."

Whatever the explanation of Daddy's catnip, his strange and even spooky appeal for the fair sex, poor Rose certainly was dazzled. She was worse than dazzled, the sickness of love was upon her, her fever was high, her pain was great. She'd become very friendly with Mother, but far from diminishing her feelings toward Daddy it seemed to make her love him all the more. She'd smile with affection at Mother and say, "You're so sweet," then turn and stare at Daddy and a pinkish film of tears would start to form in her eyes and she would blink and look away.

It was rather pathetic even to Doll and me, although we were more fascinated and delighted than pitying. The more Daddy teased Rose and joked around with her the more lovesick she became. She sighed as if the world were ending, stared off pale into space at nothing, stumbled around the house in confusion and crept off into corners with a handkerchief to her eyes. In those first weeks she didn't go out on Thursdays and Sundays at all, she'd stay home and stand for hours watching in the window to see if Daddy would come up the driveway in the Ford. And when he did, she'd catch her breath, lift her hands and make little feeble, helpless gestures, then more likely than not run and hide in her room.

It was plain something had to happen, something had to give, and Doll and I were waiting for it with a keen anticipation. Rose was fighting a losing battle and the time soon would come when she wouldn't run and hide and weep in her room; we knew this and had our eyes carefully fastened at various keyholes. "She's going to kiss him," said Doll, "that's what I bet." I myself expected more than a mere kiss, although I wasn't sure exactly what.

We knew at supper that night something was going to happen very, *very* soon. Not only was Rose gazing at Daddy like a motherless calf, she spilled the turnip greens, dropped the biscuits and wept twice. Mother was frowning at her in puzzled worry, trying to make it out, and finally she said: "Rose, you're in an awful dither tonight. What's the matter with you, honey, are you sick or something?"

"She's all right," said Daddy. "She's just *non compos mentis* temporarily, that's all."

"Is that it?" asked Mother.

"No, Ma'am," said Rose, in a voice so tiny we could hardly hear her. "I'm fine. I had a little headache this morning, but it's gone."

"You look sick if you ask me," said Mother. "Are you sure you're feeling all right, hon?"

"Yes, Ma'am," said Rose. "I feel just fine."

"Well, the way you look I hate to leave you with the dishes and all, but I'm supposed to go to a meeting of the Garden Club this evening. Will you be all right?"

"Oh, yes'm," said Rose, "just fine."

In those days Mother used to drive a car and go places by herself even at night and nothing much was thought of it. But on this occasion Daddy loudly cleared his throat in the distinctive way he had and said he'd take her. "Er . . . ah-HEM! No . . . no, darlin'. I'll drive you, you've got no business behind the wheel of a car. You don't think about what you're doing and you'll run into a telephone pole."

"I think about what I'm doing all the time and I've got as much business behind the wheel of a car as anybody," answered Mother. "And besides, I want you to stay and help Rose with the dishes, even if it isn't a man sort of thing to do. All this stuff about what men do and what women do is so silly. Don't they realize people are people? And the creative power, the force behind the universe that makes everything possible, this force, this unlimited creative power of life, do you think it cares whether a person is a *man* or a *woman?* Of course not. So you can help Rose with the dishes, the poor girl isn't feeling well."

"Mmmm-mm," said Daddy with a grimace. When Mother went into one of her things about the creative power of life his eyes usually glazed over and he almost always gave up on whatever it was. It was one of her greatest weapons against him. He directed a nervous glance at Rose, who sat with her blonde head bowed over her plate, then shrugged and answered: "All right, darlin', whatever you say."

Thus, Mother wasn't in the house that night and as a consequence Daddy was attacked at Thermopylae. Doll and I were ready in the darkened living room, our eyes glued at a crack in the sliding dining room doors, me above in what I thought was the better viewing position and Dolly below.

She complained bitterly about it but I was older and age had its prerogatives. Later I was to regret being up above because the dining room table blocked my view at a crucial point.

Rose struck before Mother was ten minutes out of the driveway and even though Daddy was nervous and on guard she took him totally by surprise. He was having a final half-a-cup of coffee (he never to my knowledge had a cup of coffee in his life, it was always half-a-cup) and Rose was clearing the dishes when all of a sudden she placed a hand on his shoulder, turned sideways, sat down on his lap and wound her arms tight around his neck.

"Oh, oh!" she cried. "Oh, Mr. Hillyer, I love you, I love you so much! I've tried but I can't help it, I love you so much!" Daddy stared groggily at her as she pulled her head back and moved her lips within a few inches of his own. "Please kiss me," she whispered. "Will you kiss me?"

Doll and I, eyes wide with delight, peeked through the crack in the dining room doors. It was so wonderful and wicked we could hardly bear it. What would Daddy do? Would he kiss her? Would he do more than that?

For what seemed a very long time Daddy didn't do anything at all, he just sat there with a groggy look on his face staring with a half frown at the cornflower eyes six inches from his own. In order to stare at her he had to tilt his head back and handsome man though he still was it made him look a bit like a bewildered rooster. I think in all fairness to Daddy he really didn't anticipate anything as violent as this and the full soft breasts mashed against his chest and the eager pink lips waiting for a kiss momentarily *threw* Daddy, derailed him, rendered him in one of his own favorite terms *non compos mentis*. Finally, however, he managed to clear his throat and say to her:

"Ah-HEM! Now Rose, get off my lap. What are you doing, girl? Are you crazy?"

"Yes, crazy about *you!*" said Rose. "Kiss me, Mr. Hillyer!"

"Why, I'm not going to kiss you, you crazy girl. Now I'm telling you again, get off of my lap. Come on, Rose, get up. Now you get up I say, and stop this!"

"No, no!" cried Rose. "You don't understand, I *love* you! It's real love and I can't help it! Please kiss me, Mr. Hillyer, I love you, I love you so much. . . ."

At which point Rose put her head down on Daddy's shoulder and began to cry. Big sobs came from her, miserable sobs the authenticity of which could not be doubted. She also kept a very firm grip on Daddy. Her arms were wound tightly around him and Rose was strong, she was against him like glue.

"All right, all right," said Daddy in a shaken voice. "All right, now calm down, Rose, the children will hear you. Calm down, let's talk about this thing, let's discuss it."

"Don't make me . . . me . . . me . . . get up!" sobbed Rose.

"I won't make you get up right away, if you'll calm down and discuss it," said Daddy.

Rose did calm down and they did discuss it for quite a while as she sat glued immovably on his lap, one arm still around his neck and a hand on his shoulder. This discussion, which was followed with an absorbed interest by Doll and me as we peeped from the living room, was actually rather repetitious and got nowhere. Daddy kept insisting that Rose stop acting crazy and get off his lap and Rose kept insisting she couldn't because she loved him so much. It was a stalemate and I had about decided nothing much more than this was going to happen, when something did.

What happened was that Daddy tried to get up, he made an effort to rise to his feet and dislodge Rose from her perch on his lap, but Rose was a big girl and strong and she didn't want to let go of him. She flung her other arm around him, leaned her weight forward, and Daddy grabbed out with one hand at the dining table; then they half sat and half sprawled on the floor in such a way they were out of my line of vision.

But they were not out of Doll's line of vision. She was down near the floor and could see them much better after they fell out of the chair, she could look right under the dining room table and see exactly what was transpiring. And the little skunk wouldn't let me look, she moved her shoulders and body in such a way as to block me. Doll for all her angelic sweetness could be a very, very stubborn little girl; this was *her* viewing spot and I couldn't have it.

Tantalizing silence in the dining room. Then a deep sigh from Rose and a soft remark from her in a very different tone. "Oh, Mr. *Hill*yer!"

"What are they *doing?*" I whispered.

"He kissed her," said Doll. "Boy, did he kiss her!"

"Let me look—move, let me look!"

"No, this is *my* place!"

I'll never know why Daddy and Rose didn't hear us whispering at that dining room door; I guess maybe they were a little preoccupied.

"Doll, *please* let me look just for a *second!*"

"No!"

It was one of the most frustrating experiences of my entire childhood. I could only see a part of Daddy's back and shoulders and the bottom half of Rose on the floor, her dress twisted up far above her knees, so far I could see her white panties. And then a little gasp of delight and wonder came from Dolly.

"What is it?" I whispered.

"Buddy, this is amazing, it really is, you wouldn't believe it."

"What *is* it?"

"One of her titties is out," said Doll in an awed whisper.

And *that* was too much, I could endure no more. I am afraid I did the sort of thing big brothers often do to little sisters; I grabbed Doll around the waist, hauled her back, shoved her over on the floor and stole her place.

Eagerly, I put my eye at the crack and I saw at once that more was going on than Doll had said. Not only was one of Rose's titties out of her dress, Daddy had a firm grip on it, his hand was right over it. At the moment he wasn't kissing her, he was staring sternly at her, his eyes a trifle red and glary, as his hand squeezed the titty, which was plump and round and had a large pink nipple on it surrounded by what seemed to me a huge circle of lighter pink. Wow!—what a show! But alas, the show was almost over. Daddy's eyes became even more red and glary, he bit his lips together hard beneath his clipped moustache, took his hand from Rose's titty and grabbed her by the shoulder and said:

"All right, that is *enough* of this nonsense, and *I mean enough!* Get up off that *floor,* Rose, and put your *damned tit* back in your dress! Put it *back,* damn you, or as sure as *God made little chickens* I'll take off my belt and give you a *whipping!* Do you *hear* me, girl? *Get up!* Get *up* and cover yourself *properly this instant!*"

Crumpled and crushed by his anger and making little half-crying noises of dismay, her blonde hair over her face and her breast hanging out and cruelly indented by the material of her dress, Rose got to her hands and knees. Few people could face up to Daddy when he was really mad, and he was mad in that dining room. His anger no doubt was directed as much at himself as at Rose, but that didn't make it any less real. He was in a red-eyed rage.

"Goddamn you, girl!" he said, as Rose clambered to her feet and stood before him with meekly bowed head and with trembling fingers pushed her breast down into her dress and brassiere. "Goddamn you, anyhow! You've made me make a fool out of myself, damn your hide, but let me tell you I am standing at the pass of Thermopylae and I won't budge! The very idea, my own home with children in the house, to say nothing of my wife—ohh-h, you had better believe I am standing at Thermopylae, you little nut, you had better believe it! What are you, crazy? A man is *supposed* to be a fool like this, everybody knows that, but a woman is supposed to have some control and sense! Are you a nitwit? What's the *matter* with you?"

Later, Daddy got his humiliation under control and talked in a very different manner to Rose. He sat her down at the dining room table, held her hand, put an arm around her shoulders and spoke to her in a way that reduced her to total abject tears.

It was a gift Daddy had, perhaps his greatest gift, the power to affect and sway others by his own emotion. Aside from his verbal abilities, which were considerable, he was also a great performer, an extraordinary actor able to generate overwhelming emotion and fire. He could say the most extravagant thing and invest it with total truth. Of course he believed every word he was saying, that was a part of his gift, absolute conviction, but above and beyond conviction his delivery was that of an artist. His warm Dixieland baritone would rise with vibrant power and fall to a dramatic near-whisper—it was enough to make a person's hair stand on end to listen to him. What a King Lear he would have made! He certainly wrecked poor Rose; he reduced her to a sobbing and pitiful pulp, and he wrecked my sister Dolly, too, as she listened with me at the dining room doors.

Daddy wept easily. An arm around Rose's shoulder, her hand in his, his eyes slowly filled with tears as he spoke to her. "Rose, Rose, Rose," he said, "you poor miserable little child, don't you know I love you? Do I have to put my hand on your body or kiss your pretty lips to prove it? You are beautiful to me, Rose, don't you know that? I've loved you since you first came here, darlin'. And don't you know Mrs. Hillyer loves you, too, that she's already taken you into her heart, and that that woman's heart is as wide as the blue sky itself and as deep as the stars? Do you know what a friend you have got there? Do you know she would fight for you like a tiger, that she would fly to your defense in an instant and fight for you with all the courage in her soul if anyone tried to hurt you? Is *this* any way to repay her trust and love for you, given so freely out of the sweetness of her heart? Are you ashamed in your soul, as I am ashamed? Are you sorry for your foolish selfishness, as I am sorry? Yes, yes, darlin', I know you are . . . don't cry, honey, don't cry. But let me warn you, damn your hide, this is Thermopylae and I am standing here. Do you hear me, damn you, I am standing at Thermopylae and the Persians shall not pass! And by God if you ever do anything like this again I'll fire you so fast it'll make your head swim, and that is no idle threat! Now you get your tail out of here and go wash those dishes, and for God's sake stop crying!"

Soon after Rose left for the kitchen weeping penitent tears, Daddy gave a profound sigh and sat back weakly in his chair at the dining room table. He gazed out at nothing for several seconds, then whispered aloud: "Whew-w! Rough, rough!"

Doll and I found the whole thing thrilling beyond measure. We tiptoed out of the living room and up the stairs. At the top of the stairs Dolly paused and brushed a tear from her eye and whispered: "Isn't Daddy wonderful? He wanted to kiss her some more and play with her, but he didn't, because he loves Mother and all of us, and he loves Rose, too. Isn't he wonderful? Isn't he great?"

"Wonderful?" I asked. "He kissed her and played with her titty and I don't see anything so wonderful about that. He probably was afraid Mother would come back early and catch him, or afraid to get tangled up with Rose for fear Mother would catch him later."

"You know, Buddy," said Dolly, "sometimes you make me sick."

I smiled thinly as she gave me a venomous glance and walked off down the hall. Doll didn't speak to me for a week. However, looking back on it I would say her venom, although justified, was somewhat misdirected. I didn't mean what I said any more than Daddy himself meant a lot of the things he said. Some emotions are too strong to be expressed, they expose too much, they reveal too much, especially at thirteen. Doll misread me, I wouldn't have admitted it then even under torture, but I felt a powerful secret admiration for the heroic account Daddy gave of himself when Rose attacked him at Thermopylae.

4

Rose wanders in a wilderness, lost

ROSE'S GLOOM WAS extreme while it lasted, which was about a week. Some skeptical souls might feel her remorse was hypocritical, since her penitence did not change her behavior very much, not then and not later. However, I believe Rose felt a real shame and even despair at her feelings. As she said to me one night about a week after Daddy rejected her: "I am awful unhappy. Can I get in bed with you a little while, do you mind? Buddy, I am wandering in a wilderness, lost."

While Rose wanders in a wilderness, lost, I must borrow the reader's ear for a brief word, reluctant as I am to interrupt what might prove to be a rather amusing little narrative with intrusive editorializing that risks attaching more importance to it than it deserves. A brief word, that is all, and we will get on with the early autumn moon, let it rise.

It seems to me a character such as this girl I am writing about is especially susceptible to miscomprehension for reasons having to do with that disturbing and frightening mystery known as *sex*. I daresay the reader already has gathered Rose had some failings in this area, but the interpretation of those failings can vary enormously and that is what concerns me now.

To be sure, the girl must speak for herself and the reader must judge her for himself. It is not a thing I myself can do or would want to do; I am only a vehicle or tool here, the teller of this tale.

Nevertheless, this is a book unlike others I have written and I cannot claim an icy objectivity toward the characters portrayed in it, however desirable such aloofness might be as a general rule. And I must confess that includes the girl I call Rose, who cannot strictly be said to be a wisp of my imagination.

No, not strictly. Such a thing is impossible in a book of this kind. A character cannot be invented out of the air from nothing and neither can experiences that have any meaning. Rose is bound to be based on a person or persons I have known, on human observations I have made in situations similar or perhaps even identical to the situations in this narrative, on human experience I have lived through and know as I know the lines of the palm of my hand—*that* much I can say, anyhow, because it is true of any work of fiction if we grant even a modest ability on the part of the writer, even a minimum gift in the telling of a real and true story.

What I am saying is this: the girl I call Rose could not possibly have been a mother's helper in our house, of *course* not, we know they all had "excellent moral character"—but she is no figment of my imagination, not in a million years, and since I feel a fondness for her, since I love her whatever her faults, I am most reluctant to expose her naked and bare without even a word.

Yes, she *does* become pretty naked and pretty bare as that autumn moon rises, and I am loath to see her so vulnerable to harsh judgment and cruel condemnation. Surely a brief word in her defense is permissible? The truth itself, I am afraid, might get lost in the shock of her nakedness and bareness, it might get lost and wander in a wilderness, and who would want that?

Now, about this girl. A number of things are bothering me, bugging me, preventing me from getting on with this little narrative, for whatever it is worth. They are: Tobacco Road, moral imbecile, nymphomaniac, and bitch. The word "nymphomaniac" seems to me especially inapplicable. First of all, "nymphomaniac" is a filthy word, a scare word, a male-chauvinist word. If one is not speaking of a psychotic creature in an insane asylum or an unfortunate woman with a pituitary tumor or some such thing as that, then the word has practically no meaning at all. It can be used to describe rather ineptly and misleadingly a neurotic girl who is actually frigid and who in vain struggles to obtain relief by means of compulsive promiscuity—that is about the only meaning the word has.

Well, I happen to know the girl I am writing about in this book was *not* frigid—far from it, good heavens no. And if a "neurotic" person is a person isolated by fear and unable to make human contacts and feel affection or love for others, then she was not neurotic, either, but the exact opposite. To call such a girl a nymphomaniac seems to me utterly idiotic, and yet I am sure some perusers of this book will describe her as precisely just that: "Grim pornographic fantasy of a Tobacco Road nymphomaniac." Well, *c'est la vie*, the perusers of course are entitled to their opinion just as I am entitled to mine. As Harry Truman said, if you can't stand the heat get out of the kitchen.

To make myself perfectly clear like another of our great Presidents, I am not saying this girl's morals were those of a middle-class Southern product of a finishing school and I am not saying she was a prim cold-blooded Victorian, but she was no gothic Tobacco Road moral imbecile and her sexiness was within a normal human range—high-normal maybe, but normal; I am sure there are countless thousands of girls and women in this country as sexy as Rose, and some even sexier.

And I will venture the thought that they suffer from it, too, just as this girl did. Our family oracle had a theory relevant to this thought, and slightly cuckoo though she was she knew a thing or two:

"What no one understands, Brother, or very few, is that we live in a barbaric world. The day will come when they will look back on us in pity and horror. You tell me Rose is bad, Daddy tells me Rose is bad, everybody tells me Rose is bad, and you're all wrong. Because you see, Brother, we live in barbarism and Rose in not a barbarian. Rose is a Greek."

That might be the whole answer right there, but of course Mother was swayed by her love for Rose. She couldn't be objective where her heart was concerned, not even slightly. Mother wouldn't even believe Rose actually *did* anything, much. "It's a bunch of fuss and feathers," she said. "Rose just flirts, that's all. She *is* a horrible flirt, I admit."

No, I am afraid *some*thing was wrong with this girl, in fact undoubtedly something was wrong with her and I have often wondered what it was. As the song says, "Why you ramble, no one knows." Perhaps a perceptive reader can tell me what was wrong with Rose because I truly don't know, and that is one of the reasons I am now putting down on paper these recollections after so many years, aside from my hope this memoir might provide a little passing amusement for those who pick it up.

Of course, there need be no mystery. A simple answer is possible, a very simple answer indeed. Some readers of fair sense and good will would no doubt give such an answer, on the order of: "She was a complete little bitch, that's all. Why does it puzzle you? Didn't you ever run into a little bitch before?"

Well, bitch is not as bad as nymphomaniac and I suppose Rose *was* pretty damned bitchy, but I can't really accept it. The word "bitch" implies a predatory quality, an intent to wreak harm, the use of sex for power, a lascivious and unloving exploitation of the emotions of others, a cold sexuality without real feeling, a lewd meanness of the heart and soul—that is what a bitch is, and this girl simply did not have such things in her. It puzzles me because it isn't true, she was not a bitch. I don't know *what* she was, to me this girl is a mystery and I am quite serious in asking some wise reader to explain her to me, if he can.

In fact, I will make a solemn promise to reply to any letters that are not purely abusive; just write care of the publisher of this book. I will listen with interest to any halfway reasonable theory; I will even listen to a *semi*reasonable theory, and I suggest offhand the following areas for consideration:

Was the girl I call Rose merely "like us all," as Mother said, except more so? Was she one of those odd adults who remain inside a perpetual child? Was she a Greek in a barbaric world as Mother also said? Did she simply have "no moral sense," as Daddy said?—I don't like that view, but he expressed it and my father was no fool. Was she in some strange unconscious way an advance echelon of women's lib? Was she an injured and damaged child of dire poverty who dreamed of ice-cream cones she'd never had, was it a hunger of the soul that drove her? Was she some weird variety of emotional and sexual artist, whose craft had a kind of beauty even as upsetting and disturbing as it was to everyone around her? Was she a wonder or a horror of nature?

Other areas of consideration might occur to the thoughtful reader. Be that as it may, any replies will be gratefully received and politely answered, and the fundamental question is this: what *really* made Rose behave as she did, what made her ramble?

No more apologies, no more questions, enough! However, since my night of nights with Rose was not only one of the most important experiences of my life but also fundamental to whatever comprehension I have of her as a human being, I believe I should fill in as conscientiously as I can the circumstances surrounding that night.

About a week after her rebuff by my father, Rose became so depressed one night she couldn't sleep, she was tossing and turning and crying with gloom in the awful September heat, so she got up and pitty-patted down the upstairs hall in her nightgown, went into my room and crawled into bed with me for a little solace and company and confessional chitchat about her lost love for Daddy.

To call her behavior "indiscreet" would be a massive understatement. In the churchgoing, puritanical, Bible Belt, middle-class and genteel South of that time and place such a thing as crawling half-naked in a flimsy little nightgown into bed in the dark of night with a thirteen-year-old boy was simply unspeakable. And, I suppose, her act on the face of it even in this day and age was inexcusable: having tried the father and been rejected, she tried the semiadolescent son—or so it appeared; in reality it was not quite like that. I am sure Rose when she went into that room and crawled into my bed did not have even the remotest notion of depraved seduction on her mind.

And in actual fact no such "depraved seduction" occurred, although I would be the first to admit a few fairly sexy events did transpire, as the early autumn moon rose in September heat over the big white oak in our yard and Daddy slept peacefully downstairs on the other side of the house and for once, thank God, did not have insomnia in reverse.

Yes, fairly sexy, I have to admit that, but more significant things than sexy things happened on the night of nights Rose came to my room. That was later, after she'd left my room and returned to it, at which point she pulled off her small miracle by causing the "iron of pity" to strike a child's cold flinty heart and send forth sparks of human sympathy.

Now I have nothing against sex, not in the least, I think sex is wonderful, beautiful, great, more fun than a barrel of monkeys. However, an awakening of human sympathy, I believe, is more important than the mere existence and unreasoning function of whatever God has given us below our bellybuttons. This is an unpopular view in our day and age, I realize, but it is mine. It is a hairy little bastard, this view, but it is mine.

Onward and upward with the early autumn moon, it will rise very soon and mercilessly as it must because that is how early autumn moons are. After all, at my age the spirit quails before eternity and looks for life. Perhaps some readers would prefer to skip the next few chapters and get to the "funny" part of this book? Watch out for the lady in that early autumn moon, there is snap in her tits, believe me, and I am not talking about Rose.

Well, no more apologies, but then I have got to present the reasonable and true facts both inner and outer. And in all fairness to Rose, she was not accustomed to sleeping alone and that is not meant to be a joke—as a child on a poor dirt farm she had never slept by herself; a private bedroom on such a farm was unheard of. To sleep alone seemed unnatural to her, a morbidly lonely thing to do. One of her first questions to my mother when she came to the house was: "You mean I have the room all to myself?"

Besides, again in all fairness to Rose, at twelve-and-three-quarter years of age I was extremely precocious in some ways but the precocity was by no means consistent and I was physically still very much of a child. I was fairly tall for my years but a very thin and undernourished-looking little boy with a thick shock of bright red hair and green eyes, in my own opinion horribly ugly and covered with all kinds of dreadful freckles. At summer camp at nine I'd almost died of "walking" typhoid and pure homesick heartbreak for my lost mother—where was she, where had my angel gone to leave me there to waste away and die in that camp, helpless without her love? In delirium I saw her face like a cameo in the sky and in a daze of fever looked for her in empty cotton fields and pine woods, and nearly died. As I put it in another book:

"For years on years, he had looked, with an aching heart and an unending hope. He climbed every hill and mountain, in the day and in the night, eyes lifted with yearning to the deep blue sky and the velvet stars, where angels spread their wings and fly."

As a result of this illness, which kept me out of school for half a year and left a more or less visible indented line across my teeth that people though was caused by braces, I was actually retarded in some ways. I looked younger than I was, I was not even quite adolescent, although it is not accurate to say there were no signs whatever of puberty. I was at that brief stage at the very end of childhood, which is not one thing and not the other either.

To be a trifle clinical about it in order to convey a true picture of the situation, some not insignificant traces of pubescent hair had appeared—yes, bright red, a "magnificently beautiful" shade according to my mother, although I myself loathed the color of my hair then and loathe it still, but fortunately it is getting a little dingy nowadays under the light of that early autumn moon. To continue this clinical description, I might add that that endowment which defines the male, if it does not necessarily ennoble him, was still of modest dimensions but had undergone in recent months and even weeks an alarming increase of both girth and extension and could not be dismissed as altogether negligible even though it wouldn't have won any prizes at a county fair.

To complete this true picture of the situation: strangely enough, although I knew all about such matters or thought I did, I had never experienced the soul-shaking thunder and lightning and bioelectric display of what is called on all sides today "orgasm"—and gossip, I am afraid, is no substitute for experience in this mysterious kingdom of human existence and I did not really know what this was; I thought it on a par with urination and had no idea on earth it could upset a person. And I did not know girls and women were capable of it. That might sound hard to believe, but it's true, I didn't know they could.

Sunday school at the First Baptist Church of Glenville did not pass out very much detailed information on such matters and what I'd picked up in the gutter was not too reliable, although the best of it had an approximate accuracy. I'd heard all the usual legends about it, that the father spit in the mother's mouth and the baby was born out of the mother's bellybutton, that it was born out of the mother's pussy the same night the mother and father "did it"—there was a little lilting song, "Ha, ha, ha! Ha, ha, ha! Won't take it out till the baby comes!"

But the account in which I placed the greatest faith was that given me by one of my little filthy pals, a boy named Hollis slightly older than myself who cursed obscenely and smoked cigarettes all the time even in front of his parents, a thing I'd have given worlds to do—he'd flick ashes at them with his fingernail as if to say, "There, how do you like *that?* I am not bothered by all the things you try to worry and upset me with, not a bit! I am what I am and I do what I do, and all your grown-up screaming and carrying on doesn't hurt me in the least—*flick!* Now watch me take a drag on this butt . . ."

I was awed by the filthy Hollis, totally awed by him. To smoke a cigarette like that in front of Mother and Daddy was my dream, to blow smoke at them with calm aloofness and cool independence—but it was impossible, they'd both hit me over the head at the same time. How did the obscene Hollis pull it off?

One day the filthy, cigarette-smoking Hollis took me out to our garage and told me in a low, bloodcurdling tone how babies are made. The father, he said, put his "dilly" into the mother's "cock" (an odd authentic Southernism, by the way; the word in Dixieland describes not a man's intimate parts, but a woman's) and peed about two-thirds of a glassful of hot soapsuds into her, which caused her to groan horribly because it burned her and hurt her something fierce. Exactly nineteen and a half inches up inside her "cock" there was a big bloody hen's egg and the scalding soapsuds washed it off and melted its leathery shell in about thirty minutes, and this made the nasty thing turn into a fish with a tail, but it kept growing and lost its tail and finally turned into a baby and came out of her nine months later with all kinds of blood and three gallons of piss pouring down while she screamed her head off. Like most born liars I was very gullible. I believed every word of this macabre account of human reproduction, which actually of course is not wholly inaccurate.

The reverse meaning of the hideous word "cock" in the South is rather bizarre—why do they have it backward? Or do we in Yankeeland, in our ignorance "cock-deep" in frost and rime, have it backward? An interesting philosophical puzzler, but in any event, in the South a "cock" is a pussy, or it sure was when I lived down there. Now, a "prick" is universal . . . but to hell with it, where is that moon?

Coming up over the white oak in our yard, slowly and remorselessly as the lady in it limbers up her hips for a little early autumn action—and watch out for her, there is snap in her tits, all right, snap aplenty. She is no bitch, but there is snap in her tits and power in her behind.

I can't resist a slight divagation, which has for me a certain charm and also relates in essence directly to the thrilling climax of this book itself—well, I hope thrilling; this is my aim, anyhow, that is what I have in my sights. A scene of breathless suspense: Will Mr. Right shoot Rose or will Daddy and Mother and I talk him out of it? But no *more* divagations, for God's sake, or that moon will never rise.

Just this last one, the original divagation, which I said relates in essence to the climax of this book. I was thinking of an interesting and amusing and true little tale, a story employing the hideous word "cock" that my father used to love to tell, the story about Old John Washington. This was not a story Daddy would even dream of telling to a girl or a woman, but he told it to the boys and I heard it many times. The story goes as follows:

Sometime back around the turn of the century, the shrewish wife of a character named Old John Washington suspected him of fiddling around with an attractive "high yellow" girl who worked for them, so one day when the girl was there she told Old John she was going downtown and would be gone three hours. But she came back in about twenty minutes, and sure enough there Old John was in the bedroom with his britches down and mounted on the "high yellow" and going like a billy goat. "Ah, ha!" she said. "I set a trap for you and I caught you red hand!" Whereupon the reply: "Woman, you set a trap for Old John Washington and bait it with cock, and you'll catch him every time!"

Daddy loved this story, he liked the style of it, and "red hand" was one of his favorite terms. He was a great little trapsetter himself and whenever he caught me at some piece of scoundrelism he'd say: "Ah, ha, Brother, I set a trap for you and I caught you red hand!" He liked the style of it, just as I myself at thirteen liked the style of those scalding soapsuds as described by the filthy Hollis.

Now, if I can get back to the important part of this story, which is the girl I am writing about, I was saying I am certain Rose had no idea whatever of depraved seduction on her mind when she came to my room that night in hot and humid September long ago. It wouldn't even have seemed possible. Fairly tall for my age but very thin and still not recovered from the near-fatal nightmare of Camp Sacarusa, terrified of revealing the emotions which ravaged and tormented me and determined to conceal them because they were too unbearable even for me to know much less the world, I looked very young and was very young, and about the Kingdom of Sex very ignorant and naïve.

I am sure Rose thought of me as a complete child in a physical sense and that it didn't occur to her I was capable of real folderol or that I would even have any serious interest in it. Of course her innocence in coming to the room hardly excuses her behavior after she got there, but even that, I must admit, seems to me innocent in a way. At least she was not trying to hurt me—and depraved seduction, I submit, is sadism, just as pornography itself is sadism, a deliberate and cold-blooded and hateful attempt to degrade the human image, to diminish humanity and particularly the feminine half of it, to tell us with a whining and nasty and cowardly complaint life is not worth living, which I do not believe for one moment as I see right now that early autumn moon rise over that white oak.

It will get here, it will shine down soon, I have only a

couple of final points to make to complete this true picture of the situation. It must be said my relationship with this girl, even before the night she came to my room, was not that of a child to a nurse despite my few years. It is a fact I was very precocious in some ways and Rose talked to me and related to me pretty much as an equal.

It is also true I was the child in our family with whom she had by far the strongest tie, even before she came to my bed and wound up so very naked and very bare in the light of the moon. Rose was fond of my sister and little brother, she'd play with them for hours on end and never tire of their company, but I was older and more capable of being a companion to her, better able to listen with attention and understanding to her endless accounts of this, that and everything in the world that had ever happened to her. As I told Mother when she first arrived, she talked a *lot*—get her started and she'd go on for hours, telling every tiniest microscopic detail of whatever it was. I don't know what her I.Q. might have been, I am no expert in such matters, but she sure had a hell of a memory and I imagine her basic intelligence must have been quite high. At any rate, she could talk a cat down out of a tree and I was one of the very few people who really could listen to her, except Mother and of course later Mr. Right. Daddy couldn't; he'd tell her, "Oh, Rose, shut up, you're yacking my ears off. It gives me a swimming in the head to listen to you."

Finally, child though I was, I amused Rose, and at times horrified and fascinated and bewildered her. Until the night she came to my room, she couldn't quite make me out and sometimes would stare at me in a deep puzzlement. Once she said to me rather sadly: "I *think* you love me, Buddy, I really do. But I don't know, you scare me sometimes, you give me a chill right down my backbone and then I think you hate me."

I remember another occasion when she told me I was *crazy.* She couldn't bear ugliness, meanness and cruelty and I often took advantage of this weakness in her, if weakness it was. I'd make up things, tell her about a perfect cold-blooded murder committed with black widow spiders or about bad boys who took five cats and destroyed them by putting firecrackers up their asses. One day I gave her some such lovely piece of misinformation and she sighed in distress and said:

"You're nice, Buddy, you really are and that's the strangest thing of all because you're real bad, too, just *awful.* Your mother is right, there's something dangerous in you. The very idea, telling me in all seriousness a man in Peru ate his little niece, and even worse made smoked pork chops out of her! Now you just get this straight, you little redheaded thing, I don't listen to such stuff and I don't pay it any mind, I just turn my back, and look away. And that's what I'm doing to *you* right now, Buddy, I am turning my back on you and looking away! You are *crazy,* a hoot owl hasn't got a thing on you! If you don't love me, then just keep your mouth shut about it!"

The night was hot and very sticky as it often is in September in this burningly sunny and humid area of America the beautiful—magnolia country it is, cotton-pickin' land, where little girls on dirt farms were ashamed to wear flour sacks to school and hid in the woods and cried. It was very, very hot. I had only a sheet across me and no bedclothing of any kind, I was naked.

It was late when she came in, very late, at least one or one thirty in the morning and I was sound asleep. The first I knew of her presence was when I felt a hand on my shoulder and heard a sniffle of tears in the dark. Like most children I awakened very slowly and at that hour it was still dim in the room, the moon had not yet come up; I couldn't think or see clearly and for a moment believed it was my mother come to complain of an argument with Daddy.

And that was not an unreasonable surmise. I have not yet given a complete picture of the strange relationship between my parents. They were kind of like Georgia and Georgia Tech on the football field, or Army and Navy. Or to change the metaphor, like a cat and a dog, a lion and a tiger. Despite the love between them my father and mother had many arguments, in fact they had an almost continuous argument and she always came to *me* to complain. I was her weapon, her atomic bomb against him—and they didn't even have atomic bombs in those days, they hadn't invented the damned things yet. "Brother, do you know what *that man* said? Wait till you hear the cruelty and total inhumanity of it. . . ."

Well, that is getting a little grim and it is a story I will never tell. This one despite its defects and superficiality is better, as I am sure my father would agree. Mother is at rest enfolded in the creative power of the universe, but Daddy as I write these words is still here at eighty-two and still has catnip, and I hope and expect will live to read this book and be amused by it, although he won't like my saying he put his hand on Rose's titty, which of course he never did, that's mischief. Or goosing her as I describe later, that's worse mischief.

"Wait till you hear the cruelty and total inhumanity of it. . . ." No, that is a story I will never tell, I am telling it well enough here and now! Suffice it to say the conflict between my parents, despite the love between them which made it worse, could be slightly dreadful—and *I* was Mother's intended atomic bomb, God help me! Luckily they hadn't invented such things in those days and I never even went off like a firecracker. However, it was this, the war in our home and not mere walking typhoid, that caused the illness in me both Rose and my mother correctly described as dangerous. What is a child who loves both his parents to do when he sees them day by day tear at each other like a lion and a tiger?

Of course a lot of the time, as in nearly all of this particular narrative, they were just having fun. As I explain later, their fights were one of their greatest recreations. I do believe it was often a form of love play.

Let the autumn moon rise, the lady in it isn't fearful, her power does not lie in her tits and behind but elsewhere, if she has power at all. Rose has wandered in a wilderness, lost, for more than long enough, let us look for her in the light of that early autumn moon and see if we can find her.

5

Rose stumbles into paradise, and is found

ROSE DIDN'T STUMBLE when she walked down the dark hall, she stumbled later when I put that sophisticated proposition to her: "And by the way, Rose, since you're here in bed with me and everything, can I touch your pussy?"

The sophisticated proposition, however, came somewhat later in the night. When she first arrived I didn't even have the vaguest dream of such a thing. I thought she was Mother, I was sure it was Mother when I heard the sniffle of tears and a feeling of dread ran through me.

But it wasn't Mother come to complain about Daddy, it was Rose in what seemed to be a funny little white nightgown. Later as the moon rose and shone down through the window I got a better look at the nightgown, a thin, worn relic from the past with faded patches that did not match the original material. It was a child's nightgown really and hung down only about halfway between her hips and knees. But I could hardly see her at first, she was a dim figure and I couldn't see her or hear her and I couldn't grasp what she was doing at night like this in my room.

"Did I have . . . I mean, did they have a fight?" I asked, half-awake. "Is Mother sick?" A thin mumble seemed to be saying no, this was not the case. I slowly gathered Rose had come to my room because she was terribly blue and in despair and wanted company. "Buddy, I am wandering in a wilderness, lost, just like in the Bible." As she sat on the edge of the bed and explained in a faint, sad little voice how unhappy she was, I gradually awakened and began to understand her.

"Do you mind? I won't bother you, you can go on back to sleep. I'll just lie here a while and maybe it'll help me get to sleep myself. I can't stand to be alone right now and that's the truth. Can I get in bed with you a little while, Buddy, do you mind?"

"Well, I don't have any pajamas on," I said, "it's so hot."

"Oh, that doesn't matter," she answered. "I won't look at you, Buddy, and I can't see you in the dark, anyhow. Besides, you shouldn't be modest with *me*, I'm your friend, not your enemy. Please . . . can I get in bed with you a little? I'm awful unhappy."

"Well . . . all right," I said reluctantly. I was almost pathologically modest as a child. It had been a terrible problem going in swimming naked at Sacarusa with the other boys, I was horrified when I found out that was what we were supposed to do. It is a thing one never fully recovers from and that is why to write a book is to wander in a wilderness at least for a while.

Of course, people in all walks of life face this difficulty every day all the time. It's one of those fundamental problems, exposing yourself bare-assed—do I dare to eat a peach? shall I tell her I love her? suppose she laughs? Oh yes, it's a fundamental problem with infinite applications in all the secret places where we live. If you expose that poor helpless thing, someone is liable or even certain to kick it; but if you don't, you will never communicate with another human soul, you will never touch another heart or hand, and that is *truly* pure sheer hell. Better to tell her you love her and take a chance. If she laughs, she is hurting only herself, not you. But enough philosophical speculation, the weight of it is too great for the small vessel of memory, mischief and imagination in which it sails, let's get on with it, let's tell this story.

Carefully, cautiously, afraid even in the dark she would see my limp sleepy little "dilly" with its surrounding traces of scarlet fleece, I opened the sheet just enough for Rose to get under it and she crawled into bed with me, put an arm around my waist and lay her blonde head beside me on the pillow with a relieved sigh.

"Oh, Lor-r-rd," she said, "it *does* help being near somebody, having a person to put your arms around. I've been *awful* unhappy, Buddy, just *awful.* Now . . . you go on back to sleep, I'm sorry I woke you up."

I think she really meant for me to go to sleep and she was quiet for a while, but when Rose had something on her mind she couldn't be silent for long and she soon began again to talk about the depth of her unhappiness, how dreadful it was, how terrible her pain. I was wide awake now and listened to her.

"Oh, Buddy," she whispered, "you don't know how it hurts to have a broken heart, what a terrible feeling it is, and I've had a broken heart so many times. Men, I don't understand them, I can't see through them, I can't figure them out and they break my heart, that's all. I can't find Mr. Right, Buddy, I can't find him no matter how hard I look, all I find is a whole pile of Mr. Wrongs. I can't locate him, Mr. Right. I've given up looking, they break my heart all the time, Buddy, men do, and I can't stand it no more, I just can't. But this is the worst ever because it isn't his fault. No, it's *my* fault, oh yes it's my fault, I was bad, oh God I was bad—now you wouldn't believe I could be bad like that, but Buddy I was horrible. I can't tell you *who it was* but do you know what I did? I sat on his lap and got a holt of him and wiggled and wuggled my ass on him and was worse'n you could know, a child like you. Why, I let one of my tits fall out deliberate on purpose and practic'ly smacked him in the face with it and I was squirmin' my ass on him something awful, and I let my goddern skirt come way up so he could see my drawers, oh I was the smart one I was hopin' it would *stir him up,* Buddy I was *just terrible,* why I was *disgustin'!*—but to get back serious to what I was sayin', it is not only, Buddy, the loss of him . . ."

Rose, as a result of moving into the home of "rich folks," was trying systematically and earnestly to change her countrified speech, thus from time to time such things as "it is not only, Buddy, the loss of him" came from her.

Rose's accent, her drawl, her country talk were far more extreme than I have indicated or could possibly indicate in writing; it would have been very difficult for a person outside the Deep South to comprehend a lot that she said, and I am sure it would wear out the reader in no time if I tried to reproduce literally her manner of speech. I can come very close to *what* she said but I cannot reveal *how* she said it, the best I can do is suggest it and that I am afraid is a limitation of writing. In any event she was ashamed of what she called her "trash" way of talking and worked hard and with some success to change it. When she first came to the house there were many more "ain't's" and "nary's" and "lookee yonders" and even more extreme countryisms in her speech. She tended when she got excited to revert to this somewhat, but after some weeks in the house when she was calm she sounded almost like any other Southern girl.

". . . no, Buddy, it is not only that, his loss, but the awful mem'ry of how bad I behaved on that *occasion.* Why, it has just made me *ill,* Buddy, I don't even hardly want to eat nothin', I really don't, it makes me practic'ly puke to look at food, and me I got me a good appetite. But *I* don't want to eat nothin', I *don't,* I'm *ill.*"

Of course I knew perfectly well what she was talking about, but just to make conversation I asked her the cause of her misery and to my surprise she at once blurted it out. "It's your *daddy!* I'm so much in love with him I'm out of my mind!"

No doubt she wanted and needed badly to talk to someone about it and that was her reason for coming to my room. After swearing me to everlasting secrecy, she told me all about it in great detail, including certain information I found slightly shocking, such as a story of how Daddy had come into the kitchen one day and goosed her. Daddy evidently had given Rose more provocation than Doll and I realized.

"He really got it in there, Buddy, and I mean *deep.*"

"I don't understand you, in deep where?"

"Why, my asshole, where do you think? That's what a goose is, don't you know that? Of course through my dress and he was only joking, but he really got it in there, his finger almost hurt me. That daddy of yours is the biggest joker who ever lived, but I guess this *was* a little dirty and later on he apologized, held my shoulder in the most nicest way and said he hadn't ought to of done that, it come over him and he couldn't resist because I have such a *beautiful* ass. How about that, that's what he said, his very words,

'Rose Honey Cup, you have got a *beautiful* ass, darlin', and I just *couldn't* resist goosing it. The beauty of it *overwhelmed* me, but I shouldn't have done that and I won't any more.' Buddy, I am tellin' you, that daddy of yours knows how to make a girl feel good and I love him, I just love that man.''

Yes, Daddy had given Rose more provocation than we realized, he himself in part had brought on the attack at Thermopylae. According to what she said he'd made several such joking passes at her and I believe her. She told me at interminable length about the whole thing. In a tireless whisper with one arm around me and her soft blonde hair spread beside me on the pillow, she related in tiniest detail the entire epic, then having done so she summed it up for me, gave me her interpretation of the over-all meaning and result of it, including remote future possibilities.

''Oh, he might return my love someday,'' she said, ''you never know about them things, but I can tell you this—*not* while I'm in the house, he just won't. Joking around and goosing was one thing, but he won't do nothin' serious, not your daddy, not while I'm here in the house with his wife and children, he just ain't that kinda man. And maybe he wouldn't do nothin' even later if I ever saw him. What it all amounts to is I am madly in love with him and can't help that, but it's a lost love, Buddy, a tragic lost love because not only is he married he's a *good* man and won't have nothin' to do with me, I can't get him and if I don't watch my step real close he'll fire me. He don't call me Rosebud or them things no more, he's friendly but he just calls me Rose now and he don't put his arm around me no more neither, or nothin' like that. I can't get him, Buddy, he'd fire me if I done anything again and you don't know how that kills me because I love him so, I can't help it, I just love that man. But I admire him, too, I pratic'ly worship that daddy of yours. You wouldn't understand it, but most men if they can get a girl they go ahead and get her—I guess to hell they do just like a dern rabbit, then of course later they'll tell her she's no good when they done the same thing theirselves! Why, I get so pissed off at them men sometimes, the way they act, I almost don't feel like bein' nice to them no more! They talk about good, but *they* ain't no good, practic'ly none of 'em! I'm tellin' you, Buddy, nearly all of 'em will get a girl if they can, and later explain her *she's* no good. Heh! Them men, ain't practic'ly *none* of 'em no good, but they *talk* about good, that's all they do is talk about it like a bunch of monkeys! I get so pissed off at 'em, I really do, Buddy, I just get so pissed off at 'em I could hit 'em with my pocketbook! But not your daddy, he *is* a good man, he don't just talk about it he *does* it, and I'll tell you something on account of it I love him *all the more deep*. Oh I sure do, and one of these days when I ain't here no more I'm gonna come back to this house, by golly, and pay that man a love call, and who knows, we'll see! But right now it's a tragic love, Buddy, a lost love even though I'll love him as long as I live and that's a fact. Me, I like men even if they *are* a bunch of monkeys, but I couldn't care about no other man right now, this thing has hurt me so much I got no interest, not a bit. Maybe I'll get over it sometime but I don't know when or how, I love that man so much I could eat him right up without no salt or pepper. But I'm talkin' your head off, ain't I, I better be quiet now and let you get some sleep. You shut your eyes, honey, and I'll just lie here a while and maybe sleep a little, too."

But Rose didn't want to sleep, she wanted company and wanted to talk about her lost love for Daddy. It soon started up again and as she chattered on about him I was extremely conscious of her woman's body beside me, despite my few and childish years. I'd been conscious of her woman's body from the moment she got into bed with me and put her arm around my naked waist.

Rose had little modesty with anyone and practically none whatever with a child—she lay there beside me in complete unselfconsciousness with an arm around me, her skimpy nightgown up almost to her waist and her bare leg against mine, and her soft round breast mashed against my arm and side. The breast had a very disturbing effect on me: it felt like a magic, soft, warm little pillow and seemed to cause a tingle where it touched me, a kind of electric tingle that I liked and didn't like at the same time.

When I later saw them naked I didn't think Rose's titties as I called them were exactly pretty, they were too strange and disturbing to be pretty to me then, but actually Rose's breasts were very handsome, perhaps her best feature, although as Daddy said she also had a beautiful behind. Her breasts were large with big nipples and they were very firm; she didn't need a brassiere and often didn't wear one, which in those days was not merely daring but damn near crazy—it was one of her favorite tricks to wear no bra and put on a dress or blouse of such thin material her nipples would stick right through it and make little eye-popping dents. And male eyes popped all right, in those days such a thing as this was wild, out of sight, around the bend.

However, the soft titty mashed against my arm and side, distracting though it was, was not the most disturbing thing I sensed as I lay there listening to her chatter about Daddy. I also was very aware of a strange scent that emanated from her, a powerful odd fragrance that made me dizzy and unable to get my breath. As I believe I have said, Rose, for an ignorant country girl, was downright fastidious about her person and the scent that came from her was mixed with the smell of Ivory soap. I'd heard the water running into the tub in the bathroom at the end of the upstairs hall that afternoon, she'd had a bath; but the feminine scent that came from her had a power far beyond mere soap and it had a most disturbing and upsetting effect on me.

Of course we have a lot of horror about this, millions of dollars—good God, probably *billions* of dollars—are spent because of it. Bite this little tablet, chew it up and crunch it in your stinky mouth or no boy will ever kiss you . . . or if he does, he'll shriek in revulsion and rush off and brush his teeth with calfshit to take away the taste of your fetid lips. *That's* how horrible you are! Bite that tablet, you revolting girl, suck on that mint, squirt your loathesome dripping armpits and spray your reeking vulva and vagina with a cooling mist that has blossoms in it or no man will ever want you—but if you do what we advise *regularly* Prince Charming will come along and fuck you and take you to lollipop land.

It is not the most stupid thing I ever heard of in my life, but it ranks high, the incredibly nasty and lying stuff that comes over the Pukey in regard to this matter of a "human girl person." What a crass appeal to fear, what an abominable lie. How do they do it? How can anyone eat rotten hog brains day after day and not throw up? It is utterly disgusting what comes over the Pukey, and that is why I have refused to write for the goddamned thing even though they have offered me all kinds of money to help them sell their pussy sprays and the other moronic nonsense they shove down the suffering gullet of this naïve great country.

It is true the organs of creation and elimination are in juxtaposition; that is God's plan. Of *course* a girl should wash herself, and so for heaven's sake should a man!—but that is all that is needed, honest soap and water . . . maybe, on a very hot day, a *little* deodorant under the arms, I don't want to be unreasonable about this. But to the fairer half of humanity I have this piece of advice: leave the area between your legs alone, honey, it is *all right,* there is nothing wrong with it and don't let those lying hucksters scare you, the way it is is what makes real men love you and protect your children and bring home the bacon and hold your hand when you aren't feeling well, don't waste your money by squirting God-awful chemicals with synthetic rose blossoms on it, you yourself are a *real* rose blossom and the way you smell is *great.*

The knowledge was not in my head when Rose came to my room and lay her woman's body by my side, but all in the world I smelled was the perfectly normal scent of a healthy young woman's human person on a hot September night, and a young woman who at that had had a bath not too many hours before. Today, as can readily be perceived from my peroration against the Pukey, I would find the odor of her "girl human person" a beauty of nature, but I sure didn't then.

As I felt about her soft mysterious titty mashed on my side, I liked it and didn't like it at the same time. Part of the scent, the musky part of it, seemed to come in some degree from under her arms, but most of it plainly and unmistakably came from the forbidden place down between her thighs. The odor was weird, out of this world. It was a bit like chinaberries mixed with locust flowers, but in addition there was a powerful heady musk not unlike my mother's French perfume, although Rose was wearing no perfume. She'd had a bath around 4 P.M. but it was now something like two in the morning and it was hot; there was also, to tell the truth, a definite but not strong fishy smell and a stronger tinge of sharp ammonia, which I assumed in a weakish horror to be traces of dried pee-pee on the hairs of her pussy.

I am probably making it sound as if it were repulsive to me then, for which I am sorry because that is not quite accurate. *Disturbing* is the word, disturbing and upsetting, and just a little scary. It was also, however, strangely fascinating. I couldn't understand the true nature of the matter but I knew I had come upon something remarkable, something unique, something true—this, then, was what a *real grown human woman* smelled like. I'd noticed a distantly similar scent from my sister during games of "Doctor," but to compare poor little eleven-year-old Doll to Rose was like comparing a molehill to Mount Everest. The powerful scent that emanated from her was headying, dizzying and very strangely disturbing: more than the soft breast against my arm and side, it caused me to feel a wobbliness in the knees and a weak emptiness in the pit of my stomach. It also caused, most disturbingly of all, a peculiar tingle in my no longer quite-so-limp or sleepy "dilly."

Yes, *that* one was waking up, bravely struggling upward from the swamp of innocence and peering around blindly in the murk in response to an immemorial signal—"Where is it? Where is it? It is somewhere around, I know it is somewhere around, where is it?" As I lay there half-hypnotized by the primordial scent of her body with her bare warm leg against mine and her arm around my waist, a thought beyond my years came to me, a daring thought that made my head reel by its very boldness, a truly brilliant ratiocination.

After all, there she was in bed with me, it was dark, no one could see us, Daddy and Mother were sound asleep far away—it was a heaven-sent opportunity, that little child's nightgown was only about six inches below it, if she would open her legs I could put my hand between them and touch her. I swallowed, glue in my mouth and an awful weakness in my knees. It was a thing I suddenly wanted very, very much to do, and somehow it had to happen.

How could I ask her, how? Yes, how? The problem was

to find a dignified way to bring it up, a composed and mature manner of expressing it so she wouldn't think I was just a child. Perhaps casual and offhand with true sophistication would be best, just lightly as if it were nothing, a casual request as if it were almost a continuing part of the conversation. Yes, that was the ticket if I could only find the right place to fit it in with calm, unruffled sophistication.

The opportunity came only moments after the daring thought had entered my mind. Rose had temporarily veered off the tiresome subject of Daddy and was telling me how *understanding* I was, how wise beyond my days on earth. "Buddy," she said in a tender whisper, "I'll never forget how nice you've been to me tonight, how sweet and kind you've been listening to all my troubles. Now, I know you love me, I . . . I'm sure you do, I never *really* doubted it, and it's done me more good than you can know to talk to you. You understand it, you do, you don't blame me for loving your daddy when I can't help it, you understand it and forgive me, you really do. Do you know, you're a *lot* smarter than your age, Buddy, do you know that?"

"Well, that's what they all say," I replied with cool sophistication. "And by the way, Rose, since you're here in bed with me and everything, can I touch your pussy?"

Thus the sophisticated proposition was finally put to Rose, as the September moon cleared the white oak in our yard. She was stunned into silence for a moment or two, but not for long. "Why, Buddy, shut your mouth!" she answered. "What an awful thing to say, and where did you get any such idea as that, anyhow?"

"I'm curious to see what it's like," I said. "Can I touch it?"

"No, you can't! And you ought to be ashamed of yourself, saying such a nasty thing, a child your age!"

"Can't I touch it a *little*, Rose, not a lot, just a *little* to see what it's like?"

"Of course you can't! I'm . . . I'm *shocked* at you, Buddy, real shocked! Now you be quiet or I'm going back to my own bed!"

I have no doubt Rose was genuinely startled, if not so shocked and horrified by my language as she pretended.

Such words as "pussy" and so forth hardly fazed her; she used them often herself when speaking to me and my sister and little brother. "Wash your ass," she'd say when giving a bath to Waski. "Come on, now, wash it, you can't go around with poo down there, there are little bugs in it and they'll make you sick. Take that cloth and wash your ass good this very second, Waski, or I'll go tell your Mother!" The reader of course has already heard her, this was how she talked to us children. But I have no doubt the sophisticated proposition startled and disconcerted Rose.

"Buddy, will you *shut* up? Are you out of your mind?"

However, as I kept nagging and arguing and pestering her, her shock wore off and she gradually shifted her position and began discussing the sophisticated proposition with me in a slightly different way, as if it were a very bad idea but not a total absurdity, as if it were a most unwise move but a thing that could conceivably happen.

"Oh, stop it, Buddy, stop arguing at me," she said. "What do you want to touch it for, anyhow? Haven't you ever seen Dolly? Mine is just like hers."

"Yeah, but yours is all grown-up," I said, "it's got hair on it."

"Well, that's the only difference, otherwise it's the same. Besides, I don't even have much because I'm towheaded, and towheads don't have much hair down there."

"Rose, what you say can't be true. You could have a *baby,* and Doll could *never* get a baby out of her. And I never even saw Doll much, she won't let me look at it. I saw her friend Elizabeth's better than I did hers, and I didn't see Elizabeth's much either. She just whisked her dress up, then pulled it right back down."

Rose laughed. "What did you see?" she asked.

"Well, I saw a kind of little slit between her legs, with sort of fat lips, and . . . well, a little jigger in the middle like an orange pip. That's all I saw."

Rose laughed again. "That's all you saw? Buddy, that's *it!*"

"But that *can't* be all there is to it!" I said. "Where do babies come from? There's got to be an opening in it somewhere, a place where babies can come out. Well, don't laugh, Rose, isn't that true? Well, *isn't* it?"

"Yes, it's true," said Rose with a smile I could see in the moonlight. "You're crazy as a hoot owl, Buddy, you really are, wanting to touch my pussy and giving me all these arguments. The things that go on in your head and come out of your mouth are something else, I never met anybody like you at any age. Now listen, look. I know you're curious like any child and want to know, but Buddy, I can't let you touch me down there, your daddy and momma would fire me, they'd think I was awful."

"But I'd never tell *them* about a thing *like this*, that would be the dumbest thing in the world!" I said. "*Please*, Rose, let me touch it, I want to see what it's like. You said I was nice to you, can't you be nice to me? Isn't turn about fair play? I listened to you talk about Daddy for the longest kind of time, can't you let me touch it a *little* just once? *Please*, Rose, won't you let me? I'm *curious*. It would be real sweet and nice of you, if you would . . . *please*, Rose . . . "

I didn't believe she would agree and I was pleading and whimpering piteously at her just for the sake of argument. I didn't know then that Rose had a chronic and fundamental difficulty saying no to any male, even a very young one. She wasn't aroused or interested in me, she just couldn't say no to me, it was a failing she had. To my surprised delight, she cleared her throat and replied:

"*Well*, I guess it wouldn't really matter all that much, you're just a child. And I know children are curious, I was myself when I was small. If I let you do what you want, will you cross your heart not to tell your daddy and momma?"

"Oh, yes!"

"And then you'll shut up about it, and not ask no more?"

"Oh, yes! Of course!"

I am absolutely certain Rose at this point did not have any kind of lustful interest in me, but she *had* become quite solemn. In an awful suspense I watched her give it a final moment of grave consideration, then saw her stumble as she reached for the hem of her thin, worn cotton nightgown. She didn't think the touch of a child's hand could affect her, but she was wrong. "Well, all right then," she said. "And remember, don't tell nobody. You promised, Buddy."

"Oh, don't worry," I said, as she half sat up in bed and

pulled the nightgown above her waist. It was happening. A slight ringing noise was in my ears and I had trouble breathing as she pulled the nightgown even higher around her waist, lay back on the pillow, opened her legs and said: "Now, not much, Buddy, just so you'll know, okay?"

In the moonlight, which was now brighter in my room, I could see plainly her belly and navel and not too far below her navel an inverted triangle of short and rather curly hair that was darker than the hair on her head. This wasn't any revelation, I knew of course grown women had hair there, but the actual sight of it gave me a queasy sensation. And there seemed to me to be quite a bit of it; she'd said towheads didn't have much hair down there, but if this was not much then brunettes must have an awful lot, I thought, they must be hairy as bears. Slowly, I put my hand on her stomach near her bellybutton, which reassuringly looked very much like my own, then I took a deep frightened breath.

In part it was my imagination, but the scent of her body seemed infinitely stronger now; veritable waves of dizzying, hair-raising scent seemed to come from that mysterious and scary area between her legs. The thing made me nervous. It would be too much to say I was really afraid of it, but it sure made me nervous.

"I thought you wanted to touch it?" asked Rose.

"I do, but I'm just looking," I replied.

"You can't even see it in this light."

"I can see it a little."

"Buddy," said Rose, with a smile in her voice, "every girl and woman has one just like mine. You wanted to touch it, go ahead and touch it—it won't hurt you, there's no way it could hurt you."

"I know that," I said, "what do you think I am, dumb?"

There was no way out of it. Slowly, I moved my hand over her warm stomach toward the mysterious thing about which I'd wondered all the thinking days of my life. Of course it wouldn't hurt me, not in a direct sense, but this was a forbidden thing and who could tell what subtle dangers and oblique pitfalls might lurk in there?

However, when my fingers encountered the outer limits of it—short, curly hairs that were silklike but not as fine as the hair on her head—curiosity overcame my apprehensions.

My hand moved on to a padded mound which was covered with hair that was very curly and considerably thicker. The mound seemed to me very prominent, like a little hill, and I pressed it with my fingers and discovered that although it was soft there was hard bone beneath it, I could feel a kind of ridge.

Very fascinating. I was so interested I didn't even mind the scent of it even though it was very strong. My fingers moved on to the odd division in the middle of it and I felt the same little jigger I'd noticed in Elizabeth, the little thing kind of like an orange pip. I moved my fingers lower and encountered the plumpish sides of the division, which also had short, curly hair. The area in the middle was not exactly wet but it was not exactly dry either, moist I guess was what it was and that was most interesting. With great curiosity, totally fascinated, I moved my finger back to the little orange pip and touched it in an effort to determine its nature and properties—*very* interesting, it was a rubbery and slippery little thing and it darted away from my fingertip in a rather clever way, I couldn't pin it down. At this moment Rose reached for my hand and pulled it away. "That's enough, Buddy," she said, in a voice that did not sound quite like her.

"Why, I didn't even touch it!" I said indignantly.

"Yes, you did."

"I practically didn't at all! That wasn't a *fair* touch, Rose! You've *got* to give me a *fair touch!*"

I felt her stiffen in the bed as she turned to me and brushed back with one hand blonde wavy hair from her forehead. "Don't tell me that, you dern little redheaded thing!" she said, in a voice that did not sound like her hardly at all. "You remind me of them men. I don't 'got' to give you nothin'!"

"But . . . but . . . but *Rose!*" I cried. "Don't get *mad,* why are you mad? I only want to touch it so I can see what it's like, and I *didn't!*"

"Well," she said in a quieter voice, "you touched it, that's it."

"I don't know why you are mad at me, you said I could. Do you want *me* to get mad at you, too? Did I *hurt* you, is that why you're mad?"

"Buddy, I am not mad at you."

"Then why are you talking to me in that tone? Now there is some justice in my position, Rose, you will have to admit that. There is some justice in my position when I ask in all politeness for a fair touch."

"Well, you had one. You had a fair touch."

"Oh, yeah? Then tell me this, how could a baby get out of there? I didn't feel any place where a baby could come!"

Now she seemed weary, preoccupied, almost sad. "Well, it's there," she said. "That's where a baby comes from if a girl can have them."

"But *where?*" I asked. "I didn't feel anything like that!"

"Buddy, it's *there* a little below where you had your finger, just take my word for it."

"But Rose, that is the very thing I am most interested in! I want to see how a baby can get out of it! Now you don't *have* to, but if you're nice you ought to give me a fair touch and let me feel where a baby comes from!"

"Oh, Buddy, stop fussing at me! I already was nice to you, I let you touch it and I don't *want* to be touched there no more, it bothers me! You don't understand it but a thing like that can stir a girl up. You just lie back and be quiet now."

Rose herself said it—"a thing like that can stir a girl up." But I don't believe she thought even now it was possible for the touch of my hand to have any serious effect on her, although it already had. I fussed, complained, fretted and nagged at her relentlessly with all kinds of arguments until finally she sighed and said: "Oh, all *right!* Give me your hand and I'll show you the exact dern spot they come from, if you have just got to know!"

With another weary and what seemed to me a rather angry sigh, Rose took my hand and put it between her open legs, seized my middle finger in her own fingers, pushed my finger down and said, *"Here,"* and a tingle of shock went through me as my finger sank effortlessly into warm flesh. The sensation was shocking, but also very pleasant, the flesh fit softly around my finger like a warm ring. I noticed something else that was rather interesting, the whole area had become more moist, it wasn't wet but it was more moist; my finger seemed to be covered by a kind of thin slippery substance, it had gone into her very, very easily. However, as I felt the soft folds of flesh firm if not tight around my finger I was extremely puzzled by a basic question.

"Rose," I said, "no baby could possibly be born out of here. It seems to be kind of deep, but it isn't really any bigger than my finger."

Rose didn't answer. She was probably, I thought, still mad at me because of the way I'd demanded she do what I wanted. But she'd released my hand and I might as well examine this mystery while I had the chance. I pulled my finger almost out of the warm flesh and pushed it back in, then did it again, and once more, and again, fascinated by the way it seemed to close upon my finger, and *follow* my finger if that is the word. As I did this, I discovered an even more interesting thing: not only did it fit exactly around my finger, she had muscles in it down there—I could feel the soft ring slowly tighten on my finger, loosen and tighten again.

However, I was still very puzzled. No baby could get out of this place, not even possibly, it was much too small an opening. I'd seen newborn babies and they were little, but their heads were far bigger than this thing and I did not see how on earth they could get out of it. The flesh did seem to have strange folds in it, when I moved my finger to the side I could feel them, and maybe it would stretch a little bit, but it would have to stretch a *tremendous* amount for a baby to get out of it. With an absorbed and fascinated interest, I continued my examination, Rose herself forgotten. It *was* deep or seemed to be. Was it nineteen and a half inches deep, or had the filthy Hollis exaggerated? Curious to know if I could get to the bottom of it, although I didn't think I could, I pushed my finger in a little harder, afraid of hurting her, but still felt no bottom, just warm, unending flesh.

"Rose, how *deep* is it?" I asked. "Is there a bottom to it?"

Silence. Finally, I heard a tiny swallowing noise from Rose, then in a strange little voice she said: "I dunno. I guess so."

"There's got to be, it seems to me," I said, and pulled

my finger almost all the way out of her and pushed it back in quite harder as far as I could, and at that point Rose grabbed my wrist and said: "Buddy, quit that!"

"I'm sorry," I said, "did I hurt you?"

"No, you didn't hurt me, but quit it."

"Well . . . if I didn't hurt you, why do you want me to quit it?"

"Because it's stirring me up something *horrible.* Now please quit."

It was strange and a little scary, definitely a little scary. She was telling me to quit but at the same time holding my wrist with a grip of iron so I couldn't move. What was the matter with her? I began to be a little afraid. "Well, let me go, then," I said.

Rose didn't reply and she didn't move. Her hand continued to grip my wrist like iron. Finally, she took a long deep breath and when she let it out I could feel her sweaty leg tremble against my own. She seemed to be in some kind of misery or pain. Her hand remained gripped hard on my wrist; there was no way I could get my finger out of her, she was quite a bit stronger than I was myself and I could not have moved my hand. She took another long deep breath and a little shudder ran through her body.

"Oh, God," she whispered, "this is awful of me, just awful."

A long silence ensued. I lay propped on an elbow with my finger sunk in warm flesh and looked at the lower half of her pale body in the moonlight and listened to her breathe. She was breathing peculiarly; I could see just below her ribs her stomach rise and fall in the moonlight, her navel tilting slowly up and down. I couldn't see her titties, to my disappointment they were still covered by her thin cotton nightgown, but I could see all of her stomach and a part of her ribs, and her abdomen and diaphragm were rising and falling faster than normal. She seemed to be out of breath but she hadn't exerted herself in any way, all she'd done was just lie there.

How long would she keep this up? In silence and frozen motionlessness, we both lay there in the hot humid moonlight, her hand gripped on my wrist and my finger in her. From time to time I could feel the soft ring slowly tighten and then loosen on my finger, and now it gave me a slight case of the creeps. I'd noticed something else that didn't set too well with me. The area between her legs was not just moist now, it was wet, the entire thing was wet, very wet, even the short curly hairs around it were wet. I definitely began to get the creeps. This had been extremely fascinating at first, but now I wanted out of the situation. Why didn't she *say* something? Why was she making those little funny swallowing noises? Why was she sweating so much? I could feel both her arm and leg all clammy with sweat—what was *wrong* with her? I wanted out of the situation, I'd had a "fair touch," oh yes, very fair, that was plenty, more than plenty. I made up my mind to demand that she release my hand and let me take my finger out of her, but then another little scary gulping sound came from her and she said in a tiny helpless voice:

"Buddy, this is horrible of me, just horrible, but there's nothing I can do. Will you please help me a little?"

I had to feel sorry for her she seemed in such distress, but I didn't like it. Doubtfully, I asked, "Help you?"

"Yes . . . will you help me a little?"

Even more doubtfully, I asked: "What do you want me to do?"

"I'll . . . I'll show you," she whispered. "Just put your finger back here for a minute." Her hand guided my finger back to the little strange pip and she pressed my fingertip on it and moved it forward and then backward. "Do this a little," she said in a whisper I could hardly hear. "Just a little, like that. Not too hard and not too easy, like that . . ."

It was the weirdest business I'd ever heard of. For some peculiar reason known only to herself and the devil she wanted me to rub the damn little thing with my fingertip. I didn't like it, I didn't like it one bit, the whole episode had become weird as hell, but I saw no way out of it.

"Like this?" I asked.

"Yes," she whispered, "like that, exactly like that."

"All right," I said, "for how long?"

"Buddy, only for a little."

It was more than a "little," or so it seemed to me—actually I suppose the rubbing of the pip only went on for two or three minutes. But it was quite a bit more than a "little," and it was hard to do because the damn thing was so slippery, it kept darting away from my fingertip, or seemed to. She began breathing harder almost as soon as I began it and as I kept it up she breathed even harder as if she was out of breath completely, and from time to time little funny sounds sort of like a kitten meowing came from her.

It was scary. I don't want to exaggerate, I was not really frightened, much less terrified, but I was certainly bewildered and bothered. She was breathing as if she'd run a mile and had one arm around me so tight I was nearly as out of breath as she was; her arm was locked around me like a band of steel, I couldn't breathe, and her other hand was clenched on my shoulder so hard it hurt. As I have said, Rose was very strong for a girl. More than my shoulder hurt, the angle of my hand was awkward and my wrist ached. On top of all my other problems, rubbing the little pip was difficult, I kept losing it, it was so elusive and slippery I could not keep my fingertip on it or so I thought.

"Where *is* it?" I asked. "I can't find it."

"You've *got* it!" cried Rose in a choked voice. "Keep on, Buddy, just for a little, please!"

On and on it went, my wrist hurting and Rose breathing harder and harder and now making not only little mewing sounds but little groaning sounds as well. She was also sweating even worse, perspiration was running off her in streams, I could see streaks of it on her belly and legs in the moonlight. Suddenly a louder groan came from her followed by another even louder groan and that was enough for me—I'd had all I wanted of this weird business, to hell with it!

"Oh *please,* Buddy!" she cried in a strangled voice. "I am in just a minute, *don't stop!*"

"But my wrist is tired," I said wearily, "it hurts. How long do I have to do it?"

"Just a *little* more . . . *please,* Buddy, I almost am right now . . . do you love me a little? I love *you* . . . please, not much more . . ."

It struck me then as slightly ironic, although I did not know what over-all significance it might have had: before *I* had been whimpering piteously, and now *she* was. Perhaps it is in fact an unfortunate recurring theme in the relationship of male and female in our own society, especially if one of them is thirteen years old, but of course Rose had only herself to blame for that. She'd hardly been wise, but then how can a girl be wise if she can't say no?

With a weary and disgusted sigh, I resumed rubbing the elusive little pip and made a real effort to keep my fingertip on it and rub it fairly hard, since that seemed to be what she wanted. It was—soon thereafter, Rose gave a low, dreadful groan and to my astonishment began lifting her hips in such a way I could hardly maintain contact with the pip even though I was concentrating on doing just that.

And then she gave a loud bloodcurdling cry that could easily have awakened Doll in the bedroom next door: "OHH-HH-HH!"—it was awful, I could feel her entire body trembling all over and the little pip throbbing and pulsing as if it were alive under my finger. It really and truly gave me the complete creeps, I'd had enough, *more* than enough, and I determined to get out of that mess no matter what she said—but then her arm loosened around my waist, her hand slipped from my shoulder, her blonde head fell back on the pillow, and she pushed away my hand and closed her legs tight together with a kind of weak shudder.

To say the least, I didn't know what to make of it. Obviously, she'd had some type of a fit. I'd seen a rather homely adolescent girl on a local Glenville bus once have an epileptic seizure and that was what this was, not the same but similar to it. Rubbing girls on that little pip made them have a fit. As I lay there relieved that Rose's fit was over, I felt a certain amount of pity for her—she'd wanted to do it, but it was clearly an awful and painful thing to endure.

So I thought at first. I soon found out the truth was otherwise. Rose took several deep, deep breaths, as if she'd been sixty feet down in the ocean, then she put a limp hand on my stomach and her head limp on my shoulder. I felt her lips touch my cheek and heard her whisper: "Oh, God, that is heavenly, heavenly. Oh, Buddy, I can't tell you how heavenly that is, how beautiful, it's paradise. I love you, I love you so much. Oh, Buddy, I love you . . . "

It seemed to me a strange thing for her to say after having had such a frightful fit. "I love you, Buddy. . . ." what on earth had "love" to do with her ghastly behavior? To listen to her made me want to vomit.

Writers, in my view, are or should be prophets as well as mischief-makers and storytellers. It is true the writer owes his reader whatever gifts he might have, but he does *not* owe it to the reader to tell him comforting and reassuring lies; on the contrary—the writer owes it to the reader not to reinforce his prejudices but to destroy them, to strike them if he can with a terrible swift sword, to smite them with truth and knock them down. Prophets are without honor, it is a thankless calling, but it was ever thus and cannot be otherwise. A great book or even a good book or even a soso fair book cannot be written by reinforcing lies, it can only be done by telling some readers sometimes things they do not want to hear.

Many readers of "average intelligence and good will" would, I believe, find the preceding pages rather amusing and slightly pathetic. Others, I am sure, would find those pages shockingly nasty and in very "bad taste." Well, good taste is not a thing I have ever been famous for, it is not my forte or strong point hardly at all. But I feel a certain sympathy for those disgusted and nauseated readers.

I really do. The fact is, at thirteen I reflected with an especially gruesome horror the values of a society which condemns sexuality in general and condemns specifically and savagely the sexuality of its fairer half. Is the trick I have played on the reader—I hope for his diversion and amusement—apparent now? The source of the power of the lady in that early autumn moon is not located where I said but in her viewpoint, which permits the boy's reactions to make a mocking and horrifying comment on the very values he is reflecting.

If those pages are disturbing, then that is why the pages are hardly erotic at all. The offense of the lady in the moon does not lie in a description no matter how graphic of a grown girl allowing and even half compelling a thirteen-year-old boy to masturbate her; the real crime lies in that lady's underlying sympathy for the dreadful girl. In actual fact the boy did *not* masturbate her, for *that* she could have gone to her own lonely bed; but mere physical relief was not what she wanted, it was incidental to a thing far more powerful and for that thing another person is needed. It was a shared not a solitary act, which makes it "worse." There is no doubt of it, the underlying sympathy is the *real* crime. If I condemned Rose now as I did at thirteen, if I dismissed her human feelings as on a par with an epileptic fit, then those readers shocked by the preceding pages would congratulate me on having upheld our moral standards in the face of all the "pornography" nowadays.

"*Moral* standards?"—now that is funny, and let us not be deceived by the apparent liberalization of our age. Hateful pornographic movies, books and magazines are merely the other side of the coin, another angle of Queen Victoria's forbidding face. The Good Queen is far from gone; it is not surface appearance but underlying attitudes that really count—and underlying attitudes have not changed all that much.

"*Moral* standards?"—very funny. Half the human race is not fully human—that is a moral standard? A girl who becomes aroused and foolishly commits an act of love with a young boy is a filthy creature for whom one should feel no sympathy—this is a moral standard? Time will tell whether or not such standards are moral, time will tell if "the day will come when they will look back on us in pity and horror." I believe that hour will arrive, I believe the day will dawn when pussy sprays are a thing of the past and that is my prophecy.

Even a soso fair book must have a prophecy, a vision of a better world and a better life! The theme of this story *does* have a considerable importance and will be with us for a long time, but the above is all I claim or want for this small work itself, that it be at least a soso fair book able to provide a little passing amusement for those who pick it up. There would surely be no point in writing deliberately a book that has no value whatever, isn't that so? And thus I have made my prophecy that pussy sprays have got to go, they have got to go and they will go, they will vanish into the murk from whence they came.

The truth of what happened that night when Rose lay her head on my shoulder and told me she loved me is obvious, whatever those who think her filthy might make of it. It is as plain as the autumn moon in the sky what had occurred.

"I love you, Buddy . . ."

It seemed to me a strange thing for her to say after having had such a frightful fit. However, barbarian though I was at thirteen, if I had been asked if Rose meant it when she whispered that she loved me, I would have had to say yes, she meant it without qualification in her heart and soul. I would have had to admit that even then because it was so overwhelmingly and unmistakably true, but in the nastiness of my own little heart and soul I did not have the remotest idea of the value or meaning of her emotion. Not then—the night of nights was not over, but not then.

As I said, it's as obvious as the moon in the sky. I had not found Rose, I had located only a part of her and could not begin to comprehend even that small part. I knew little of the world and less about the truly hard-to-find places where people live or die, survive or perish. But this did not hold for Rose herself, no matter how unwise, how stupidly kind, how childish, how naïve she might have been. With her far greater resources than my own, she had stumbled into paradise, and was found.

6

Rose rocks the cradle

AS NATURE WOULD have it and man has arranged it, Rose cooled off in about five minutes and the horror of her deed dawned on her like a sickish sunrise with hideous mustard clouds and dangerous tornadoes lurking not far off. "Oh, GOD!" she cried. "What have I *done??*" Oh, Buddy, forgive me, I didn't mean to do that, I *didn't!* Oh, Lord, next thing I'll be robbing a cradle completely! Ain't there no *limit* to how bad I am? What if your *daddy* had come in here? Ohh-hh, oh Lor-r-rd, I got to get out of here, I got to get out, ohh-hh, ohh-hh . . ."

A hand clasped melodramatically but with real fear on her forehead, Rose sat on the edge of the bed shaking all over, I could feel her body tremble beside me. She was too upset at this point to realize the real and deadly danger she was in; the only thought in her head was to get out of that room, to put distance between herself and the scene of her horrendous crime. As I felt her body tremble with fright, I couldn't help but feel a bit sorry for her, flint-hearted little child though I was.

"Rose, you shouldn't feel so bad," I said. "It was *my* idea."

"You don't understand," she answered. "Oh, God! I know I'm bad, but I never thought I would stoop as low as this! I got to get out of here, I got to get back to my own room in my own bed! Buddy, you won't tell nobody, you won't do that, will you? You do love me a little? I hope you do, cause I got to tell you good night, I got to get out of here!"

Rose stood up on trembling knees in her nightgown in the moonlight. I was glad her fit was over but a little disappointed she was leaving, I had hoped to see and examine her titties, which interested me almost as much as her mysterious pussy. But it was late and I was sleepy and tired so I said: "Good night, Rose. And don't worry, I won't tell a soul about this."

Rose was too upset to realize at this point the danger she was in, but a wince did come on her face as she stood there in the moonlight in her thin, worn cotton nightgown. "I sure hope you don't," she said in a sick little voice. "They'd think I was awful and I sure was. But I didn't mean to, I really didn't. Promise you won't tell, Buddy."

I promised solemnly to say nothing to anyone and a few moments later heard her close the door and then heard her bare feet pitty-pat off down the upstairs hall. She couldn't wait to get out of there and put space between herself and her sin.

Unfortunately, however, or fortunately depending on the point of view, this was not the end of my night with Rose. As I have said, the night of nights Rose came to my room was not only one of the most important experiences of my life but was also fundamental to whatever comprehension I have of her as a human being, and that is why my account of it forms a fairly substantial fraction of this narrative. The night of nights had not ended, it had only begun.

However, other events of even greater importance did occur after that night and we will get to them in due course. The time of the "damnable commotion" and the epizootics and all the rest is not far away, we have remaining only a couple of chapters in which Rose first rocks the cradle in the deep and then robs it and falls herself into pure sheer hell—and that last *was* fairly sexy as opposed to rather amusing and slightly pathetic; and this is no trick of mischief, that robbing of the cradle was *fairly sexy*, or so it sure seemed to me at the time.

Why my mother never noticed on the following morning the traces of lipstick on the cigarette butts in that glass I'll never know. Daddy with his Hawkshaw the Detective instinct would have noticed instantly. But Mother didn't. Perhaps it was her faculty for not seeing certain things, the gift she shared with Rose for turning her back, and looking away. She was upset, though; I remember her pale and worried face staring down at me as Southern morning sunshine warmed the room.

"I am deeply shocked at you, Brother. The very idea, stealing and smoking Rose's cigarettes and reading something till all hours, probably something nasty since you won't tell me what it was. Do you realize it's eleven thirty in the morning, that you've laid here in bed like a lizard half the day? This isn't *you,* Brother. You must be sick or you wouldn't act like that, I am going to have to give you a dose of castor oil or calomel. Which one do you want?"

Rose swore that when she left my room she'd had no intention of going back to it and I believe her. However, the fact is, quite apart from moral judgments, her behavior had been most unwise, even more unwise than it might appear. At the age of thirteen I was an incorrigible and inveterate blabbermouth, whose middle name as my father often said was braggadocio. True, I'd promised Rose I wouldn't tell and in a childish way thought I meant it. But not in the least, the truth is I was dying to tell Doll, palpitating in eagerness to stun her with it, downright feverish to take her aside and flabbergast her more or less as follows:

"Doll, wait till you *hear* what happened! Now you won't believe this, but last night Rose came in my room and got in my bed and I put my finger in her pussy! I did, Doll, right to the bottom, I could feel her backbone, and it got so wet you wouldn't believe it, there was about a quart of pussy juice pouring all off it! Then I rubbed a little jigger in it and she sweated and snorted like a horse and had a horrible fit, her eyebrows were scrunched all down and her eyeballs were rolled up and she groaned like she was dying and frothed at the mouth! How do you like that, Doll? What do you think of it, and do you know what it means, hmmm? You aren't like that *yet,* you're little, but you *will* be. You see it's what happens to a grown-up woman when somebody puts his finger in her pussy and rubs that little jigger. I hate to tell you this, Doll, but someday a man will put his finger in you and rub your little jigger and you will sweat and snort and have a horrible fit just like Rose. How do you like that, hmmm? Well, Doll, that's how life is and that's why it's my duty as your brother to tell you so you'll know: it's *awful,* Doll, but that's how it is, that's how the world turns as it circles the Sun . . ."

Ghastly as it sounds, that's very close to what I would have told Doll if Rose hadn't returned to my room. I wouldn't have intended my sister to run at once to my mother with this terrifying information, or at least I wouldn't have exactly intended that, but Doll beyond any doubt would have done so immediately and it is not hard to imagine the effect of some such question as the following: "Mother!—Buddy says he put his finger in Rose last night and rubbed a little jigger in her and she snorted and had a fit, and he says *I* would too if I was grown-up—is it *true,* would I sweat and snort and froth at the mouth and have a horrible fit like he says?"

When Rose returned to her own room a dreadful case of the jitters overwhelmed her. She got herself a Camel and was about to light it when the jitters hit. The horror of what she'd done had already staggered her but it staggered her again with multiplied effect as an additional realization came to her—she had gotten into bed in the dark of night with a thirteen-year-old boy and allowed him to play with her most intimate female parts and then had made him masturbate her . . . *and that boy was going to tell them all about it on the following morning!* Of course he would! A boy able to invent stories about a man in Peru making pork chops out of his little niece couldn't possibly keep such a thing as this to himself, not even possibly! She was in deadly and grave danger and on the following morning almost certainly would be fired and sent packing from this house—it would take a small miracle to save her, and that was the plain truth!

Such were Rose's thoughts, she told me later, as she stood there by the bureau in her room on shaking knees. I would tell Dolly, of course, that was who I would tell, Dolly, and she would run to her mother, and Mrs. Hillyer weeping would go to Mr. Hillyer, and Mr. Hillyer in a fury would throw her out of the house in five minutes, she would lose the only real home she'd ever had, she'd be sent away in contempt by people she loved. . . . Rose was so staggered she almost fell right down to the floor in a faint, so staggered she forgot the pack of half-empty Camels and the five or six wooden country matches in her trembling hand.

Tornadoes indeed lurked in the mustard clouds of that sickish yellow sunrise. A person about to be taken out and hanged, she said, couldn't have felt much worse. As the realization came to her that even though she had to try there was *no way* she could make me be quiet about this her eyes filled with tears and she began to cry—she was doomed, hopelessly doomed, I would surely tell them the awful and disgusting thing she had done and she would lose her place, be fired.

Rose of course was absolutely dead right. Rose was right, there was *no way* she could make me keep my nasty little mouth shut about a great filthy thing like this. And yet we know she did, she made me keep my little mouth shut like the lips of the Sphinx until this day when it no longer matters, because a small miracle occurred. And that I believe is the most important thing by far that happened on the night of nights when Rose came to my room and got into my bed in naïve innocence and childlike despair, unable to endure the wilderness of life without love.

I didn't hear her bare feet pitty-pat in the hall when she returned, but I heard the door softly open and knew it was her and was very annoyed; I was tired and had almost gone to sleep in those few minutes she'd been away. She had come back, I was sure, in order to coax me into fiddling around again with that damnable little orange pip or whatever it was, and I'd had *enough* of it; it had been interesting at first but I didn't want to bother any more with the little stinky and nasty thing. After all, "Doctor" was a great game but who wanted to play it all night? I sat up in bed and crossed my arms sternly like Daddy as her nightgowned figure cautiously shut the door and tiptoed across the room toward my bed. All I needed was Daddy's straw hat on the back of my mop of red hair tilted a bit the side, and a rolled up copy of the Glenville *News-Tribune* in my hand; I didn't have a clipped and just barely graying moustache, but my lips were bitten together in a thin Daddylike line as she came in the moonlight toward my bed.

I was about to say: "Go away, Rose, and leave me alone, it's late!"—when I realized she was crying. Tears were on her face, I could see them in the moonlight, and she was biting her lip in an effort to control herself. She was also trembling very badly, I could feel her body shake as she sat beside me with hesitation on the bed. What seemed to be some matches and half a pack of cigarettes fell unheeded from her hand to the sheet as she reached for my own hand, took it and squeezed damp fingers on it and said in a tiny voice:

"Buddy, I didn't mean to come back, I didn't, but I have to ask you, as bad as I've been please have pity on me and don't ruin me by telling them what I did. I know it was bad, it was bad and dumb. But mostly it was dumb, Buddy. I didn't really mean you no harm, I'd never want to hurt a hair on your head and that's the truth, I love you, I wouldn't want to hurt you ever. But everybody would think I did, they'd think I was an awful girl, they'd despise me and hate me."

At this point she began to cry aloud in such a way I was afraid Doll would wake up and hear her. Clutching my hand and trembling all over, she asked in a broken voice: "Do you hate me, Buddy? I've tried to be good and nice to you, do you hate me? Do you think I'm awful?"

Now, sympathy was a thing I regarded as wishy-washy, despicable, blubbery, loathesome and deadly dangerous, as perhaps I have already indicated—the lack of it, an inability to feel it or allow myself to feel it, was the very illness from which I suffered. An emotion like that was too dread to be permitted to exist, it exposed too much, it revealed too much, it hurt too much, far too much—I was *not about* to let this girl reduce me to helplessness in such a way, not about to, *never!* She could cry all she wanted to and I wouldn't listen to her, not for a moment, but already Rose's small miracle was on the way. It was coming, with a mercilessness the lady in the autumn moon could match but not surpass; the beginning of a terrible ache was in my throat and the start of a truly intolerable pain was in my chest as I listened to her cry and heard her ask me if I hated her.

However, I was fighting, I was fighting hard, and I am sure my answer seemed a little cold to her. "*No,* Rose," I replied, "I don't hate you and I don't think you're awful, exactly. Besides, what are you worried about? It was *my* fault, not yours, I'm the one who thought of it, like I told you already."

A discouraged and despairing little sigh came from her. She stared at me in helplessness for a moment, then put her other hand on my knee and said:

"Buddy, you don't understand. They'd blame *me,* not you. And they'd think I was awful, a disgustin' girl, which I am but Buddy, please don't tell them. Please don't. I can't get no other job—and that ain't even the most important thing, but I *can't.* I really can't, Buddy, it's a depression goin' on, they ain't no jobs. I know cause I looked and looked and couldn't find nothin', nothin' at all. Now I ain't just tryin' to make you feel sorry for me, but I weared out my shoes lookin' for some work, Buddy, I was hungry, real hungry, and I didn't have no place to stay, but I couldn't find no job nowheres because there just wasn't none. All I could of done was to be, to be a . . . well, you wouldn't know about it, but I couldn't do that, never, I couldn't . . . there wasn't nothin' I could do, till your Daddy helped me and gimme this place, which saved my life in more ways than you could know. . . ."

Her words, and even more the tone of her voice, the way she said them, were having a most disturbing effect on me, the pain in my throat and chest was getting worse, but I was curious to know what this thing was Rose could do and yet couldn't and I was not ready yet by any means to let her destroy me. "What is it?" I asked. "This job you could have got?"

Rose paused for a moment as if afraid to answer, then replied: "Well, maybe I ought not to tell you this, but it's called being a whore. Girls let men do it to them, you know, put it in down there, for money. Some girls I knew did it, but I couldn't."

"Why not?" I asked, with genuine interest. Again Rose must have felt she was doomed, it was hopeless. Another little despairing sigh came from her.

"You *do* think I'm awful, don't you," she said in a wan voice. "Maybe I am, I guess so, if I can act like this with a child. Prob'ly that's what I ought to do, be a whore. But I can't, Buddy, I just can't, it would kill me, I would die."

I understood it even then, in a way. Rose could not charge

money for such a thing, she was far too intent on giving it away even to dream of selling it. Whatever she was, she was not and never could be a whore. I understood it, that she couldn't do this, but I was curious what these girls earned and I asked her:

"Why not, Rose? Do they make a lot of money? How much do men pay them for doing it?"

Rose swallowed audibly and in a very discouraged voice replied: "Well, in that house in Birmingham, where this awful fella Richard and another man wanted me to go, it was three dollars."

"*Three* dollars?"

"Yeah, but you only got to keep one of 'em, that house keeps two."

"One dollar, hmm," I said. "How many men do they do it with in a day?"

"Oh, a lot, Buddy, I dunno. Ten or twelve, I guess, maybe more."

I sat up in bed. "Ten or twelve? That's a *lot* of money, Rose. What do you make working *here?*"

The sound of tears had come back in her voice. "You know what I make, Buddy. Room and board, and twenty-five dollars a month."

"Rose, you'd make that much in *two days* being a whore. Do you realize that? Twelve men a dollar per man a day, sure, two days."

The thought in my mind was actually one of grudging admiration—or let's say semigrudging admiration, I was very bothered—that she would work so hard in our house for so much less money than she could have made working for that awful fella Richard in Birmingham, but again she misunderstood my attitude. She'd won already really, her small miracle basically had arrived, but she didn't know it. A choking sound came from her as she tried to hold back tears.

"Buddy, I don't want to be no whore, I *can't!* I might be bad, I know I'm bad, but I can't be no whore, I just can't! And besides, that ain't really why I don't want you to tell them, just because I can't get no job—folks won't let me starve—the real reason is I *love* it here, I love your whole fam'ly, and I don't want to have to go!" Weeping again and struggling with only partial success to control herself, Rose clutched my hand in both of hers. I'm sure she felt it was now or never; the hour was late, I was only a child and tired. "Buddy, if you like me even a little bit, please don't tell them. Don't tell Doll, she's a little girl and would tell your momma for sure. Don't tell nobody, not a soul, if you do your daddy will fire me right off. Buddy, I know I'm no good, I'm a bad girl but I can't help it, please have pity on me and don't tell! Please don't tell, please don't. . . ."

Thus Rose destroyed me, although I already was ruined and all she had to do was deliver the *coup de grâce.* To change the metaphor to something a bit more positive and hopeful, I believe one thing. Hardhearted souls see the gates of heaven in those rare moments when the merciless iron of pity strikes fire from that lump of frozen flint. I certainly did; as my illness was greatly alleviated if not cured I saw the celestial gates shining and beautiful with forgiving angels and little cherubs flying all around. I saw the gates themselves as I looked into Rose's tearfilled eyes in the moonlight and felt her pain as if it were my own. It was beautiful and unbearable; I burst into sudden semihysterical tears, flung scrawny arms around her and for quite a while struggled in desperation to control myself and act like a man. Finally, with as much solemnity as I could summon, I said:

"Rose, they could stick splinters under my fingernails, and I will *never* say a word! I will *never* tell them, because . . . I love you!"

Rose knew I meant it and put her head on my shoulder and sobbed aloud. It was, I think, a rather moving moment, the bad boy and the bad girl sharing together an instant of real love, reaching across an awful void and touching hands. There is no doubt of it, the night of nights with Rose was one of the most important experiences of my lifetime. I was hardly cured of my illness, but I would never be quite the same again, not after seeing those gates with the angels and little cherubs flying around. As I said, an awakening of human sympathy is more important than the mere existence and unreasoning function of whatever God has given us below our navels. It's a hairy little bastard, this view, but it's mine.

My sister like most children was a very sound sleeper, but it's still a wonder to me she didn't hear all this carrying on and wake up. It's an even greater wonder to me she didn't hear the carrying on that occurred not too long thereafter. Daddy himself conceivably could have heard *that,* all the way downstairs. Rose just naturally and inevitably caused commotion, it was a failing she had.

I was happy but worried, the sobbing head on my shoulder was not nearly so heavy as the burden it partially replaced, but the noise she was making as hot tears splashed on my neck and trickled warmly down my shoulder concerned me. "Rose," I whispered, "you'd better not cry so *loud,* Doll will hear you!"

"Oh, Buddy!" she cried, in her normal voice, not a whisper. "You *do* love me, I knew you did, I knew it! You love me and understand me even if you're a child, you do, I knew you did and I love you, too!"

"Rose, be *quiet!* You'll wake up everybody in the whole house!"

Gradually she did quiet down, but I felt for a long time hot tears splash down with wet warm trickles on my neck. I also felt her breasts on my chest squashed against me like soft magic pillows and now I noticed a curious change in my entire point of view toward her: somehow, the womanness of her, even the mysterious scented place between her legs with the little peculiar pip and all the rest of it, no longer seemed alien or disturbing at all. *That* was the way girls and women *were,* no more.

The realization came to me with startling speed. If I loved Rose herself, then why couldn't I love everything about her? It was merely the way a woman was, and the way a woman was was beautiful, especially one like Rose who loved me. And whom I loved, too; hadn't she showed me the gates themselves with angels flying around? How could I have thought—as, horror of horrors, I did—that the little pip was strange and unnatural? It was part of her, that was all, she'd been born with it, just as I had been born with the things I myself had, which some young girl who did not love me would find equally strange and unnatural.

Very fast, with great speed, it all came to me: the thing that counted was Rose herself, nothing else mattered, nothing at all, just the person who talked, smiled, cried, held me in her arms and loved me. Just Rose, a "girl human person" as she later said to me in dismay, that was all that mattered, just Rose who held me in her arms and mashed soft warm little pillows against my chest.

It can happen in other ways, no doubt, but thus real desire can be born. I thought I'd experienced something like it already, but I had merely been playing "Doctor." A sudden and truly powerful weakness came into my knees.

"Rose," I whispered, "will you do it with me?"

There is *no* doubt about it. Rose had really and truly rocked the cradle.

7

Rose robs the cradle and falls into hell

"*DO IT WITH* you?" asked Rose softly. "You mean . . . *do* it with you? Is that what you mean, Buddy?"

"Yeah," I replied, "that's what I mean."

I felt an almost imperceptible tensing of her body, then Rose lifted her head from my shoulder, propped on an elbow, gave a little sniff at her waning tears and smiled in amusement. It was perhaps an illusion but I thought I could see a little twinkle in her eyes from the light of the moon. Whether I saw it or not I'm sure if there had been sufficient illumination from that distant lunar body a twinkle would have been there. Sincerely inviting to go to bed a girl who had a fundamental and chronic difficulty saying no was dangerous business.

"Will you, Rose? You don't have to worry now about my telling anybody, because you know I won't. We could do it now and nobody would ever know. Will you do it with me?"

Again she smiled, put her hand on my cheek and said: "Too bad you ain't a little older, Buddy, or I sure would, I'd have this dern nightgown off in a wink. But Buddy I am afraid you are just a little too young."

"I'm not all that young," I said. "Will you do it with me? I'm serious, will you, Rose?"

Rose smothered a laugh, then moved her hand to my shoulder. I could see her smiling in the moonlight, her lips pressed together and puckered in a way she had when something struck her as especially funny and she half wanted to hide her amusement. I've since known several girls who sometimes smiled in this way and it always seemed to me very charming, very beautiful. Her voice was gentle when she spoke, "Buddy, you couldn't," she said. "You're too little. Besides, that would really be terrible of me. What I've done is bad enough, God knows. But we couldn't, anyhow, you're just a child."

I was a trifle hurt by her laughter. "I'm not just a child," I said, "and we could do it if you'd just stop laughing at me. I've got one!"

"You've . . . got one?" asked Rose solemnly. Suddenly she giggled, a rarity for her. Rose laughed in a number of ways, but almost never giggled. This was a giggle. "Is that so? You've got one, huh? Well, I'll declare, how about that?" Again she giggled.

"Yes, I've got one!" I said angrily. "It might not be as big as Daddy's, but it's there!"

The noise of several smothered giggles came from Rose, but when she spoke her voice was grave. "Well, I don't want to hurt your feelings, I don't intend to laugh at you in a mean way, Buddy, I really don't."

Up until this moment I had been *extremely* cautious about one thing: to keep her away from all contact with or knowledge of my little "dilly," which more than once during the night had lifted its head from the swamp and peered around. Its head was bravely lifted right now, unaware of its supposed incompetence; the dilly thought it was a perfectly adequate match for anything that might come along, and ironically enough the mindless thing was more or less correct.

But until this moment in near-pathological modesty I'd carefully and cautiously kept it hidden, a hand protectingly over it or a sheet between it and her. Now I discovered my modesty as far as Rose was concerned was gone, vanished, it no longer existed.

"Okay, you want to see it?" I asked. "You can see it, I don't care, and you'll be surprised. It's bigger than you think, Rose."

I half opened the sheet, but Rose didn't bother to look down. Hand on my shoulder, she smiled into my eyes in the bright moonlight. "Buddy, you've lost your modesty with me," she said. "That's nice, it's very nice. You see what love can do? You love me, so you're not modest with me now."

"No, I'm not," I said, and pulled open the sheet that was still partly between us. "Here, look, Rose, you'll be surprised."

Rose *was* a little surprised. Not much perhaps, but a little. The dilly at least made her to do a slight Laurel and Hardy double-take. She glanced casually down it, turned her head half back toward me, then glanced at it again. After a moment, her hand moved down and her fingers closed lightly on the dilly. For several seconds she was silent, her fingers clasped around me. "Hmmp," she said. Her fingers squeezed slightly tighter, then she released me, gave me a little pat on the leg and pulled the sheet over me.

"Got to cover it up," she said. "Don't want the pretty little thing catchin' a cold."

"Well," I asked, "isn't it bigger than you thought?"

"Oh, I dunno," answered Rose in a lazy, amused voice.

"What do you mean, you don't know? Come on, Rose, talk sense. What do you *think?"*

Rose, who had been staring up at the ceiling with a little smile, turned her blonde head toward me. "I think you're a cute boy," she said.

"Cute?"

Cute was what people said about babies. I half turned away from her, really hurt. I had trusted her and she'd laughed at the dilly. I still loved her but I was hurt.

"Buddy," she said. I felt her arm around my shoulder and her voice in my ear. "I didn't mean it that way. Now really I didn't. You're older than you look, and . . . and one of these days you're going to be a man."

"I'm older than you think right now," I said. "We *could* do it, Rose."

She smiled again, put her hand behind my head and kissed me on the cheek. "Well, it's a compliment to me you want to. But I *don't* think you'd like it, Buddy, I really don't. I reckon maybe you *could* do it a little and a thing like that can be terrible upsettin' to a child, I happen to know. Besides, your daddy and momma would hate me a lot, they'd despise me and they'd be right to. It would be an awful thing for me to do, a helpless child like you."

She thought I was too young. It was very disappointing, I almost felt like crying. How could I make her change her mind, how could I make her say yes instead of no? "Well, I'm not as young as you think," I said.

"You're pretty young," she answered with another smile. "You're smart way beyond your age and just think you're old. But don't worry, you got nothin' to fret about. You wait a little while, some girl will do it with you, I'm sure of that."

Crushed, I replied: "I don't think they will. You won't and they won't, either. I'm not good-looking, Rose, that's the trouble."

"You're not good-looking? Why do you say that?"

"Why do I say it? Good grief, Rose, look at me, skinny and everything with freckles all over and disgusting red hair. I'm horribly ugly, Rose, that's obvious, and I'm sure girls won't like me."

"Haven't heard anything so silly in a week," said Rose. "I think you really believe it. Lemme tell you girls don't go just by looks, that's the least important thing in a boy or man. And besides, you ain't horrible ugly, you're horrible crazy. Sure, you're thin like some pore little sparrow and that's what kills me, it's why I keep beggin' you to eat somethin', but your freckles are real cute and your hair is plum beautiful just like your momma says. I'd give *any*thing to have hair that pretty shade instead of my own towhead stuff, and so would practic'ly any girl."

Could she be right? *Never.* "Maybe . . . a girl," I said, "but it looks *pretty stupid* on a boy. And you can't tell me those freckles aren't disgusting. Redheaded people are very ugly, Rose. Their skin looks like a plucked chicken that's been sunburned, and that's a fact. They're *nauseating.*"

"Well, they *are* kinda mottled, them freckles!" said Rose. "Ha, ha, ha, ha! You'll get a girl sometime, Buddy, maybe with one leg or her titties cross-eyed, she'll like them freckles of yours, wait and see!"

"Ha . . . ha . . . ha," I replied. "I just wish you had more *respect* for me. We *could* do it, Rose, if you'd just quit laughing at me."

"Hey," she said, in a cheerful mood now, her fears and tears forgotten, "look what's on the bed, my Camels, how about that? Shows you how much the pure piss was scairdt out of me, I clear forgot the dern things—and here's some matches, too. I don't even remember bringin' 'em in here. I'm tellin' you, Buddy, I was scairdt pure pissless and there ain't no other way to put it. All of a sudden I just knowed you'd tell Dolly, I just knowed you would. You got a glass in here, Buddy?"

I was bitterly disappointed that she wouldn't "do it" with me. When I asked her I'd been sure she would. How could I make her say yes instead of no? How? With a wisdom beyond my years the thought occurred to me I could never do it by cold argument. Never, the thing to do was *stir her up* somehow. Put my finger back in her? No, she wouldn't let me. Her titties, maybe . . . if I played with them, would *that* stir her up? Possibly.

"Yeah, I got a glass," I said. "Right here on the table."

"Well, I'll smoke me a Camel, then go on back to my room and you can get some sleep," said Rose, who knew I was hurt and disappointed but ignored it. "Hand me the glass, Buddy, I'll use it for a ash tray."

I reached to the table by my bed and gave her the glass, then watched her strike a country match to light her Camel. Rose was not a real smoker; in the orange light of the match she gave the cigarette little shallow puffs, then with her pink lips shaped like an O blew out smoke with a faint whistling sound, watching it solemnly as if that were the point of the whole thing. She shook out the match, set the glass down on the floor, lay back on the pillow and put her free arm around my shoulders.

"It's so nice to lie here and talk with you," she said. "I love you a lot, Buddy, even if I can't do what you want. And I can't, it would hurt you, it would hurt you in your mind and I've bothered you enough already."

The powerful weakness of real desire had come again in my knees. In the half-blinding light of the match I had gotten a pretty good view of Rose in her thin nightgown, which was a curious garment she must have owned for years. It had six or seven old-fashioned buttons that opened from the top to the bottom. A couple of buttons were missing and several were unfastened. Her breasts were more than half-exposed; I saw behind the smoking and sputtering match a cleft that seemed to me deep as the Tallulah Gorge, a fantastic valley formed by two pale, pink-lighted, giant mounds, on one of which I could see a part of a big pink circle. So her "titties" seemed to me then, giant soft mounds; in reality, Rose was full breasted but not abnormally so. At that time, however, her breasts were larger-than-life-size to me and the sight of them half-naked brought back the powerful weakness in my knees. I wanted badly to put my hand on that soft living Tallulah Gorge, but was afraid to do so. She'd said no and might get up and leave.

"Rose?" I whispered.

"What, Buddy?"

"Will you tell me something?"

"Well, I dunno, depends on what it is."

"I know, but will you tell me, no matter what it is?"

"Mmm, well, that's not playing fair . . . but what is it?"

"How *old* were you when you first did it?"

Rose laughed. "Oh, Lord, I dunno."

"How old were you?"

"Buddy, I don't remember. I was real young."

"You really don't remember?"

"Well, I remember. I was young."

"How young?"

"Buddy, what does it matter? I was real young."

"Rose, won't you tell me? I want to know."

"I don't know why you're asking that. What do you want to know for?"

"I just do. How old were you?"

"Well, I was eleven if you have got to know. Eleven, almost twelve."

"That's younger than me. Who did it to you?"

"My daddy," said Rose in a casual, matter-of-fact voice.

"Your daddy? You mean your *real* daddy?"

"Yeah, my real daddy. Let's talk about something else."

"But Rose, your real daddy—that wasn't very nice of him, was it?"

"No, it wasn't very nice. He was drunk."

"Did he do it more than once?"

"Let's talk about something else."

"But he did it again?"

"Whenever he had a few drinks and could catch me,

sure. Until I was fourteen and run off with Charles, who said he'd marry me but all he done was got me sick."

I was shocked by this casual information Rose gave me about her daddy. I didn't know such a thing was possible—how could a father "do it" to his own daughter? "Well," I said, "that daddy of yours sounds pretty bad, Rose."

"He wasn't that bad, he was just very poor. Very, very poor, you don't know how poor we were, Buddy. I didn't have a dress to go to school one year, so I didn't go. Momma, that was before she died, sewed up flour sacks, but I was ashamed, other children could see the labels. I cried and hid in the woods and wouldn't go."

I couldn't believe it—no dress at all? Such a thing was unimaginable and yet she seemed to mean it, it was no joke. "Your mother," I asked, "really made a dress out of flour sacks?"

"Yeah, she did, it was all we had. And I couldn't stand it, Buddy. I wanted them to think I was beautiful, I couldn't stand them to see me in them flour sacks . . . that's all it was, just flour sacks sewed together with the labels showing. I couldn't stand it, Buddy, I have always been real vain, I ran in the woods and hid and cried, and dreamed about ice-cream cones. Daddy took me into Gadsden once and bought me one and I've dreamed about them ever since, both when I'm awake and when I'm asleep, too. I dream about them even nowadays, about a big cool place where there's lots of ice-cream cones and I can have them. Isn't that funny, Buddy, a grown girl like me dreaming such a child thing?"

For a moment I couldn't answer. This was another world, a world I knew nothing about—*one* ice-cream cone in her entire childhood? "Do you mean," I asked, "that's the only time you ever had an ice-cream cone, that day he took you into Gadsden?"

"Maybe I had one some other time," she answered, "but that's the only time I ever remember having one. It was chocolate, and boy was it good. I cried and cried when it was gone. But when Momma give me that flour-sack dress was worse, that was a real bad year. We didn't have nothin' to eat lots of times, nothin' at all, not even hoecake and sorghum syrup which is what we ate a lot. There was days we didn't even have nothin' that year, and it's an awful feelin' to be hungry, Buddy, just about the most awful feelin' in the world. My daddy was the least of my worries. You can't blame him much, he was so lowdown and miser'ble nothin' mattered. He could get drunk on raw moonshine and screw me 'n' my sister Lunette and it didn't hardly make no difference, except of course it upset me and her somethin' terrible. It's an awful feelin' to do it with your own daddy, but we had worse worries than him."

Once again Rose had touched my no longer quite-so-flinty child's heart. What a world she had come from. How could she be as she was and come from such a life? It was a rather profound question actually and later was to puzzle deeply the new doctor whom Mother called in when Rose got her great epizootics. How could Rose be as she was and come from such a world as the one she described, a world of dismal incest and near-starvation?

Yes, once again she'd touched my flinty heart. I put my hand on hers and in a slightly shaking voice said: "Rose, I feel *real* sorry for you. You must have had . . . a *very* unhappy childhood."

Rose gave my shoulders a squeeze. "Love you so much," she said.

"Well . . . at least you're not hungry around *here.*"

"No," she answered, "no, I'm not." She was silent for a long moment as if thinking, then turned partly on her side toward me and said: "You know, Buddy, you wanted to know where babies come from, and I put your finger in down there and told you that was where I could have them. But I'll tell you somethin', a real sad secret you mustn't mention. That dern Charles reminded me of it, because it was his fault. Buddy, the truth is, I can't have babies, never in my whole life, I can't no matter how long I live. It's very sad . . . I mean, it really is. And if you want to know I think a lot of my troubles come from this because it bothers me a lot mentally in my mind. What it is, is a rare medical thing. You see, Buddy, there are these little rubber tubes in a girl with a tee-ninecy hole in the middle of 'em—" Rose abruptly paused, and asked politely: "But do you want to hear about this? Does it make you sick to your stummick or anythin'?"

"Oh, *no,*" I replied, all ears. Little rubber tubes in girls was just the sort of thing I wanted to hear about.

"Well, then, as I was sayin', it's a rare medical-type thing. There are these little rubber tubes in a girl and I don't know exactly how they do it, but babies come down them. I mean at first when babies are real small, real, real, small, so small you can't even see 'em. And somehow or another, they come down them little tubes, I guess they sort of swim. But once in a long while a girl gets this rare type thing wrong with her, a sort of ailment kind of, and when that happens them little tee-ninecy holes in the little rubber tubes shut up real tight, they seal right up and she can't never have a baby no matter how she tries."

Rose, of course, as I later learned, didn't have any "rare type" disease, she had merely caught gonorrhea from the dern Charles. The disease later was cured completely, but she had gone untreated for several years and as a result her Fallopian tubes were damaged and she was permanently barren. I didn't know this at the time but I understood she couldn't have children, and I also understood this mattered a great deal to her. As she herself said, it bothered her a lot mentally in her mind.

"Well," I said, "that's too bad, Rose, I know you like children."

"Yes," she answered, "I like them, and you know what I was thinkin' when you said that sweet thing to me, you know why I've told you all this? I was thinkin', maybe them doctors don't know so much, maybe sometime them little rubber tubes will open up even though they say they won't, and I'll have a baby of my own, which is what I always wanted even when I was real small. A livin' baby that would cry and need me, a pretty little baby I could hold in my arms, all mine. And I was thinkin', if them doctors are wrong and they don't know everything, if they're wrong and I ever have a baby of my own I'd want it . . . to be a boy. . . ."

Rose paused, tears in her voice. She knew too direct affection, love too untrammeled and plain, sometimes made me draw away, but mostly she hesitated, I think, because her emotion was so strong she couldn't speak. Her voice had begun to break when she got to the livin' baby that would cry and need her.

"Well, Buddy," she finally said, as I knew she would, "don't mind me sayin' it, but if it wasn't a girl, I'd want it to be a real sweet and pretty boy like you, smarter than me. I love you so much, Buddy, I just love you a lot."

That was what did it, I believe, her damned maternal instinct, and maybe what her miserable father had done to her on that horrible one-mule farm when she herself was a helpless child. The robbing of the cradle and the fall into pure sheer hell came very fast after she told me if the doctors were wrong and she ever had a baby she would like it to be a "real sweet and pretty" boy like me. Real sweet and pretty, my freckled ass! Curse the moment that idea came into her blonde head! Curse that moment, and curse it twice!

"I love you, too, Rose," I said, "and won't you do it with me? I want to, Rose, I really want to a lot. I want to because . . . I love you. Unbutton your nightgown, Rose . . . please, unbutton it, I love you."

"I love you the same, just as much the same way," she answered, "and you have really been wonderful to me tonight, I'll never forget it." Rose sat up in bed, stretched out her arms and sighed. "Well, I'll smoke me one more Camel, then go on to bed and let you get some sleep. It must be awful late, the moon is goin' down."

Yes, the moon was going down and the robbing of the cradle and the fall into hell happened very fast. When Rose struck the match to light her final Camel, I saw again begin the sputtering orange flame the pale living Tallulah Gorge between her titties and this time put my hand there. She was slightly negative, a trifled bothered and distracted from her cigarette, but didn't make me take my hand away and after I pleaded with her for a while she unbuttoned her thin relic of a child's nightgown and let me feel and see her breasts in the remaining moonlight. She wouldn't turn on the lamp on the table by my bed, but she let me touch them and look at them in the light of the moon and I have always considered it one of the most generous gestures she made on the night of nights, because I think it *did* "stir her up" and I think she knew it would and knew it would make it harder for her.

Like a thin frog on a lily pad, I lay in the moonlight on her practically naked body, her soft breasts in my hands and my head between them. Rose's breasts to me at that time were too strange and upsetting to strike me as pretty or beautiful, but they fascinated me enormously. One amazing thing about them was their incredible softness. I'd thought a woman's titties were much harder and firmer, almost like a grapefruit or a cantaloupe, but they weren't; they stood out on her chest but they were very soft.

It gave me a whole new idea about girls and women, an appreciation of the fact that however great their spiritual or mental or emotional qualities they did not have the physical strength of men, not even a strong girl like Rose. If their breasts were so soft, they could be hurt very easily—a man could hit with his fist a woman's breast and hurt it badly. And that would be a terrible and loathesome thing to do, I remember shuddering inside at the very thought. No doubt I had long ago absorbed this attitude from my father—that a man who would strike a woman ought to be horse-whipped—but Rose's breasts, so soft and vulnerable, made me understand why and how he felt that way, why he always was so courtly and protective toward the beautiful half of humanity.

Another thing about Rose's breasts that fascinated me was her nipples, and also the lighter circles around them, which seemed to me huge but were pretty much normal. The nipples at first impressed me as disappointingly insignificant, but I soon learned that if they were gently pinched they would become much larger and stand up like little hard acorns. It was a fascinating phenomenon: the lighter pink, silver-dollar-sized circle would shrink in and wrinkle and the nipple would stand up in it—this must be what happened when a baby sucked on it for milk, no doubt.

Thus an inspiration beyond my days came to me: why not emulate a baby and see what would happen . . . maybe the nipple would get even bigger or some other intriguing thing would occur, maybe it would *stir her up* . . . hmmm, why not?

"Now look," said Rose, in a voice not quite like her, "I

said you could touch them and look at them in the moon, but that's all."

"Well, that's all I'm doing."

"No, you are doing somethin' more, and I don't think you better."

"Does it hurt you?" I asked slyly. Yes, sir, I was *right.* Sucking her nipples like a baby stirred her up, I'd had a hunch it would. It stirred her up plenty, I could tell. Cold argument would never do it, this was the way to make her change her mind and say yes. Innocent as a lamb, I repeated the question with a gentle commiseration: "Does it hurt, Rose?"

"Well . . . no, it don't hurt, but I don't think you better."

I kept on and Rose didn't stop me. With both hands on one of her soft breasts, I held the little acorn nipple in my mouth and ran my tongue around and around it. I could feel a slight roughening or wrinkling of the light pink circle and the nipple did seem bigger. A faint sigh came from Rose, then a weak whisper: "Buddy, don't. Please don't." I kept on for a while, then moved to her other breast to see if its nipple would behave in the same way, and it did. I heard a deeper sigh from Rose and a little swallowing sound. She was breathing differently, too, I could feel her chest swell and subside under my hands as I continued to suck and nibble at the little hard acorn. I heard another swallowing sound and the realization came to me that Rose was helpless. All I had to do was ask.

"Rose," I whispered, "open your legs, just a little."

Yes, she was helpless, I noticed a tiny little flinch in her body beneath me as her legs prepared to do as bidden. But the legs didn't move, Rose was *not* helpless, not quite. As I said, it was her damned maternal instinct, and maybe what her miserable father had done to her when she herself was a helpless child. But mostly it was her damned maternal instinct. A "real sweet and pretty" boy like me—curse the moment that idea came into her blonde head, curse it twice! Instead of her legs opening as they'd been bidden to do, I felt her hands grab me by the shoulders with strength and shove me back.

"Will I *ever* learn!" cried Rose in a voice loud enough

to wake up not only Doll but Waski in the bedroom across the hall. "I told you to quit it, now quit it like I said! Get up offa me! Get up!"

"But I want to!" I said in a voice as loud as hers. "You can't . . . you can't *stir me up* like this, and not do it!"

Since time began, I wonder how many girls and women have heard that complaint. Rose I am sure had heard it more than once, and it set her slightly boiling. "Oh, *can't* I? Well, you just get your little redheaded ass offa me right now! You hear me! Get your ass offa me!"

She was not really angry, not exactly, but she was firm. I had no choice. Whimpering with defeat and loss, I rolled off of her like a thin frog on my side. Next thing she was sitting on the edge of the bed *buttoning her nightgown!* It was awful! I wanted her! The dilly wanted her! Why was she being . . . cruel to me and the dilly! Would it help maybe if I clutched her hand and cried?

"Rose, please! Don't button up! Rose, this is hurting my feelings, it's hurting my feelings a lot . . . Rose, please, don't you understand? This is hurting me, the way you're acting. . . ."

In silence, as I pleaded with her, Rose buttoned her nightgown and gathered up her cigarettes and matches. Finally she turned to me and put her hand on my arm and said:

"All right, I know it hurts you. But it would hurt you worse, Buddy, if I did what you wanted. It would hurt you in your mind in ways you don't even know, and I won't do that to you. I won't, do you understand? I won't."

I understood. She wouldn't. "Okay," I said, wan and robbed. "Just tell me this, Rose. How . . . how old do I have to be?"

"Older than you are," she said gently. "Now, give me a real sweet hug good night, hmmm?"

"All right," I replied, and put my arms around her and felt for the last time in this way her soft breasts against my chest like warm magic pillows. Loss, loss, loss! Cruel robbery! I'd almost had it, the dilly was nearly there, and she was taking it away.

"Well," sighed Rose, her arms around me, "back to my bed of lonesome hell. All I can say, is if I'm gonna act like this and rob a cradle like I done tonight, I gotta get myself up, and go out. Your daddy don't want me and you're too small, and I'm gonna get myself up and go out, and look for Mr. Right. He's out there somewhere and I'm gonna find him!"

As I said in perfect truth, no "depraved seduction" occurred. And Rose did rob a cradle and did fall in her own lonely bed into the hell of life without love. It happened just as I said, I never lie, or not often. Of course another interpretation could have been put upon it, but then interpretation is everything, isn't it? Surely the reader must know from his or her own experience of life that *I* have not invented mischief, that the truth is often the exact opposite of what it appears.

While mischief is on our minds, there is a minor aspect to it I wanted to mention. I am thinking of thistles. And to be honest about it, on rare occasions in my scribbles mischief is thistles. Yes, I have planted a plot or two of thistles in my day and the good Lord willing intend to plant and water a few plots more before I'm done.

What is a thistle? Well, it is a particularly diabolical imitation of hay that is meant to deceive domesticated beasts. All writers, who are really wild and untamed animals sort of like wolves, must take care not to be run over by a stampeding herd. And that is where thistles come in. You see, thistles are not only inedible, they have little tiny thorns in them, and the thorns stick in the mouths of the leaders of the herd and thus they are distracted and maddened, and in their angry hoof-stamping distraction the wolf slips off like a shadow and gets away.

Thistle-type mischief, however, is strictly a minor thing. The wolf is usually wandering in deep snow so far outside the dangerous herd there is no problem. It's extremely minor, most mischief is there because the truth cannot be presented but must be discovered. Nevertheless, occasional though it is, thistle mischief is more than subterfuge for the sake of subterfuge; it exists in reality to prevent the theft of the soul.

Now to compare a wolf to the soul might seem strained, but there is a little wolf in us all if we do anything that is the least bit exceptional. And millions of people do exceptional things every day. The businessman who sticks out his neck and takes a chance on a new idea has done something exceptional. The mother who takes action to become more than a dependent housewife has done something exceptional. There are myriad examples and all of these wolves not only need thistles, they grow them, too.

Vanity is the great destroyer, success not failure! After all, the man who damns you merely wants to steal your money, and money can be made no matter how loudly he brays. But the man who praises and flatters you wants to inflame your heart with vanity and steal your soul. For them both, thistles!

But not in this book, it's a small work and thistles aren't neccessary for it. The reader knows by now not to accept unquestioned *any*thing I say, since the truth is often the exact opposite of what it appears and must be discovered by you and me. But not in this little book. Show me a thistle in it and I'll eat it myself!

It is a fact, I never lie, or not often. The writer who lies to his reader is not only a poltroon but a bad writer besides. I don't lie, the truth is nearly always there waiting to be discovered, which it must be because if it is merely announced it isn't the truth at all. Isn't it so?

Rose did rob the cradle, didn't she? And she did fall into her lonely bed of hell, isn't that true? And it was "fairly sexy" when the boy played with her titties, wasn't it? There were no lies. Rose had a fundamental and chronic difficulty saying no to any male, but it was not a total impossibility for her to do so—after all, as I said very plainly, she was no moral imbecile from Tobacco Road, and no nymphomaniac and no bitch, either. My portrait of her provides overwhelming evidence it would be *impossible* for her to rape a child, isn't that true?

Mischief is a means of discovering the real truth, it is not a lie. There were no lies, not even about the capacity of the dilly, which tempted Rose far more, I believe, than she revealed—not two weeks passed before the filthy Hollis showed up one afternoon and took me out to the garage and told me he'd learned about the greatest thing in the world. "It's making me *sick!*" I cried. "Hollis! It's making me *sick,* I'm going to faint, I'm having a heart . . . heart . . . heart attack!''

It was a heart attack Rose had spared me for reasons of her own. ''Well, Buddy,'' she said, as I felt her soft breasts against me and her arms around me for the last time in this way, ''back to that empty bed. I don't understand this sleepin' alone, it ain't natural, people ain't supposed to sleep alone. But back I go. Good night, honey, love you.''

Good night, indeed! It was almost dawn, the night of nights was over and I was sound asleep in peace long before, I am sure, Rose found rest in her lonely bed.

8

Rose gets herself up and goes out

A FEW MINUTES before noon on the following day, which happened to be a Thursday, I stopped by my mother's room as she had ordered me to do. I'd washed my face, combed my hair and put on a freshly laundered pair of khaki pants and a white shirt, but I still looked a little peaky from the long night before.

"Did you speak to Rose yet?" asked Mother.

"No, I haven't seen her."

"All right. You *don't* look well. This isn't punishment, Brother, I don't believe in punishment, it's for your health. Come on with me to the kitchen. I'll give it to you there and at the same time you can apologize to Rose for stealing her cigarettes."

Rose wasn't in the kitchen. Doll and my little brother were there eating hamburgers and drinking milk. "Where is Rose?" asked Mother.

"She's upstairs in her room," said Doll, "getting herself up."

Mother had a bottle of castor oil in her hand. She carefully, even reverently, set it on the kitchen counter and walked to the refrigerator for an orange. "Doing what?" she asked.

"Getting herself up. That's what she said."

"She's going out," said Waski.

"Out?" asked Mother, with a little frown. "Oh, yes, it's Thursday, isn't it. Well, all right. Come here, Brother."

"What did he do?" asked Doll.

"Never mind. Come on, Brother, waiting won't help."

In deep gloom, definitely feeling peaky, I slumped across the kitchen and took the quarter of orange from Mother's hand, then watched her pour out with careful reverence an enormous tablespoon of castor oil. My mother had great faith in castor oil. She had faith in any kind of laxative, but greater faith in the more powerful ones. And castor oil, believe me, is powerful, I had enough of the damnable stuff in my childhood to know.

"All right, here, take this and swallow it all down. Be careful not to spill it or I'll give you more."

I groaned. "Ohh-hh, Mother, do I *have* to?"

"Yes, Brother, you have to. It isn't punishment, it's for your good. When you do such things as you did last night, I know you're not feeling well, you must be sick."

"What did he do?" asked Doll. "Something real bad?"

"I bet he stole money again out of Mother's pocket-book," said Waski. "That's what he always does."

"Shut up, you little muddy-eyed brat, or I'll kill you!" I said, as I held the spoon of ghastly castor oil in one hand and the slice of orange in the other. The orange was a humane touch of Mother's. Since the taste of castor oil was so dreadful, she always let me and Doll have a slice of orange with it. The idea was to eat the orange afterward and thereby take away the hideous taste of the oil. For years and years Dolly and I couldn't abide the taste of an orange; it reminded us of castor oil, and in fact practically tasted like castor oil.

"Don't speak like that to your little brother and go ahead and take that medicine right this second. Go ahead, Brother, I am waiting."

I took a deep breath, pinched shut my nose with the hand in which I held the quarter of orange, opened my mouth and as quickly as possible swallowed the castor oil—or tried to swallow it; the trouble with castor oil, aside from its horrible nauseating taste, was that it was so thick you couldn't swallow it.

"Geccch, yehh, guhhhh!" I said.

"Stop gagging like that and putting on a show, and swallow it! Swallow it, Brother!"

"I am!"

"Swallow it all, don't you dare spit any of it out."

I gulped for the third or fourth time in an effort to get the filthy oil down my throat, then dropped the tablespoon to the floor and crammed the slice of orange in my mouth, shuddering all over. Doll and Waski watched with bright happy eyes. All of us loved to see the others punished, of course—or have their health benefited by medicine, as the case may be. It was nothing but routine childish *Schadenfreude,* joy in the misfortunes of others, but when Mother noticed it it upset her terribly. She had a theory we all loved each other and she couldn't understand how one of us could smile with soft delight when another one suffered.

"Gahdamn stuff!"

"What did you *say?"*

"I said ahh-hh damn stuff."

"No, you didn't say that, Brother."

"Yes, I did, Mother. Your hearing aid isn't working right. I said, ahh-hh damn stuff, that's what I said."

"No, Mother—" began Doll in a prim little tone.

"Shut up, Doll, I'll cut your guts out!"

"Children, children!" said Mother. "Be quiet, both of you! I have a headache and I am not going to listen to you fight. Is that clear?"

Saying "goddamn" was a thing Mother wouldn't put up with. I was afraid she was going to give me another tablespoon of the castor oil, or a teaspoon of it anyhow. In a grave, sincere manner I said to her: "If you thought I said something else, Mother, even though I didn't, then I apologize, I'm sorry. I won't say it again, even though I didn't really, not exactly. You ought to get your hearing aid checked, Mother, it isn't working right lately. But I apologize, anyhow."

"All right," said Mother, "and while you're apologizing, you can apologize to Rose, here she comes." Mother could see her; we couldn't, we could only hear strange and hitherto-unknown high heels clicking down the hall toward the open kitchen door. Odd, I thought. What kind of shoes did Rose have on, anyhow? "Hello, Rose, dear," said Mother, with a slightly strained smile. "Going out for your afternoon off, hmm . . . my, you're . . . looking pretty."

Even Mother was startled and disconcerted. Doll and I and Waski were flabbergasted. We stared in open-mouthed wonder at Rose in the kitchen doorway. She had on all kinds of make-up—bright red lipstick, pink rouge on her cheeks, powder, stuff on her eyes. But even worse, the clothes she had on were fantastic, the outfit she was wearing couldn't be believed. It was the first time we witnessed this phenomenon: Rose had "gotten herself up."

"Well . . . well . . . that's . . . quite an outfit you're wearing, Rose, very *gay,*" said Mother. "Come on in, dear. Brother has something to say to you."

At that moment we heard the Ford in the driveway. It was Daddy. Occasionally, not often, he came home to lunch. I wondered right away what he would think of the clothes Rose was wearing.

"Buddy has something to say . . . to me?" asked Rose. Her eyes of deep cornflower blue were fixed politely on me and there was no trace of fear in them, she knew I wouldn't betray her, that I'd said nothing and would say nothing about the night before. However, she was a little pale beneath all the make-up and I'm sure she wondered what it was all about.

I stepped forward and said: "Rose, I sneaked in your room yesterday afternoon and stole three of your cigarettes and smoked them last night. This was very immoral of me because it is thievery, they were your cigarettes, not mine. I am sorry, Rose, I apologize."

"Well," smiled Rose, "that's all right, Buddy."

"Now," said Mother. "How much does a cigarette cost?"

"Oh, now, it don't matter. . . ."

"I want to know, Rose. This is serious, the boy has got to be taught to respect other people's property, especially their personal possessions. How much does a cigarette cost if you buy only one, and can you buy just one?"

"Yes, Ma'am," said Rose, "you can buy just one down at that thrift drugstore. And they're a penny a piece."

"All right, he smoked three. Brother, when you get your ten cents allowance on Saturday, you will pay Rose four cents. The extra penny is for her trouble."

"No, now Mrs. Hillyer, don't make him pay me. . . ."

"He will pay you, Rose, this is for his character. And besides, they were your cigarettes, you are entitled to be paid."

We heard a noise at the back door and then an astonished exclamation: "Ye gods and little fishes!" It was Daddy, hunched forward and staring through the curtains of the back kitchen door.

Rose hadn't turned around, her eyes were still fixed on me and a little smile was on her face. She gave me a wink as if to say: "I knew you wouldn't tell on me, and don't worry, I won't take your four cents." Despite all the make-up and outlandish as her clothes were, even outrageous, she looked to me very beautiful at this moment and I felt a sadness that the night of nights was gone and would never return, a sadness I feel to this day. She looked very beautiful indeed if slightly out of her mind.

"Good God!" said Daddy as he entered the kitchen, a rolled up Glenville *News-Tribune* in his hand. "What in the hell have you done to yourself, Rose?"

Rose turned to him with a little smile. "Nothing," she said. "I got myself up, that's all."

Daddy put both hands on his hips, still holding the rolled up newspaper. His straw hat was tilted backward and to the side, as usual. I never saw him wear it straight. "Got yourself *up?*" asked Daddy.

"Yeah," answered Rose. "I'm goin' *out.*"

Thumbs on hips, Daddy stared at her. "Um-hmmm," he said. "Well, that is the damndest outfit I ever saw in my life. You walk down the street like that and they'll put you in jail, Rose."

"Why, they won't either," said Mother. "She looks *pretty.* And I wish you wouldn't pick on Rose all the time. It's cruel and mean the way you pick on the poor girl constantly like that. Don't listen to him, Rose, you look very pretty, even beautiful."

"You're sweet," said Rose, with a little smile at Mother.

"Hmp," said Daddy. Shaking his head, he walked on into the kitchen, pulled out a kitchen chair and sat down at the table. "All right. All right. If you've got time before you go 'out,' get me half-a-cup of coffee, Rose. Not a cup, a half-a-cup, dear."

"Why, sure," said Rose, "always got time to get you a half-a-cup, but one of these days I'm gonna give you a *whole* cup and see what happens."

"Mmmumm," said Daddy with a little growl. He ignored jokes about his foibles, such as never having a cup of coffee, but always half-a-cup.

"Buddy stole Rose's cigarettes and smoked them," said Doll. "Mother gave him a dose of castor oil and he cursed it, Daddy, he took the Lord's name in vain, then claimed he hadn't said it. He lied, Daddy, he really ought to be ashamed of himself, *I* think."

"You mustn't be a tattletale, dear," said Mother. "It's none of your beeswax."

"But it's true, Mother," said Doll sweetly. "Buddy lied . . . in his teeth. As his sister I have to say that, because I *love* him and a thing like that ought to be . . . *corrected.* Don't you think so, Daddy?"

Doll was still furious at me because of what I'd said about Daddy at Thermopylae. She wasn't ordinarily as vicious as this, although for a little sweet angel she could be pretty vicious, I have to admit that, especially if you annoyed her. She could fight back tooth and nail, that little girl, I still have scars she left among the freckles.

"Umm-hmm," said Mother. "Ummm-hmm."

"What's all this?" asked Daddy, as he lifted his head above the unfolded Glenville *News-Tribune* like a bear coming out of hibernation. "What's the little skunk done now?"

"Just a moment, just a moment," said Mother, and she turned rather frostily to Doll. With a sweetness equal to Doll's own, she said: "You mustn't be catty and scheming and calculating and Delilah-ish and Jezebel-ish toward your brother, dear, because you *do* love him, even if you said it just now with total hypocrisy. You love Brother and Brother loves you, and I cannot understand why you both act the way you do. When you behave like that, Frances, you are making a mockery of the most beautiful feelings in your own heart, don't you know that, don't you understand that?"

"Yes, Mother," said Doll meekly. "I'm sorry, I was trying to *help* him."

"Umm-hmm," said Mother. "Well, I think you do at least sense a little of what I've said. I hope so, one can only throw bread on the waters and hope something gets it other than the turtles. I *hope* you listened to me, because our love for others is the only wealth we have, it is all we have got, the only thing we own that is worth a dime. Now if you and Waski have finished your lunch, and I believe you have, then run on and play. Run along now, both of you, I wish to speak to your father. *You* stay, Brother."

Actually, my treacherous little sister's words—which under other circumstances could have gotten me into real hot water; Daddy had a "thing" about cigarette smoking, as Doll well knew—didn't seem to have registered on Daddy. He wasn't listening to her. He was pretending to scrutinize the Glenville *News-Tribune*, but he was peering over his reading glasses and the paper itself at Rose as she heated up and poured out his half-a-cup of coffee. Thank God Rose's "outfit" distracted him; Doll had been out to slay me, that little angel was after my jugular vein. If there was one thing that made Daddy's eyes turn into red glaring marbles with veins in them like road maps, it was cigarettes, or "coffin spikes," as he called them. He smoked them himself, that was why.

Half surreptitiously, Daddy's gaze followed Rose over the tops of his reading glasses and over the uplifted Glenville *News-Tribune*. His brow had deep, doubtful furrows and his mouth was clamped tightly shut. I knew the expression well and could interpret its meaning without any difficulty, as could all members of the family, including Waski. It was Daddy's this-house-is-a-morphydike expression.

Some relative or other had once been taken by a real estate man to look at a house that was conventional in some ways but had several "modern" architectural features—a strange porch, a peculiarly sloping roof and unsymmetrical windows. The relative, who was an old coot set in his ways, had stared in disgusted skepticism at the place and said: "This house is a morphydike."

Daddy liked this story a great deal; it wasn't in a class with "red hand" but he liked the story and told it often, and even more often used the expression itself. It seemed to sum up the doubt he felt about life itself. Or perhaps, more accurately, the world. A morphydike, otherwise known as a hermaphrodite, in this context was not an individual possessing the reproductive organs of both male and female, but rather the philosophical essence and spirit of doubt itself. Rose's outfit was plainly to Daddy a morphydike and I had no doubt when I saw his face he would tell her so in a while.

It was quite a rig and it was news to everyone. Rose had gotten her first month's pay a few days before and had asked for a couple of hours off to do some shopping, but we hadn't seen what she bought. Now we saw it—or part of it anyhow, the outfit seemed in some degree *assembled.*

"Here you are, half-a-cup!" said Rose with a cheerful smile. It was amazing how untired she looked. She couldn't have gotten more than a couple of hours' sleep, but you'd never have known it to look at her. Rose, as Mother often said, had an enormous vitality, she never got tired.

"Hmm-mmm." Daddy was staring at Rose's skirt with his morphydike frown. The skirt was made of a strange, pink, semi-shiny and very thin material with about a dozen tiny little flowers that could have been rosebuds sewed on it. The job was neat but the effect was bizarre. The little flowers had been cut out of some other material, they were of cotton. I have no idea what the skirt was made of—some kind of imitation silk, rayon I suppose. But the most arresting feature of this skirt, as Daddy pointed out, was not its design but its fit. No bathing suit ever revealed the contours of the feminine posterior with a more perfect candor than that skirt. It concealed nothing . . . well, almost nothing.

"Rose," said Daddy, "that's a pretty stylish skirt you're wearing. The thing I don't understand about it is how did you ever get it *on?*"

"Well," said Rose, "it has buttons." She lifted a frilly arm—we have not yet gotten to the even more incredible blouse she had on—and turned a hip toward Daddy and indicated a row of buttons in the pink material. The buttons were red and black and looked like small ladybugs.

"How can those buttons stand the pressure?" asked Daddy.

"There are more on the other side."

"Turn around, darlin'."

Rose slowly turned. A soft smile was on her face. She was always pleased when Daddy paid attention to her, and she seemed especially delighted that he'd noticed her new outfit. As she turned her back to us, Daddy winced at the sight of the plump, round cheeks of her naked-looking behind. "Good God, they'll put her in jail," he said, and turned to Mother. "Now honey, you'll have to admit that skirt goes pretty far, it goes almost all the way to Chicago."

"Well, it *is* a little tight," said Mother. "Maybe you ought to let it out a little, Rose."

"No, this is the style," said Rose. "It's meant to be clinging."

"Clinging isn't the word for that skirt," said Daddy, "clinging doesn't even begin to come up to it. Why, Rose, you might as well not have anything on at all. Why don't you just walk down the street naked?"

It was not much of an exaggeration. Rose's very feminine and attractive behind was revealed almost as plainly as if she were naked. The soft rounded curve of each buttock, the cleft between them, the abrupt termination where her behind ended and her legs began—it was all there plain as day and she seemed to have on no underwear of any kind, not even a slip. The skirt even today would cause taxi crashes on Fifth Avenue. Rose in a way was a pioneer far ahead of her time.

"Oh, it's not *that* bad," said Mother. "It's just a little too tight, that's all. No one will notice unless they have such thoughts in the first place."

"Who doesn't have such thoughts?" asked Daddy.

"Well, I don't," said Mother. "A lot of people don't." She glanced at me. "Brother doesn't. But I want to talk to you about him. Are you through criticizing Rose?"

"Another question on my mind is this," said Daddy to Rose. "It doesn't puzzle me as much as how you got that skirt on without popping all the buttons off it, but it worries me—Rose, where did you get that peculiar shirt or blouse or whatever it is?"

"It's half a dress cut off," replied Rose. "I already had it. Do you think it's peculiar?"

"It isn't peculiar," said Mother, "it's pretty. And I don't think all this criticism is called for. What Rose wears is Rose's own business. Don't listen to him, Rose, the blouse is pretty."

"You're sweet," said Rose. "But I'll admit it's different.

I like to make up my own styles sometimes and they're different."

"That's got to be a combination of half of *two* dresses," said Daddy, "or rather, a combination of a *fourth* of two dresses. What do the purple buttons fasten, anyhow?"

"Nothin'," said Rose. "They just go across my chest like a military uniform."

"I never saw a military uniform with buttons on it *side-ways,*" said Daddy. "Would it be for a soldier who's lying down?"

"Will you stop picking on her?" asked Mother.

Rose's blouse, which was white, had a horizontal row of cloth-covered purple buttons just below her breasts, which strained against the semitransparent material and jiggled whenever she moved. She had on no trace of a brassiere and not only did her nipples make pronounced dents in the material they were half-visible through it. It seemed to me even the pink circles around her nipples could be made out through that thin blouse. Today of course such things are hardly unheard of, but Glenville in 1935 was another age, another world. A blouse like this with its peekaboo features was bound to cause whistles, cries, shouts and even worse on the street. My perception was determined by that time and maybe it was not *quite* as bad as I remember it, but it was bad, it was almost outrageous enough to get her arrested; Daddy had been only half joking when he said that. The blouse did, however, have modest sleeves, which seemed to have come from some other blouse or dress; they were full and frilly and of a different shade of white.

"Well, I don't want to crush your spirit, honey," said Daddy. "I admire it, I admire the audacity of it. And as a matter of fact that row of horizontal buttons looks kind of pretty, somehow or other. And you yourself are beautiful as always. If they put you in jail, let me know and I'll come down and get you out. I'll bring a bathrobe so we can make it home."

"Oh, be quiet," said Mother. "Nobody's going to put her in jail. You have a nice time, Rose. And I'm glad you're going out on your day off for a change, it'll do you good."

"Hmm-mm," said Daddy doubtfully. "How do you propose to get downtown, Rose, assuming that's where you're going?''

''It's where I'm going,'' said Rose. ''I'll take the bus.''

''Well, I'll give you a ride if you want, in about a minute.''

''You're not eating lunch?'' asked Mother.

''Just half-a-cup of coffee. I never eat, you know that. It's pitiful. My nerves can't tolerate food, darlin', just can't tolerate it, that's all. Not eating and reverse insomnia are my curses. Let's go, Rose, let's hit the road.''

''All right, I'll get my rose and my pocketbook.''

''Your what?'' asked Daddy. ''Your rose?''

''Yeah, my rose,'' said Rose. ''From your garden, Mrs. Hillyer, if you don't mind.''

''Not at all, dear,'' said Mother. She turned to Daddy as Rose walked across the kitchen in her new high-heeled shoes, which were of black patent leather and very shiny. She wore little tiny shoe socks and no stockings; her legs, another of her good features, were bare—but the skirt did come down to her knees in a manner approximating the style of that day. It nevertheless was a startling outfit that poetically at least was outrageous enough to get her arrested.

''Now honey,'' said Mother to Daddy, ''I want to talk to you about Brother. Do you know what the boy did? He stole Rose's cigarettes and smoked them and stayed up practically all night reading something nasty. I'm sure it must be something nasty because he wouldn't tell me what it was. Now will you tell your father what it was you were reading, Brother?''

''I don't like it,'' said Daddy. ''This house is a morphydike.'' There it was, *morphydike.* I'd expected him to say it to Rose, which in effect he had. Thank God he was thinking about that rather than the cigarettes.

''What dear? What are you talking about?''

''That getup of Rose's. I don't suppose they'll really arrest her, but if she walks down the street like that she's going to have an army following her.''

''Now I want to talk to you about Brother, this is a serious problem. Did you hear what I told you?''

''Yes. Don't smoke cigarettes, son, they are coffin spikes

and will kill you, and don't read at night, it bothers your Mother."

"All right, Daddy, and I'm . . . sorry."

"I don't like it. I don't like it a bit. This house is definitely a morphydike. Where's she *going*, for instance? She doesn't know anybody in Glenville, where's the girl going?"

"She's going out," said Mother. "What's so complicated about that?"

We heard Rose's high heels coming back down the hall and a moment later she appeared in the kitchen doorway, a big black shiny pocketbook in her hand, a red rose in her blonde hair.

"What is that in your hair?" asked Daddy.

"A rose," said Rose.

"Why have you got it in your hair?"

"Well, because I'm goin' out," said Rose. "It's sort of a . . . sort of a *motto.*"

"A motto?"

"Well, yeah. It's a motto, kind of. And it'll help people get to know me easier. They'll say there comes Rose with her rose. If my name was Daisy, I'd wear a daisy. If my name was Violet, I'd wear myself a bunch of violets. It's a motto, kind of. Of course mostly I wear it pinned on my dress. But when I *really* want to get myself up, I stick it in my hair, that *gets* 'em."

"Umm-hmm," said Daddy, a slight glaze in his eyes. "I see."

"I think it's a . . . cute idea," said Mother. "It looks pretty, too. But . . . you yourself are the thing that's pretty, Rose. You don't *really* need a flower stuck in your hair, honey."

"You're so sweet," said Rose. "But I like it there."

"Ah-HEM!" said Daddy, loudly clearing his throat in the manner he had when something bothered him. "May I ask, Rose, where exactly you're going? I don't mean to pry, but . . ."

"Well, just out, that's all."

"Just out?"

"Yeah, just out. I'll be back at midnight like you said for me to be, when I first come here."

"Um-hmm. Well, it's none of my business, but do you have any remote idea *where* you're going?"

"It certainly *is* none of your business," said Mother. "Don't answer him, Rose. And for the last time, stop picking on her!"

"Well, midnight, that's twelve hours," said Daddy, "it's only noon now. And twelve hours is a long time, I was just wondering how she's going to occupy those hours or if she herself knows—"

"Of course she does! Now leave her alone!"

"Well, I don't know *exactly,*" said Rose. "I just thought I'd mosey down the street and look around. If I don't meet nobody, maybe I'll go to the picture show or something, or get me some barbecue."

"All right, all right, to hell with it," said Daddy. "Mrs. Hillyer is right, it's your life and none of my business. Get in the car, honey, and I'll take you downtown. I just want ten seconds more with this boy."

Rose smiled at me and Mother. "Bye-bye," she said. We all watched her walk out of the back kitchen door. Her hips already were swinging softly from side to side. A vision of her walking down the main street of town flashed through my mind—she wouldn't go to a picture show and she wouldn't buy her own barbecue either, she'd meet somebody.

"Well, I shouldn't have nagged at her like that, but the girl worries me," said Daddy. "And you'll have to agree that outfit is pretty wild and wooly, hon."

"Yes, but she's such a goodhearted thing," said Mother pensively. "I admit those clothes really aren't very modest, but Rose doesn't know any better, she's never had any advantages. And in her somehow or other it all seems innocent, just like a child. That girl couldn't hurt anybody even if she tried, she's so goodnatured and kind you can't help loving her. I've never seen a mean impulse in her yet and I don't think I ever will. There's just no meanness in her. She's a very unusual girl."

"Well, we'll see how it turns out," said Daddy. He stood up, rerolled the Glenville *News-Tribune*, adjusted his straw hat backward on his head and to the side, then glanced down at me. "Keep your grimy paws off of cigarettes, you little rat," he said, as a brief reddish glare came into his eyes. Daddy could make his eyes go bloodshot in a split second and I shrank before his gaze. I wasn't the only one afraid of that glare. I saw him use it many times to intimidate rowdy gucsts at Mother's hotel—few, very few, could stand up against his anger and when they did there was sure to be a fight. It was a terrifying glare because the anger behind it was no bluff. Daddy, for all his extravagances and eccentricities, was a formidable man. I saw him more than once fly like an infuriated terrier at drunken, obscene-talking hotel guests twice his size; he did it both with and without the hotel blackjack, his eyes red and glowing with rage. It was as if all the frustrations of his life would suddenly boil up in him and explode. He was a formidable man and no one to trifle with, and although he and I were very close friends, little sons who were atomic bombs meant to blow him up got on his nerves.

"All right, Daddy," I said meekly.

"If I catch you smoking cigarettes again, I will skin you alive and throw your carcass to the crows, and I mean it," said Daddy, the red eyes riveted on me. Then he turned to Mother, bent over, lifted his straw hat, kissed her and walked from the kitchen out onto the back porch toward the Ford in the driveway, one hand on his hip and the rolled-up newspaper in the other. I sighed with deep relief. Rose had distracted him, I'd gotten off very easy.

"Now Brother," said Mother, "what nasty thing were you reading last night?"

"Mother, it hurt my feelings when you suspected me or I'd have told you already. It was nothing but *Huckleberry Finn.*"

"*Huckleberry Finn?* Is that the truth?"

"Yes, Mother."

"But you've read *Huckleberry Finn* three or four times, at least."

"I know, I'm reading it again. I'm reading all of Mark Twain's books again. You know how much I like his writing, Mother."

"Well . . . yes, yes, that's true." She paused, a little frown between her eyes, which were a paler and softer blue than Rose's. Something seemed to be bothering her, nagging at the fringes of her mind. "Well, I know you wouldn't lie to me *seriously.*" Again, she paused. Something was definitely bothering her, something she couldn't put her finger on or didn't want to put her finger on. Finally, she moistened her lips and said in a very small voice: "Brother . . . was *Rose* in your room last night?"

I stared at her blankly. "Rose? No, Rose wasn't in my room, why would Rose be in my room?"

"Well, I don't know," said Mother. "I don't know . . . you acted a little funny this morning. I just thought . . . maybe she came in and talked or something."

It was eerie. She *had* noticed the lipstick on the cigarette butts, she *must* have . . . but she chose not to be aware of it. Turn your back, and look away. On some level of her mind, she knew Rose had come into my room and kept me up most of the night, but the knowledge was not in her conscious possession and thank God for that. So it seems to me; I suppose she could have just made a wild intuitive guess that happened to be right. Mother was spooky in this way, she could come up with the truth on the basis of very little information at all—maybe she'd seen Rose wink at me, or maybe just the glances between us gave her the feeling something had gone on the night before.

"Well, as I said I know you wouldn't lie to me *seriously,*" said Mother. "And *Huckleberry Finn* is fine. But I don't want you reading nasty things and inflaming your mind, Brother. You don't know it, but you're almost at the age where nasty things could inflame you. And those are very powerful emotions you are not old enough to handle. I still can't get over your bringing home that horrible little comic book."

Some weeks before Mother had found under the shirts in my bureau a little filthy comic book, which consisted of obscene drawings of characters from newspaper comics. This one featured Dagwood and Blondie and Mr. Dithers, Dagwood's boss. Mr. Dithers came to dinner and insisted on fucking Blondie, which he did while Dagwood watched google-eyed with his tongue out and smashed his meat. Then Blondie mounted Dagwood and Mr. Dithers maniacally screwed Blondie in the ass while she said in a bubble: "Ohh-hh, poke 'em in me deep, boys, I'm comin' in both places!'' Needless to say, this little filthy comic book appalled Mother to the core. She couldn't *believe* it. How could such things *exist?* I got castor oil for it and three days later calomel, too. I was real sick.

''Mother,'' I said, ''it was *Huck Finn.* I don't even look at those filthy, horrible things any more. I give you my solemn word it was *Huck Finn.*''

''Well, I know you wouldn't lie to me seriously,'' said Mother, ''you are a good boy at heart. And that is far more important than mere brilliance, Brother. Why, you can be the most brilliant person who is practically around anywhere and if you have no heart it doesn't mean a thing. That is what kills me about Daddy, he is a very gifted man but he is mean and cruel. Did you *notice* how he picked on Rose and kept picking on her? Wasn't it disgusting, didn't it revolt you, Brother? Honestly, that man, what I go through with him you cannot imagine. . . .''

Rose was up and out and rambling, and I myself thanks to castor oil and a few gray filthy fibs was off the hook.

9

Rose hears strange voices in the night

DURING ROSE'S FIRST month at our house, Doll and I and my little brother followed her around like puppy dogs, we were in her company almost continuously and spent many hours of each day with her. However, school then started and we didn't see as much of her as before. There was also the fact that she was now going out on Thursdays and Sundays, whereas previously she'd stayed home.

Despite Daddy's apprehension an army would follow her down the street, nothing much seemed to come of it on that Thursday when Rose first got herself up and went out. Where she went nobody knows, least of all what happened—Rose very seldom talked about her outings, she gave us few clues as to where she went and what she did and who she saw. It made Daddy suspicious because it was not characteristic of her. Rose chattered endlessly about everything else under the sun, why was she so "mum" about her outings?

I knew of course she was looking for "Mr. Right," but whether or not she was having any luck in finding him was a mystery. On that first Thursday when she began her search, she returned shortly before midnight in good spirits and seemingly none the worse for her excursion. Daddy mentioned it in the dining room the next morning while Rose was in the kitchen fixing breakfast. This led to a brief, inconclusive and slightly acrid argument between my parents.

"Well, she came back," said Daddy. "I let her in last night about five of twelve and she seemed chipper as a bird. I didn't notice any bruises or broken bones."

"I don't know why you make such an issue of it," said Mother. "It's her day off, why shouldn't she go out? She's not a slave here. Anybody's entitled to days off and I don't know why you're carrying on so about it."

"I am not carrying on about it, dear."

"You certainly are. All this sarcastic business about bruises and broken bones . . . what does that *mean*, anyhow?"

"Nothing, dear," said Daddy. "Don't fret about it."

"I'm not fretting about it, I just don't like it, that's all. I don't like this streak of viciousness in you that keeps coming out. Bruises and broken bones, huh! Now I don't want to get in an argument and spoil everybody's day, but may I ask what you've got against this poor little girl?"

"I have nothing against her, dear. I am extremely fond of Rose, as you well know. I love Rose, I love every hair of her crazy blonde head; you know that and I don't know what you're riled at, I don't know what you're talking about, I don't understand you, your meaning eludes me, dear, it passes me by like a shadow in the night."

"Oh, the pretense you put on! You know perfectly well what I mean, I mean that sinister remark you made—bruises and broken bones, now what kind of thing is that to say?"

Daddy sighed wearily and looked up at the ceiling as if asking the Lord to witness the injustice of it; then with superpoliteness he replied: "It just popped into my head, darlin'. If the comment distresses you I prostrate my dog body at your feet in humble apology and implore you to find it within you somehow to forgive me."

"Well, all right, I apologize, too, I shouldn't have said that about the streak of viciousness, although at times you puzzle me so much I don't know whether I'm coming or going. How you can have the sympathies you do and be so cruel is beyond me. And while we're imploring I'd like to implore *you* to stop picking on Rose. For heaven's sake wait till she does something bad before you jump on her."

Daddy threw his napkin down on his plate. "All right!" he said. "All I am saying is that a girl who would wear clothes like that is going to get in trouble sooner or later! That's all I'm saying!"

"She just wants to look pretty," said Mother. "But we

won't argue about it any more, there isn't any point, you are beyond reason."

"So are you, dear," said Daddy.

"Oh, be quiet, I don't want to talk to you. I have nothing to say to you."

It was a polite dispute rather than a real Mother-and-Daddy argument, but it was fairly acrid—quite a bit of mild hate flashed back and forth between their eyes as we children sat there hunched over. As I have said, such arguments occurred between them on practically a daily if not hourly basis. This particular argument or polite dispute was inconclusive and so was a similar brush between them on Sunday when Rose got herself up and went out again. After that, over a period of four or five weeks, disputes about it dwindled until one disastrous evening when Rose heard strange voices in the night.

And so did the rest of us. It was about ten thirty and we were all in bed, including my parents. I was awake, however, and so was my father. Soon after the voices began everyone in the house was awake. From somewhere in the bushes and the trees of the vacant lot behind the house we heard a sudden infuriated shout:

"You son of a bitch, what are you doing here?!" And then an equally infuriated answer:

"I'd like to ask you the same question, you bastard!"

And then an exchange of gargled shouts, insults, oaths, threats and accusations:

"I told you to stay away from her, goddamn you!"

"You got no right to tell me to stay away from her, I knew her before you did!"

"She told you to leave her alone, didn't she?"

"Like hell she did! You're the one she wants to get rid of!"

"That's a lie!"

"You're a liar yourself!"

"I'm no liar, she wants to get rid of you, you ugly bastard, and you know it!"

"She doesn't want to get rid of me, it's you she wants to get rid of! And don't call me an ugly bastard or you'll be swallowing a mouthful of teeth!"

"You'll swallow teeth yourself if you don't leave her

alone, you low-down ugly bastard, I'm not afraid of you! Go on, throw one, throw one!"

"I'll throw one, you son of a bitch!"

Then followed grunts, groans, soughing noises and a great crashing in the bushes. I was up out of bed peering down from my window trying to see what was going on. Evidently a furious fist fight was in progress down there somewhere. But there was no moon that night, it was dark and they were back in the trees and bushes. I couldn't see the fighters even though I could hear them well. The grunts, groans, heavy breathing and crashing in the bushes went on for three or four minutes, until suddenly the kitchen light and the light on the back porch blazed on and I heard Daddy's voice, very loud and very angry:

"All right, I have got a Parker shotgun here and it is loaded and the trigger is cocked and wherever you birds are and whatever you are doing you had better get the hell out of here goddamn quick if you don't want to get shot and you birds had better believe I mean it!!!"

A sudden trembly silence ensued. The grunts, groans and crashing noises had stopped totally. *Thump! thump! thump!* went my heart—would Daddy shoot those birds with his Parker?—as the trembly silence continued; then sudden other crashing noises as the birds whoever they were took off in a great hurry for somewhere else. Daddy's anger was most convincing.

"And do not come back, you sons of bitches! Stay away from my house and home and my wife and children or I'll blow your goddamn heads off!!!"

Daddy had said he "loved" Rose at Thermopylae and on numerous other occasions, but what is love? It is only a word and a four-letter word at that, often as meaningless as other expletives of similar length. But it is probably the best word we have in the English language to express certain human capabilities and therefore we have got to use it. I think Daddy did love Rose, and I think he didn't want to fire her, despite the pressure her presence in the house and her behavior outside it put upon him. I'm sure it was because of this reason he didn't speak to her that night in his anger, but turned off the porch and kitchen lights and went on back to bed. Call it fondness, call it affection, call it pity, call it love, in any case he went on to bed.

Perhaps it is worth noting that in the South—I think this is accurate, although it also applies to the northerly areas of Yankeeland—a man's home is supposed to be his castle. This was certainly true of the South I knew as a child. My father could have shot those men cold dead and no charges of any kind would have been made against him. They had outraged his home and it was no joke, however harmless and amusing it might seem in recollection. I wouldn't have been in the least surprised to hear that Parker go off and neither I am sure would those birds in the bushes, they got the hell out of there as fast as they could go. It was a serious thing and Doll and I expected Rose to be fired.

In the dining room the next morning, Doll and I and Waski waited anxiously to see what would happen. Mother seemed very upset but Daddy himself appeared calm. He sat there reading the Atlanta *Constitution* while Rose finished making breakfast in the kitchen. From time to time he would say, "Hmp!" or "Hmp, how about that?" in reaction to some piece of news in the paper. But when Rose came in with scrambled eggs and bacon and toast and took her own place at the table, Daddy put down the paper and stared expressionlessly at her. Rose, who was extremely pale, smiled at him but got no reaction. In a quiet, extra-polite voice, which was a very bad sign, he said:

"Well, Rose, my sleep was a little disturbed last night, and so was Mrs. Hillyer's, and I imagine so was the children's too. How about you? Was your sleep disturbed?"

Rose answered solemnly: "Yes, Mr. Hillyer, it was. I . . . I heard strange voices in the night."

Daddy stared at her for a long time, his fingers drumming on the tablecloth. Finally he asked, "*Strange* voices, Rose?"

The innocence Rose projected was unqualified, total. She could lie like a child about certain things. Her blue eyes opened wide with pure blamelessness and she said with simple sincerity: "Yes, sir."

"You mean you never heard those voices before?"

"Oh, *no*, sir, *I* never heard them voices. I don't know who they were, they're strangers to me, whoever they are."

"Now wait a minute, Rose—"

"Maybe we shouldn't discuss this in front of the children," said Mother, who already was in a snit. Her lips were pressed together and I could see her hands twisting and untwisting her napkin.

"There is nothing the children shouldn't hear," replied Daddy in an icy tone. "Besides, they heard it already. We all heard it. Now Rose, stop behaving as if you're Bopeep. Those men had a fight last night in my yard because of some female in this house, and it *wasn't* Dolly or Mrs. Hillyer."

"Yes, but I don't know who they was," said Rose in a failing voice, "they was strange voices to me, I never heard 'em before in my life, I swear it."

"How is that possible, dear?" asked Daddy, with an aloof, chilling politeness. It was one of his deadliest weapons, the aloof, chilling politeness, and he was also giving Rose a restrained version of the red-eyed glare—restrained, only men received it full blast. "Are you suggesting those men came here to visit *Dolly?* Or my *wife,* perhaps? Was it because of Mrs. Hillyer they were cursing each other profanely, knocking down all the shrubbery in the neighborhood and breaking each other's jaws and noses? Is that your suggestion, dear?"

Rose couldn't take it. Her lip trembled, she squinched her blue eyes shut tight, bowed her blonde head and began to cry. "No . . . no, it was . . . I dunno, maybe it was Foster . . . I was so upset I couldn't hear 'em, I dunno. . . ."

"*This* is the cruelest, most inhuman thing I have ever seen in my life," said Mother. "Is it Rose's fault if two men fight about her?"

"That isn't what we're discussing," replied Daddy. "That isn't the point."

"It certainly isn't!" cried Mother. "The point is you are being brutal, brutal to this poor girl!"

"I am *not* being brutal to her!" yelled Daddy. "Now that isn't true! I am not being brutal to her a *bit!*"

"Oh . . . oh . . . oh!" wept Rose, a hand over her tightly shut eyes. "I think . . . maybe . . . one of 'em . . . was Foster . . . but I don't hardly know him!"

"Oh, *shut* up, Rose!" said Daddy. "Shut your mouth and quit crying!"

Meanwhile, of course, we children were watching in fascinated awe, horror and delight. My little brother had his mouth wide open and his auburn tresses flopped from side to side as he turned his head as at a tennis match to follow it all. Waski's hair was still long and it had been even longer—it was so pretty Mother had had trouble bringing herself to cut in, until one day he came home in anger and said someone had called him a girlie-boy. In those days, of course, long hair on boys, even young ones, was rare. I, too, was following the proceedings with a keen interest and suspense, although I was sure now that Daddy had told Rose to shut up he wouldn't fire her. Doll also was following the struggle with an absorbed concentration; her eyes, which were a darker sapphire than Rose's own deep cornflower blue, were opened wide and the tip of her tongue was on her lip and she was hunched forward so as not to miss a thing—later, in adolescence, she wrote poetry, but at eleven she was a tough little girl, although so angelically beautiful and innocent-looking my father often would stare red-eyed at her, turn away, put a hand on his heart and say some such thing as: "Walking the earth, an angel!"

We were all actually having a grand time. And so in a way were Mother and Daddy; they were having one of their battles, and that was fun if it didn't get too serious—battles were one of their greatest enjoyments. The only person at the table who wasn't having much fun was Rose, who sat there weeping and bowed, her blonde hair hanging almost down in her cereal bowl. She obviously believed Daddy was going to fire her and the thought filled her with despair; she was making quite a lot of racket as she cried.

"Ohh-hh! Ohhh-hh! OHH-HH!"

"God damn it, Rose, *shut* up! Quit bawling like a calf and eat your corn flakes!"

"I . . . I . . . I'm not hongry!" wept Rose, a hand still tight over her eyes and her head bowed low. In stress Rose reverted to country talk. She wasn't "hongry." I'm sure she wasn't. No doubt she'd lain awake all night wondering what to say, and finally had decided with a childlike ingenuousness that the best thing was to swear sincerely those men were total strangers.

"I'm not going to take any more of this barbarism," said Mother. "Here it is only twenty of eight and I'm nauseated already, do you hear that? If you keep this up any more I'm going to vomit!"

"Now listen!" said Daddy. "You just listen! When I have to get up in the middle of the night and defend my home with a shotgun against a couple of damned scoundrels—"

"Scoundrels? They weren't scoundrels, they were just boys."

"Boys? You say to me boys?"

"Yes! Yes, I say that to you, they were boys! Boy friends of Rose, that's what they were, boy friends of Rose! We all know that, everybody knows that, the children know it—those men out there, I mean those boys out there, they were boy friends of Rose . . . and why shouldn't she have boy friends? Do you want her to be unnatural? Don't you think she's human the same way you are yourself? It's the South, that's what it is, the South with its horrible traditions of slavery and crime and the oppression of women, who are just as good as men and just as human! Rose is entitled to her feelings the same way you are, but would you let her have her feelings, would you even let *Dolly* have her feelings, whom you love and adore? No! No, because you were brought up down here and you don't know anything else! And when I try to talk to you seriously, when I try to explain to you the unlimited creative power of life, how beautiful it would be if we all just gave up this hopeless struggle and simply loved each other from our hearts, when I try to explain that what do you do?—you *mock* me!"

Daddy's shoulders were humped, his eyes a trifle glazed. "I don't intend to mock you, dear," he said mildly. "I respect your philosophy. It's beyond my comprehension, but I respect it."

Mother turned to Rose: "Rose . . . listen to me. Don't pay any attention to that man, you are not going to be fired as long as I have breath in my body, not for such an innocent and human thing as having boy friends. You can have boy friends, honey, you can have all the boy friends you want!" She turned back to Daddy. "And as for you, as for you, I am just waiting to see how you'll bring the niggras into this, that'll be your next move, I am sure, the niggras—"

"Now *wait* a minute! I never said a *word* about the niggras, and you misrepresent me *constantly* on that point. Damn you, darlin', I am *not* antiniggra!"

"Oh, *yes you are!*" declared Mother. "*All* Southerners are, they drink it with their mammy's milk—hate, pure ignorant hate, just because of skin being a little different! Why, they'll look back on us in pity and horror! We're complete barbarians and have the nerve to call ourselves civilized! And let me tell you, one day the South is going to pay a price for this, one day a bitter price is going to be paid. It's breaking the laws of life itself, that's what it is. You can't put yourself against the creative power that makes everything work and expect to get away with it, never! One day a price is going to be paid, a price of blood and misery, and that's the truth. In fact if you ask me, we are already paying that price day by day, paying it every hour by the barbaric and miserable lives we lead! You are *not* going to fire this girl, not while there's breath in my body or strength in my little finger left to squeeze a trigger and shoot you with truth right between the eyes!"

Well, Daddy had said at Thermopylae that Mother would fight for Rose like a tiger if anyone tried to hurt her, and he wasn't wrong. His eyes had long since glazed over. Daddy sat at the dining table with his head tilted to the side and downward, lips pressed together beneath his clipped and slightly graying moustache, his fingers softly drumming on the tablecloth. Finally, he said, "Hmmm," and looked up wearily. The truth, which I didn't know then and didn't realize for years, was that Daddy himself believed a great deal that Mother said. He didn't accept her views on practical matters, but it was not sarcasm or irony when he said he respected her philosophy, it was the truth.

"You are right, darlin'," said Daddy, quiet and calm now. "Rose, I am sorry if I abused you, humbly sorry and I do mean humbly. But may I say just one thing? I'll admit I'm a Southerner, I was born here and I don't know what else I could be. And as a Southerner I was brought up to believe a man's house is his house, ignorant though that is of me, and I don't want strange men fighting in my yard and scaring my children. I assume you didn't invite them here, that they just came, since you've denied knowledge of them—''

''No, that's not true,'' said Mother. ''She said one of them was Foster.''

''Just a moment, darlin'. What I'm getting at, Rose, is that I wouldn't want any young girl or woman living in my house to be traipsing out at night to meet strange orangutans to discuss the New Deal with them, do you understand me?''

''Now I am *not* going to listen to that!'' said Mother. ''Here we have an intelligent conversation and you bring in orangutans!''

''Darlin', *please,''* said Daddy. ''May I finish? All I'm saying to Rose is that in case she might have a clue as to who those fellows might be, the scrappers in our bushes, would she please henceforth be so kind as to ask them to stay off the premises? That is all I am asking, Rose, will you do it for me, dear? If you have any least dim notion who those birds are, will you ask them to be so gracious as to avoid my home in the future?''

''Yes, sir,'' said Rose feebly.

''Amen!'' said Mother, a happy smile in her eyes. Strangely enough, Mother often had trouble reading Daddy, perhaps because her emotions were so entangled and involved with him. The rest of us knew when he told Rose to shut up he wasn't going to fire her, but Mother thought he would, she thought the Southern dragon was going to eat poor Rose.

''Amen!'' said Mother, with a little triumphant smile. She'd won, she'd shot him with truth between his Dixieland eyes and saved the innocent maiden from his smoke and flames. That was all she'd wanted to do: prevent Rose from being fired. As I have said, Mother loved Rose more than any of us and when her affection was committed there was no limit to which she wouldn't go. This was the cause of her outburst, although she believed everything she said and she said it many times.

10

Rose has epizootics

ABOUT FOUR OR five weeks after we all heard strange voices in the night, Daddy got a call one afternoon from the police. Rose had been arrested and was in jail. Daddy was on duty at the hotel at the time and he had to phone the day clerk to come relieve him so he could go up to the courthouse and spring the insane creature. Several men had been arrested along with Rose and also were in jail. Another man had been badly beaten up and was in the hospital.

It was a Thursday and as usual Rose had gotten herself up and gone out. It wasn't clear what happened but it seemed she went to a number of inexpensive restaurants and cafés of the type called honky-tonks. The question of who she was with or wasn't with was controversial, but she appeared to be accompanied by a large, beefy man named Horton. At any rate it was a fact she and Horton wound up at the same time in a place called the Apple Tree Café.

Rose herself practically never drank whisky or beer or anything alcoholic, but Horton did. Horton drank a lot. He'd had fourteen or fifteen beers that afternoon, and when Horton had that much beer in him nearly anything was possible, because as nice a man as he was he had one bad fault: a terrible temper.

And that afternoon Horton got mad, some sort of argument started, about baseball or something, and he had a horrible fight with several other men. Fat as he was, he was quick as a cat and very strong; he knocked all of them down, half killed one of them and demolished the Apple Tree Café.

As it happened, I knew this man Horton fairly well; he occasionally came into the lobby of the hotel. The house in which we lived in 1935 and part of 1936 was only an interlude; throughout most of the Great Depression we lived at Mother's hotel, an antique structure of some sixty rooms called the Grand Royal. This fat man Horton sometimes would come in the lobby and sit in one of the rockers and drink a Coca-Cola and smoke a cigar. Daddy didn't like him at all. He was reputed to be a part-time bootlegger and was known to be violent. "He knocks them down with a beer bottle," said Daddy. "But that doesn't satisfy him. After he knocks them down, he stomps them."

I myself kind of liked Horton. He was very soft-spoken and had a shy, almost boyish smile even though he was a florid-faced man of about forty with a paunch like a big watermelon. He talked in a soft high tenor voice with an extreme Southern drawl and he was funny, he had a kind of lazy humor. His name for me was "Peckerwood," a shortened Dixie version of redheaded woodpecker. An uncle of mine also called me this, a rich uncle who lived on a high hill with rock gates.

I liked fat old Horton even if he did hit people with beer bottles and stomp them, and Rose must have found something in him she liked, too. She sure bit the hell out of Dave's finger when he hit old Horton with the blackjack. I liked him, he'd beckon me over with a lazy wave of one of his ham-sized hands and sing softly in his high tenor voice: "Heah a dime for you, Peckahwood. Brang me a iiice cold dope 'fo Ah melt and run all ovah the flo'." He'd then let me keep the nickel change. "Set yo'self up, ole buddee-ee, you look like you burnin', too. Ah don't see no smoke but yo' haid on fiah already."

I liked Horton but Daddy despised him, he didn't like Horton a bit and once in trembling fury had told him to go chase cats, scram, go home, get out of the lobby, the rocking chairs were for paying guests and not for loafers. Horton was three times Daddy's size and I was afraid he'd hit him over the head with his Coca-Cola bottle and stomp him, but he didn't, Horton just laughed uneasily and waddled out. As I have said, it was a thing I saw more than once. My father, when angry, was not only fearless; he seemed to have an inner force that made people very reluctant to face up to him, even honky-tonk stompers like fat Horton. "Here I stand, sir, and you'll either have to back off or kill me." The man who makes it necessary for you to kill him must always be formidable and the rage beneath the surface in my father was high. Of course to marry a rich woman and see her turn out to be slightly cuckoo and find yourself practically broke and running a less than grand or royal hotel with an intended atomic bomb for a son would irritate anybody. Horton wisely waddled out, reluctant to face a manslaughter charge.

It was this, I think, Daddy's intense dislike of Horton and not the fact that she'd been arrested and put in jail, that got Rose in real trouble. She was in trouble all right, in such trouble Daddy didn't say a word on the matter at suppertime. It was too serious to discuss in front of us children. He was icily polite not only to Rose but to Mother and the rest of us, a very, very bad sign.

After supper, Doll and I heard him arguing angrily with Mother behind their closed bedroom door. This bedroom, which was across the hall from the living room at the front of the house, was also a kind of sitting and sewing room and a study room for Mother, and she and Daddy usually had their most serious arguments and conferences there.

We couldn't hear Mother but Daddy was talking louder and we could catch fair-sized snatches of what he was saying. Being arrested and put in jail, he declared, was perhaps not wholly Rose's fault, that remained to be seen, but regardless of that he didn't want in his house a girl who would run around with a drunken bully bootlegger like Horton.

"Now you see it isn't just funny fun!" he shouted. "That's what you thought it was, funny fun, Rose and her rambles! Well, it isn't funny fun, here she is running around with a brute like Horton, a fat rascal who has half killed a dozen men in this town! He'll really kill somebody before he's through, the mean pig-eyed son of a bitch, and you keep telling me Rose finds something good in people! What's good in Horton, huh? Nothing! Rose doesn't find good in him because there isn't any, and she is finished! I am going to fire her and that's that!"

The argument went on for about an hour. When Daddy

shouted in fury we could hear him, but mostly we heard only snatches in the living room across the hall, where we huddled in fear for Rose. We didn't dare creep closer and eavesdrop at the door in a situation like this; Daddy had a sixth sense about such things, there was a lot of Hawkshaw the Detective in him and some Sherlock Holmes, too, and he might suddenly yank open the door and catch us. We trembled in the living room convinced that this time it was all over for Rose, who had done the dishes and was up in her bedroom weeping.

Daddy had gotten her out of jail without difficulty; he held an honorary, unsalaried job on the Glenville Civil Service board, which appointed town policemen. However, the arresting officer wasn't there and disorderly conduct charges were still hanging over Rose. Trouble with "the law" was a thing extremely frightening to her; she knew girls who had no "rich folk" friends and had been put behind bars and kept there.

But Daddy had said nothing whatever to reassure her when he got her out and fetched her home. She told me in tears on the back porch after supper that he'd been even more icy in the car than he was in the dining room; he didn't speak a word to her all the way home. "Not a word, Buddy," she said, weeping. "He just stared ahead and wouldn't talk to me! Oh Buddy, my day has come, he's gonna fire me! And I haven't done a thing, except bite that policeman when he hit Horton—except for that I haven't done a thing, not a thing, nothin'!"

But Rose in childish fear didn't admit to Daddy and Mother she'd bitten anybody. She swore in tearful sincerity she hadn't done a thing, nothing at all, she was just standing there hoping they would stop all that horrible fight, she was just standing there and crying out to Horton to stop it and quit knocking those men down, when the policeman came in and started hitting Horton on the head something awful with a blackjack. As for why he'd arrested her—why, just to be *mean*, there couldn't be any other reason because she hadn't done anything.

That's what she told Mother and Daddy. After about an hour of furious argument with Mother, Daddy had gone upstairs and brought her down. We saw him lead her weeping into Mother's bedroom-sitting room, hand on her arm and his face grim.

At this point, curiosity overcame caution and I did sneak up and listen at the door for a few minutes, long enough to hear the above protestation of total innocence. I also heard a sobbing Rose swear among other things that she hardly even knew this man *Horton,* that her date that afternoon wasn't him at all but another man, a fellow named *Phil* who drove a bakery truck. Phil was her date, but no, it wasn't Phil that Horton beat up so bad, that was *Norris,* and why he'd beat up Norris she had no idea, they were arguing about baseball or something.

No, no, no, she hadn't had a date with Horton and Phil and Norris all at the same time, of course not, she didn't even know Norris hardly or at least she knew him only a little tiny bit, he'd once given her a lift downtown in his taxi because that was what he did, he was a taxi driver and was separated from his wife, which was why she wouldn't give him a date, he had a wife, that fellow Norris the taxi driver, and of course she wouldn't have anything to do with a married man, never!

Daddy finally gave up on her and came out of the bedroom. As he put on his hat we heard him say: "All right, Rose, if you want to keep acting like a child even though you're nineteen years old, I'll just go downtown and hunt up Dave Wilkie and find out for myself precisely what happened in that café. And as for your toothache, I am sorry about that but I must admit I am at a loss to comprehend how and why the two of you blame *me* for it! Frankly I think Rose has more important things to worry about than a damn silly toothache!"

Little did Daddy know the consequences of Rose's toothache. It was her first attack of epizootics. The truth is, Rose would never have made it through the winter in our house without epizootics.

Dave Wilkie—who, yes, turned out in apple blossom time to be Mr. Right—was the policeman who had broken up the brawl in the café and arrested Rose. We all knew Dave well and we'd known his wife Lois even better. Dave's wife, who had been killed several years before in a freak accident, was supposed to have been a remote and distant cousin of Mother's by marriage.

She came from a good family down on its luck and Dave was somewhat beneath her on the intricate social scale of Glenville; his own people had been honest but poor farmers, not impoverished tenant farmers like Rose's people, but poor. What Mother called with unintentional snobbery: "Good honest plain stock." We ourselves were good honest *fancy* stock, I suppose. Mother didn't intend to be a snob; she tried all her life to be a liberal and believed she was an extremely dangerous radical, a real threat to the Southern way of life, and perhaps she was.

From whatever stock Dave Wilkie came, fancy or plain, he had only a high school education and was unemployed in the early, most terrible years of the Great Depression. He was a skilled carpenter and knew something about construction and wanted to be a builder, but there was no building going on in those days. He could get nothing. To eke out an existence until times got better, Dave's wife Lois had worked as a seamstress and she did quite a lot of sewing for my mother. I remember her and Mother discussing and spreading out dress material in the Wilkies' tiny living room, while Dave himself sat there miserable with his hands folded and his head bowed. Dependence on his wife almost killed the man. Such things were very common in the Great Depression, in comparison to which the "recessions" of today are a party picnic of abundant prosperity and economic well-being. Those who didn't live through it cannot imagine it, they cannot conceive what the Great Depression was like. Hitherto honest wives and mothers sold their bodies for a dollar to feed hungry children; strong men wept and fell broken to their knees—and Dave Wilkie was almost one of the latter. My father, who had influence on the Civil Service board, had gotten Dave his job as a Glenville policeman, which turned out to be a rather fortunate little coincidence.

The freak tragedy of Dave's wife occurred only a few months after he joined the Glenville force. An old and rotten balm of Gilead in the Wilkies' back yard blew over in a windstorm and crashed down through the back porch and broke Lois's leg and hip. Five days later she developed an embolism and suddenly died at thirty-six, leaving Dave alone with a young boy. He was a shy man with women and had never remarried.

I didn't believe Dave would arrest Rose for no reason any more than Daddy did, and I wouldn't have believed it even if she hadn't told me she bit him. I knew Dave well, he often came into the lobby of the hotel to have a drink of water or simply to get out of the weather. A lot of times we'd sit and talk, mostly about his young son, Tom, who played football for Glenville High and was so good, a scout from Georgia Tech already had mentioned a possible scholarship. Dave doted on his son as much as any father I ever saw; when he talked of Tom his real character was plain.

On the surface, Dave was a tough and hard and bitter man, with a temper even worse than that of the fat bootlegger Horton. Before he became a policeman he too had gotten into honky-tonk brawls and he was deadly dangerous. He was a broad-shouldered, powerful man with fists bigger than Horton's, and as I said an even more violent temper. One rumor was that he'd gotten in a horrible fight with a man bigger than himself who'd done professional prize fighting—according to the story, Dave had hospitalized the man, he was supposed to have broken five or six of the man's ribs, one of his arms, and knocked out eight or nine of his teeth.

That was on the surface and even below the surface: a hard and bitter and violent man. Those years of unemployment did something to him. Dave, like many Southerners of that time and indeed many Southerners of a later time, hated Negroes and he could be cruel to them. He wouldn't hesitate to beat an "uppity nigger" into a pulp with his club or blackjack. As I said, on the surface and even below: a hard and bitter and violent man. The truth I believe is that Dave Wilkie had an illness that needed to be cured, and I believe it is also true he wanted it to be cured.

I believe that is so, because I don't think Dave was truly an evil man. His brutality—a raw violence beneath a child-like gentleness—was typically Southern and I am convinced the man wanted desperately to be relieved of the injury he had received, to have his painful affliction healed and that this was why he felt initially as he did about the girl I call

Rose. Mother had another theory, but I think I am closer to it, although in a sense she said the same thing.

There was other evidence to support an opinion Dave was not a truly evil man. His adoration of his handsome son, a talented running back and a very personable boy much brighter than Dave himself, was one such piece of evidence; the man had raised this boy alone between the ages of fourteen and seventeen, and he had done it with a fatherly devotion that was quite remarkable and unusual. Dave was genuinely and truly unselfish toward his son. The very way he said "my boy, Tom" was kind of touching. A man who could love a son that way could not be truly evil—that is what I was thinking in the Atlanta airport not too long ago while waiting for an Avis rental.

I might add that Dave Wilkie had no cold-blooded cruelty in him; I saw no such thing in him when I knew him in those days long ago. He didn't beat the mortal hell out of blacks if he felt there was no need for it; there was no sadism in him.

Other police on the Glenville force God knows were worse. I heard the black bellboys at the hotel talk about it, I was very friendly with them and knew how they felt . . . or thought I did, today I wonder about that. The impression I got was that they respected Dave but did not fear him. There were certainly others they did fear, others they feared so much they'd cross the street to avoid.

It could truthfully be said that the Dave Wilkie I knew in the depths of the Great Depression was a man who by his own lights was fair. He was at heart a kindly man, gentle to children and almost pathetically polite to women. I remember how deferential and even reverent he was to Mother when he'd see her in the lobby. This is a thing most Southern men have toward women and maybe it is old-fashioned of me but I have got to believe it has a certain value. Until women lift a thousand pounds and run the hundred-yard dash in nine seconds flat, it has got to have a value. If it has no value, why are men strong? What are they to protect, merely themselves?

I knew Rose had bitten him, but I would have been certain anyhow Dave wouldn't have arrested her without a reason. Of course as it turned out she'd tried to hit him over the head with one of her high-heel shoes and had bitten his finger. It was a bad bite, she bit the hell out of him right to the bone. She'd become utterly hysterical at the sight and sound of the leather-covered blackjack smacking down on Horton's semibalding head—for which Dave as an officer of the law could hardly be blamed. What else could he do when a drunken man in a wild rage was tearing a restaurant to bits and half killing people?

As I pointed out it was a fortunate coincidence for Rose it was this particular policeman upon whose finger she fastened her "once in twenty years" teeth—that was what Dr. Winton said, once in twenty years he saw teeth like hers. Dave knew she was practically a member of our family and he told Daddy that since the girl had never been in trouble before and since the bite on his finger was undoubtedly more hysterical than intentional, he would drop the charges.

Daddy, who was infuriated at having been lied to, said no, haul her into court, make her pay a fine—but Dave refused. "Now, Mr. Hillyer," he said, "you wouldn't want her to have a record of arrest and conviction. Besides, the girl was real upset, she didn't mean to bite me or even hardly know she did it. You tell her it's all right, I forgive her."

When Daddy got back to the house, I have no doubt he'd made up his mind to fire Rose. But in the meanwhile the toothache about which she had complained had become much worse. A swollen lump half the size of a golf ball had appeared on her jaw and it was obvious she was in severe pain. We were all back in the kitchen and Mother was worriedly putting cold compresses on her face when Daddy stomped in.

"All *right!*" he said. "Now why didn't you tell me you bit Dave? You little liar, you bit his finger to the bone and tried to hit him on the head with your shoe. Now that's the sort of lie I'd expect from a small dimwitted child, Rose. Didn't you know I was bound to find out about it? And don't you know if Dave wasn't a good and kindhearted man, you could go to jail for this?"

"Oh, *be quiet!*" said Mother. "This girl is suffering dreadfully, look at her jaw, look at it! She has a terrible toothache, look at the swelling, it's like a chicken's egg.

The poor thing . . . how does it feel, Rose, does the ice help?''

''Ohhh-hh, ohhhh-hh,'' groaned Rose, ''ohhhh-hh, it *hurts,* Mrs.Hillyer, it hurts so *bad!* Ohhh-hh, it's *killin'* me, Mrs. Hillyer!''

''Mmmmm,'' said Daddy. ''Well, I'm sorry she has these epizootics, but I still don't see why she told me such a damn silly lie. How about it, Rose? Don't you know the difference between truth and falsehood even slightly?''

''She's suffering terribly and I will not allow you to cross-examine her, grill her and pick on her!'' cried Mother. ''I won't allow it! And you're not going to fire her, either, not if I have anything to say about it! Why, it's completely unjust. It wasn't her fault those men fought over her this time any more than it was when they fought over her the last time. How is she to blame?—men *like* her, that's all. And in any case this is no time to pick on her and torture her. Where's your sense of proportion? Look at her, look at her jaw, look how she's suffering, the poor child. How does it feel, Rose, you poor baby? Does the ice help a little, hon?''

''Ohhh-hhh,'' groaned Rose, ''a little, I guess . . . ohhh-hhh.''

''Fiddlesticks!'' said Daddy, and turned and walked out with a disgusted look on his face.

It was the first of Rose's epizootics, but not the last. She was up all night moaning and crying and Mother was up most of the night with her, putting compresses on her cheek and holding her hand. She wept and groaned the whole night through, as much with terror as with pain. Rose had never been to a dentist in her life. The very idea of it frightened her out of her wits.

But she obviously needed a little dental attention. The swelling became worse during the night despite all the ice put on it. Early the next morning, Mother and I took her in the car to Dr. Winton, our family dentist. Daddy had washed his hands of the whole thing and I went along to help. It was the Christmas holidays and luckily I was home and available.

I say luckily because Mother needed all the help she could get, from me or anyone else. ''Be calm, Rose, try to quit crying!'' she said, as she started the Ford with a heave of shifted gears at about ten after eight. Daddy in disgust had taken a taxi to the hotel. Rose was in such pain and so exhausted and terrified she could barely sit up in the car seat. She was clutching one of my hands with both of hers and she kept whispering: "Oh, Buddy, that dentist will kill me!" She was also crying. Rose could cry like a little child with boohoo sobs and that was what she was doing as Mother drove the Ford on a slightly wandering path down the driveway and out onto the Summerton Road. "Ohh-hh, boohoo-hoo-hoo-hoo!" wept Rose. As I said, she'd never been to a dentist in her life and she was convinced all kinds of horrendous things were going to happen to her—and unfortunately, in this case, she was right.

Dr. Winton, who practiced regular dentistry and did not do difficult oral surgery, could not help her. This was what we finally learned, at which point we had to drag her back to the car and take her to another dentist named Addison. But that is getting ahead of events; it took quite a while even to determine what was wrong with her. We got there before Dr. Winton arrived and sat there for what seemed an interminable time in the waiting room, Rose weeping and trembling in every limb despite everything Mother said to reassure her.

Finally, Dr. Winton, a white-haired man who talked in a gruff way to hide an extreme reluctance to inflict pain, arrived. Rose took one look at him and shrank down in her seat, ashen. "You know," she said—and she really said it—"you know, it's funny, it's the strangest thing, Mrs. Hillyer, but it doesn't hurt any more, let's go home."

Mother persuaded her that to leave now wouldn't be wise. However, when the nurse opened the door of the inner office and Rose saw the dental chair with its equipment, her eyes popped, she planted her feet and began to take steps backward—Mother and I combined stopped her but we couldn't make her go forward. "I'm not goin' in there!" she said. "I don't like the looks of it and I'm not goin' in there!"

The nurse tried to be firm with her, Mother tried to be firm with her, even I tried to be firm with her. No effect, the dental chair horrified her. Dr. Winton himself finally came out to reason with her. "Now, young lady," he said, "be calm. First of all, let me tell you I am *not* going to hurt you."

"Yes, you are," said Rose.

"No, I am not."

"Look, you can't kid me," said Rose.

"Now listen, calm down and listen. I am *not* going to hurt you, I give you my solemn word I am not. All I want to do is look at you."

"Oh, yeah?" asked Rose. "Well, you can look at me right now."

"Don't talk foolish, dear, don't talk silly. I mean look in your *mouth,* so I can see what's *wrong* with you."

Dr. Winton finally persuaded her, but when she realized she was supposed to go in there alone she balked again and this time wouldn't budge. She flatly refused to do it, not alone. "If Mrs. Hillyer and Buddy come in with me, I guess I might. But I ain't goin' in there all by myself! No, sir! Wild hosses can't get me in there!"

"All right," said Dr. Winton with a shrug. "If that's the only way she'll let me look at her mouth, then all of you come on in. Just try and stay out of the way."

When Rose finally sat down in the dental chair she stared with popped eyes at all the terrible equipment and made little whimpering noises like a crying puppy. "Oh-oh-oh-oh," she said. As Dr. Winton stepped around in front of the chair she demanded that Mother hold one of her hands and I the other. We took a good grip on her, but when Dr. Winton came at her with two of those horrible instruments—actually a harmless exploratory dental pick and a little dental mirror—she wriggled wildly and got halfway out of the chair.

"Rose, sit *still!*" said Mother. "He's not going to hurt you, he just wants to look!"

"Ohh-hh, ohh-hh," whimpered Rose.

"I am getting a wee mite weary of this," said Dr. Winton. "Now listen here, young lady, do you want me to help you or not?"

"Ohh-hh, ohh-hh," said Rose, "it's just that . . . ohh-hh . . ."

"I think the only way you can examine her, much less work on her mouth, is under general anesthesia," said Dr.

Winton. It wasn't the only time we'd hear this remark that morning. Dr. Addison, the oral surgeon, would say it more than once.

"Now Rose, stop acting like a child!" said Mother. "I am getting very outdone with you! You're nineteen years old, you're not a baby! Behave yourself, do you hear me?"

"All right, all right," said Rose. "I'm sorry. I'm sorry, Doctor. But please don't hurt me, now you said you wouldn't!"

When Dr. Winton at last got a look in Rose's mouth, his white eyebrows lifted in surprise. "Hmmph," he said. He turned the mirror this way and that, probed with the pick, drew back, adjusted his glasses, bent forward and did it some more. "Hmmph," he said again, then stood back and put a hand in his shock of white hair, startled eyes on Rose. I was wondering what awful thing was wrong with her teeth. Probably many of them would have to be pulled. Country people, I knew, had very poor teeth because of their diet, although Rose's teeth were an even pearly white and looked fine as far as I could see. For the third time, Dr. Winton said, "Hmmph."

"What's wrong, Doctor?" asked Mother.

Dr. Winton turned to Mother. "Is it true she's never been to a dentist?"

"That's what she says," answered Mother. "Have you, Rose?"

"No, Ma'am," said Rose. "I never had a toothache."

"I guess you haven't," said Dr. Winton. He shook his head in disbelief and again turned back to Mother. "Her trouble is an impacted and abscessed wisdom tooth. But except for that, the girl has teeth I don't see once in twenty years. She hasn't got a cavity in her mouth, not a single one. And not only that, she has a model bite, her gingiva is pink, healthy, shows no trace whatsoever of periodontal disease. The girl has perfect teeth. I am telling you, I don't run into a mouth like this once in twenty years. For some reason she is immune to tooth decay." Dr. Winton turned back to Rose with what seemed to me a kind of resentment. "You're a fine one to be afraid of dentists," he said. "You don't know it, but you're a very lucky young lady."

"Then why have I got a toothache?" moaned Rose.

"Your toothache has nothing to do with decay. What you have is a partly extruded wisdom tooth for which there isn't room in your mouth. Of course the net result is the same and I know it's painful."

"It'll have to be pulled, won't it?" asked Mother.

"Yes, she'll have to get it extracted, but I can't help you with it. I don't do this kind of oral surgery, you'll have to go to Addison. Frankly I have to tell you it'll be a little difficult. Considering the nerves of this patient, it might be an excellent idea to take her to the hospital and put her to sleep."

"Oh, no!" cried Rose. "No, no, no—not the hospital!"

Rose was more terrified of the hospital than she was of a dental chair and that was the only reason her impacted wisdom tooth ever got extracted that morning. At the next dental office, she didn't have Mother and me to hold her hands, Dr. Addison wouldn't put up with such foolishness; but we heard what was going on in there—the moans, groans, bloodcurdling gasps and screams. We also heard Dr. Addison threaten several times to stop if she didn't sit still and be quiet. "You will have to go to the hospital and get general anesthesia!" he yelled. "I am not going to put up with this! Now shut up, and quit squirming! How can I get this damned tooth out if you keep jumping all over the chair? Sit still, that's my last warning to you!"

In fairness to Rose, it was a very bad extraction and today undoubtedly would be done under anesthesia in a hospital. Of course she had Novocain shots but even so it was gothic. The tooth was deeply imbedded sidewise in bone and its roots were abnormally large and curved in such a way it couldn't be pulled; bone had to be obliterated and the tooth itself ground in pieces and broken into bits. The operation took an hour and a half and would have been a God-awful experience for anyone, much less a country girl who'd never been to a dentist and thought they were torturing fiends out to kill her.

When it was finally over, Rose was so shattered she couldn't walk unassisted. Daddy had to come help Mother and me take her home. In the car she kept whispering: "Never again, never again." By the time we got home she literally could not stand on her feet and Daddy had to carry her in his arms from the car into the house and up to her room, where she lay on her bed groaning and moaning for four or five days.

Rose's pain was real but her fear was worse; she was terrified half out of her mind the awful wound in her jaw wouldn't heal and she'd have to go back to that monster dentist and he'd do even worse to her—the very thought would start her moaning and weeping. Rose had had enough of "rich folk" dentistry and medicine, enough to last her the rest of her life. It was because of this she later concealed with such wild-animal guile what Daddy called her "great epizootics."

11

Rose has great epizootics

INEVITABLY, THE QUESTION of firing Rose got buried in all the misery of the terrible pulling of the tooth. Daddy didn't bring it up again and in a week or so Rose was well. Her errors—running around with a brute like Horton, being arrested and put in jail, biting Dave on the finger and lying about it—were overlooked if not forgotten.

However, Rose was no sooner her old self than the commotion resumed. About three weeks after the terrible pulling of the tooth Daddy almost fired her again and this time it took "great epizootics" to save her.

There was, as I have said, quite a lot of Hawkshaw the Detective in my father and one morning he stopped me in the hall and said in a low tone: "Come with me, son, I want to show you something. *I have found suspicious footprints in the flower bed beneath Rose's window.*"

It was true there were indentations that looked something like footprints in the flower bed.

"See that, son? Now this is a *heel,* see, and *there,* that's the ball of a foot. *Someone has been walking here.*"

"Well . . . they're not very plain," I said.

"That is because it rained recently," answered Daddy. "The rain has obscured them. But you could still take plaster casts of these footprints, then you could match the plaster casts up with whosever shoes they are, and that way you could catch him . . . understand?"

"How would you find him?" I asked.

"Well . . ." said Daddy. "Well, what I mean is, you could prove it was his shoes if you did find him. But look at *this*, Brother, this is even more interesting than the suspicious footprints. Look at this mark here, and look at that mark over there. Now wouldn't you say those marks are the marks of a *ladder?*"

"Well, I don't know," I replied, trying to sound like a fellow detective although if Rose had done anything I didn't want her to get caught. "No, I don't know, Daddy. I think the rain has obscured them."

"True—but if you look sharply, you can see that those marks are the marks of a ladder. Now let's go back to the garage and see if the ladder *has been tampered with.*"

"Okay," I said, "good idea."

When we got to the garage and inspected the ladder which hung along the side, Daddy's eyes narrowed and he said: "Umm-hmm, I thought so. This ladder has recently been tampered with. Look at it, Brother, some person or persons unknown have *unquestionably tampered with this ladder.*"

"Well, Daddy," I said, "that's very interesting. But how can you tell somebody has tampered with it, just by looking at it?"

"The paint is flecked off here, freshly," said Daddy. "See? No doubt about it. You have to have sharp eyes to observe these things, son, but they're there."

Oddly enough, as events later proved, Daddy was dead right about the suspicious footprints and the ladder. As I said, there was more than Hawkshaw the Detective in him, he had some Sherlock Holmes, too. However, the evidence at this point was hardly conclusive and I believe he was just looking in desperation for an excuse to get rid of Rose. Daddy liked Rose, he was genuinely fond of her, I think he even loved her, but life with her in the house drove him crazy. It was, as he said, a monkey and dog show.

Since Rose's recovery from the terrible pulling of the tooth, a number of maddening things had happened. Not things big enough to fire her about, they were small things, but they were maddening. The "callers," for example—the phone, it kept ringing, ringing, ringing, night and day. If Doll or I answered, a low male voice, furtive and husky and conspiratorial, would ask to speak to Rose . . . the voices varied, but they all sounded the same, somehow. If

Mother or Daddy answered, the callers usually would hang up without a word. It drove Daddy wild.

But the "followers" drove him even wilder than the "callers." One afternoon a very scruffy-looking man followed Rose home right up to the door and wouldn't go away even when Mother went out and spoke to him. He kept hanging around out there and it scared Mother, the man had a funny look in his eye. She telephoned Daddy at the hotel and he came racing home in the Ford. The man saw him turn into the driveway and took off across our yard. Daddy clamped on the brakes, jumped out of the car and yelled at the man:

"Come back here, sir! Come back here, you!"

The scruffy man didn't even look around, he kept going on across our yard and the Humprey yard next door and the O'Neal yard on beyond. Daddy took off after him and chased him quite a ways but the scruffy man ran like a deer and Daddy couldn't catch him. "He ran like a deer," said Daddy. "I couldn't catch the rascal."

Two days later, a young boy no more than eighteen followed Rose home. He left when Mother asked him to, but he was surly about it. Rose swore she hadn't spoken to him or encouraged him in any way to follow her and that she had no earthly idea who he was. We later found out his name was Billy and that he wanted to be a fireman.

On the following day this boy Billy was back, or so Doll said. She saw him out in the vacant lot creeping around in the bushes. Mother didn't see him and neither did I, but Daddy found two freshly stamped-out cigarette butts behind a big oak tree and this proved he was there. "No, darlin'," said Daddy, "your little angel eyes didn't deceive you. The rascal was there. I'm going to buy some buckshot for the Parker. This place is under a siege."

It did seem like a siege. A few days later, the scruffy-looking man was back, out there in the front yard peering around a tree trunk with his hat down over his eyes. This time, Mother called the police as Daddy had instructed her to do, and they caught and arrested the man, who turned out to be an unemployed bricklayer with a wife and four children. He said Rose had flirted with him down at the grocery store, he declared she'd put her hand on her hip, winked at him, turned around and shook her tail at him. Rose denied it indignantly; she swore she'd never even noticed this man until she looked around and saw him following her home. It doesn't make any difference but I believe her about the scruffy bricklayer. Rose didn't put her hand on her hip and wink at him and shake her tail at him, the vibrations she gave off were so powerful she didn't have to use such crude methods as that.

These "followings," as Daddy called them, didn't even occur on Rose's days off, they happened as a result of her merely going in her ordinary clothes down to the grocery store to buy eggs or butter or something. Daddy said: "It would be understandable, maybe, if she was 'gotten up.' This is hellish. They go after her even when she's normal."

Therefore, I think that Daddy, as a result of the maddening callers and the even more maddening followers, was looking for an excuse to fire Rose when he came upon the suspicious footprints in the flower bed beneath her window. However, unbeknownst to him and to Mother, Rose hadn't been well the past couple of days, not well at all. She let on to Mother and Daddy she merely had a little bad cold and it was nothing, but Doll and I knew she was sick, she told us so and we could see it. She had a fever, a bad cough and was so weak she could hardly drag herself around to do the housework. I told her she ought to tell Mother she was ill and ask her to call a doctor, but the suggestion appalled Rose. She swore us to secrecy and with the cunning of a little wild animal hid all the symptoms of her illness from Mother and Daddy, dismissing her cough as an insignificant trifle.

"This ladder has unquestionably been tampered with by a person or persons unknown," said Daddy, "and there could only be one reason: to get up into Rose's bedroom. That wraps and seals it, son, let's go speak to your mother. I'm getting rid of that girl. This country couldn't stand King George and I can't stand Rose. Give me liberty from this monkey and dog show or give me death."

Daddy took me along to Mother's room to back him up and support him, but I didn't. To his annoyance I knocked the pins out from under him by agreeing with Mother that dim footprints didn't prove anything, they might be perfectly innocent and not suspicious at all.

"Very well," said Daddy with an icy calm. "I know I'm right but I don't give a damn. Even if this evidence proves nothing, I am firing her, honey, and this time you are not going to talk me out of it. I don't like to do it, I'm very fond of Rose, but she's crazy, she's out of her head. Life with her in this house is a *total* monkey and dog show! All kinds of scruffy-looking characters following her home, strange voices in the night, brawls in honky-tonks, the phone ringing day and night and now footprints and ladder marks in the garden—I've had *enough* of it. I am fed to the gills with it and I am firing her!"

"Well," said Mother, who was on the verge of tears, "I realize it's a problem, she does seem to cause an awful lot of commotion . . . but honey, give her one more chance. The truth is, Rose doesn't mean any harm. She doesn't intend to cause trouble, I'm sure she doesn't . . . those men follow her and fight over her, it just happens."

"I am sorry, darlin'," said Daddy. "I don't like it any better than you do, but either that girl is leaving this house or I am myself."

Daddy went upstairs to fire Rose and found her lying half-conscious in bed with a very high temperature. She couldn't answer him coherently and her forehead was blistering hot. There was nothing to do but call the doctor. Mother called a new man named Dr. Martinson who arrived about half an hour later, examined Rose and said she had influenza complicated by double pneumonia and her life was in very grave danger and she would have to be taken to the hospital immediately without delay. She was a very, very sick girl.

"Her life . . . in grave danger?" asked Daddy in dismay. "How did she get so sick so quick? If she wasn't feeling well, why didn't she tell us?"

It was terrifying to us all. I remember Rose half-conscious strapped to a stretcher being carried down the stairs from the second floor by white-coated ambulance attendants. She was aware of what was happening and was trying to grab at the banisters to stop them. To go to the hospital was infinitely worse than being taken to the dentist.

In Rose's view, being put in the hospital was equivalent to being put in the cemetery. Many country people of that time and place fully shared her opinion: one went to the hospital only to die. When she caught a glimpse of Doll and me in the doorway of the living room she feebly cried: "They're takin' me to the hospital! Buddy, Dolly . . . don't let them! Help me! Help me!"

Rose did very nearly die; Daddy did not use the term "great epizootics" casually or lightly. In those days, double pneumonia was a fatal disease more often than not. There were no antibiotics and not even the sulfa drugs and usually in a day or two or three the last drowning breath would be taken and that would be that. Rose's survival I am sure was due to her having as Dr. Martinson said a constitution strong as an ox, a kind of supervitality that could survive almost anything, but Mother and Rose herself ascribed it to the wonderful Dr. Martinson. I never liked this Dr. Martinson, I didn't like him one damn bit and felt he did nothing whatever except stay out of the way and let Rose herself fight and beat her illness, which in all fairness to him was probably about all he could have done in those years. He took credit for it, however; he didn't disagree with Mother or Rose that it was his marvelous medical skill that pulled her through.

This doctor was not our regular family doctor, but a new man Mother had found, a former Yankee who called himself Dr. F. Robert Martinson. I have never cottoned up much to people who call themselves Initial Something Something, although they probably have their reasons for it. The man had a sallow, unhealthy-looking complexion and a little spade-shaped gray beard that I didn't like either, but for some reason I really don't remember this man's face very well. He was new to us and we only used him for Rose's epizootics, but he'd been in town five or six years.

This Dr. Martinson was probably a good doctor as doctors go but I don't think his practice amounted to much in Philadelphia or wherever it was. His practice certainly didn't amount to much in Glenville. The other doctors seemed to respect him, but he was a cold and hateful man and people didn't like him. Somehow or other he had met and married a well-to-do Glenville widow. He was about fifty years old and spoke in a superior, half-sneering manner that was very unpleasant. There was also something a trifle lewd about him, as witnessed by his Venus de Milo remark about Rose. Tragically, this doctor and his wife committed murder-suicide around 1946, right after the war. People said he'd lost a fortune in the stock market.

Rose was far too ill to have visitors at first, but after four or five days she got a little better and Mother and I and Daddy and Doll and Waski went to the hospital to visit her. She was still very ill and so feeble and weak it seemed an effort for her even to hold open her eyes. She wept when she saw us and whispered: "Pray for me."

The new doctor took us to a small empty waiting room, sat us down and said: "As you see, she's better. The girl is strong as an ox fundamentally and I think she'll make it if she can get through another day or two. That is, without complications. One trouble is she had tuberculosis as a child—"

"Tuberculosis?" asked Mother in alarm.

"Yes, there's scarring in both lungs, worse in the right than in the left but considerable in both. The disease is arrested but—"

"She has t.b.?" asked Mother. "Should she be cooking food and taking care of children?"

"I didn't say she *has* t.b., Madame, I said she *had* it. Please listen more attentively. The girl is quite recovered from the disease and there's no reason she shouldn't cook food or take care of children. I mentioned it because the scar tissue in her lungs makes the prognosis of pneumonia somewhat more guarded for her. Not insofar as the pneumonia *itself* is concerned, no, not that, lung tissues regenerate and the girl has in fact a larger oxygenating capacity than most people and that is what has kept her alive—no it is not that, but the prognosis is guarded in *this* respect: serious bronchial infection of a chronic variety *can* cause a recurrence of the tuberculosis. Is that clear?"

"No," said Daddy. "What do you mean, *recurrence?* If the tuberculosis can come back, then how can you say it's safe for her to handle food and take care of children?"

"You weren't listening carefully," said Dr. Martinson with a little smile. "I said *chronic* bronchial infection, and *chronic* means over a period of months or even years. That *could* cause a recurrence. But it's very unlikely. Except for her present illness, this girl is *very* strong and healthy. If she throws off this pneumonia she'll almost certainly make a complete recovery and there'll be no problem.

"Then why bring it up?" asked Daddy. "Why worry us with a lot of medical gobbledygook that doesn't mean anything?"

"Honey, *please,*" said Mother, "you're embarrassing me. Go on, Doctor, tell us how Rose is, we're very interested."

"Because 'medical gobbledygook,' sir, is my job. It's my duty to inform you of possibilities, no matter how remote."

"All right," said Daddy. "What are the odds of this pneumonia causing her tuberculosis to recur?"

"I'm not a gambler, Mr. Hillyer, I practice medicine."

"Well, I know you're not a gambler, but give us some idea how remote this remote possibility might be. Would you say, sir, the odds are ten thousand to one against it?"

"I said the possibility was remote. The odds would be high against it, naturally, of course."

"Ten thousand to one?"

"Well . . . assuming a complete recovery . . . well, a good recovery . . . perhaps somewhat higher."

Daddy stared at him for at least five long seconds, his eyes a trifle red and glary. He'd taken an instant dislike to Dr. Martinson. In fact, Daddy couldn't stand the man, he couldn't endure him. Finally, with an icy politeness he said: "Thank you. We appreciate being advised about it. Very kind of you."

"Go on, Doctor, we're extremely interested," said Mother.

"There's not much more to say, Madame. As I pointed out to you, the girl's oxygenating capacity, the oxygen-extracting capability of her lungs is what I mean, her *aeriferous* capability is perhaps the best way to put it—"

Mother had told me nine hundred times to build up my vocabulary because it would be a great aid to me in the ministry, and although I didn't have the foggiest notion of being a preacher I liked words the same way Daddy did and used to spend hours looking up meanings in the dictionary and even sometimes writing them down. This doctor gave me a couple of good ones then and later, but I couldn't find them all in our regular dictionary. My uncle, however, the one who called me "Peckerwood" and lived on a high hill, was an eye, ear, nose and throat doctor, and I found the words in his office. I enjoyed this aspect of Dr. F. Robert Martinson, but Daddy didn't. Not hardly at all.

"Her *what?"* asked Daddy.

"Her lung capacity."

"That isn't what you said."

"Very well, I said aeriferous, sir."

"Spell it," said Daddy.

"Well sir, heh-heh-heh-heh, there's no need to spell it. It simply means she can breathe more deeply than most of us."

"Then why in the hell didn't you say that in the first place?"

"Honey, will you stop that? You're embarrassing me terribly," said Mother. *"Please* continue, Doctor. You were saying . . ."

"Well, I was saying, if I may be forgiven for it, that the girl has a larger *aeriferous* capability than most women her size or even many men—she can breathe deeper than most of us and that is what is saving her life. And let me tell you she was a sick girl. Her illness was grossly, almost criminally neglected and I must say I don't understand how that occurred."

"She wouldn't tell us she was sick, Doctor," said Mother.

The man, who really was impossible, stared at Mother as if she were not only an unmitigated total fool but an evil fool as well. Daddy had turned his head away and was drumming his fingers loudly on the maple arm of the Hardy Hospital waiting room sofa, his mouth a thin line beneath his moustache and his eyes hooded with weary dignity. If there was ever a man calculated to irritate Daddy to the core, it was this Yankee Dr. Martinson. Daddy didn't like Yankees anyhow because they were unnatural and didn't know how to pronounce words correctly, but a fancy-word-using Yankee like this one who stole his verbal thunder was downright unbearable. "Loathe the rat," he said later in the car, "loathe that rat, just loathe him totally. He ought to be hanged."

"*Well*, now, Mrs. Hillyer," said Dr. Martinson with a half-sneering smile that was meant to be friendly but wasn't at all, "I should think ordinary powers of observation would have suggested to you the girl was seriously ill."

"She hid it from us," said Mother. "She was afraid of the hospital."

"Afraid of the hospital?"

"Yes. Deathly afraid of it. Her people were poor tenant farmers and she doesn't know anything about doctors or hospitals or dentists or practically anything—we had the most horrible time you could dream of when she had to have a wisdom tooth extracted. She thought the dentist was trying to kill her."

The doctor stared at Mother in disbelief. "That girl grew up on a tenant farm? That girl in bed in Room 506? Are you trying to tell me that girl is a product of the Southern hookworm and pellagra belt?"

"Well, her people were extremely poor," said Mother. "She almost starved more than once as a child. And when she had food I'm sure it was awful, although they might have grown some vegetables. But you know what they mostly eat, those poor dirt farmers, hoecake and hominy grits, not a balanced diet at all."

"Exactly, and that's why she couldn't possibly have come from such a farm," said Dr. Martinson.

"Excuse me," said Daddy, "are you calling my wife a liar?"

"No, but I find it incredible, that girl—"

"My wife is telling you the truth, sir. I myself know it for a fact. Rose's people were impoverished. She grew up on the worst type of tenant farm and I am sure sorghum and hoecake and grits are precisely what she ate. However, she did leave home at fourteen and her diet then no doubt improved."

"By fourteen the damage is usually done," said Dr. Martinson. "She *must* have gotten protein somewhere as a young child, if only sporadically. But even so she has got to have a fantastic constitution, almost miraculous if you ask me. Aside from her illness at the moment, she's a very strong girl, a very healthy specimen of a young human female—do you realize the girl is five nine, in normal health probably weighs a hundred and thirty-five pounds, is almost as strong as a man and has a figure better than the Venus de Milo?''

Rose, sick as she was, had sent out her vibrations to him. His comparison of poor sick Rose to the Venus de Milo was so lewd I blushed. Daddy didn't like it either, I saw him frown as he stared at the doctor and sized him up. I am sure Daddy and I had the same thought in mind: if Rose got well, there might be trouble with this bird, a doctor who concerned himself with the figure of a desperately ill pneumonia patient. However, it wasn't *what* the man said but rather the *way* he said it; there was something lewd in his eyes.

''Yes. Rose is very pretty,'' said Mother. ''But I think she's even more *attractive* than she is pretty. If you look at her close she isn't really beautiful. What she has goes beyond being pretty and beautiful.''

''I'm afraid you weren't listening attentively to what I was saying. Pretty isn't the point. The point is you don't as a rule grow up like that on a diet of sorghum and hominy grits. She did have a better diet from fourteen on but she got protein somewhere as a child, if only part of the time. Of course part of the time isn't all of the time and obviously she does have a very strong constitution, her recovery from tuberculosis alone shows that. Yes, her constitution is strong and I am now even more sure she'll recover from this pneumonia and get up from that bed. The prognosis is *good.*''

''What you say is extremely interesting, Doctor,'' said Mother, ''and most encouraging. I understand from what you've said Rose will get well and we . . . we *don't* have to worry about her having had t.b.?''

This man really was impossible. He smiled again at Mother as if she were an unmitigated total idiot to be concerned about the welfare of her children and said with an amused lift of an eyebrow: ''No, you don't have to worry about her infecting your dear little kiddies, Mrs. Hillyer, she's healthier than they are. Ha ha ha ha!''

''That's all I want to know,'' said Daddy. ''Let's get out of here before I come down with the epizootics myself.

Thank you, Doctor, for your discourse, it was fascinating, no doubt."

"Yes, thank you very much, Doctor," said Mother. "We are more grateful than we can say and it was most interesting indeed."

Looking back on it, I would guess the man probably had some ability as a doctor. The other doctors seemed to respect him. But he certainly had a severe personality problem. People said that he took drugs; I don't know that he did, but people said he did, that he shot needles into himself all the time and put things in his behind, too, little things that melted and made him feel good.

Whether that was true or not he was insufferable; but this was why Mother liked him—he was a Yankee intellectual and couldn't stand the South, even though he'd married a Southern woman with money and lived in the depths of Dixieland very comfortably and with very little effort. Some people said he was Jewish, but the man was a German Lutheran, there was nothing even remotely Jewish about him. I really didn't like him a bit. I didn't mind most of Rose's boy friends, Horton for example, but this one I minded. He was a damned fool and didn't have enough sense to appreciate her. I disliked him so much he seems like a ghost to me; I can't even remember what his face really looked like, all I remember is a graying spade beard and a rather sallow complexion—and teeth, oh yes, he had crooked, yellowish teeth from which the gums had receded and his breath did not smell like new-mown hay.

No, this Dr. Martinson didn't appreciate Rose, although I am sure on one occasion he took advantage of her, maybe serious advantage right in our house while making a professional call. He certainly looked guilty slinking down those stairs. If he hadn't done something wrong, then why did he slink like that and why did he jump nervously and look at me with fear when he saw me staring at him?

But I suppose this unfortunate man (after all, he did come to a sad ending) was not as bad as I am depicting him. He probably was not quite as pompous and obviously hostile as I remember him, and probably not as unattractive in appearance as I have suggested—many women, of that time anyhow, would have considered him "distinguished-looking,'' with his trim little graying beard and his injured collie-dog eyes behind the glasses, which had a little nineteenth-century ribbon going down to his lapel not far from his unvarying white carnation.

A flaming Yankee ''liberal'' who later when he got to know her discussed Karl Marx with Mother, and a little black silk *ribbon* on his glasses—how about that? And he wore tailored clothes, too, mostly black, and I suppose some girls and women would be impressed. Rose was, damn her. I really didn't like the man. To tell the truth, I was jealous of him. The very thought of him touching Rose made me sick.

It's sad but true, I hated that son of a bitch so much I can't even remember his face. Of course the real reason I hated him was because of what he did or tried to do later during the crisis of the great, gaga epizootics, but I loathed and despised him even before that. I was hurt and sick inside at Rose for liking him—what did she see in this *rat?* and that was what he was just like Daddy said, a miserable *rat!* After all, why did he blow out his brains and those of his wife, was that an accident, was it caused merely by losses in the stock market? What did she see in him? How could she possibly like a miserable and hateful man like this one? How? Why? Because he had ''saved her life'' by doing nothing and because he had a little black silk ribbon hanging from his glasses?

As Dr. Martinson, F. Ralph, rat or tortured man or whatever he was, predicted, Rose recovered from pneumonia and got out of the horrible hospital bed in which she'd expected to die. From the time of our visit her recovery was very fast; she came home four or five days later and was in bed at the house another four or five days, then began to make a complete recovery, to regain her strength and the fifteen pounds she'd lost. We knew she was getting well, Doll and I, when one day she confided to us:

''Oh, he's so kind, so gentle inside, and so unhappy with that rich wife who doesn't understand him, her being a Southerner and everything, and what a bedside manner he has got—so gentle and kind beneath the professor way he acts! What a bedside manner, why it does me good just to see him sit there all solemn and go pokin' in his bag like he's gonna cure me, which he did of course. And even more important he *loves* me, like a patient I mean, the other day he got tears in his eyes just listenin' to my heart beat—he tried to hide 'em but I saw 'em, and after a little bit he says to me, 'You know, you are beautiful?' Now wasn't that a nice thing for a doctor to say to a patient, wasn't it? What could cheer a girl up more? And would you believe that poor man thinks nobody likes him? That's what he says, nobody in the world likes him! Well, *I* like him and I don't see why he's unpopular, he knows more about medicine than you could shake a sheep's tail at—why, I used to be *afraid* of doctors, but I'm not any more, I love them! You wouldn't believe this, but a good doctor like him could *operate* on me right now and I wouldn't even be scared! And besides all his *vast* medical knowledge, he has the most kindest heart inside beneath the professor way he acted at first till I made friends with him, the most kindest heart—he wants justice in the world, and he has got some real interestin' ideas. Justice, that's what he wants and he talks about it all the time, justice for everybody and especially for niggers. And I think that's real *nice* of him because niggers don't have a very good life, you got to admit that, to be a nigger is sometimes practic'ly fatal, but the wife of course don't understand alla that, *she* thinks niggers are just so much black-assed dirt, which anybody oughta know better if they been on their ass their ownselves—but that's the cause of his *profound* unhappiness, Buddy, you and Doll, that's the cause of it, his profound unhappiness, that no-good mean wife with all her Southern prejudices against niggers and everything. She *hates* him, that's what he says and I believe him, and *why?* You tell me, why should that woman hate a wonderful man like him? Look at all the medical knowledge he has got, and his clothes—oh Lord, I never saw such clothes! And handsome, a good talker, got lots of ideas and things to discuss, I don't know what's the matter with that woman, she's out of her mind! Heh! Well, *she* might not understand him, but *I* do, and I love him, I really love him a lot. And besides, he saved my life, I wouldn't be here but for that man, he snatched me from the jaws of death."

Rose was getting well. About a week after she came

home, Dr. Martinson stopped by to check up on her and he was in her room for at least forty-five minutes—and not only that, it was the most indiscreet possible time of the day: during the dinner hour when we were all home, including Daddy. We were all having supper while it was going on, this forty-five-minute checkup. Daddy himself said: "Hmmm-mm . . . wonder what that doctor is doing up there for so long? I hope Rose hasn't had . . . a relapse."

I'd heard Rose rattle on about him the day before and I knew what he was doing or thought I knew and I got away from the dining table on the excuse I had to go to the bathroom. But I didn't go to the bathroom, I posted myself in the darkened living room and watched the stairs. I saw Dr. Martinson leave, black bag in his hand and his shoulders hunched. He slinked down those stairs and gave a nervous start of fright when he saw me staring at him with narrowed eyes, hands on my hips like Daddy. And Daddy himself as a matter of fact was *right there.* He was suspicious, too. His voice sounded loud and clear from the back of the hall:

"Everything all right, Doctor?"

Again, the doctor jumped with nervousness. Maybe he didn't take complete advantage of Rose right there in our house, that would have been a crazy risk and he probably wouldn't have had the nerve, but he did *something* up there in that room that sure wasn't medical. He looked over his shoulder at Daddy, who stood with hooded eyes by the dining room door, napkin in hand and thumbs on his hips just like me. It must have been a little unnerving to the man, those two pairs of hands on the hips and the two pairs of narrowed Hawkshaw eyes.

"Oh, yes! Yes! " he said. "Just fine! A few more days . . . a little more rest . . . she'll be perfectly healthy. . . ."

As the doctor fled out of the front door, Daddy strolled up the hall toward me, napkin in his hand and thumbs still on his hips.

"What do you *think,* Brother?" he asked in a low, conspiratorial tone. "What was he up to in Rose's room all that time?"

"I don't know," I said. "But you better watch him like a hawk, Daddy, if he comes back again."

"He is not coming back again," said Daddy. "I have had enough of that son of a bitch and his beard both."

Unfortunately, however, it wasn't the last we saw of Dr. Martinson. Mother called him again when Rose got the great, gaga epizootics that caused Daddy to exclaim: "She does it on purpose!" Before that, however, Rose was hired, mired and fired on a cold and icy February morning.

12

Rose
is hired, mired and fired

NOUS VERRONS CE que nous verrons, but already Daddy had observed enough to cause his eyes to resemble maps handed out free by that good Gulf gasoline. He certainly had and it'd petrified him. To see a person endure and courageously survive disastrous epizootics both creates and augments emotions of affection, involvement and even investment as far as that person is concerned. I watched Daddy struggle with it day by day. He'd intended to fire Rose, but her great epizootics had saved her. How could he fire her now after she'd bravely conquered death itself?

And yet, could a leopard change its spots or Rose her petals? What next? What kind of damnable commotion would she create tomorrow? And what could be done to forestall that coming commotion, frustrate it, defuse it? Perhaps . . . just perhaps . . . a very . . . very . . . *solemn warning?* . . . a rigid finger in her face inches from her nose and two reddened road-map eyes boring into her like augers?

"Whew-w-w!" said Daddy one morning at breakfast over a half-a-cup of coffee, as Rose sang happily in the kitchen doing the dishes, her old self. "Would you believe the bill that goddamn hospital has sent us? Would you believe it? Look at it, darlin'! Look at it! They're trying to destroy Christian civilization, and they aren't even Jews or Arabs!"

"Lord in heaven," said mother, slightly ill. "How can they charge so much?" In shocked consternation she adjusted her glasses and examined again the slip of awful paper in her hand. "This is absolutely horrible. How are we going to pay it? I'm not rich any more, do they think I'm still rich? Write them a letter and tell them Ben stole all my money and we can't pay any such bill as this."

"That won't do any good, darlin'. A hospital is the cruelest institution known to man. They have hearts of fire-hardened steel up there, darlin', fire-hardened steel."

"This is *awful,*" said Mother. "How are we going to pay it?"

"We can't," said Daddy. "We are ruined. And I'm the fool who went around saying you shouldn't marry for money, but it's just as easy to love a woman who has got it. Darlin', we're wiped out. Rose has wiped us out with her epizootics. That's all she wrote. Ruination. Rose has ruined us, and I knew she would the minute I saw her perched there on the sofa in the living room with her frizzy blonde hair all poking out and her blue eyes so innocent. That insane creature has *wiped us out.* I thought that goddamn doctor's bill was bad, but this is the end. There's nothing left but the river."

With a dismayed shake of the head Mother handed the hospital bill back to Daddy. "Well, we'll just have to pay it," she said in a wan voice. "We'll manage, somehow. Pay them by the month or something, or maybe borrow it from the bank, except I hate to do that. The trouble with borrowing is you have to pay it back, that's the catch."

"A shrewd observation, darlin'," said Daddy. "You're on the track this morning even more solidly than usual."

"Tra-la-la-la!" sang Rose as she came into the dining room with a sunny smile to get the rest of the breakfast dishes. It was a Thursday and Rose was always in a grand mood on Thursdays. Pretty soon, after making the beds and doing a little ironing and vacuuming, she'd be patting on powder and rouge and putting on her finery in the process of getting herself up to go out. "Oh, what a beautiful day, even for February! Tra-la-la-la! I never would of knowed I was in the hospital, and I thought I was gonna croak and kick the bucket, how about that? Ha ha ha ha ha!"

"*We* know you were in the hospital," said Daddy. "And Rose, before you get yourself up and go out, may Mrs. Hillyer and I have a brief word with you in Mrs. Hillyer's sitting room? Say, in about ten minutes?"

"Sure," said Rose a little nervously. "What did I do?"

"Nothing yet," said Daddy, "as far as we know. That's what we want to have the brief word with you about, dear, to insure that you *won't* do anything."

"I don't do anything, Mr. Hillyer," said Rose with a little smile of perfect innocence. "I really don't. You see my bark is worse than my bite."

Mother had said that one time and Rose kept repeating it—her bark was worse than her bite. It explained everything beautifully, all she did was bark. Daddy finally—not on this occasion but later—stopped it by telling her: "Yes, but your bark is horrible. It's shattering eardrums all over Glenville. Quit barking, Rose, you're deafening me, I'll need a hearing aid like Mrs. Hillyer if you keep it up."

About a month after she was snatched from the jaws of death, Rose was hired, mired and fired early one morning in the midst of a February ice storm. Daddy had warned her and he warned her fairly. I know he did, Doll and I heard the whole thing down in the crawl space under the house. I had discovered that by creeping along on hands and knees in the dry crumbly dirt under Mother's bedroom-sitting room it was possible to get one's ear next to the hot-air register and hear with perfect clarity the conferences and arguments up there. Just like you were in the room. On the morning the hospital bill came, Daddy took Rose in there, sat her down on the horsehair sofa next to Mother, and said:

"We all love you, Rose. Even more now, since you've bravely surmounted all these epizootics. We admire you, we esteem you, we hold your hand with love and affection, we have an *investment* in you, and I don't mean a mere investment of money, although God knows we have that, too. I mean a human investment, we care about you, you matter to us. But I said all of this better in the first sentence of these remarks. We love you, Rose, but we are raising children in this house, innocent and unformed children who know very little about life or the world, and we just can't have the sort of thing going on that was going on before. We can't have it, Rose. *I point my rigid finger right at your nose, Rose, and I stare unwaveringly into your big blue eyes and I say to you—we can't have it, Rose!* Now. All right. All right. Er-r, ah-HEM! Now. Can you behave yourself in the future or *not?* That is the question, Rose. That is the mortal-coil-shuffling question. To behave or not to behave. To suffer the slings and arrows of outrageous fortune and keep your skirt down, or to hoist it in the light of the moon and make whoopee, that is the question, the coil-shuffling question. *Can* you behave or *can't* you? If you can, we'll be happy to have you stay with us, but if you can't, if it simply isn't in your nature to suffer the outrageous fortune of chastity and good behavior, then I am going to fire you, Rose, because I have no choice, and I say it in front of you and Mrs. Hillyer and I mean it. I point my finger directly at your nose, Rose, and I look right in your beautiful blue eyes and I tell you this is a final warning. Do you hear me, dear?"

Rose of course heard him, and she assured him with grateful tears there would be no more trouble, no more strange voices in the night, no more nothin'. She had finally learned her lesson, learned what really mattered, being at death's door had made a changed girl out of her. "It's a fact, Mr. Hillyer," she said. "Why, I don't even want to go out no more, I mean go out like I used to. I was lyin' there in that horrible hospital bed practic'ly dyin' and I thought, what was I runnin' around for? I thought, what do all that matter, *nothin'*, if I ever get out of this dern bed all I want to do is *live!*"

"Well, if I may make a suggestion," said Mother, "I don't think you ought to wear those *clothes*, Rose. I'm afraid they're . . . well, provocative to men. I know you don't realize it, but clothes like that *disturb* them. Would you mind if I helped you change the style of your things a little bit?"

"I'd love it!" said Rose.

Sadly, however, if sadly is the word, Rose wanted more than just to live. Any cow could live and chew its cud and she was not a cow, but as she herself put it "a human girl person." Rose hadn't changed at all, she'd just suffered and been badly frightened, which made her "condition" *worse,* not better.

About a week after the rigid-finger-road-map-eyed final warning, the reverse insomnia hit Daddy a cruel blow and he woke up one morning about a quarter to five and went down to the kitchen and had half-a-cup of coffee, glanced at the Glenville *News-Tribune* of the day before although he'd already read it, considered a piece of dry toast and rejected the idea, then groaned wearily at the thought of another day at the damned hotel, stood up, adjusted his winter fedora on the back of his head and a little to the side, put on his overcoat since an ice storm was in progress, went out to the back porch on his way to the Ford, glanced down and saw smiling at him on the porch floor a pair of stark, empty, naked shoes.

Now, as I have said several times, there was a lot of both Hawkshaw the Detective and Sherlock Holmes in Daddy, an awful lot. When he had originally found the suspicious footprints and telltale marks on the tampered-with ladder, he had been foiled in his intention to fire Rose by her great epizootics. Therefore, he had done the next best thing—he had bought a length of chain and a padlock and had locked down immovably the ladder, which hung on iron pegs on the side of the garage.

And that is what trapped the culprit! The rascal couldn't get the ladder because *Daddy had changed it down.* There they were: stark, empty, naked shoes of the rascal smiling at him on the porch! The sneaky scoundrel had come there to the back door and Rose the insane creature had tippy-toed downstairs and let him in, and then the pair of them had tippy-toed back upstairs to her room and that's where they were right now!

Daddy raced back into the kitchen and down the hall and up the stairs, his face grim and his eyes beyond question bloodshot. I think I heard him going up the stairs and I certainly heard him when he began banging and banging on Rose's door.

"Rose! Rose! Open this goddamn door! Open it this instant! Do you hear me? Open this door or I'll break it down!"

Rose finally, after many muttered incoherent delaying remarks, unlatched the door and Daddy burst into her room, looking hither and yon for the culprit. But no one was there. Rose was *suspiciously stark naked* and scared to death besides; she was standing there with a sheet half around her and her blue eyes popped wide open—but the culprit wasn't there. Daddy looked under the bed, he looked in the closet, he even looked behind the bureau. No culprit.

I'd gotten up and crept part way down the dark upstairs hallway—it was black as midnight at that hour in the winter—and I heard him shout: "All right, Rose, where is the son of a bitch? I saw his stark, empty, naked shoes smiling at me right on the porch and I know he's here! Where is he? Where have you got him hid?"

I heard Rose's voice feebly protesting no one was there, really and truly, and she had no idea whose shoes they might be. She might even have gotten away with it, except that Daddy with his instinct noticed her window was wide open in midwinter. "Hmmm-mm," he said, "I notice that your window is wide open in midwinter. Now that's strange, Rose, don't you think?"

The next thing that happened didn't even take any detective ability to speak of, because as Daddy walked toward the open window he heard from somewhere down below a wretched groan. He stuck his head and shoulders out of the window and there dim in the light from Rose's room he saw lying on the frozen icy ground a young boy holding his leg and moaning, naked as his stark empty shoes except for a pair of undershorts.

"And who, Rose, may I ask, is that?"

"Well, it's Billy," said Rose.

"And what, may I ask, was Billy doing here?"

It was a rather silly question but Rose gave him a straight answer.

"Well, Mr. Hillyer, Billy's very poor, he don't have no money and there wasn't no place else to go. He's *very* poor, Mr. Hillyer, he don't have no job and what's more his Daddy whips him all the time and calls him no good. I let him in because I feel real . . . sorry for him. That's all it was. Nothin' happened, Mr. Hillyer, we just talked. Billy's a nice, sweet boy and wants to be a fireman. You'd like him. . . ."

"Ye gods and little fishes," said Daddy wearily, "a fireman. Well, you've done it, Rose. I warned you, but you've done it anyhow and I guess I knew you would."

"Done *what,* Mr. Hillyer?" asked Rose. I'd crept down the hall far enough to peek around the door jamb. In her distress, Rose had the sheet only partly around her and one titty was out. "Nothin' happened, I *swear* it didn't, we just talked."

Daddy sighed and shook his head, then adjusted his winter hat and folded his arms across the overcoat. Sadly, he looked at her. "Put on some clothes, Rose," he said, in a voice as gloomy as I ever heard from him, "you're naked as a jay bird. When you're dressed, come on downstairs. I'm afraid your friend Billy is injured. Where are his clothes?"

Rose began weeping and the sheet slipped from her shoulder and her other titty was exposed; they both were exposed, and they were very naked, very bare. It was the last time I saw Rose's breasts in this world, and the memory lingers on. "Under the mattress," she said, her head bowed and her pretty breasts staring at Daddy and me like gentle eyes. "I hid 'em there so you wouldn't be mad. But nothin' happened, Mr. Hillyer. Besides, he wants to marry me, he *loves* me. I can't marry him, he's too young and hasn't got no job, but he wants to marry me, he loves me, he's a very sweet boy . . . now you wouldn't hurt him, would you?"

"Give me his clothes," said Daddy.

An hour later, after an ambulance had come and taken away Billy, who had broken his leg in jumping from Rose's window down to the frozen ground, I listened in sorrow at the dining room doors and peeked through a tiny crack. Daddy, Mother and Rose sat at the kitchen table. Tears were on Mother's cheeks and Rose herself was softly weeping.

"Well, what can I say?" asked Daddy. "Rose, I warned you. I warned you, honey, didn't I? Now *we* can't have boys sneaking in our house at night and tippy-toeing up to your room and jumping out of your window and breaking their leg, *can* we?"

"No . . . no," wept Rose, "and . . . I got a confession to make, Mr. Hillyer. What I said before wasn't really so. Billy and me, we wasn't . . . just talkin'. And I'm sorry, I know it was bad . . . but I love him and I'm only a human girl person and I can't help it. Won't you and Mrs. Hillyer forgive me? Please don't fire me, I love you all so much and I don't want to have to go. . . . "

Daddy was silent for a long, long time, his gaze down

on the kitchen table and his hand on his forehead. When he finally looked up at her his eyes were not in the least red or glary but behind a film of tears their normal brown. ''Rose, darlin', you break my heart,'' he said. ''But I am only a human man person myself of the father variety. It breaks my heart, but pack your bag, baby, and get the hell out of my house. Rose, as of this instant you are hired, mired and fired!''

13

Rose has great, gaga epizootics

DADDY HAD SAID "as of this instant" and meant it, but Rose didn't leave our house that instant or even that day or even that week. Rose never saved her tiny wage, she spent it on her finery. On the day she was fired she had two dollars and fourteen cents to her name. After considerable discussion with Mother, Daddy agreed it would be cruel and inhuman to throw out on the streets without notice a practically penniless girl who had no job and nowhere to go.

"All right," said Daddy to Mother, "we'll give her a two weeks' notice. That will enable her to find another position. But get this straight. I don't mean two weeks and one day, I don't mean two weeks and one hour, I mean two weeks."

Three weeks later, Rose was still in our house. Daddy was beside himself; he said he was going to blow a gasket and I believed him and so did Mother and everyone else. "Is there no way," he asked, "to get *rid* of this girl? Are we stuck with her for *life?* I am going to blow a gasket!"

At first, Rose looked seriously for a job. She got up every morning and went out in chaste clothes Mother had helped her alter and "restyle." Her method was to go up and down the main street of town into and out of all the offices and stores, regardless of what kind of offices or stores they were. She'd walk in and say: "I'm lookin' for work. Do you have anything for somebody who's willin' to work hard?" Since she was inexperienced and there were few jobs to be had anyhow, her method naturally failed. After about a week she became discouraged and her efforts slackened off. She still went out looking but confessed to me she sometimes just wandered around. There was no point in asking for a job, they'd only tell her no.

One night at supper, ten days or so into the two weeks' notice, Rose toyed with her food, ate almost nothing and finally put her napkin beside her plate. "I've tried," she said. "I just can't get nothin'. It takes the heart out of you, they look at me like I'm crazy."

"Well, you aren't crazy but you're childlike," said Daddy. "You can't get a job on Broad Street like that, Rose, you don't have any skills or training or experience. I'll put an ad in the *News-Tribune* for you for housework. That's what you know a little about and that's your best bet. The kind of job you've got here—or rather, had here."

"An excellent idea," said Mother. "Aren't you going to eat anything, Rose?"

"I'm not hungry," said Rose. "I can't eat anything, I haven't been able to eat since I got fired. I think maybe I'm sick."

"God forbid," said Daddy. "You're not sick, Rose, forget it. Don't get any notions in your head, you're not sick."

"Yes, sir," said Rose.

"She does look a little peaky," said Mother.

"No, she doesn't," said Daddy, "she's fine, *fine*. She's perfectly healthy, don't give her ideas."

"Well, I'll do the dishes then I'm goin' on to bed," said Rose. "My stomach hurts."

After Rose left the dining table, Daddy said: "Her plan is obvious, plain as day. She's going on a *hunger strike*. The question is, how do we foil her?"

"She's just nervous and worried," said Mother. "And you would be, too, if you had no job and no place to go. But you had a good idea about an ad in the paper. What she needs is a position in somebody's home like she's got here. And Rose is a good cook and housekeeper, we ought to be able to find something like that for her."

Unfortunately, we couldn't, although Daddy put an ad in the *News-Tribune* on the following day. There were a limited number of families in Glenville who could afford domestic help in 1936, and those who could preferred to hire walk-in blacks for almost nothing. Besides, Rose's reputation was known to many around town. No one wanted her.

In the meanwhile, Rose continued to complain she had no appetite and her stomach hurt. Mother marked this up to nerves and so did Daddy. True, from time to time he said she was laying the groundwork for another attack of epizootics, but he didn't really believe this and when he finally blew a gasket he thought he was rid of Rose at last.

It happened three weeks and four days after Daddy had fired her. At supper that night Daddy ate in silence his usual meagre meal, then put down his napkin, cleared his throat and said:

"Well, I have got news for you, Rose, and I want the whole family to hear it. I blew my gasket this morning and called long distance to Tennessee and spoke to Cousin Hop and you'll be glad to know, Rose, I have found you a job!"

"Tennessee?" said Rose.

"Yes, Tennessee," said Daddy. "A lovely state!"

"Well," said Rose, "what kind of job is it?"

"Ahh-hh," answered Daddy, "you'll like it. It's a fine, *outdoor-type* job."

"You mean a *farm?*" asked Rose.

"No, no, not exactly," said Daddy. "It isn't a farm in the sense that it's a farm. Not at all. It's a . . . dairy establishment. You'll like it! I'm sure you'll like it because it's so . . . *peaceful.*"

Rose bowed her head and began crying.

"Honey," said Mother to Daddy, "Rose was born on a farm and she has terrible memories of farm life. Now I don't think—"

"Just a minute, Rose, you don't understand," said Daddy. "This isn't a dirt farm like the one you were born on, it's *nice*. A neighbor of Cousin Hop's, I talked to him on the phone, a very fine man . . . and a beautiful dairy establishment, not a farm, damn it! Stop crying! Do you hear me, Rose? You've got nothing to cry about, they're kind people and you'll get thirty dollars a month—that's a raise! A beautiful herd of Jersey cows, modern milking equipment, why it's ideal, you'll just do some housework and help a little with the milking."

"I don't see how you can call it ideal," said Mother,

"knowing what you do about Rose's childhood. Don't you realize what the word 'farm' means to her?"

"I don't give a hoot in hell's hollow what it means to her, I have blown a gasket on this thing!" said Daddy. "And it's high time somebody did! She can't stay in our house forever! I fired her, damn it! She's got to leave someday and it's going to be *now!* Besides, this isn't a farm like she's thinking, it's a dairy establishment, *damn* it!"

"It sounds like a farm to me," said Mother. "Calling it a dairy establishment, that's just words and trickery and flummery."

"Words and trickery and flummery or not she's going there tomorrow on the bus! It's settled! I personally am going to put her on it and wave my handkerchief good-bye! It's settled, damn it! And I must say we've been more than fair to you, Rose, and it's pretty selfish and mean-hearted of you to sit there and cry like that and make me feel guilty. You haven't even been trying to get a job these past ten days and you know it. Now stop weeping, you are wasting your tears."

"I'm not crying because of *me,*" said Rose. "I'm crying because of *somebody else.*"

"What?" asked Daddy.

"Well, I was born on a farm myself . . ."

"What? What?" asked Daddy.

". . . and I hate to think of the baby being born on one."

"What baby? What baby? What baby are you speaking about?"

"Mine," said Rose as the tears ran down.

"Yours? What'd you say, Rose? *Yours?"*

"Yes, *mine,*" said Rose. "I am going to have a baby."

Daddy stared at her in a condition he himself described as "poleaxed," his head forward and a numbed emptiness in his eyes. "Good God Almighty," he said. "This is a catastrophe, they won't hire her."

"Children," said Mother, "leave the room. Brother, you go up to your room, Doll, you go to yours, and Waski, go to yours. And stay there until I tell you you can come out."

My little brother was unnerved by all of this and did as he was told, but Doll and I did not. Daddy, we knew, was too thunderstruck to think about us. We went loudly up the stairs then crept down them again and tiptoed into the living room and listened and peeped through a crack in the dining room doors just as we had done on the night Rose attacked Daddy at Thermopylae. It was very exciting. Rose pregnant!—this was the most marvelous development yet. Evidently, the doctors *had* been wrong and those little rubber tubes had opened up after all and Rose would have what she wanted most, a baby of her own! Of course there was no father to help take care of it, but Rose's dream had come true, she would have a little livin' baby that would cry and need her, a real baby of her own to hold in her arms. It was great, wonderful! In breathless fascination, Doll and I crouched in the dark living room and peeked and listened.

"This is a total catastrastroke," said Daddy. "That's what it is, a catastrastroke out of the blue. And as of this moment I am stumped, I admit, I am stumped and treed both and I don't know where to go, the hound dogs have got me surrounded and treed."

"Poor thing," said Mother to Rose, "don't cry. I know you feel awful, but don't cry, honey, nobody's perfect. Why, people make this mistake all the time, it could happen to any girl. How far along is it?"

"Well," wept Rose, "I . . . I think about three months."

"Um-hmm," said Mother. "Who's the father, dear? Billy?"

"Well, I . . . I . . . I don't know," said Rose. "It couldn't be Billy, I didn't know him then . . . maybe it was . . . but no . . . I'm not sure, you can't be sure about a thing like that, I'm really not sure."

"I know it's embarrassing," said Mother, "but who were you . . . exposed to?"

"Well, now, Mrs. Hillyer, I . . . ahh, that's kinda hard to say. I'm not sure . . . the truth is I'm really not sure."

"You're not going to get anywhere with that line of questioning," said Daddy. "The problem is, what are we going to do?"

"*That's* why I'm asking her who the father is," said Mother. "It's the most vital question of all, the matter of responsibility. Someone is to blame for this, not just Rose, some boy or man is also to blame."

"Well, I wouldn't want to blame nobody," said Rose.

"It isn't a matter of your blaming, Rose. He is responsible as much as you are. Now, tell us the truth. Who's the father, dear?"

"She already told you, she doesn't know," said Daddy.

"But she must have *some* idea . . . unless . . . unless . . . was there more than *one* person, Rose?"

Rose was weeping in a handkerchief. "Ohh-hh, Mrs. Hillyer, I . . . I'm not really sure."

"Mmm-mm," said Mother, with a tiny little frown at Rose, "that does pose problems, if there was more than one. Rose, really, you shouldn't act like that."

"Oh, I know," wept Rose. "But I didn't, really. Honestly I didn't, Mrs. Hillyer, I'm not as bad as you think. There was only one, but you see he's out of town and didn't leave no forwardin' address and I don't know where he is, that's why I'm not sure."

"Hold the phone," said Daddy, *"hold the phone!* No forwarding address, huh? I have a little sneaking hunch I forgot something, in fact I am sure I forgot something! In the shock of this brilliant move I have forgotten the most important thing of all!"

"What did you forget?" asked Mother. "What do you mean?"

"I forgot that Rose will lie like a child," said Daddy. "She just doesn't want to go to that farm. The girl's no more pregnant than I am!"

"Yes, I am," said Rose.

"No, you're not," said Daddy.

"Yes, Mr. Hillyer, I am."

"All right," said Daddy, his eyes gleaming with Sherlock Holmesian triumph. "Tell us, Rose. What makes you think you're pregnant?"

"Well, I haven't had my period for three months and my stomach is getting big," said Rose.

The Sherlockian gleam faded and again Daddy stared at her with a slightly poleaxed expression. But then he pulled himself together and said, "I don't believe it."

"It's so," said Rose.

"All right. All right, damn it! We've seen you with your clothes off around here, stand up and pull up your dress, and let's take a look!"

"*Honey,*" said Mother, shocked.

"She doesn't have to take her panties off, we can see her stomach with her panties on. All she has to do is pull up her dress and let us see her belly. I guarantee you this girl is not pregnant! She's lying like a little child just like she always does!"

"This isn't the Middle Ages!" said Mother angrily. "To ask her to expose herself like that is the most barbarous thing I ever heard of!"

"I've seen her without her clothes," said Daddy. "Good God, the morning Billy jumped out of her window she was running around her room naked as a jay bird. And I'm not asking her to take off everything, just to show us her goddamn belly."

"Well, even so, the proper thing is to take her to Dr. Martinson and have him examine her, that's the proper and civilized thing."

"I've had enough bills from Dr. Martinson! Now she can show us her stomach—Rose, stand up and pull up your dress!"

"You don't have to, Rose," said Mother.

"Well, I don't mind," said Rose in a weepy voice, "if you just *won't* believe me . . ."

"*Now,*" said Daddy triumphantly, "you will see, she's lying like a little child the way she always does. That belly will be flat as a pancake."

Rose, however, was not lying like a little child. In weary defeat, Daddy stared at her swollen abdomen as she stood before him sniffling and weeping and holding her dress six inches above her navel. There was no doubt about it. Her stomach below her bellybutton protruded plainly and unmistakably, I saw it myself through the crack in the dining room doors—the baby had grown to about the size of a large grapefruit.

"Yes, I'd say you're about three months pregnant, maybe a little more," said Mother. "Put your dress down, Rose." She turned icily to Daddy. "Well, are you satisfied? Now that you've called her a liar and shamed her completely by forcing her to expose her body to you, are you happy? Hmmm?"

"Take her to Dr. Martinson in the morning," said Daddy.

"I have been poleaxed and I am in a *non compos mentis* condition and I am going to bed. My apologies, Rose, you aren't a liar at all, you're as truthful as the Virgin Mary but I don't believe in this case the Holy Ghost is the father. Good night, everybody!"

After breakfast the next day, Daddy sent me, Doll and my brother from the table and announced his decision to Rose and Mother. There was no way I could eavesdrop on this conference but I found out later what he said. Rose would have to have the baby in a home for unmarried mothers. He was sorry, but she couldn't have it in our house and that was all there was to it.

But epizootics is a pathological condition and Rose of course wasn't pregnant at all. Dr. Martinson had her in the hospital all afternoon doing tests and having other doctors examine her and I didn't find out about it until that night around nine when Rose, Mother and the Doctor came back to the house and had a conference with Daddy in the living room. I was alone, Doll had been sent to bed. I was supposed to be upstairs studying but I wanted to know when Rose would have the baby so I crept downstairs and listened.

Rose herself was sent up to her room after a few minutes. She was crying so much it was impossible to have a conversation with her there. She was close to hysteria; the thought of having to go back to the hospital and have a major operation scared her half to death. Mother later had to go up to her room and spend a good part of the night with her. As Mother said, it wasn't just fear of the hospital and an operation that upset Rose, she was also heartbroken. She'd honestly believed she was pregnant; that by a miracle the little rubber tubes had opened up and she would have a baby. To have it turn out to be some *thing* that might possibly be cancer, a *thing* that would have to be cut out with a knife was too awful and horrible to bear. It was all an empty dream, and it broke her heart and frightened her almost literally out of her wits. What Rose had was not a baby but an ovarian cyst, and she'd undoubtedly had it for many months, perhaps for years.

"I am not surprised you thought she was pregnant," said Dr. Martinson to Daddy. "An ovarian cyst can look very much like pregnancy. Her case is a little atypical because it caused her no trouble for such a long time, but that can happen, too. As for malignancy, I don't think so at all and neither does Dr. Hardy. It's very unlikely, I probably shouldn't have even mentioned that possibility to her.''

''No, you shouldn't have,'' said Mother in a rather cold tone. She no longer seemed quite so enchanted with Dr. Martinson. ''It was needlessly cruel and I can't imagine why you did it. She thinks it's cancer and she's going to die.''

''Well, I told her it was very unlikely. We are practically certain it's a cyst and that it's nonmalignant, I told her that in clear English.''

''I also don't know why you had to tell her it's a *major* operation and that Dr. Hardy will have to open up her entire abdomen. Why terrify her? What was the point of that?''

''She's an adult, Mrs. Hillyer, I was merely giving her the facts.''

''Well, it's a disaster,'' said Daddy. ''I don't know what to say. I am floored, Doctor. I suppose, however, if it isn't malignant and she can get through the operation all right it might be better than her being really pregnant. She doesn't even know who the father might have been; it probably could have been a number of people, if she'd been pregnant in the first place. Maybe this is better.''

''Oh, it's definitely better, beyond question,'' said Dr. Martinson. ''A fatherless child, an ignorant girl with no job, no money, no home. It's fortunate, a blessing really, and a stroke of good luck for another reason I want to mention to you. Of course any major operation is dangerous, but she's strong as a horse, she can take the operation. Unless, of course, something goes wrong or it turns out to be malignant after all.''

Mother was totally disenchanted with Dr. Martinson. She was now staring at him with icy dislike. ''This conversation is making me a little sick,'' she said. ''I think I'd better go upstairs and try to comfort that heartbroken and terrified girl. If I listen to much more of this, I'll vomit on the rug.''

''Honey, that's no way to talk to the doctor,'' said Daddy. ''He's merely doing his job, dear.''

''Well, I am attempting to,'' said Dr. Martinson with a

thin grieved smile. "I am sorry the truth nauseates you, Mrs. Hillyer, because before you leave there's a bit more of it I'd like to put to you. This operation provides a therapeutic opportunity that I feel is quite important in regard to this particular girl, who suffers not only from an ovarian cyst but from a certain psychoneurotic condition as well. This operation could be of enormous benefit to her."

"What do you mean?" asked Mother.

Dr. Martinson turned to Daddy. "Are you able to endure a little medical talk, Mr. Hillyer? I don't want to offend you."

Daddy now seemed almost friendly to Dr. Martinson, perhaps because he was so delighted Mother didn't like him any more. "You won't offend me in the least, Doctor," he said. "Not a bit, I'm quite interested in what you have to say."

"Very well. First, about the girl's history. This is nothing to be alarmed about, she is quite recovered from it, but we have learned that the girl had gonorrhea at fourteen and the disease did irreversible damage to her Fallopian tubes. Evidently she's been very promiscuous since early childhood, she has no control over her sexual impulses. But the point I'm getting at here is that she's permanently barren, she can never conceive a child."

"Go on, Doctor," said Daddy.

"Yes, go on," said Mother quietly.

"Now about this operation," said Dr. Martinson. "We have an option situation here, or at least in my medical opinion we do. First let me explain what an ovarian cyst is. It is a fibroid growth and although cysts generally are nonmalignant they can grow to enormous size, incredible size—historic records exist of ovarian cysts weighing as much as a hundred pounds and even more. Of course they couldn't operate on them in those days."

"That's fascinating," said Daddy. "What a case of epizootics. She does it on purpose! You can't convince me she doesn't do it on purpose! That girl is a genius when it comes to epizootics."

"Let me continue, please. As I was attempting to say, ovarian cysts can grow to gigantic size and therefore they must be removed as a lifesaving procedure. The affected ovary of course is destroyed. Many surgeons these days, in my belief often quite unnecessarily, also remove as a matter of routine both the uterus and the other ovary, even if they are not diseased. Do you understand me so far?''

''Perfectly,'' said Daddy.

''I am thinking particularly of the other ovary. As a rule, I don't believe in removing it. The woman's hormonal system is profoundly disturbed, she is subject to possibly serious depression, she loses many of her secondary sexual characteristics—for example, her breasts might shrink and become flabby, facial hair might appear along with a coarsening of the features, and of course her sexual drive is greatly diminished, especially in a girl or young woman. The trauma seems more profound in youth, but it can be serious at any age. For these reasons I am opposed to removing the other ovary, as a *rule.* Do you follow me?''

''I am ahead of you,'' said Daddy. He glanced sidewise at Mother, who was listening intently, a hand to her chin. ''Go ahead, Doctor, pray continue.''

''There is also of course the fact that removing the other ovary sterilizes the woman. But *this* girl can't have children, anyhow, so that is no factor.''

''No, it isn't,'' said Daddy.

''Now . . . may I speak quite frankly with you, Mr. Hillyer?''

''Please do,'' said Daddy.

''I have of course observed the girl in treating her.''

''Of course.''

''Well, I think we both know her.''

''Yes, we know her.''

''What are you talking about?'' asked Mother. ''I don't understand all this mumbo jumbo and the funny looks on your faces. What are you getting at?''

''Mrs. Hillyer,'' said Dr. Martinson, ''this girl is sick in more ways than one. Let's face the truth about her. She is an extreme psychoneurotic with uncontrollable sexual impulses. She borders on nymphomania and it would be a mercy to spare her the suffering she causes herself and others. I recommend as a therapeutic measure the removal of her second ovary. It is ethically and medically the only proper decision in this case and I suspect your husband agrees with me."

"Reluctantly, I do," said Daddy. "It would be a blessing to her and everyone else. The girl is oversexed and I say—*spay* her!"

Mother stepped forward and said in a trembling voice: "Over . . . my . . . dead . . . body!"

Both Daddy and Dr. Martinson stared at her in surprise, especially Daddy. I, too, was startled. Mother often got angry at Daddy, but not like this. She was trembling all over and a fire was in her eyes. I have never seen her more deeply outraged, her contempt for Daddy and Dr. Martinson was boundless. Both of them seemed to shrink in their shoes as she asked with an icy calm:

"Are you human beings or are you some kind of male monsters? Is there no limit to which you won't go to keep your illusions about yourselves? You'd go so far as to mutilate a helpless girl who has no means whatever to defend herself, you'd go that far? Don't you think I know what you've just said and don't you think I understand the dreadful and revolting crime you have just conspired to commit?"

The scene would have been funny if it hadn't been so serious. It really was like throwing holy water on a pair of devils. As I said, both of them seemed to shrink in their shoes as Mother let them have it. This was especially true of Daddy, but even Dr. Martinson was intimidated by the calm fury and ice-cold moral indignation of her words. In consternation, stricken, Daddy tried without complete success to return her relentless gaze. "Well," he said, "well, now, darlin' . . ."

"I thought I knew you," said Mother, "I thought I did. It doesn't surprise me to hear this sadistic man propose such a thing, but I thought I knew you better. I thought in your heart you were a good and kind man. Well, let me tell you, I can't believe the monstrosity of what I've just heard in this room and I won't forget the shame of it until the day I die. A defenseless girl depending on you for protection, and you propose to mutilate and destroy her. How *dare* you suggest such a thing? How dare you even *think* of it?"

"Well, now, darlin'," said Daddy in a voice not at all like him, "give me a chance to defend myself. . . ."

"I can't believe you really meant that," said Mother quietly. "I can't believe you meant it or I'd want to die. You aren't a male monster, this man is but you aren't. Look me in the eye, and tell me this. We have in this house a girl of whom you say you're fond, a girl who's never had a chance in life, a girl for whom you say you feel love and sympathy. All right, look me in the eye and tell me, do you *really* want to take Rose's womanhood away from her when it's all she has got?"

Daddy moistened his lips once, then moistened them again, then gave a wincing flinch as Mother turned her head away from him, put her hands over her face and began to cry. In the meanwhile, Dr. Martinson was standing there with his hands half-raised and his sallow face almost as pale as Daddy's; he kept half opening his mouth as if he were going to speak, but he didn't say anything. Neither for a long time did Daddy. Finally, he put a hand on Mother's arm and said:

"Honey. Honey, please . . ."

"I don't believe it. I love you and I don't believe it. You couldn't have meant that, you couldn't have. . . ."

"Well," said Daddy, again in a voice not like him at all, "I hadn't thought about it . . . that much. I was just thinking . . . well, it's an idea, the girl *is* oversexed, and . . ."

"Rose *isn't* oversexed!" said Mother. "That is ridiculous! If you're going to talk nonsense, then I don't want to talk to you at all. Rose is exactly the same as the rest of us, except more so."

"Well, I know, more so," said Daddy. "That's the problem. I was thinking that . . . well, maybe she'd be better off."

"Better off?" asked Mother in a quiet fury. "How could she *ever* find love and happiness, if you did what you're talking about? Are you *insane?*"

"Now, may I say, I am against that particular procedure," said Dr. Martinson, "as a general rule. But in a case of near-nymphomania, it doesn't seem monstrous to me at all, but medically advisable." He'd finally gotten up the nerve to say something. Mother and Daddy ignored him.

"Well, now, I admit," said Daddy, "I admit, honey, it would be . . . it would be cruel. Yes, it would be cruel. I was just trying to help her, but for this particular girl it would be . . . cruel. If Rose wasn't attractive and pretty . . . if . . . well, it would probably be bad for almost any young woman. I don't know exactly what I was thinking about . . . of course a lot of women have that operation and it doesn't bother them, I don't believe . . . I mean they feel fine. Rose wouldn't, though. You are right about that, for her it would . . . well, I didn't *think* about it. The doctor said it and it sounded reasonable, but I didn't think it through. And you are right, you are dead right, completely and totally right, it would be an awful and horrible thing to do. I am sorry, honey, forgive me, I didn't mean it."

Having disposed of Daddy, Mother turned with an unearthly calm to Dr. Martinson and stared at him as if he were a bug upon which she intended to step. The doctor still had a pale frightened look on his face and his hands still were half raised in the air as if to ward off a blow.

"I will not cry like a woman," said Mother. "I didn't cry because of what you said, but because my husband seemed to consider it. You can't make me cry like a woman, a woman has just as much sense and self-control as a man. And you get this in your head, you get it in your head and you keep it there. I don't have much money any more, but I can raise quite a few thousands of dollars if I have to and I want to tell you this. If you do what you were talking about to that girl, then I will hire lawyers and sue you for malpractice for every penny you have got. I'll hound you in every court in this state, I'll do my level best to ruin you. Do you understand me?"

"Yes, I understand you, but you have misunderstood *me* completely," said Dr. Martinson.

"I understand you perfectly," said Mother. "You leave that girl alone, you wretched man, or you will be sorry."

Dr. Martinson smiled foolishly, almost as if Mother had just paid him some sort of compliment. "Actually, of course," he said, "I won't operate. Dr. Hardy will operate, I don't do major surgery, he'll operate and of course he'll be guided by your wishes in this respect."

"Let him be guided not by my wishes and not by Rose's

wishes," said Mother, "although I am sure they are identical. Let him be guided by the wishes of the creative power of life itself, because that is what has spoken through me tonight. And thank God it has, you should both thank God it has, I have saved you from committing a terrible and sickening crime. And I am humble, don't think I am proud, I need that power, too. We all do. Without it, we might as well be dead and gone, existence without it has no meaning."

Mother always went off the deep end, sooner or later. From this point on the conversation became pretty incoherent and repetitious, but it didn't matter. She had accomplished her goal, the victory was hers.

About five minutes after Mother said the creative power of life had spoken through her, I heard the sound of crying in the kitchen and a moment later the kitchen door opened, flooding the darkened dining room with light. It was Rose in her thin cotton nightgown, the same child's nightgown she'd worn on the night she came to my room. A glass of water was trembling in her hand.

"Shhh!" I whispered, my finger to my lips.

More than the glass of water in Rose's hand was trembling, her legs also were trembling as if she might fall and her face was a deathly white. The stark terror in her eyes was dreadful to behold. I was afraid she would faint and wondered how she'd gotten down the back stairs in such a condition. Quickly, I tiptoed over to her and put my arm around her waist and led her into the kitchen and shut the door. The water half spilled from the glass in her hand and she put the glass on the kitchen table and leaned against me, weeping.

"Buddy, I'm goin' to die," she whispered. "They are goin' to operate on me and I am goin' to die! I have got cancer and they are goin' to cut me all up, I am goin' to die!"

"No, you are not, Rose!" I said. "You are going to be all right!"

"I am goin' to die!" she cried. "They are goin' to cut me all up, they are goin' to cut my stomach all open and I'm scared! I'm scared, Buddy, I'm so scared! I don't want to die, I don't want to die!"

I was trying desperately to think of some way to make her less frightened and I said: "Rose, you are not going to die, you are going to get well! And I'll tell you what. If you die, then I will too! I'll jump in the river and drown myself if you die! And I wouldn't make that promise unless I was sure you're going to be all right, now would I?"

"What?" asked Rose. She drew back from me in alarm and stared at me with worried eyes, her own fears for the moment out of mind. But new fear came into her eyes as she stared at me in shock. Suddenly she cried out in a voice loud enough to be heard through the dining room in the living room: *"Mrs. Hillyer! Mrs. Hillyer, come here! Will you come in the kitchen please right away?"*

"What's the matter?" I asked. "What are you calling Mother for?"

Rose had one of my hands in both of hers and was squeezing and resqueezing it in semihysteria. I still was afraid she would faint. There was no color in her face at all. "Ain't it bad enough for me to be sick like this without you talkin' like that?" she asked. "Ain't that bad enough? It's what my Daddy done, and Buddy you mustn't say such a thing! That's the most awful thing a person can do, you mustn't say such a thing!"

The kitchen door opened and Mother looked inside. "What's the matter, Rose? What's the matter, honey?"

"Mrs. Hillyer! Mrs. Hillyer, Buddy says he's goin' to drown hisself in the river if I die! Talk to him, tell him he shouldn't say such things or even think them!"

Mother stared at me in brief puzzlement, then her frown cleared and she walked over to Rose and put an arm around her shoulders. "He won't drown himself, he just means he loves you," she said. "Come on, Rose, I'll take you back upstairs to your room. The doctor gave me a pill for you so you can sleep, and I'll stay with you as long as you want me to."

Rose's fears for her own fate returned and she began weeping again as Mother led her from the kitchen. "Please stay with me, Mrs. Hillyer," she said. "I'm so scared. I'm goin' to die, I just know I am. They're goin' to cut open my whole stomach and he says maybe I got cancer . . . please stay with me, Mrs. Hillyer, don't leave me alone."

Mother did spend a good part of the night with her, sitting in a chair by the bed and holding her hand. I believe I said this narrative would reveal in time that Mother loved Rose more than any of us, and it was certainly true. They had a similar philosophical outlook and similarities of personality as well. But there were big differences between them. Rose was outgoing, vivacious and related to people of all kinds with great ease; Mother was shy, deaf, introverted and suffered from hypersensitive nerves and other afflictions. And of course, unlike Rose, Mother never rambled. No, she never rambled insofar as boy friends are concerned, not in her entire lifetime. She was a Southern lady and my father was the only man she ever knew. And yet in the real and deeper meaning of the word Mother *did* ramble and she and Rose had a lot in common.

Perhaps it is now clear why I can't really remember Dr. Martinson's face. I can't even remember the man's real name, although I have searched my head for it for a month now. What is more, "Martinson" doesn't sound right for him, it isn't ugly enough—would "Martin*gale*" be better? F. Randolph Martingale, M.D.? Or maybe F. *Ranson* Martingale, M.D.? Probably.

But Martinson will do, it doesn't matter what the son of a bitch is called, he is a ghost anyhow no matter what name I give him. Murderers tend to fade. And that of course is what he was, a cold-blooded killer. I really hated the murderous bastard and when I heard he'd shot his wife and blown out his own brains I was pleased. It couldn't have happened to a more deserving fellow. Rose to be sure found something in him to admire, but then and now she had greater resources than I.

However, I suppose it's foolish to hate a dead man just because he tried with diabolical malignance to ruin a helpless girl's life, and a girl who at that had given him moments of sympathy and love, but then of course that was her crime in his eyes. So much for F. Ralph Martinson, M.D.—may he rest in peace with his unfortunate wife in their lonely graves.

Rose was admitted to the hospital on the following afternoon and scheduled for surgery the next morning at nine o'clock. Dr. Whatever-his-name-was, after thinking over

Mother's remarks to him, withdrew in a huff from the case and Rose became the patient of Dr. Hardy, who talked with Mother and Daddy about the other ovary and agreed with them there was no medical reason to remove it if it wasn't diseased, which it almost certainly was not. And one ovary, he said, was as good as two; the pituitary would simply signal the one ovary to work a little harder, which it could easily do. If Rose survived the operation without complications, she would be as much of a woman as she'd ever been.

At noon on the day of the operation, we all waited in the Ford outside the Hardy Hospital and watched Daddy pace back and forth on the sidewalk. He couldn't endure the waiting room, he said. From time to time he would go up the steps of the hospital to ask for news, then come back and pace again, hands clasped behind him and deep corrugations on his forehead.

Daddy had done a total turnabout on the question of the other ovary and now insisted he had never seriously considered such a thing, he was just entertaining the thought because it was an idea and interesting "in the abstract." In a way I believe this is true. He probably would have changed his mind after thinking about it, Daddy often jumped at "interesting" things and later drew back from them. It couldn't really have happened with Mother on the scene. If the man had spoken to Daddy alone as the result of a shrewd guess Mother would be opposed, that wouldn't have worked either. Daddy wouldn't have kept quiet about such a thing, he'd have gone to Mother and told her what had been proposed and the end result would have been the same.

The only way Dr. What's-his-name could have carried out his intent would have been to say nothing to Daddy and Mother and then tell Dr. Hardy the girl's employer and moral guardian wanted the uterus and other ovary removed, which conceivably might have worked but also could have gotten him into a hell of a lot of trouble. He had to clear it with the people responsible for the girl and in this Mother frustrated him. The man was really quite angry; I understand he went around town telling people we were crazy Southern idiots lacking all moral values, that we kept a nymphomaniac in our house for a pet. Well, *c'est la vie.*

However, although Daddy had convinced himself he never would have agreed to such a barbarous mutilation of a helpless girl, I think it bothered him. The idea *had* interested him, as indeed it might have interested many men of that time and place—and, for that matter, perhaps a few men of our own enlightened age. What could be a simpler way to cure a "nymphomaniac"? Butcher her a little, that would fix her up. As a matter of fact, I am told on good authority that the indiscriminate removal of undiseased ovaries and perfectly healthy uteri in those days was *very* common and I wonder why that was—a bit of male barbarism, perhaps?

Perhaps. Just possibly, and I think the words "spay her!" haunted and bothered Daddy. As he paced back and forth outside the hospital, he avoided looking at either me or Mother who sat beside me pale and silent on the front seat of the car.

Dolly and my little brother were equally silent on the back seat, except for one constant question we all asked many times. Waski kept asking why was it taking so long, and so did Dolly, and so did I. Mother, who was so frightened and worried she could barely speak, could only tell us it was serious, that was why it took so long, but Rose would be all right, she was young and strong and would live.

Finally, after Daddy had made God knows how many trips up the hospital steps only to come back out and pace again, he disappeared inside for about five minutes, then reappeared and came slowly down the steps, one hand on his hip and his hat in the other. Very slowly, he walked toward the car and from some distance away I saw tears in his eyes. This was not unusual with Daddy, he often had tears in his eyes and it was impossible to know the meaning of it, very hard to know if the news was good or bad. But Mother was afraid. She leaned over me and I felt her body tremble as Daddy reached through the window and took her hand.

"Well," he said, "I thought I'd seen the limit, but these are the most great, gaga epizootics she's ever had."

"How is she?" asked Mother.

"Fine," said Daddy.

14

Rose meets Mr. Right at last

SO IT WAS Rose survived the long hard winter and met and married Mr. Right in apple blossom time. A "friend" had saved her. Daddy himself had said it: "Do you know what a friend you have got there? Do you know she would fight for you like a tiger, that she would fly to your defense in an instant and fight for you with all the courage in her soul if anyone tried to hurt you?"

But Rose herself never knew. I never told her a word about the worm that crawled up the stalk whimpering at thorns he himself had invaded and hungry to destroy the beauty she had, I never said anything to her about it and neither did anyone else. Why desecrate her beautiful pity for that poor man? I think he strained even her. When she was reduced to having to admire his clothes, Rose was in trouble.

Nevertheless, her resources were large, she did find something to admire and more importantly something to pity in that sick individual, and for thanks he dubbed her a nymphomaniac and tried to murder her. It's amusing in a grim way that *this* man called *her* a psychoneurotic! Well, *c'est la vie*. Much that appears to be the truth is not, much that appears false is the truth itself. *C'est la vie*.

But although Rose never knew about the Big Battle of the Other Ovary, I think she knew she had a friend. Who else sat with her and held her hand until four in the morning? Who else took her to the hospital and gave her the courage to let them cut her all up? Rose knew. "Buddy," she said, "your mother is a saint. She is the most beautiful person who ever walked the earth."

Well, it's a view of Mother, and who am I of all people to disagree with it? But Mother did have her drawbacks, such as trying to make human atomic bombs and other infernal machines as well, she was no saint—but that has nothing to do with this story, does it? And a story, if only by implication, is or should be not merely a story but a vision of a better life and a better world, isn't that true? Isn't it true no matter what sharks who eat their own entrails might say? I think it is true, I think Rose was right, I think a certain beauty did exist on this earth at the moment my mother stepped forward and said in a trembling voice: "Over . . . my . . . dead . . . body!"

Well, I said I was not objective about the people in this book and that was no lie. The reader of course can make his or her own evaluation of what happened without assistance from me, but perhaps my opinion has some relevance since it seems I myself am kind of a character in this book despite my efforts not to have it so.

Would the reader believe I wrote those God-awful chapters of her in bed with the boy eighty-seven times trying to get *myself* out of it?—and *couldn't?* What a struggle! As Daddy would say, it wore me to a nub.

But Rose knew she had a friend, she knew it very well. Of course she loved Daddy more than any of us, more than Mother, much more, but then that was her nature, that was the way she was. A rose is a rose is a rose, as the immortal Gertrude said, and it can't be anything else, it cannot lose its petals or its beautiful scent in the summer air, until of course real winter comes as it does for us all whatever kind of flower or growth we might be.

Let's get back to our story. There is no need to wander in a wilderness again. After all, we are out of that bed with her, thank God. But I do believe the older self is a character in this story and perhaps it should be so. Occasionally comments of the older and presumably wiser self might be very important and even essential if the truth itself is to be revealed. Be that as it may, it can't be helped. Writing a book, I am afraid, is like riding a bear—even if the beast is bridled it goes off sniffing and snuffling on its own.

But let's get on with it, it's almost April, I want to get this thing done and relax a while, go down South and visit the Old Man, sit on the patio and have a drink or two of sippin' whiskey with him, titillate him a little about this book and *stir him up*. Of course he might hate it, you never know. I told him he's practically the damned hero of it, but you never know.

The bear sees the barn, let's get on with it and take a whispering jet to God's country no matter what we find down there—an outraged old man or an amused old man—because that is something beyond control, and I can quickly explain that, before we get back to Rose. It's worth explaining, too, an interesting insight that only took me thirty years to arrive at. You see, writing a book is like riding a bridled bear, but a book itself demands an altogether different metaphor—in the classic philosophical conundrum used to startle and stimulate freshmen in Philosophy I, a book is like the tree that crashes in silence to the ground if no one is there to hear it fall; it does not exist until another person picks it up and reads it and brings to it *his* or *her* creative power. All the tree alone can do is crash soundlessly to the ground, because a book is a symbiotic creation of writer and reader and unread has no existence at all. The writer, therefore, can only control *half* of a book, the writing part of it. The other half, the reading part, occurs miles away in another head and is totally beyond the writer's control and in fact is none of his business. So let's get on with it, let's crash to the ground Yankee sugerbush or Dixie hackberry or whatever, let's get back to our old love and finish her story and go see Daddy while he still can lift a glass.

Okay, where were we? Let's see, we'd just gotten through with Rose's last and greatest epizootics and everything had turned out all right. Rose had her operation, Daddy said she was "fine," and she was. There was nothing wrong with her second ovary and Dr. Hardy didn't touch it. In due course, she got well. As that other doctor has said, she was a very strong girl with a tremendous vitality and will to live, and her recovery and convalescence were uneventful although her complete recuperation took a while.

That was to be expected, the time needed for her to get back to her old self. A serious major operation involving massive abdominal surgery, following so soon a near-fatal bout with influenza and pneumonia, was not a thing one got up from immediately. She was weak and unable to do much work for many days even after she was up and around. Spring arrived and the crab apple in the yard was in bloom before she was truly herself again. "What a winter," she said.

Daddy agreed with Mother it would be cruel and inhuman treatment, after all of Rose's pain and difficulty, to send the poor thing off to a farm, even a dairy establishment. Of course something had to be found for her, she couldn't live with us forever. After all, she'd been fired. Daddy didn't say much about it until she was recovered and even then he found himself unable to give her an ultimatum, but he was still determined somehow or other to get rid of her.

Daddy was determined to get rid of Rose not only because of the damnable commotion she had caused and which doubtless would return when she was herself again, he was determined for another reason I was not wholly conscious of for many years. Let us leap briefly far ahead into the future:

"Bedroom eyes, Brother! Bedroom eyes! Not crude and obvious, not lewd or anything like that, but *bedroom eyes*—gentle, delicate, feminine, little looks and gestures and moves you couldn't put your finger on. Why, I had to fight her off day and night, that thing you call Thermopylae was nothing. I give you my word it was only the beginning. Son, you don't *know* what a menace that girl was, what an artist, what a maestro! She could give you *one look* with those big blue eyes of hers and it would have more effect than another woman taking off all her clothes and jumping on top of you! Your Mother, you and the other children in the house—and bedroom eyes all the time! I don't know how the hell I ever survived it. It drove me crazy and wore me to a nub. For some reason the little nut loved me and she never wavered from it. Son, she had me sweating blood. Of *course* I couldn't have her in the house the way she was acting, sneaking boys up in her room and all the rest of it, but the worst thing of all was those bedroom eyes looking at me with love day and night. How I ever resisted her, I'll never know. It was a strange thing, son. The little nut loved me with all her heart even though she adored Mother. Now how do you figure that out? And I'll tell you something else—do you remember that day she came and paid us a love call? She told me then if she had a man like me she'd never run around again, her rambling days would be gone. And I kind of believed her, son, I kind of believed her. What do you think of *that?*"

Thus spake Daddy not too many months ago, when we recalled Rose on a visit I paid him in October of the year 1971, about thirty-five years after the events of this story and that is a very long time. And yet time is an even stranger thing than the fact that Rose could love Daddy with all her heart even though she adored Mother. Some events which happened last week seem to have occurred in the dim past, but other things which happened many, many years ago seem to have happened yesterday.

One beautiful April morning Daddy finished his breakfast coffee, put down his napkin very carefully just so by his plate, crossed his arms and said: "Beautiful day, isn't it, Rose?"

"Oh, beautiful, just beautiful!"

"How do you feel, dear?"

"Wonderful!" she answered. "Perfect, good as I ever felt!"

"You are completely recovered, I take it?"

"Why, just like I was never sick," said Rose. "All I got is a big old scar on my stummick and it don't bother me none at all. That Dr. Hardy can operate on me *any*time!"

"Good, good . . . I am delighted to hear that. After you have done the dishes, I'd like a word with you and Mrs. Hillyer in the sitting room if you don't mind. Now don't be alarmed, Rose—just a word, a *friendly* word, that is all."

I had to go to school and couldn't eavesdrop on this conference, but a shaken Rose told me that afternoon what he'd said. He pointed out to her that he'd gotten her a good job on a dairy farm and she'd refused it because she didn't want to work on a farm, she hated farms. All right. He'd gotten her a job in a cotton mill and she and Mother had refused it because she was afraid of mills and machinery. All right. He'd gotten her a job as a waitress in a café and she and

Mother had turned it down because it wasn't a good environment, men drank in there and the other waitresses were wild girls and it was a bad atmosphere for her.

At which point Daddy took out five ten-dollar bills and ten five-dollar bills and said: *"All right,* Rose, now here is a hundred dollars. You've cost us hundreds of dollars already that we can't afford, but here is a hundred more. It is four months' wages, Rose. Now I hate to take this action but if I don't you'll be in our house forever, and I fired you, damn it. I fired you for good reason, goddamn it, and I have got to tell you you have got *one week* to make other living arrangements. I don't care where you go, go to *Alaska,* go to *China*—you have got one week, Rose!" Here, Daddy stopped, put a hand on his head, closed his eyes, gritted his teeth and groaned, and then said: "No. No, I can't give you any ultimatums, I couldn't stick to it, anyhow, what's the use? Not a week, not a week. But Rose . . . Rose . . . *please* try and find somewhere else to live. Will you do that for me, darlin'? Will you please someday move out? We love you, honey, but will you please move out?"

As I said, Rose was shaken. "I don't blame him, Buddy," she said, "Lord knows I don't. Him and your Mother have been kinder to me than anybody could dream, I'd be dead twice over if it wasn't for them. But where am I goin' to go? It bothers me so much I feel like I'm goin' crazy. There just ain't no jobs worth havin'. I'll have to take one of 'em though, work in a mill or as a waitress. Come walk with me in the yard a minute and help me think."

It was true there were no jobs worth having. Unskilled labor in a cotton mill meant long hours of grueling boredom that destroyed both the mind and the spirit in exchange for pitiful pay. A job as a waitress in a honky-tonk was hardly desirable either, although Rose had worked as a waitress in Birmingham and this was probably what she would have to do. In the yard, Rose held my hand as we stood by the blooming crab apple and watched two hummingbirds dart in and out among the blooms.

"Ain't they the prettiest things," she said. "Look at 'em, they don't worry about no job or where to go. I wish I was a hummin' bird myself. Sure would make things a lot easier. Just fly around crab-apple blossoms and have a lot of fun. What am I goin' to do, Buddy?"

"I guess you'll have to work as a waitress," I said.

"I done that already and it got me in worse trouble than you could know, it dern near got me killed. I got to think of somethin' else. Let's go look at your rabbit pen."

About a year before there'd been some big horrible argument between Mother and Daddy with me at the core of it, and the result was my rabbit pen. Daddy had taken me off in the Ford up to the high-school hill, stopped, sat there in silence, glanced at some people half a block away, said, "Those people are looking at us." He drove another block, stopped the car, gripped the wheel until his fingers were white, turned to me in tears and said: "Your mother can love you all she wants to, son. It's all right with me. I love you, too, even if sometimes I don't act like I do." Soon thereafter Daddy hired a man named Jake Storey to build me a rabbit pen.

"Why don't you have rabbits no more, Buddy?" asked Rose, as we stared at the empty tin-roofed pen, which consisted of about eight separate hutches. It'd cost Daddy forty dollars, a good sum in those days.

"Well, they're dumb things," I said. "I got tired of them."

Rose smiled pensively as she reached out and touched the chicken wire. "Did you know when I was a child we had pretty near five hundred rabbits?"

"Five *hundred* rabbits?"

"Yep, five hundred, we sure did. It was my daddy's dream. He was goin' to get real rich raisin' rabbits. There was this nice man, Mr. Siles, we rented from him, the farm, share-cropped for him, and he was goodhearted. He once sat me on his lap and put his finger in my drawers, but he was a nice man. He loaned Daddy some money to get started on the rabbits and Daddy got a whole mess of orange crates, got 'em for nothin' or practic'ly nothin', and we growed stuff for the rabbits and boy did we have rabbits. We had rabbits all over every which a way. It was what killed Daddy. He didn't drown hisself till a long time later, but it was them rabbits killed him."

"How did the rabbits kill him?" I asked.

"They killed him because he thought he could sell 'em but nobody but country folks eat rabbits, Buddy, and they ain't got no money to buy 'em. That was what killed Daddy. We had to eat all them dern rabbits our own selves. Every dern one of 'em, and it took about four years to eat 'em all up."

Hmmph, I thought, quite interesting. Rose was five feet nine, weighted a hundred and thirty-five, had a great figure and perfect teeth—that doctor had said she got protein somewhere, and she had. It was those rabbits.

"I got awful sick of rabbit," said Rose, "oh boy did I get sick of rabbit. But later on after Mother had died and Daddy wasn't doin' nothin' but drinkin', I sure would of been glad for a little rabbit stew, believe me. You know, I oughtn't to of told you about what Daddy done to me when I was a child. Until them rabbits ruined him, he was a real good man, Buddy . . . poor and ignorant, he didn't know nothin', not even that city folks don't eat rabbits, but he was a real good man. I loved him a lot, I loved him an awful lot and so did Lunette until she died."

"Your sister died?"

"She and Momma both died of t.b. I was lucky and didn't get it."

"Mmm," I said. There was no point in telling her she'd had t.b. and recovered from it. "What was your mother like?"

"A saint just like your own mother," said Rose. "She's up in heaven right now. There's no doubt about it."

Poor as her people had been, the life Rose had led on that tenant farm evidently had not been altogether inhuman. She had loved her parents and they had loved her. Rose had not come out of a vacuum but out of a rural South that whatever its faults and failings contained some human wealth as well as five hundred rabbits.

"I'll go see 'em at the café tomorrow," said Rose, "and ask 'em for that job. It won't kill me."

On the next day Rose went to the honky-tonk and got a job as a waitress. She then looked for and found lodgings, room and board for a few dollars a week in the private home of a respectable widow who took in several boarders. This was on a Friday. She was supposed to go to work at the café on Monday morning and intended to move from our house to the boardinghouse on Sunday afternoon, but she never did either of these things. Late on Friday night at about ten of twelve she came to my room in a state of great excitement and woke me up.

"Buddy," she said, "wait till you hear what has happened! It's a miracle, I am saved! I have met Mr. Right at last!"

"Wha-at?" I asked, half-awake.

"I have met Mr. Right, Buddy, I'm saved! I don't have to go work at that honky-tonk or live in that boardin' house, I'm saved, I have met Mr. Right! I met him early this afternoon and spent all afternoon with him and all evenin', and he loves me, I know he does, he is Mr. Right! And who do you suppose he is? That policeman who arrested me, the one I bit! He is Mr. Right!"

"Dave?" I asked. "Dave Wilkie is Mr. Right?"

"*Yes!* He is, he's Mr. Right! Buddy, this is the most wonderful day of my life. I have lived through the worst winter there ever was and it was worth it all, I have met Mr. Right in springtime and he loves me, he is goin' to marry me! Wait till I *tell* you how it happened, just wait, because this will thrill you pink. I was walkin' down Second Avenue not half a hour after I found a room in a boardin' house, not half a hour, and I saw him comin' toward me on the sidewalk, that same policeman who arrested me, the one I bit! Well, I was a little nervous at first seein' him, but as he come up he smiles and says hello. Buddy would you believe it, I knew almost right then he was Mr. Right, the second he smiled and spoke to me! My knees just went all weak, I got butterflies in my belly right then—not the way you think, not because he's good-lookin' but because of the way he smiled and the way he says hello. Well, I smiled back at him and says I was glad I run up acrost him because I wanted to tell him I'm sorry I bit him. 'And how is your finger?' I ast. And he held up his hand and I took it and took a look. 'My, my,' I says, 'you have got a scar, mmm, that is sad.' And he laughs and says it wasn't nothin'. And we got to talkin', we got in a conversation, a big long conversation right there on the street! Fifteen minutes, twenty minutes! We was talkin' and talkin'. He told me his wife had been killed in an accident! Right off, he told me he was a widower and lived alone with his son! He told me he hadn't remarried because he hadn't found the *right* person, but that he didn't like bein' a bachelor and he asked me if I myself was married! And I says no, not me, and he looked at me for a long time, the longest kind of time, then says real quiet, 'Well, come on acrost the street and let us get a cup of coffee.' All of this, Buddy! That's how quick it was! He was thinkin' just what I was, and when we crost that street I knew for sure he was Mr. Right—it wasn't just his tellin' me about his wife bein' dead and askin' if I was married, I knew it because of the way he held my arm, real gentle but firm—he was Mr. Right, I had met him at last!"

"Has he asked you to marry him? Has he asked you *already?*"

"No, not already, but he's goin' to! Let me tell you what happened next. We were in the coffee shop talkin' and talkin'—mostly *I* was talkin', and he listened. We had three cups of coffee, we was in there in the coffee shop nearly a hour! And I finally says, 'Are you on duty?' And he says yes he was, but he got off real soon and did I want to go somewhere and get dinner with him, and I says yes, I sure did! Well, we went up to the police station and got his car, a Chevrolet almost new, and we drove around a while because it was too early to eat. First we went out to the fair grounds. . . ."

Rose had total recall and she told me everything that happened on her date with Dave, the various places where they parked and talked, where they went to dinner, what they had to eat, the places they went then in the car. Two things seemed to impress her the most.

"First, he never got tired of listenin' to me. I talk an awful lot and sometimes men get tired of it and tell me to shut up. Twice I ast him if he minded me talkin' so much and he says no, he loved to hear me talk. That's what he said, Buddy, them were his very words! But more than that, in all them hours, Buddy, do you know what? The only thing he ever done was hold my hand, now how about that? He didn't even try to kiss me! All he done was hold my hand while we sat and talked, that's all! He didn't even kiss me when he took me home, and he'd spent all day with me and bought me a T-bone steak that cost him a lotta money! He shook *hands* with me, that's what he did, and he says, 'Thank you for a wonderful evenin'. Can I see you in the mornin', it is my day off'—he loves me, he loves me, Buddy! This is the happiest day of my life, he is comin' here tomorrow mornin' at nine and I bet before the day is over he asks me to marry him! And don't you know I'll sure say yes! I have met Mr. Right at last, Buddy, I have met him at last!"

Dave didn't ask Rose to marry him on the following day, but he did ask her on Sunday afternoon; thus she never moved to the boardinghouse and never went to work in the honky-tonk on Monday morning. She had met Mr. Right in the nick of time.

Needless to say, we were all very pleased, especially Daddy. But Mother was pleased, too, we all were. Dave Wilkie came that Sunday night in his best suit and in effect more or less asked Daddy for Rose's hand. The whole family was there, it was a gala occasion the night we got rid of our pet "nymphomaniac"—except we weren't quite rid of her yet, not quite!

"Well, Mr. Hillyer," said Dave in the calm, quiet way he had of speaking, "you and Mrs. Hillyer have been kind of father and mother to Rose, and I thought in politeness I ought to speak to you. Rose I guess has told you, we sort of fell in love at first sight, she and me. Well, almost first sight, I'm not countin' that time she bit me and I arrested her. Anyhow, I love her very much and I want to marry her and take as good care of her as I can the rest of her life. And Rose and me, since you've been a father to her when she needed one real bad, and you Mrs. Hillyer a mother to her . . . well, we'd like your blessing."

"Dave, you have got it," said Daddy.

"I think it's wonderful," said Mother. "Just wonderful. We're so happy for you, Rose."

It was a gala occasion. Rose of course began crying and ran and put her arms around Mother. It was not only a gala occasion when we got rid of the pet "nymphomaniac," it was also a tender and touching scene, marred only slightly by Daddy's cautionary word to Dave a little later on.

"You're so sweet!" said Rose to Mother. "I love you so much and I'll never forget what you done for me!"

"When do you plan the delightful nuptials?" asked Daddy.

"As soon as we can," answered Dave. "A few days. We have to get a preacher and find some little church in the country somewhere. That's what Rose wants, a little church in the country. Rose says you sort of wanted her to get a place of her own and she does have a room in a boarding-house. But I was wondering if she could stay on with you a few days more, it won't be long. Is that all right?"

"Certainly, certainly," said Daddy. "Fine, just fine."

"Can we go to the wedding?" asked Doll.

"I reckon you can," said Rose. "You're all comin' to the weddin', all of you, because we want your Daddy to give me off."

"Me give you off?" asked Daddy.

"Will you, Mr. Hillyer? My own daddy is dead, I got no relations I know of, you-all are the only family I got. . . ."

"Umm, well, all right," said Daddy uncomfortably. "All right, I'll do it if you want me to."

"Appreciate you letting her stay on a few more days," said Dave, "and glad you approve. Course I'd marry her anyhow but it's real nice to have your blessing."

"As I said, you have got it, Dave," answered Daddy. "And since I'm in the position here of being kind of giver-offer, maybe I ought to give off just a little friendly advice about Rose, if I may without being presumptuous. We know Rose very well and we love her a lot. And I'm sure you do, too, but then of course you've only known her three days."

"Yes, that's right," said Dave with a little smile.

"And that's not an awful long time."

"Long enough for me," said Dave. "I wanted her twenty minutes after I met her. I knew right away. I think I almost knew it that time she bit me. She is the girl I want."

"Well, isn't that wonderful," said Daddy. He paused and cleared his throat loudly, a deep frown on his forehead. "Ahh-HEM! Don't get me wrong, Dave. But since as you point out Mrs. Hillyer and I have been kind of like guardians, more or less, to Rose, we'd like you both to be happy, that's all. And since we do know Rose very well, I just thought a word of friendly advice might be helpful."

"Well, sure," said Dave.

Daddy again cleared his throat loudly. Now that he'd gotten into this, he didn't seem to know how to get out of it. Once more he cleared his throat, then said: "Well, Dave, Rose is a high-strung and nervous girl kind of like a thoroughbred race horse, she's a racer, a high-stepper, and marriage is sort of like pulling a plow. I don't want to be unromantic but it *is* sort of like pulling a plow. And race horses, you know, don't much like plows, unless they're handled *firmly.* And that is my friendly advice, Dave, that you handle Rose with love but *firmly.*"

Dave didn't much like it; his eyes were a trifle cold. "I'm sorry, Mr. Hillyer, I don't know what you're talking about."

"Nothing," said Daddy. "I'm not talking about anything. I'm just suggesting you handle Rose with love but firmly."

"Well, I'll do half of what you say. But Rose don't need to be handled *firm* by me or anybody. I don't even know what that means."

"Mr. Hillyer means you oughtn't to let me sleep late in the morning," said Rose, "sometimes I sleep real late. Things like that, sleepin' till eight thirty or even nine, that's what he means."

"Yes, that's what I mean," said Daddy, "exactly."

Dave's face relaxed for a moment, but then Mother said: "Well, Rose *is* nervous and sensitive and very emotional. And it takes the form of *flirting*. But I'm sure once she's married she won't do that any more. Of course not."

Dave was silent. He was too respectful of Mother to argue with her, but it was plain from his face he didn't like the conversation one bit.

"Ahhemm, well, now," said Daddy, "let me add that Rose is a fine cook, Dave, and a good housekeeper, too! Yes, sir! Her fried chicken can't be beat and what that girl can do with candied yams and turnip greens and black-eyed peas and butter beans and pecan pie just can't be beat! And what's more, she's cheerful as a cricket! You're going to be a happy man, Dave."

Dave smiled. "I'm happy already," he said.

Thus Daddy wriggled out of his ill-advised effort to warn Dave that he might have a few problems with Rose. Daddy was not convinced marriage would settle Rose down one hundred per cent immediately. It annoyed Mother very much and they argued about it later that night in the kitchen. "Why *shouldn't* it settle her down?" asked Mother. "Of course it'll settle her down. What is this cynicism, anyhow?"

"Honey," said Daddy, "I'm not saying it won't settle her down, I believe it will once she adjusts to it. But Rose is very young, in some ways still like a child, and Dave is thirty-five. I just felt he ought to be firm with her, that's all. But I should have kept my mouth shut, you can't tell a man a thing like that even indirectly."

"I'm sure there isn't going to be any problem," said Mother. "She adores him. What's more, he's perfect for her."

Rose and Dave Wilkie were married five days later in a small country church in a glade of oak and dogwood seven miles from town. We all went to the wedding and Daddy as agreed gave her away. Rose's knees trembled beneath her white dress; I could see it faintly vibrating as she stood beside Dave before the preacher and said: "I do." But she looked very happy and so did Dave.

In the car going home, we children munched wedding cake from the picnic-reception held outside the church by the bank of a crystal, water-cress-choked brook where Rose kissed everybody in sight and wouldn't let go of Dave's hand as tears brimmed and fell from her cornflower eyes. The Ford rolled along, Daddy at the wheel; chickens ran squawking off the dusty country road and farm dogs barked angrily at the Model A, in which Daddy took a lot of pride, he had a deep admiration for Henry Ford. As the chickens squawked in alarm and the dogs barked and a big cloud of red dust swirled behind us, we swallowed the last of Rose's coconut wedding cake and Daddy shook his head as if pestered by a cloud of gnats, blinked his eyes hard as if blinded by the spring sunshine, mopped his forehead with thorough, fierce pats of a wadded handkerchief and then inspired a deep, deep breath and blew it out with a shudder and said:

"Thank God we have got rid of her at last!"

"Why, honey," said Mother, "it's beautiful! Aren't you happy for Rose? Don't you think it's beautiful?"

"Darlin'," declared Daddy, "it's so beautiful I could vomit."

"Sometimes," sighed Mother, "I have trouble understanding you."

"Whew-w-w! We've thrown King George out of Connecticut," said Daddy with another deep-sea sigh. "It took everything George Washington had, and Robert E. Lee had to get in there and help, too, but by God we did it! And the best thing of all is she's *happy!* The little nut is *happy,* darlin'! Thank God and all His turtles, she's *happy!* She loves him and he loves her, too!"

"That I can understand," said Mother. "She loves him and he adores and worships her."

So it seemed. I had to agree with Mother and Daddy. There was no doubt whatever in my mind Rose loved Dave. And Dave worshiped and adored Rose herself so much it was pathetic. I have seldom seen a man so stricken and smitten by a girl as Dave was by Rose. It was true, I never lie, or not often. Rose had survived the long hard winter and had met and married Mr. Right in apple blossom time. *C'est la vie.* Say it again, Dr. Jazz, while your fingers plink the ivories and the sporting girls strut, *c'est la vie!*

15

Rose pays us a love call

DESPITE THE DEEP respect and esteem in which I hold the reader, I must say that at times readers fall down on their jobs rather pitifully. Instead of putting a little real creative whammy into the reading of a book, they slough off lazily and don't pay attention, they skim over vital information as if it had no meaning, as if words are just words and not instruments of communication. And that won't do!

As an old admirer of Mark Twain, I am reminded of a very funny thing he did once that illustrates the truth of what I've just said in the paragraph above. Suddenly in the middle of a story he was writing he inserted a poetic description of some type of bird—I forget what he called it, but let us call it a dingbat—that was *wingless* and nevertheless *hovering* in the air, and that also was *silently crooning*. I may not have the precise words, but that's the idea. Now if you are "wingless" you cannot "hover" and if you are "silent" you cannot "croon," yet this dingbat did both. Furthermore, the passage made absolutely no sense whatever, it had nothing at all to do with the story he was writing.

And no one noticed. Not one reader ever commented on it, no one wrote Mark Twain and asked him, "What the hell is this dingbat thing?" The passage was swallowed just like a piece of chocolate candy. That is why I say readers sometimes fall down on their jobs rather pitifully. What happens I believe is that he or she assumes a writer writes something just because the writer happened to write it. There was no *reason* for it, the writer just felt like writing it—"in the mood"—so he wrote it. A dingbat?—sure, it hovers winglessly and croons silently, fine, okay, that's what dingbats do, it's poetic or something.

A whorehouse "professor" piano player appears suddenly out of nowhere at the end of a description of a lyrical wedding in a country church, sure, it doesn't mean anything, no incongruity here, the writer just felt like writing that so he wrote it. And that phrase *c'est la vie*, used a number of times previously in a context of bitter irony ("... *this* man called *her* a psychoneurotic! Well, *c'est la vie*"), it meant nothing, of course not, just words that's all.

I wonder how many readers swallowed that whorehouse "professor" just like a piece of chocolate candy? To any who did I must politely but firmly say you are just plain falling down on the job. Immediately following "apple blossom time" we have "Dr. Jazz" saying again *c'est la vie* while his "fingers plink the ivories and the sporting girls strut"—and *that's* not a dingbat?

Those who were suspicious of this sentence get an A, and those who weren't go sit in the corner. After all, I can't bring this book into existence all by myself. There are no *accidents* in this narrative, the whorehouse professor was no accident and neither were the five hundred rabbits, which might not be more bunnies than a famous magazine publisher ever saw, but it's a lot of rabbits and Rose ate 'em all.

So, please pay attention and put a little creative whammy into this thing; if I present you with an outrageous dingbat, then sniff at it before you swallow it like candy. Stop and ask what a whorehouse might have to do with Rose's marriage to Dave Wilkie.

I believe my father was skeptical from the start, although he hoped Rose's happiness would last and he certainly was relieved to get her off his neck. I think he doubted this marriage; in some areas Daddy was more intuitive than Mother, who thought the marriage was made in heaven. But Daddy I am almost certain suspected otherwise; he was waiting from the first for that other shoe to fall.

However, Rose *did* love Dave and Dave *did* adore and worship her, and they seemed idyllically happy in the weeks following the wedding. Dave often stopped by the hotel and Daddy gave us reports at the supper table on how things were going. One night he said:

"Well, I have to admit they seem to be getting along just famously, not a cloud in the sky. Dave stopped by again this afternoon and says he's the happiest man in the world, that Rose couldn't be a more ideal wife. They never quarrel, she's a wonderful cook, she keeps his house neat as a pin. And he loves her a thousand times more now than he did when he married her. I tell you, I never saw anything like it. The man just talking about her gets tears in his eyes. Do you know what he said to me? He said he didn't know what he'd done that God would be so good to him to give him Rose, that all he could do was be grateful he had found and married her. The man absolutely worships and adores her."

"Well, you could see that the first night they were here," said Mother. "And it doesn't surprise me in the least, I understand why he feels that way. Dave is quiet, he isn't exactly dumb but he's a quiet and sober man, he's solemn and doesn't say much, he's quiet and mean as he is with all that policeman stuff and getting in fights, inside he is very gentle, almost too gentle. I realize there's a lot of rage in him, but sadly enough there isn't really much life force in him if you want to know, not much, but Rose has all kinds of life force, more than she knows what to do with. And she not only has all that vitality, she's also extremely warm-hearted and kind, there's no malice in her and the combination charms him. And I don't wonder, it's a thing you don't see often, a combination like that. I'm not talking about a developed thing, I'm talking about just raw life force and a lot of people who have it tend to be mean, especially when they're young, but Rose isn't like that. Any man could love her, but a man like Dave lacking in life force with a secret gentleness mixed with an awful rage, this kind of man isn't going just to love her, he's going to adore her, he needs her like he needs life itself. She completes him. And he completes her, too. Rose needs strength and love and protection, which Dave can give her. You've got to remember Rose was a hurt child, a terribly hurt child, I don't know how she survived at all—well, I do know, it was because of the great life force she has got, that and her creative powers of love which when life force is developed is the same thing. I don't know if you fully realize it but Rose is a very remarkable and even astonishing girl, a kind of human miracle considering where she came from, not finished yet she's still very young and childish, but it's there, the miracle, and Dave saw it and recognized it at once, or at least he sensed it, I don't think he could ever understand Rose really, there's not enough there, there's not enough furniture in his house if you open the front door and look inside, just a small rug and a few chairs and a little iron bed. But he sensed it, though, he sensed she's got exactly and precisely what he himself doesn't have, and that's why he adores and worships her so much."

"You have analyzed it *perfect*, dear," said Daddy. "I say that even though it gives me a swimming in the head to listen to you. The only thing that worries me when you go into the fourth dimension is whether or not you'll get out of it and return to this world. But I have to agree with you tentatively, anyhow. I must admit they seem happy as can be. I just hope it continues."

"It will," said Mother. "They're one of the most ideal couples I ever heard of. He'll love her till the day he dies and she will him, too. You wait and see. I'm certain of it."

As I said, Mother thought Dave and Rose's marriage was made in heaven, and she was wrong. However, her "fourth dimension" analysis, I believe, was close to the truth. Very close, in fact, except for one essential point: Dave Wilkie hardly "completed" Rose even though she certainly needed love and protection, as Daddy himself said in answer to Mother.

"I hope you're right, darlin'. Of course Rose needs somebody to look after her, somebody who really loves her and understands her. In a crazy way that's what she's been trying to find all along. I hope she has found it and that now she can settle down and behave herself."

"Of course she can behave herself," said Mother. "Rose is a little more sexy than some women, I suppose, but the importance of all that is ridiculously exaggerated. That man Freud is a total idiot who for all his brilliance doesn't know a thing about human nature and someday they'll laugh at his theories. The other one, Adler, is far more sensible. Sex doesn't come first, the spirit, the mind and the heart come first. What we do with sex isn't determined by sex *itself,* sex is nothing more than a blind urge and what we do with it is determined by what the spirit, the heart and the mind *tell* us to do with it. The man is a total learned idiot and it would be laughable that he's taken seriously, if it wasn't such a pathetic comment on our civilization itself. Imagine, sex determining the human spirit instead of vice versa! It's on a par with witches and handling rattlesnakes, it really is. But to answer what you said, of *course* Rose can control herself if she wants to. As childlike as she is Rose has got a good head, she is no fool. To be uneducated doesn't mean you're stupid, she is actually a very bright girl and there's no need for her now to run around and act up, she has got what she wanted. I'd bet my last nickel she'll be faithful to Dave as long as she lives."

"As long as she lives?" asked Daddy. "Mmm, well, Freud might be a total idiot, I wouldn't know, but I wonder about *that.*"

"You wonder because you're a cynic," said Mother.

"Maybe you are right, darlin'. Maybe you are right. They certainly seem to be getting along just beautifully."

"You don't mean that."

"I *do* mean it. I just said it."

"No, you didn't, you said you wonder if she's going to be faithful, and I say *yes,* she is!"

"I said," said Daddy, his fingers drumming on the tablecloth and his eyes commencing to become a trifle bloodshot, "that I wondered if she'd be faithful all her life. And I might wonder about that, with some legitimacy, darlin', about almost *any*one, damn it! What do you think the world is made out of—buttermilk and cornbread?"

"No, blood and offal!" said Mother. "Blood and offal and horror!"

"All right, all right! You're not going to get away with this! I said they were happy, I said I believed it, I said I was convinced!"

"No, you didn't!"

"Yes, I did!"

"You did not and I'll tell you why! You don't love Rose, you fear her!"

"That's a lie, damn it! I mean, that's not accurate, darlin'—and don't remind me again I said 'spay her,' I didn't mean that, I was just talking. I love Rose and you know I do, I love her little tail to pieces and that's the truth."

"Then I don't know why you express cynical doubts. Don't you know right now Rose needs our faith, not doubt? Next thing you'll be saying the house she and Dave are living in is a morphydike! That's what you always say! The world to you is six feet deep in blood, offal and horror—and I'm going out of my mind living with you!"

"I'm going out of my mind living with *you!*"

"Then we're both out of our minds, that makes us even!"

"That's right, we're even!"

"Oh, shut up, I don't want to talk to you. I have nothing to say to you."

"I don't have anything to say to you, either, dear. I don't have P-turkey to say to you."

And so forth and so on. My parents had an almost daily if not hourly quarrel of this type. But in their way they loved each other and I think at this point Daddy almost agreed with her. He felt I believe that his apprehensions were groundless, that Rose had found the love and security she needed and that marriage to Dave would settle her down. I myself thought so, I liked Dave and I believed Rose's rambling days were gone.

However, about two weeks later Rose paid us a love call and both Daddy and I saw very clearly it wasn't so. Rose seemed happy, she was adored and worshiped and protected, but she hadn't changed a damn bit. If anything, secure now with a husband and a home of her own, she seemed *worse*. I really was quite shocked at her behavior and so was Daddy, we were both shocked and distressed.

Mother at this time was finally writing her thesis for the master's degree in history that she had practically earned some years before at Columbia University. She'd decided that to live a parasite life as a so-called Southern lady just wasn't enough and she wanted to teach at the local women's college in Glenville, from which she herself had graduated as a girl.

Mother wanted to do this in order to employ her mind and her abilities, because, as she said many times, the only tragedy in life aside from a failure of the love power was a failure to use the gifts that power had bestowed. "It is a secondary tragedy, Brother, but it is a tragedy. You must use the gifts God has given you or life is pure hell. And that is why you should be a preacher. You were born for the ministry, you could move millions. Will you listen to me, will you listen to your mother who knows you? It isn't just that I hatched you, not for a moment, I am quite objective about this and I saw it in you when you were a very tiny child—those bright little eyes of yours just looked at me, it was eerie! You must use the gifts the creative power has given you or they will eat you up just like cancer, you hear me?"

In order that her gifts not eat her up like cancer and also because we could use the extra money even though as Daddy said the salary they'd pay her at Totter College was pitiful, Mother was in Atlanta in a cheap furnished apartment taking classes at Emory University to earn the final few credits she needed. She'd spent two years in New York at Columbia, and had almost completed her studies, but not quite, thus this period in Atlanta. Daddy went down every other week end to see her; she was away from home most of that summer.

Therefore, Mother wasn't at the house when Rose paid us the love call. We'd gotten another housekeeper-governess named Kate, a thin, prim old maid of about thirty whom Daddy called "Katie-bug," although the nickname in this case was totally inappropriate. We children called her at her own request "Miss Kate." She was an awful letdown after Rose. At any rate, as it happened, Miss Kate wasn't there the afternoon Rose arrived in grand new clothes and a big floppy hat with flowers sewed on it and a box of candy in her hand.

"Hello, Buddy sweetheart!" she cried. "I've come to pay you a love call! Where's your momma and daddy?"

Doll and Waski weren't there, either. I don't know where they were, maybe out somewhere with Katie-bug, but no one was there. Daddy with his Hawkshaw instinct slipped up on us a little later at an embarrassing moment, we didn't even hear the Ford; but when Rose arrived I was alone in the house practicing the trumpet, which I'd just taken up, and playing Louis Armstrong records, the old Deccas which I bought for twenty-five cents apiece.

"I ought to of phoned," said Rose sadly. "Well, let's go back to the kitchen and have a cup of tea."

"Tea?" I asked.

"Dave likes it and so do I, it's better than coffee, more refined. Your momma's got some, don't she? Come on, Buddy!" Rose put an arm around me as we walked back through the hall toward the kitchen. "You're getting so big! I hardly know you and it hasn't even been that long. It breaks my heart Dolly and Waski ain't here, will they be back soon? I brought you all a box of candy. Whitman's Sampler, best candy in the world, you'll love it, costs a lot of money! But Dave *makes* a lot, he don't care, he gives me anything I want, he just says, 'Anything you want, Rose, just tell me and I'll get it for you.' Does he ever spoil me, that man! But how you been, Buddy, how is life treatin' you? How is my redhead sweetheart who never told on me when I was bad? Do you still love me, honey, like you used to? Do you, hmmm?"

Rose made tea and we sat drinking it in the kitchen and she told me at great length all about her life with Dave, how wonderful and perfect everything was, how much she loved Tom, Dave's young son—and this gave me a moment of pause; there was something in the way she talked about Tom Wilkie that worried me a trifle. As a matter of fact, Daddy himself had mentioned Tom, not to Mother but to me. "I'm not so sure," he said, "it's a good idea for that seventeen-year-old boy to be there in the house right under her nose. But even Rose wouldn't go that far."

Daddy was right, even Rose wouldn't go that far, I was sure of that, but nevertheless I didn't like the way she talked about young Tom Wilkie. It wasn't lewd, Rose was almost never lewd, but it was overaffectionate—didn't she realize there were times to be a little cool, a little distant? I didn't like it, the way she talked about Tom Wilkie bothered me. And as she chattered on happily, other things, like little odd wrong plums in a pudding, bothered me too. Slowly it dawned on me Rose hadn't changed in the slightest and a chill ran down my backbone. What would Dave do if he caught her? What would Dave do if she caused a "damnable commotion'' in *his* house? No doubt my father had already reflected on the probable answer to such a question. What would an angry, humorless, sober man like Dave do in reaction to such a thing? The answer was obvious—Dave Wilkie would kill her, he'd take his policeman's pistol and blow out her brains.

However, I don't think Rose really meant anything by reaching down into my pants and feeling to see if the dilly had grown any since she last encountered it. I don't really think so, I think she had a genuine philosophical curiosity and also was just playing around, teasing me, having fun. For about the fifth time, she said: ''You're so big, Buddy! Why, you've just shot up, at least three or four inches, it seems to me. I hardly know you and that's the truth.''

''I've grown in lots of way, ways that would fascinate you strangely,'' I said, and it was true. My ''male manhood,'' as she called it, had increased substantially in both latitude and longitude, perhaps in part as a result of its epochal encounter with Rose herself. Soon after my night with her I'd learned from the filthy Hollis how to fiddle with it and cause it to have an epileptic fit. Didn't even make me sick any more, either, although I was convinced in long-range terms it would destroy my mind and turn me into an idiot—which some will say it did, I almost think so myself when I look at a few of the places that bear takes me; he's a filthy beast, no doubt about it, offends my Old Testament Southern morality to its ingrained core. But I can't control the creature!

Rose burst into a delightful giggle. ''Oh, *yeah?* Well, *I* know what you're talking about, you little redheaded thing!''

''You do, huh? Well, what am I talking about?''

''Your male manhood, that's what. And I don't see how that pretty little thing could have growed *much* since then, if any. It wasn't that long a time ago, Buddy.''

''It was almost a year,'' I said, ''and it's grown *plenty.*''

Again Rose giggled. ''Well, let's just see,'' she said. Smiling and having a great time, Rose leaned toward me, unbuckled my belt and—without the slightest trace of either self-consciousness or moral sense, as Daddy might say—unbuttoned my pants and stuck her hand down in my undershorts. Her eyebrows lifted in half-joking surprise and delight. "Why, *Buddy,*" she said, "goodness me! You ain't a man *yet,* but land o' goshen, Buddy, my stars, I do declare . . . hmmmm-mmm, you got more pretty red hair, too . . . and look at *these* cute things! Goodness me, my, my, my, is some girl goin' to be lucky—"

At this tender moment Daddy, who had a spooky instinct for such things, silently materialized in the doorway of the kitchen, hands on hips. We hadn't heard the car at all. Now why did he park in the front yard and sneak in the house like that? It was his Hawkshaw instinct. He often would do that, tiptoe up on me like a shadow to see what I was doing, and this time his instinct wasn't wrong. The first Rose and I knew of his presence was when we heard him say in a rather loud tone:

"Rose, what are you doing with your hand in that boy's britches?"

"Well, I . . . I . . . I . . . why, nothin'!" said Rose. "Just playin' with him, that's all. I mean . . . jokin' around!"

Daddy undoubtedly had stood there like a silent Sherlock Holmes in the hall and had heard the latter part of our conversation and knew this was pretty much true. "Umm-hmm," he said, "and when did you last check the boy's oil, may I ask?"

"Oh, well, I . . . I saw him in the bathtub last year, ha ha ha!" Quickly, Rose rebuttoned my pants, then looked at Daddy with a little innocent smile. "Really, that's all it was. I was just playin' with him."

"Umm-hmm," said Daddy, with a faint shrug. "Well, I can't deny that that's true, Rose. You were playing with him, all right."

"Don't misunderstand, Daddy," I said. "She was just joking."

Daddy gave me a sour look. "Where's Dolly and Waski?" he asked.

"I don't know. I think maybe they went out somewhere with Miss Kate."

"Buddy tells me you have a new governess," said Rose.

"Yes, and she's delightfully dull, too. There isn't an ounce of ramble in her, thank God. How have you been, Rose?"

"Wonderful, just wonderful. Do you want some tea?"

"I never drink the article," said Daddy. "But I'll take half-a-cup of coffee if you feel like making it."

"Sure, right away!" said Rose. "Just like the old days, a half-a-cup of coffee for my favorite man!"

Daddy turned to me. "Brother, keep your damn britches buttoned. Now you run on and play marbles or something. I want to talk confidentially to Rose for a while."

I left, went upstairs, tiptoed back down them and crept into the living room and on into the dining room, but I no sooner reached the kitchen door when it was suddenly whisked open before my face.

"Ah, ha!" said Daddy. "I set a trap for you, Brother, and I caught you red hand! Go up to your room, you little snoopy scoundrel, and stay there this time!"

I meekly trod up the front stairs, went to my room, opened and firmly closed the door making it slam as if angry, turned on the radio rather loudly, then tiptoed out of the room and down the upstairs hall to the narrow back stairs and crept down them into the dim-lighted pantry. This was a better listening post, anyhow. The door was thinner and I could see Daddy and Rose through the keyhole. She was telling him how wonderful and perfect things were with Dave.

"That's fine, Rose," said Daddy. "But what I want to know is, are you behaving yourself?"

"Why, sure," said Rose.

"You're not rambling any more?"

"Oh, no."

"You really and truly are behaving yourself like a proper married woman?"

"Yes, I am. Of course I am, what do you think?"

"Umm-hmm. Well, I hope so. Dave's a good man, honey. You're lucky to have him. And he might take it seriously amiss if you don't watch your p's and q's."

"Oh, I watch 'em," said Rose, "and don't think I don't know I'm lucky. Why, he spoils me, gives me things all the time. Huh, *you'd* never do that. By the way, Buddy tells me Mrs. Hillyer's in Atlanta."

"Yes, she is. I'm afraid she'll be away most of the summer."

"That's too bad," said Rose softly. "You must get lonesome."

"No, I have the children and Katie-bug to keep me company."

"Is she nice?"

When Rose asked "Is she nice?" she half bowed her blonde head to the side with a graceful motion and with an artful innocent casualness idly put her hand on Daddy's arm. It was a maestro gesture even the Pope might have accepted, if His Holiness hadn't happened to know Rose, but of course Daddy was acquainted with her. Her hand like a white lily was just below his elbow; the fingers were not clutched or tightened, but they were there, like slender petals of a lily around his arm—a spontaneous gesture of ingenuous affection, that was what it was. But she could time such things to a split second . . . now the lily fingers released the arm, she was idly interested in the material of his suit and casually pinched it with her thumb and forefinger as she hummed with her blonde head bowed a little country music tune. Perhaps "A Satisfied Mind" . . . ? Had that come out then?

"Nice?" asked Daddy, as he looked down at her hand with a little frown. "Who do you mean?"

"The new girl," said Rose in a voice that had become strangely soft. "This one you call . . . Katie-bug. Like I guess you used to call me . . . Rosebud." The blonde head lifted and cornflower eyes stared at Daddy. "You remember that?"

"Err-rr, err-rr, ah-hh-HEM!" said Daddy. "Well, now, err-rr, ah-hem, she's dull as dishwater, like I told you. A nasty old maid, not a woman of your proportions, honey. Forget it. She hardly stalks the earth at all. The children don't like her a bit, but she means well I suppose. Rose, get your hand off my arm."

"Why?" asked Rose. The lily fingers closed again gently but firmly below his elbow. "Do you mind my havin' it there?"

"I just told you to take if off, didn't I?"

"Yes, you told me," said Rose. "But I still love you. I'll always love you. Even more now, even more since you were so sweet to me when I was sick. I'll love you as long as I live."

"Rose," said Daddy in a rather feeble voice that didn't sound like him, "your gratitude is touching. I appreciate it, but please take your little fingers off my arm."

"Mr. Hillyer," said Rose in a voice that didn't sound like *her,* "you know, it's not the same now that I'm not workin' here. I made up my mind a long time ago that when that happened one of these days I would pay you a love call. That's what this is, a love call."

Daddy took Rose's hand, moved it from his arm, put it down on the kitchen table and said: "I see. A love call."

"Yes, that's what it really is. You see, I got a confession to make. Dolly told me on the phone Mrs. Hillyer was in Atlanta." Again, big blue eyes lifted and stared at Daddy with soft love. "I thought maybe you'd be lonesome with her gone, and would want to see me."

"Now wait a minute, hold the phone, stop the presses," said Daddy. "What do you *mean,* it's not the same now that you're not working here?"

"Buddy might come back down here," said Rose, her blue eyes fixed softly on Daddy, "he's awful sneaky. Let's go in the front sitting room and talk in there."

"You mean . . . my wife's bedroom?"

"Yes, the sitting room, in there."

Daddy stared at her for a long, long time, his mouth compressed into a thin line beneath his clipped moustache and his forehead a mass of worried wrinkles. Finally, he shook his head back and forth in slow grief and said:

"Rose, you are the most insane creature I ever ran into in my life. You not only bake the cake, honey, you cut it into forty-seven pieces and serve it to midgets. Now how in the hell can you come to my house and sit there on your behind and act like that?"

"Act like what?" asked Rose. "I'm not actin' like anything. I love you, that's all I said. I love you just the way I did, I've loved you all the time, don't you know that?"

"Rose, Rose, you've married another man!"

"Well . . . yes, I know. But I loved you before I did him, a long time before. What has *he* got to do with it?"

Daddy stared at her with a poleaxed expression. "What

has *he* got to *do* with it? Rose, he's your *husband!* You stood up there in front of a preacher and married him! Don't you realize what a husband *is?* For God's sake, Rose, he's your husband and he *loves* you—doesn't that mean anything to you at all?"

It was clear to me as I peered intently through the keyhole that Rose was becoming very upset. Her voice had changed, her lip was trembling, she was on the verge of tears. "Of course it does," she said. "I know he loves me, I know that."

"Then how can you come here and behave like this? Don't you have any moral sense at all? Don't you love this man?"

"Yes, I love him," said Rose. "You know I do."

"Then how on earth can you act this way? The man worships and adores you, Rose!"

Rose suddenly burst into tears. "I know! I know!" she cried. "I know he does, don't you think I know that!?"

Daddy bowed his head and made a church of his hands. In bewilderment, he stared down at his folded hands as Rose wept bitterly, a hand over her tightly shut eyes and her body half turned away from him. He finally took a handkerchief from his pocket and gave it to her. "Here, honey," he said, "you're ruining your make-up."

"Lot of good it did me," said Rose.

Daddy sighed heavily. "I can't make you out, honey," he said. "I admit it, you have got me baffled. Totally baffled. I hate to say it, but you really don't seem to have any moral sense, not even a grain. You don't seem to realize a thing like this is wrong."

"I can't help it if I love you," said Rose. "How can I help that?"

"You have *got* to help it, for crying out loud! You are married to another man, a man you yourself called Mr. Right! Now is he Mr. Right or isn't he?"

"Well, yes," said Rose, "he's Mr. Right."

"Then what are you doing here with *me* when you're married to Mr. Right?"

"Oh, quit tellin' me I'm married to him, I know I'm married to him, you don't have to tell me!"

"You have got me baffled," said Daddy wearily. "I can't

make head or tail of you, especially tail, but your head is a mystery, too.''

''You're the one's got *me* baffled,'' said Rose. ''I can't get nowhere with you no matter what I do. And I love you so much. Oh, Mr. Hillyer, instead of all this talkin', won't you put your arms around me just once and kiss me? That's all I ask, just kiss me a little, it would mean so much to me if you would! I don't work here no more, it would be all right now! Dave would never know and Mrs. Hillyer's in Atlanta, she'd never know either. Who would we hurt? Please, will you kiss me? I love you so much, please. . . .''

Daddy was thinking hard, or in his own words, ''sweating blood.'' Through the years he had picked up quite a bit of Mother's lingo and now he said in a grave voice:

''Rose, you have got what is called a 'fixation' on me. I suppose I was kind to you when you came here, I gave you a home and joked with you and it caused you to get a 'fixation' on me. Now I'll tell you what this means. I am a substitute *father* for you, that is all this is.''

''Like hell,'' said Rose. ''You ain't no daddy to me, that ain't what I got in mind one bit! I didn't come here to see no daddy, this is a love call and I want you to kiss me!''

Daddy blinked his eyes and rubbed his clean-shaven jaw, a slightly crestfallen look on his face. Well, this was Mother's specialty, anyhow, that type of analysis—so he seemed to be thinking. ''Mmm,'' he said. ''Well, maybe it's not exactly a father fixation. Doesn't seem so. But I imagine it started that way.''

''I'll tell you how it started. It started because I fell head over heels upside down out of my mind in love with you, that's how it started. And I still am in love with you, that same way even more. Mr. Hillyer, Buddy's goin' to come down here, let's go in the sitting room.''

''Um-hmm,'' said Daddy, ''and kiss a little, huh?''

There was a tinge of irony in his voice. I didn't believe he would go in that bedroom with her, but hope returned to Rose. Her blue eyes stared softly at him and she said, ''Yes.''

''That's all you want, just to kiss a little?''

''Well . . . yes.''

''You wouldn't take off your clothes and get in the bed

with me? Now, tell the truth, Rose . . . you wouldn't do that?''

Rose moistened her lips, hesitated as if uncertain how to answer him. Finally, she said: ''Sure I would, if you wanted me to. I love you.''

Daddy nodded slowly. Could I be wrong? Would he go in there in Mother's bedroom with her? ''Well,'' said Daddy, ''that's an honest answer, I have to give you that.''

Rose stood up, put her hand on his arm and said in a soft voice, ''Come on, let's go in there.''

Nonplused, in what seemed to me practically a *non compos mentis* condition, Daddy stared at her groggily, pretty much as he had done in the early stages of the attack at Thermopylae. Again, despite the handsomeness he still had at a youthful and vigorous forty-five, he looked a bit like a bewildered rooster. But once more, as had happened when Doll and I peeped through the dining room doors, he set his jaw. ''Rose,'' he said, ''I am not going to do it. Don't think I'm not tempted, as I told you long ago you are beautiful to me. I'm a man like any other and of course I'd like to go in there, but goddamn it this is my home. I'm not a perfect man and often I'm not even a good man, but I am more of a man than that. I won't defile my home, my wife, my children, myself and you. And what is more the fellow you married is a friend of mine. Now in this day and age people do all kinds of things and it doesn't seem to bother them. Maybe I am being silly using words like defile, maybe I ought to just say to hell with it and take you into that bedroom, a lot of men would. . . .''

''You don't love me,'' said Rose in bitter disappointment. ''If you did you wouldn't talk like that.''

Daddy clenched his jaw and went on: ''As I was saying, a lot of men would. They'd take you in there, honey, and pull off your clothes and have a lot of fun with you, and maybe that's what I ought to do, maybe I'm a fool. But I can't do it, Rose, I can't and I won't. I'm sorry you feel the way you say you do about me, sorry for you and Dave both—''

''The way I say I feel? It ain't the way I *say*, it's the way I feel. I love you, that's all there is to it.''

"No. You have a father fixation, Rose, and you aren't grown-up yet. You're still rambling, that's all this is."

"Is it?" asked Rose. "Well, I'll tell you this. If you loved me, I'd never run around again. If I had a man like you, my ramblin' days would be gone."

For several seconds Daddy gazed at her with puzzled eyes. "Hmmp," he said. "Tell me this, Rose. If you feel that way, why did you marry Dave?"

Rose was silent for a long time, her head bowed. I was beginning to think she wouldn't answer the question at all, but finally without looking up she replied: "I loved him. I loved him a lot, I thought he was Mr. Right."

"You don't love him now and you don't think he's Mr. Right any more, is that what you mean?"

Again she was silent for a long time, then she lifted her blonde head and looked at Daddy and said: "Well, talkin' to you makes me see something I didn't know before. I still love Dave, I love him a lot, an awful lot, but he don't never laugh with me like you do, I don't have no fun with him. All he does is buy me things and close me in. It makes me feel like I might as well of gone to work in that house in Birmin'ham. He buys me things all the time and watches me like a hawk and it closes me in."

"Closes you in?" asked Daddy. "You mean . . . he's jealous? Is that what you're saying?"

"Sure he's jealous. Course he is. If anybody just looks at me he wants to kill them."

"Have you given him reason to be jealous? Tell the truth, Rose."

"No, I have not," she answered, "never. Not the least bit. But I sure wish he'd stop closin' me in."

"Um-hmm," said Daddy, "I thought you'd say that. May I ask, Rose, why you came here today? What was the purpose of your visit, dear?"

Rose shrugged. "To pay you a love call," she said in deep gloom. "And a lot of good it done me, too. I have real love for you but you don't want it."

"I happen already to have a wife I love," said Daddy, "which fact never seems to bother you. The curious thing, though, is that in one breath you tell me you've given Dave no cause for jealousy and in the next breath you admit you came here today to pay me a love call, which means doing your level best to seduce me. How can those two things go together?''

With the simplicity of a child, Rose replied: ''That wouldn't make him jealous, he wouldn't never of found it out.''

''People find it out, Rose, they find it out. I am afraid trouble lies ahead for you, honey. How'd you get here, anyhow?''

''I took a bus,'' said Rose sadly. Her shoulders were slumped, gloom and misery were in her blue eyes. The love call, alas, had failed, as she had anticipated it might. ''Dave is learnin' me how to drive, but I ain't got no license yet.''

''Well, I'll carry you back home to your unfortunate husband, for whom I feel a considerable sympathy at this moment. You don't even know your conduct is wrong, what is there to say? You are a child, Rose, and not only that you don't have a lick of moral sense, not even a lick. You come here to pay me a damned love call and serenely tell me you haven't given your husband a bit of cause to be jealous. Good God Almighty, talk about a moral pretzel! All I can say is I hope Dave doesn't shoot you sometime. Come on, I'll drive you home.''

So it was Daddy and I began our wait in fearful expectation of the storm that was sure to come. I was shocked and worried as he was. Young as I was I felt it, Rose's guiltless and childlike immorality was outrageous; Daddy was right, she simply had no moral sense, none at all. Of course we'd already long before had ample evidence of her failing and we ought to have known she wouldn't change and that a probable tragedy would be the result of her marriage to Dave Wilkie. So I felt and so did Daddy. Rose hadn't changed a bit, not in the least. A leopard couldn't change its spots and neither could a rose its petals. Her behavior that afternoon redemonstrated it to us both and we waited in apprehension for the coming storm, because neither of us wanted to see her blonde head blown apart.

As time went by and the storm grew nearer, our apprehension turned into acute anxiety, a bone-chilling fear for her life. Dave would shoot her if he caught her and she was behaving with a crazy indiscretion as if she wanted just that—the affair of the two cute little catfish, for example; she practically rubbed his nose in it, nothing could have been more obvious. What was the matter with her? Was she a total fool? Didn't she know Dave Wilkie was a proud and violent man and that the way she was acting was terribly dangerous? With increasing anxiety and fear for her life, Daddy and I pondered it. Maybe she *was* psychoneurotic, maybe she was a nymphomaniac after all. Neither of us could figure it out, all we knew for certain was that the marriage of Rose and Dave began to go to hell in a bucket on the day she paid us a love call.

16

Rose catches two cute little catfish

DADDY EVENTUALLY QUALIFIED his judgment significantly, although he did not wholly withdraw it and I suppose in a superficial sense such a judgment is not totally incorrect—after all, he was a married man and it was on the face of it pretty naïve and childish and naughty of Rose to go there and try to seduce him.

Why, it was shocking. Such behavior could get a girl shot! At thirteen, I have to admit it, I fully shared and endorsed my father's view that Rose had no moral sense, even though I had seen her with my own eyes rob the cradle and ought to have known better. *C'est la vie!*

Yes, it is a dingbat, a hell of a dingbat, the most silently crooning dingbat yet seen in these pages. I though she had no moral sense at thirteen, but later, much later, I came to see Rose's love call for what it really was: a frantic appeal for assistance, a desperate cry for help, a cry that went unanswered and left her no alternative but to put her life in jeopardy, to lay her very existence on the line in order to save a thing far more important to her than life itself.

We missed her, we children. Lacking in moral sense or not, Rose was great fun to have around the house and we all missed her, especially Doll and I, but my little brother Waski missed her, too. Often he would sadly say such things as: "I wish Rose hadn't gotten married and gone off. I like her a *lot* better than Miss Kate."

We were all very pleased when one day Rose telephoned and invited me and my sister and brother to go with her and Dave on a Fourth of July picnic. "Whoopee!" said Waski right in front of Miss Kate herself, who stared at him with pursed mouth and slightly popped eyes; she suffered from an overactive thyroid, poor Katie-bug. "We're going to see Rose, we're going to see Rose, we're going on a picnic with her! Good-bye, Miss Kate!"

Rose was infinitely more fun that the dour and sour Katie-bug, whose nickname was so inappropriate as to be ludicrous, but of course only Daddy called her that. She didn't like it, but she had to take it from him. "If I couldn't call her Katie-bug," he once said to me and Mother, "I'd strangle the poor damn creature and put her in a paper bag and throw her in the Poggawog River." Mother called her Kate and got along with her fairly well.

Katie-bug insisted we children address her formally as Miss Kate—she wouldn't answer if we called her anything else. There's no question of it, the immoral Rose was much more fun; she'd play all sorts of games with us all day long, tell us amazing stories of fascinating things that had happened to her, make jokes and take us off on hikes in the woods, but Miss Kate did none of this. As Daddy said, she was dull as dishwater.

Out of sheer boredom Doll and I once peeped on Miss Kate while she was taking a bath, a thing we wouldn't have dreamed of doing to Rose. I had discovered there was a good-sized chink in the lathes and plaster of the ceiling of the upstairs back bathroom, and that by crawling to the very rear of the attic it was possible to look right down into the bathroom below. We watched her sit on the toilet and pee, then watched her take off all her clothes and bathe and wash herself with meticulous care in the tub.

"It's taking her an awful long time," whispered Doll. "I think she's making doo-doo."

"No, she's just peeing and thinking," I said. "We'd smell it if she was making doo-doo."

"Yeah, I guess we would," whispered Doll.

I've often wondered how Miss Kate—a thin, tight-mouthed, peeved and popeyed creature whose favorite expression was, "Make haste! Make haste, children, make haste!"—would have reacted if she'd glanced up and seen those two pairs of eyes staring down at her. She'd probably have screamed her bloody head off.

"Look," I whispered, "she hasn't got any titties at all, hardly."

"Got nipples, though," said Doll.

"Yeah, but no titties. Rose's are *much* bigger and prettier, a million times nicer. I saw them that night Billy jumped out of the window."

"Hey-y-y, look," whispered Doll, as Miss Kate down below stepped out of her panties, or "bloomers," as she called them, "look, Buddy, she's got hair on her pussy."

"What did you expect, wheat?" I asked. "Of course she's got hair on it, all women do. Some of them have got hair on it practically a foot long."

"Oh, go on," said Doll. "I don't believe that."

"In Japan they do, the northern island, the Hairy Ainus. They have hair down there a foot long, Doll, really."

I didn't know it for a fact, but it sounded plausible. We had to be quiet when the tub was filled and Miss Kate turned off the water. It wasn't very interesting. We watched her soap and wash herself thoroughly in every nook and cranny, then bored by the whole thing we went away. She was clean, Miss Kate, I'll say that for her.

But dull as mud compared to Rose. We were delighted by the picnic invitation.

Although both Daddy and I had been worried that Rose's lack of all moral sense would lead to serious trouble with Dave, nothing seemed to have happened, all appeared to be well. I wondered if maybe Rose's love call was just an erratic thing that didn't mean much, maybe a sort of accidental aftermath of her crush on Daddy. I also thought perhaps Daddy's reaction had scared her a little, made her realize she was married now and would have to behave.

The Fourth of July picnic was a combined firemen and policemen affair being held a few miles out of town at a place called Silver Springs, a sort of park with a lot of willow trees and slides and swings for children, plus picnic benches and barbecue pits. I'd been there before. Daddy had taken me fishing there once; the springs fed a substantial stream that wandered off into fields and woodland, and there were quite a few fish in the stream, most of them catfish but some bass, too.

"Well, Buddy," said Rose in the car, "are you and Dolly

and Waski ready for some ice cream? Do you like picnics or don't you?"

"We like them!" yelled Waski. "We love them!"

"It isn't a picnic, honey," said Dave. "It is a barbecue."

"Okay," said Rose.

"Well, they are not the same thing, dear."

"I said okay," said Rose.

"A picnic is only a few people and it doesn't involve roast meat, hon. At a barbecue you have a lot of roast meat."

"Well, all I know is there's goin' to be ice cream," said Rose. "And I never in my life will ever eat enough ice cream, not if I live to be a thousand. We'll get us a plate of it soon as we get there, Waski!"

"Oh, no, you can't do that, Rose. It would spoil your appetite, hon. Get some barbecue first, *then* you can have some ice cream."

"Well, all right," said Rose.

"And by the way, hon, you remember that outing we took two weeks ago with the Elks Club? You know, down at the lake where you wandered off somewhere? Well, please don't wander off like that again, darling, it worries me not knowing where you are. Please don't do that again, hon."

"I won't wander off nowhere, Dave, I'll stay right with you. Okay, honey?"

"Okay, dear. Thank you."

All was well. Dave and Rose were perfectly happy, or certainly seemed to be. True, Dave looked a little tired and tense, there were circles under his eyes and he seemed to be gripping the wheel of the car very hard, his knuckles were white and as he talked a muscle kept rippling in his jaw. But he was very polite to Rose, he didn't seem really upset or anything. And Rose herself seemed quite happy. She was humming a little country music tune as we drove along and kept picking the petals off a daisy and throwing them out of the window like a child. "Buddy loves me, Buddy loves me not," she said, with a wink at me as each petal flew out over the road. Twice, Dave smiled affectionately at her and reached over and patted her on the hand. It was clear to me there was no real trouble between them, and I was relieved.

However, there was trouble. I didn't know it then, but there was trouble and it was bad. The incident of the two cute little catfish wasn't the first of its kind. I gathered that in the car going back. I also gathered that Rose found Dave's adoring and worshipful treatment of her a wee mite oppressive, you might even say *smothering*. It was one of the few things said on the way back: "Quit closin' me in," said Rose. "Quit sittin' on my head, I can't breathe!"

Despite her promise not to wander off, Rose disappeared during the barbecue, she vanished into thin air for over two hours. I had noticed her talking quite a bit to a large, broad-shouldered, red-faced fireman whom everyone called Buster. Dave, too, noticed this; I saw him eying them with a pale frown. Dave, however, along with several other policemen and firemen, was in charge of the barbecue pits and he couldn't keep watching Rose all the time. Frowning and worried, he came up to me about three o'clock that afternoon and asked quietly:

"Buddy, have you seen Rose?"

I said no, I hadn't, not for about an hour.

"Yeah, that's when I last saw her, too," said Dave, "about an hour ago. Now I wonder where she's gone. Funny for her to go off like this right in the middle of all the festivities. Do you suppose she could have gone off with Dolly and your little brother?"

"No, Doll and Waski are right over there playing on the swings."

"Umm, yes, so they are," said Dave. "Well, I don't understand it. Where could she go off to, and for what?"

"Maybe she went for a walk," I said.

"Yes, I think she has, and I find that just a little annoying, Buddy. I told her not to wander off like that, I made a point of telling her not to do that, and she said she wouldn't. This really isn't very thoughtful of her. But you saw her about an hour ago, huh?"

"Oh, maybe, about forty minutes."

It had been at least a full hour and Dave knew it. His worried frown deepened, his face became even more ashen as he stood there staring emptily at nothing, the muscles of his jaws rippling in both cheeks. He didn't know where Rose was, but he knew who she was with. I felt a twinge of pity for the man. He looked sick in his heart and soul. "Well," he said, "it's three now. They are already serving the barbecue. I hope she comes back soon. If she doesn't, I am going to be a little annoyed with her. This is very thoughtless of her, Buddy."

Rose came back at ten after four when everyone there had finished barbecue, Brunswick stew and ice cream. The large red-faced fireman called Buster was with her and he had an almost comical sheepish look on his face, a look that would have been funny perhaps if he hadn't been so obviously and plainly frightened as well. He kept wetting his lips and swallowing as he walked forward with Rose.

Rose, on the other hand, didn't look sheepish or frightened in the least. She seemed not to have a care in the world, although her hair was mussed, her face was sweaty, a bit of dirt was on her forehead and her dress was quite rumpled and very noticeably soiled in the back with red clay. She'd sat down somewhere, evidently, it also seemed almost as if she'd *lain* down somewhere, the red clay on her yellow dress was extremely noticeable. But she wasn't sheepish a bit, she was smiling and calm and held in one hand a bamboo fishing pole and in the other hand two little catfish on a string. Dave slowly walked up to her, very, very ashen in the face. She smiled pleasantly at him and said:

"Look, Dave. I caught two cute little catfish."

"Ahh-h, *yeah,*" said the beefy, red-faced Buster, who at this moment was more pale pink than red, "we went fishin'."

It happened so fast everyone at the barbecue was paralyzed and Dave damn near killed the man before they could pull him off, or it looked to me like he damn near killed him. As everyone watched stupidly, Dave pulled his hand far back almost behind him, his shoulder lowered at least eighteen inches, his back became rounded and humped and he lunged forward and hit the fireman Buster a terrific blow square in the middle of his mouth. Buster went back and down like a steer struck by a sledge, his eyes rolled back in his head and blood all over his face. He was unconscious, knocked out cold.

"Dave!" screamed Rose. "Why did you hit Buster?"

But she hadn't got the sentence out before Dave threw himself down on the man, jabbing hard with one knee at his groin as he did so. Then he was on him, smashing him again and again and again in the face. As his huge fists landed they made a horrendous smacking sound. I heard Rose scream again, and again. Then I saw yellow bloody teeth on the unconscious Buster's chin. To tell the truth, I became very dizzy and nearly fainted. It looked to me as if he was killing him. Finally, after the longest kind of time, people stopped just standing there watching in paralyzed shock. Four or five men pulled Dave off the man.

"Dave!" cried Rose, as he twisted free of the men and turned to her. "Are you crazy? Why did you do that? Why did you beat up Buster? You've hurt him, you've hurt him bad! Why?"

It was a very strange thing—my strongest impression, in the midst of all the screaming and blood and hitting, was of Rose's terrible distress at the fate of Buster. She was trembling with horror and astonishment as she stared down at him, unable to lift her gaze even though Dave was advancing on her with something like murder in his eyes. It was as if the thought hadn't crossed her mind that anything could happen to the unconscious and badly beaten man on the ground, and this is not an insight of the older self. The thing I remember most vividly is Rose's unbelieving distress at the awful fate of the fireman.

Whose most serious injury, as it turned out, was not the five teeth Dave knocked from his head or his broken nose or shattered cheekbone but the damage he had received in the area of the groin. Dave had hit him so hard with his knee he fractured a pelvic bone and caused the man's testicles to swell three times normal size. Of course Buster had it coming to him, catfishing can be quite dangerous in the South—a cute catfish or two can get you killed down there, easily, or it sure could when I lived in violent Dixieland, where men talk with a gentle drawl but go after your ass to get it if you touch their women.

There's no doubt about it, Buster had taken his chances and he wound up in the hospital for eight days with ice bags on his balls. But then perhaps it was worth it, Rose was quite a girl, quite an event in the life of a big beefy fireman, he wouldn't forget her. Unfortunately, he wouldn't forget Dave Wilkie either. On second thought, I don't think it was worth it, not even Rose. There's a limit, and when a man practically deballs you and knocks out five of your teeth, that's it.

"Come on," said Dave in a choking voice, as he grabbed Rose by the arm. "We are going home."

Rose's eyes snapped up to his. She was not afraid of him, a brief flash of fire leapt from her eyes to his. Softly, sweetly, innocently, she asked, "But why did you hit him, Dave, why did you beat him up? All we done was go fishin'. I swear it. Look, I caught two cute little catfish, that's the proof."

In cool defiance, her image of innocence was perfect even to the detail of a little tear in one blue eye about to fall. I was very frightened. How could she dare look at the man in this way when he was in a rage? He would grab her and break her neck, which he could easily do in three seconds. But she even gave him a little innocent quiver of her lip and something went out of Dave. A look of helpless despair mixed with an even more helpless fury came into his eyes. What could he do? Kill her, sure, but if not that, what?

Not much. He grabbed the fishing pole from Rose, broke it in half with a loud snap, then snatched the string of two cute little catfish from her, threw it furiously behind him and hit some boy on the shoulder, then grabbed Rose roughly by the arm. "Come on," he said.

"Take your hand offa me," she said with an icy calm.

"I told you, come on," said Dave.

"I am not goin' *no*where with you," said Rose, "until you take your dern hand offa my arm."

"Goddamn you, you come on with me!"

Rose protested as Dave dragged her roughly toward the car. The crowd of policemen, firemen, wives and children all watched this scene in open-mouthed shock. Even the men who were trying to revive and prop up the battered and bloody Buster looked up and watched in open-mouthed awe. As I said, Rose lay her life itself on the line and one doesn't see such a thing every day.

"Get your sister and brother," said Dave as he dragged

Rose past me through the whispering crowd. "I am sorry, we have to take you home."

Dave said almost nothing to Rose in the car as he drove us back to the house on Summerton Road, but there was a brief exchange about halfway there. Dave was squeezing and resqueezing the steering wheel, and suddenly his jaw muscles rippled and he said:

"This is the second time you done that. I told you not to wander off nowheres."

"Yeah, and you told me not to eat no ice cream, too!" said Rose. "Quit closin' me in! Quit sittin' on my head, I can't breathe!"

Dave gripped the wheel so hard the car briefly swerved. "You better not do that again," he said.

"Do what?" asked Rose coolly. "I didn't do nothin'. All I done was catch two cute little catfish, and if you don't like it, go fishin' yourself."

Dave didn't have anything else to say and neither did anyone else in that car, certainly not Doll, Waski or me, we hunched in our seats silent as mice. Rose, however, hummed a little tune of country music and stared out of the window at the passing countryside as if she didn't have a care in the world. As Daddy said, she was cheerful as a cricket. And then of course she had a reason to be in a good mood. She'd had a good day, piscatorially speaking, she'd caught two cute little catfish.

17

Rose

finds an inner peace

''*NOW I UNDERSTAND*, now I know,'' wept Rose, as Mother held one of her hands and young Reverend Jimmy Pollock held the other, ''now I see it! I just didn't want to take my responsibilities, but it's God's plan to take responsibilities! It's the bull that bought me!''

''Amen!'' cried Reverend Jimmy, a rather handsome but slightly jug-eared young preacher whom Dave had urged be present at the special meeting between Mother and Rose. ''The bull that bought you, Sister Rose! Amen! Pr-r-raise the Lord!''

''Now I understand it,'' wept Rose, a lily hand over her eyes as tears streamed down, ''I understand it, I understand it—and I have found God and an inner peace!''

''Amen!'' cried Reverend Jimmy. ''Pr-r-raise the Lord!''

Dave just *couldn't* seem to get the message, so Rose had no choice but to send him another Special Delivery. But she'd seen one man beaten half to death and she didn't want to see it happen to another one, so she picked her shots a little more carefully this time. All that happened was that she got a bowl of fruit salad dumped on her head. No one else was hurt and Dave got the Special Delivery just fine, the postman brought it right up to the front door for him and made him sign for it.

In effect, Rose told the same joke twice, and this can sometimes be quite effective—if the joke has an extra outrageous twist to it, it can be even funnier the second time around. Two elephants are not better than one elephant necessarily, but two elephants plus a pygmy hippopotamus are certainly better.

Speaking of telling jokes twice, we played an interesting game at the house the other night. I don't mean the house on Summerton Road in 1936, I mean the house on Shingle Camp Road in 1972. The game consisted of citing from memory all the possible meanings of the words "peace" and "piece." The kiddies with a little help from the old folks got quite a few of the meanings. There are a hell of a lot of them, especially of the word "piece," including of course the meaning the littlest kiddy didn't quite comprehend:

"*Slang (vulgar)*, coitus or a person considered as an object of coitus."

And that takes us back to Rose and the Reverend Jimmy, doesn't it? Good old jug-eared psalm-singing Reverend Jimmy, a man of God whom Dave hardly would have the nerve to beat half to death. As I said, Rose called her shots a little more carefully this time. Amen, Sister Rose! Amen, indeed, the bear sees the barn! Praise the Lord, call Eastern Airlines for a whispering jet, the bear sees the barn and the little red cherry is hanging on the bough—amen!

The terrible and merciless beating of Buster at the Firemen and Policemen Fourth of July barbecue made one thing very, very clear: if something wasn't done and done soon, Rose was going to get her crazy blonde head blown off. When Daddy heard about it he said:

"Well, of course it's none of my business but I can't just stand by and do nothing. I shall go to Atlanta and get Mother! There is no other way to prevent a tragedy in regard to that goddamn girl. If she will listen to anyone, she'll listen to Mother."

Daddy telephoned Dave and apologized for intruding into affairs that were not his own, but naturally he'd heard from us children about the fracas at the barbecue and he wondered if Dave had any objection if Mother spoke to Rose. "I think Mrs. Hillyer might be able to help straighten her out a little, Dave," he said. "Rose loves my wife and believes her every word is gospel. But I don't want to interfere in your lives. If I am being nosy, just tell me."

Dave was stiff and seemed mad as a stomped-on toad

frog, Daddy said, but he had no objections—sure, let Mrs. Hillyer go on and talk to her, that would be all right. After a while Dave loosened up a little and suggested they also might want to call in the minister of his and Rose's church. The minister, Dave said, was aware they were having troubles and Rose seemed to like him a lot and look up to him. She'd called on him a number of times to discuss her problems. Perhaps, said Dave, Mother and the minister combined could make a dent on Rose. *No,* he himself would *not* come to any meeting, declared Dave. He had already said all he could to Rose and his words had no more effect on her than rain on a wild duck.

Daddy took me with him for company when he drove down to Emory University to bring Mother home on the following week end. In the car going down he talked for quite a bit about the whole thing, as if half to himself although he asked my opinion on certain points.

"Well, son," he said wearily, "I hope your mother can do something. Of course Dave knows, he knows all right, but he hasn't got absolute proof, it's not the same thing as catching her red hand. He says she declares with cool injured innocence that she's done nothing at all, there's nobody in this hen house but us chickens, that's what she says. And strangely enough a man will kind of accept that, even though he knows better. The truth is, even though it's as plain as the blonde hair on her crazy head, the poor man just can't *quite* believe it about Rose. There's a remote chance she didn't actually do anything with this fireman Buster, a distant possibility that all she did was kiss him and mess around with him a little and let him fiddle with her, that she didn't actually get down to hard pan and make total whoopee. He doesn't *know* for a *fact* that she did it, and as long as she coolly denies it he can cling by his fingertips to the miserable hope that maybe she didn't. You see, son, the poor man can't believe it because he doesn't *want* to believe it, he desperately doesn't want to believe it. That damnable girl! She's got a screw loose, son, a screw is loose in her blonde head. I'm really outdone with her, the damn little misbehaving bitch, she gets a good man and look how she's acting! I'm so outdone with her I can't even talk to her. When I even look at the little nut I feel like putting her across my knee and pulling up her dress and spanking her ass with a hairbrush, whacking the hell out of it until she hollers her head off and learns a lesson. Damnable girl! But somebody ought to talk to her, it isn't too late, not yet—if we could make the little fool cut out the monkey business right now, this thing would blow over. Well, let us hope your mother is inspired! I don't know what else in God's name to do. It's a pluperfect mess, son. What we have here is an irresistible force on a dead collision course with an immovable object, and that is the exact size and substance of it. If that man catches her red hand, he'll blow out her brains and probably his own as well."

It was a tiring trip in terrible July heat and when Mother got home she took a short nap, then had one of her three daily Coca-Colas and smoked one of her seven daily cigarettes, using as was her custom a bobby pin to smoke it down to a tiny stub. Then she said:

"All right, Brother, I am ready now. Before Rose and Reverend Pollock arrive, let's do a little *emotional research.* Where's Dolly? Waski, you go get her. And where's Daddy? Ask Daddy to come in if he's finished fixing the roof or whatever it is he's fixing. Now, Brother. Before the little children get here, let me ask you this. You know Rose better than almost anybody, in some ways I think better than either me or Daddy. What is your honest opinion? Is Rose really *doing* anything now or is she just *flirting?*"

"Well," I said, "I'm sorry, Mother, I hate to say it, but . . . I think she *did* something at that barbecue."

"Are you sure about that?"

"Well, I didn't *see* her do it. But it couldn't have been clearer what happened. She didn't leave any doubt lying around. Of course Dave couldn't prove it. She said all she did was catch a couple of cute catfish, but this was a cool little insulting lie that made the truth even more obvious."

"Ummm-mm," said Mother, "sounds flounty."

"Yeah, it was flounty. One of the flountiest things I ever saw."

"Hmm. Now why would she want to be flounty about this? What is her purpose, Brother?"

"She's furious at Dave," I said. "I don't know why. He's very nice to her. But she's completely furious at him. I also got the funny feeling she was defending herself. She told him to quit *closing her in.*"

"Closing her in?"

"Yeah, she said he was sitting on her head and she couldn't breathe."

"Hmm," said Mother. "So it's kind of a defense, this thing."

"Yes. Yes, I felt that. Like she was defending herself, with her back to the wall. That's what it was kind of like."

"Umm-hmmm," said Mother, "very interesting. Flounty and furious. Back to the wall, mmm. I'm getting a vibration. Yes, um-hmm, I'm definitely getting a vibration. Youth. Extreme youth. She's not twenty emotionally, no, Brother. She's about fifteen emotionally. Rose is very naïve, very childlike. Her sense of right and wrong is not fully developed, especially about sex. Bad background, boys fiddling with her when she was a child. Different standards. A weapon for her. Suddenly has husband, wants breakfast, get up, fix supper, put out the cat. Demands, demands, it isn't fun, he's imposing on her. Responsibility! That is the one thing youth cannot endure and the mark of maturity itself, the courage to take responsibility. That is her problem, Brother. Rose is too young to accept fully the responsibility of marriage, which is an *extremely* difficult relationship even for a mature person. What do you think of that?"

"Well . . ." I said. "Rose took a lot of responsibility here in the house. I don't think she'd be mad at him like that just for asking her to fix breakfast."

"Breakfast is the least of it, Brother. It's the emotional demands people make that are so exhausting and such a pain in the neck. To be loved is a trial. That is why it takes a truly generous person to allow himself or herself to be loved. Loving a person is fun, but being loved is a pain in the neck."

"Well, she's furious at Dave about *some*thing," I replied. "I can guarantee you *that.* I didn't know Rose was capable of that kind of anger, although once or twice she talked to me a little like that—called me a little redheaded thing and told me to . . . stop doing whatever I was doing."

"Oh, Rose can get angry if you provoke her enough,"

said Mother. "She's no person to trifle with. Definitely not. But I have another thought along the lines of flounty and furious. Try this, Brother. She wouldn't actually have to *do* anything to be flounty. She could just *pretend* she did something and it would work just as well."

"I don't think she's pretending, Mother. In fact, I am very sure she isn't. Whatever her reason, she's playing for keeps, this is no game. She's not pretending."

"Well, she *could* be, though. And I really think she is. I suppose you are right to a certain extent about when before Rose was married. We'd better face it, she probably *did* do something with *some* of those boys and men, before she met Dave. Otherwise, what were all of them fighting about?"

"They probably had a motive," I replied.

"Yes, they probably did. Of course you've got to realize, if you want to be fair, that Rose doesn't have the same background as a Southern middle-class girl, not at all. Sex doesn't mean the same thing to her. But I still believe a lot of it was flirtation, just innocent flirtation. You've got to remember Rose is young, much younger than her years even though in some ways she's quite mature, actually. She doesn't realize how dangerous flirtation is, how it upsets men and makes them hotheaded and wild. They want to grab a woman if she flirts with them and Rose doesn't understand this. Don't you agree?"

"Well, I think she understands it," I said.

"No, Brother, she doesn't. Rose doesn't realize her behavior isn't just amusing, that it makes men seriously want to grab her. She thinks flirtation is just fun, a kind of game, a ha-ha thing. Whee-ee, I'm wearing silly clothes that show my hiney, and all the boys are lookin' at me, ain't I somepin'? You see, Brother, she wants attention."

I felt her approach wasn't quite on the mark, but she had great confidence in it. Mother, although slightly cuckoo and sometimes off the deep end, was far from a fool and her persistent refusal to accept the facts about Rose puzzled me at that time quite a bit. The explanation, however, I believe is very simple. She loved Rose for many reasons, but most of all for a quality I have already mentioned that they shared: an abomination of cruelty and meanness.

Therefore, in Mother's reasoning, since all evil in life came from the cruelty in the human heart and all goodness came from the power of love, and since at the same time Mother was an awful puritan who thought that to have illicit sexual relations was practically equivalent to eating human flesh, the answer was obvious—Rose wasn't cruel and evil, thus Rose didn't *really* do anything, she just flirted.

And so, despite all kinds of glaring proof, Mother held to her flirtation theory. She couldn't believe Rose could do anything truly bad, so she simply turned her back on it and looked away. "Turn your back, and look away" was the watchword of them both, the principle by which they endured and persevered despite all the terrors of a mysterious life and a brutal world. Turn your back, and look away—look away from the ugly and impossible world in which we live to a better world easily conjured into existence by the creative power of life, look away to a world of beauty and peace. Mother had picked up the expression from Rose and used it often, to Daddy's disgust. "How can I turn my back," he would ask, "when we can't pay Rose's horrible hospital bills? How can I turn my back, when scoundrels are hollering and punching each other's noses in the woods outside our house? You can turn *your* back, but how in the hell can I turn *mine?*"

Mother didn't believe Rose really "did" anything, and since I was certain she was wrong I was doubtful Daddy had achieved much by our tiring trip down to Atlanta and back again. The trip took a good three hours in those days, one had to go through every little town and avoid dogs and chickens on the highway. Great Atlanta was a long way away in 1935 and 1936, although as a matter of fact we went there often. Mother did much of her shopping at Davison-Paxon's and Rich's, and she owned property on Peachtree Street, a vacant lot upon which once had rested the Victorian home of her stepfather, who had been a mayor of the city and for whom one of its principal streets is named. Mother, as perhaps I have said, had been a wealthy heiress, she'd had quite a lot of money until Cousin Ben stole two-thirds of it and the Great Depression came, which caused Daddy sadly to observe: "I thought I was on my way downtown, on the shrewd theory you can love a rich woman just as easily as you can a poor one, but somehow I missed the streetcar and here I am sitting on the curb staring at horse buns."

Mother's love for Rose misled her, for once the family oracle was totally in error. I was very doubtful of her approach and even more doubtful when she continued her emotional research by asking in all gravity Doll and Waski *their* opinion. Of course their answers were predictable. "I love Rose," said Dolly. "She never did anything really wrong in her whole life." "I love her, too," said Waski. "She never did anything wrong at all. She's perfect."

"See there," said Mother to Daddy with a triumphant smile. "The children love her, and children don't fake their emotions, they can't. Always ask a child about some person, never an adult. An adult will lie because he thinks he ought to, but a child won't, a child will invariably tell the truth. I don't mean about facts, I mean about emotions, and nothing could be clearer than that these children love Rose, therefore she can't be bad, not really, and that's important to know."

"Darlin'," said Daddy, "I have never known a person who could be so right and so wrong at the same time the way you can do it, you are brilliant at it. Now philosophy is very interesting and you are its master, but we have a practical problem. Dave is going to shoot Rose in the head unless you talk to her and make her stop misbehaving, that is our practical problem, dear."

"Shoot her in the head? I don't think that's any sort of thing to say in front of the children," said Mother. "And you're wrong, anyway, Dave would never hurt Rose, he adores her."

"Perhaps he wouldn't hurt her," said Daddy, "but I wouldn't want to bet my life on that. Dave has a violent temper and he's a proud man and he has been taking terrible punishment. If and when he ever catches her red hand, I wouldn't care to be standing in between them, it could result in sudden lead poisoning."

"All right, let's ask Brother. What do you think, Brother? Would Dave ever hurt Rose?"

"No, I don't think so," I said. "But he might. It would be close."

"It wouldn't be close, not really," said Mother. "He'd never touch a hair of that girl's head, he couldn't."

"Um-hmm, all right," said Daddy. "But don't you think it would be preferable not to take such a chance if we can avoid it, darlin'?"

"Of course I do, and that's why we're having this meeting with Rose and Reverend Pollock—and I believe I hear a car right now on the driveway. Don't worry, we'll do something about Rose's flirting, we'll meet the problem head on but tactfully, all of us, the children too. There is nothing shameful or murky or weird about it, nothing to fear. Flirting is a thing all people do to some extent and it's harmless within reason, it's a common thing in life and Brother and Dolly and Wa-Wa might as well learn about it. Besides, I want them present because they love Rose and they will reassure her, remind her she is among friends. After all, we have no right to lecture her. She's a grown woman even if mentally and spiritually she is still in some ways a child."

Daddy wouldn't stand for it. "How can you be so right and so wrong in the same breath? This time you're wrong on two points. First, Rose doesn't just flirt, those aren't blanks she is firing they are real bullets. Second, and this I insist on, these children are *not* going to be present in a conversation with Rose and this preacher. And I intend to make sure they don't peep and snoop, either. This thing is above their heads and I will not have them involved."

"Then we won't get anywhere, it'll all be useless," said Mother. "Don't you understand? The only way to influence Rose is by affecting her emotions, because she doesn't have much mentality, not in an analytical sense. She has a very high intelligence but she doesn't use it that way, she is not an intellectual and dry reason will never move her, only her feelings will move her."

"Honey, we cannot speak frankly in front of the children and I won't have it! What's more, it would embarrass Rose and this preacher both, it would tie their tongues. This is *not* one of your good ideas, it really isn't."

"Well, maybe you are right," said Mother, as Doll and I and my little brother listened in disappointment. "I hadn't thought about it quite like that, but maybe it would embarrass them. I guess I'll just have to appeal to Rose's feelings myself, somehow or other. But you can help, too. Don't pick at her or be mean to her, be gentle and kind."

"I am not going to say a word," answered Daddy. "This is your show."

And sadly it was a show Doll and I and my little brother missed. To insure we didn't sneak around and eavesdrop, Daddy made us all go back in the kitchen and play Monopoly with Miss Kate. I saw Rose and the rather handsome but jug-eared young minister arrive and I saw them leave with Rose in tears and a handkerchief to her face, but except for a brief minute or two in the hall while supposedly answering a call of nature I missed this particular confrontation.

However, I suppose it doesn't make much difference because the tack Mother had taken was altogether mistaken. I heard in fact enough to get the essence of what really happened.

"The bull of *responsibility* that bought you, Sister Rose! That is the price you yourself must pay, you must buy back that bull! Love was given to you, Sister Rose, love and tender care, and you must return it now to your loving husband, in His name, dear Jesus, praise the Lord, amen!"

And then later of course the inner essence:

"Now I understand it," wept Rose, a lily hand over her eyes as tears streamed down, "I understand it, I understand it—and I have found God and an inner peace!"

The Reverend Jimmy Pollock was hardly a bona fide "inner peace," he did not qualify as a pygmy hippopotamus at all. What sort of "inner peace" is a jug-eared minister? It's a *piece* of mild mischief. However, three days later Daddy did report distressing news he had heard from a member of the church to which Dave and Rose belonged. On the night before at a big church supper, the Reverend Jimmy's hotheaded, part-Indian wife while back in the kitchen with Rose had flown into a rage and dumped a large bowl of fruit salad over Rose's blonde head. They were alone in the kitchen and that might have been the end of it, but Rose didn't *like* fruit salad dumped on her and besides she had a letter to mail. So, she grabbed the woman's hair and pulled it hard and made her scream piercingly, then when everybody came running in she said:

"I don't care what you think, he only kissed me like a sister even if it *was* on the mouth! And what's more, nothin' happened in that car even if we was gone three hours! Why, he is a man of God, what kind of girl do you think I am—and besides, I got a husband and I owe him responsibilities, and there he is right now, Dave Wilkie, how about that?"

Rose had not found a bona fide inner peace, but she had sure sent Dave another Special Delivery and he had to sign for it, too, right there in the church kitchen in front of the shocked congregation. But he *still* didn't get the message!

However, I am convinced that what happened next was an accident Rose did not intend. It was a disaster, two elephants and a pygmy hippopotamus thrown in. As Daddy said and I agreed, even Rose would not go that far. The thing that happened next of course was that Rose found herself a piece that was truly inner and Dave caught her red hand. The irony and the wonder is that this squalid disaster did enable Rose to find in time a real inner peace.

18

Turn your back, and look away

ABOUT THREE WEEKS after the scandal at the church, on a hot August night almost exactly a year to the day from the time Rose first came to our house, she came to our house again, wild and disheveled, her dress torn at the shoulder and her cornflower eyes rolling with terror.

It was about nine o'clock when she arrived. We were all in the living room listening to the radio, a form of entertainment almost on a par with the picture show in those days, when suddenly we heard over Amos 'n' Andy or whatever the program was a loud tapping and rattling at the front door. Rose came stumbling in before Daddy could get up and let her in; she stood there out of breath in the living room doorway with a hand on her diaphragm, blue eyes wide with fright and trembling all over.

"Dave is drunk and he's got his pistol and he's going to shoot me!" she cried. "Quick! You've got to hide me! I done somethin' terrible and he's goin' to kill me!"

"Oh, Lord," said Daddy.

"Dave has his gun?" asked Mother in a feeble voice.

"Mrs. Hillyer, I done somethin' horrible and he's goin' to kill me for sure if he finds me! He nearly did at the house, I almost didn't get away! And he'll know I've come here, he'll be after me any second, you've got to hide me quick! Please, hide me someplace where he can't find me, quick!"

"Brother," said Daddy, "take Rose up to the attic and put her in that big old wardrobe trunk of Mother's, the one she had in New York—you know it, in the far corner. Leave it open one inch so she can breathe and put that old brown car lap-robe over it, then pile those old dining room chairs upside down all around it. Camouflage her, Brother, camouflage her good—now shake a leg, boy, get moving! And Rose, don't you make a peep up there, not a sound!"

I took Rose's hand and we hurried toward the hall, but in the doorway of the living room she looked back and said: "Tell him I'm sorry! Tell him I'll go to Savannah like he wants, I'll do what he says! Tell him if he'll forgive me I'll never do nothin' like this again, that I'll be a good wife to him from now on—tell him I'm real sorry!"

"Come on, Rose!" I cried. "Come on!"

It seemed to me inadvisable for Daddy and Mother to give any such messages to Dave; if they did, he'd know she was there. I pulled her hand to make her come with me and we ran up the stairs to the second floor and then up the narrower stairs to the attic where I hid her in Mother's trunk as Daddy had told me to do. An indication of her fright was that Rose was now too terrified even to talk, she could only make little whimpering noises like a crying puppy the way she'd done in the dentist's chair. I asked her if Dave had actually shot at her and she said, "Ohh-hh, ohh-hh," and seemed to shake her head but I wasn't sure if it was a shake or a nod.

When I got back to the staircase Daddy was in the front hall talking in a quiet way to my sister and little brother. "Now Dolly," he said, "there might be bad trouble around here, nothing to get scared about, but you and Waski go up to your rooms and shut the door and get in bed and *stay* there. Do you understand me? Right now . . ."

I myself went on down the stairs as Doll and Waski went up them and when I got to the bottom Daddy said: "You come on in the living room, Brother. You are an expert liar and Dave likes you, he might believe you quicker than he would me or Mother. We have *got* to convince him we haven't seen hide nor hair of Rose if he shows up, do you understand me?" I nodded and we went into the living room.

"Honey," said Mother, "this could be dangerous, maybe very dangerous. I hadn't counted on him being drunk. A man with liquor in him might do *any*thing."

"I am very aware of that and you are damn right it's dangerous. We'd better pray he believes us, that's all."

"Honey, I think you better call the police," said Mother.

Daddy seemed for a moment about to turn toward the telephone, but then he hesitated. "No," he said, "I think that is more dangerous, not less. The worst thing that could happen is for Dave to be pushed. He'll use that pistol on somebody if he's pushed, he might even use it on *us* if he's drunk and wild and out of his head. And to judge from Rose's fear I'd say that is about the size of it."

"Oh, my God, this is horrible," said Mother. "We're just sitting here helpless waiting for a drunk man in a rage to show up with a pistol! It's horrible! Isn't there anything we can do?"

"Just sit here calm as lettuce and when he shows up lie like a rug on the floor," said Daddy. "Lie once, then lie again, and again. Of course we can also pray. The thing to pray for first of all is that he doesn't show up."

"Daddy," I said, "there's a car on the driveway right now."

"All right, be calm, both of you," said Daddy. He got up, walked to the window, pushed the shade aside and looked out. "It's a taxi. Can Rose drive?"

"Yes, I think she learned how," said Mother.

"Then she must have taken their car, that's how she got here. The question is where did she park it? I didn't hear her drive up, but of course we had the radio on. She was out of breath though, as if she'd been running. She must have had enough sense to park the car some distance from here."

We heard the slam of a car door, the sound of a departing taxi, steps on the porch and then a loud knock at the front door. "All right," said Daddy, "now be calm. Don't let him think you're frightened." He walked out to answer the door as Mother and I sat quaking in the living room. A moment later we heard him open the door and say in a superbly normal, friendly voice: "Good evening, Dave. What can I do for you?"

"You can hand over Rose, that's what you can do," said Dave. To my relief his voice was not wild and he didn't seem drunk. At the same time, however, he was not exactly calm as lettuce, the way Daddy was and the way Mother and I were, or at least were trying to be.

"Rose?" asked Daddy.

"I know she's here, Mr. Hillyer. And I'm asking you in a polite way to hand her over."

"Why, Rose isn't here," said Daddy. "We haven't seen hide nor hair of her for a couple of weeks. But come on in, Dave, come on in."

Listening to him without seeing him, I'd thought Dave wasn't in such a wild state and that he wasn't drunk, but when he walked into the living room my heart sank. His face was scarlet, perspiration ran in streams down his forehead and the look in his eyes was half-crazy. And worst of all, he had a huge pistol in his hand.

To my surprise, Mother put on an act as good as that of Daddy, who'd been really brilliant at the front door. "Why, *Dave,*" she said, "what are you doing with that gun?"

"Don't worry, Mrs. Hillyer," said Dave. "I won't hurt you or any member of your family. All I want is *that girl.* Now where is she?"

"Rose? Why, we haven't seen Rose since she was here with the minister. What's happened, Dave, what's wrong?"

"Yes, Dave," said Daddy, "what's wrong?"

Dave was standing in the middle of the living room, his eyes slewing from side to side as if searching for Rose, but now he clenched his jaw in a kind of paroxysm of fury, angrily stuck the pistol in his belt, put his hands on his hips and turned to Daddy. "What's *wrong?*" he asked. "Everything in the world is wrong! She's a complete little bitch and I'm going to kill her! Now where is she, goddamn it, quit hiding her!"

"Dave, don't talk silly, you can't shoot Rose," said Mother.

"The hell I can't! That's exactly what I'm going to do, now for the last time where is she?"

"Dave, please, listen to me," said Mother. "You can't shoot Rose, you love her!"

"I don't give a damn if I love the little bitch or not, I'm going to shoot her! I'll take her out of here, I won't do it in your house, Mrs. Hillyer, but I'm going to do it and you're not going to talk me out of it, either, nobody is! I'm going to blow that little bitch's brains out! Now where is she?"

"Dave," said Daddy, "we give you our solemn word Rose is not in this house. I swear that before God Almighty and may a lightning bolt strike me and burn me to a cinder if it isn't so!"

"You'd better not walk out in a thunderstorm, Mr. Hillyer, because you are lying!" said Dave. "I know she's here, she parked our car right up the street. Now where is she, back in the kitchen, in the pantry or someplace? I want that little filthy, crazy bitch and I'm going to get her!"

Daddy, who had been sitting calm as lettuce in his easy chair with his legs crossed, got to his feet as Dave took the pistol from his belt and walked toward the dining room. "Dave, you're invading my house!" he said.

"I know, and I'm sorry about that," replied Dave from the dining room. "But I want that bitch."

"Stay here!" whispered Daddy to me and Mother. He set his jaw and strode into the dining room after Dave.

Mother and I sat in the living room in petrified silence for a while, then Mother said: "We'd better go back there. Daddy can't handle this situation all alone. Poor Dave is beside himself, but he isn't really drunk and he won't hurt her when it comes right down to it. He loves her too much to hurt her. Don't you agree, Brother?"

Until that moment I had been totally convinced Dave if he found her would blow Rose's head off just as he said. But through the years I had learned the family oracle was seldom wrong. Even when she was mistaken there was nearly always some truth in what she said. Could she be right about this? Dave was certainly a violent man; he had a terrific temper, an ungovernable rage inside him. There was no doubt about that, I myself saw him practically kill that fireman. And yet there was something soft in Dave Wilkie—not exactly weak, but something soft. I couldn't put my finger on it, but there was something *boylike* about him, he wasn't a man in the sense my father was. For all his toughness there was something *incomplete* about him.

"I don't know," I said. "He sure *thinks* he'll shoot her."

"True," answered Mother. "He thinks he will and he has to be given an excuse even if it's flimsy, a reason, an explanation. Daddy can talk him out of it with a little help, that's what Dave wants. I imagine Daddy has already made some progress, let's go see."

When we got back to the kitchen Daddy had a pint of whisky in his hand and was trying to persuade Dave to have a drink with him. "All I'm asking is that you have a drink with me, Dave. It's the least you can do if you've got any manners at all. You invade my home waving a loaded pistol, you upset Mrs. Hillyer and my oldest boy, you crash into my kitchen looking for a girl who isn't here—now have a drink, damn you!"

"Honey, I don't think *liquor* will help," said Mother.

"You be quiet, darlin', you don't understand this, there are times when liquor is a good idea and this is one of them. Again I say: Dave, damn you, if you've got any manners have a snort!"

"Do you deny she's here in the house someplace?" asked Dave.

Maybe Mother was right. It seemed to me there was a subtle difference in the look in Dave's eyes and in the tone of his voice. Maybe it was true, maybe he didn't want to shoot Rose but wanted to be talked out of it. Well, if he'd accept a drink from Daddy and sit down at the kitchen table . . . but Mother didn't like it, *liquor* was one of her pet abominations. Glenville had local prohibition, no booze was in the town except that provided plentifully by bootleggers such as Rose's old boy friend Horton; whisky in most respectable homes in those days was a down-in-the-basement thing, and Daddy rarely ever touched it in front of Mother or any of the rest of us.

"I don't say she's here and I don't say she isn't here," replied Daddy. "All I'm saying is that if she is here she can't get away. Have a snort, Dave, and shoot her later."

"I've had a couple already, I don't need no drink," said Dave.

"Well, damn it, *I* do!" said Daddy. "And I am damned if I'm going to drink alone!" He sloshed whisky in one glass, then sloshed more in another, picked it up and held it out to Dave. "Here, damn you! If you don't take this drink, Dave, I'll be deeply offended!"

Slowly, Dave lifted his hand and took the glass of whisky.

Daddy had got him. There was nothing left but a mopping-up operation. It would take a little deftness, but that was all it was, a mopup.

"Now sit down, you can't drink whisky standing up, it's uncivilized." Daddy took a chair and banged it down hard on the kitchen floor near Dave. "Sit down, son. And you too, Mother. You can join us also, Brother. I'd give you a drink too if you were a little older."

Slowly, Dave sat down. The look in his eyes was very different now; his shoulders were bowed and a weariness seemed to have come upon him. He ran a hand through his hair, which had begun to get a little thin on top, then adjusted the pistol in the belt of his pants. Dave didn't have on his police uniform, he wore ordinary slacks and a white shirt with the sleeves rolled up to expose a tattoo on his bulging right bicep: the word *"Mother"* in a heart.

"Maybe I *can* use this drink," said Dave in a weary voice. "This has been the most awful day of my life, Mr. Hillyer. God knows that is true, the most awful day of my life."

Daddy asked gently: "What happened, Dave?"

Dave was silent for a moment, then took a swallow of his drink and said: "I'll never understand her, Mr. Hillyer. I'll never understand that girl, not if I live to be a thousand. Never. I'll never understand her, she is beyond me."

Silence. Daddy didn't say anything, and I wasn't about to open my mouth. Mother finally said: "I suppose . . . she was . . . unfaithful to you? Is that what happened, Dave?"

Dave smiled a little bitter smile. "Unfaithful, Mrs. Hillyer? That's the least of it. You can't imagine what that girl did. You'd never dream what she did in a hundred years." Dave paused to take another little swallow of his drink, then turned again to Mother. "Mrs. Hillyer, do you want me to tell you what Rose did? Do you really want me to tell you?"

"Well, yes," said Mother, "why don't you? I'd like very much to know, because then we can understand it. What happened, Dave?"

Dave paused, a miserable heavy frown on his face, then he braced his shoulders and said: "Well, I better start at the beginning. It all come on, Mrs. Hillyer, very quick. Very quick and out of a blue sky. I couldn't believe it. There never was a more amazed man than me, I almost felt like I'd gone crazy. When we was first married Rose seemed real happy, she seemed happy for quite a while, then all of a sudden she started running around. Just all of a sudden. No reason. She didn't say nothing, she just started running around."

"How did you know this?" asked Mother.

"Why, she didn't make any secret of it," said Dave. "Of course she'd look me right in the eye and swear she hadn't done a thing, but it was plain as day what she was up to. Buddy, you saw her at the barbecue, you know what I mean, the way she held them little catfish right under my nose?"

"Yeah," I answered, "like she was telling you what she'd done."

"That's right," said Dave, "like she was telling me."

"Dave," said Mother, "are you sure a lot of this wasn't just flirtation? A girl who's not accustomed to marriage and responsibility will resent her husband even if she loves him, she'll sometimes try to get back at him by flirting with other men. Are you sure that's not all this was?"

"I couldn't be one hundred per cent sure," said Dave. "That's why I didn't know what to do. But I really was sure, there wasn't no doubt."

"Shouldn't there be, Dave?" asked Mother. "Isn't it possible Rose hasn't *actually* been unfaithful to you at all?"

Dave stared intently at his glass, slowly lifted it, drank the remaining whisky and put it down. I saw Daddy's hand tighten on the pint bottle, lift it several inches and stop. Dave didn't seem to notice this. He was lost in thought. Finally he said, "She was unfaithful."

"Another drink, Dave?" asked Daddy.

"Can't hurt, might help," said Dave wearily. As if without seeing it he watched Daddy pour out a third of a tumbler of dark amber fluid, bourbon I think it was. In those days, bourbon was Daddy's drink.

"It could be a misunderstanding," said Mother gently. "Rose loves you, Dave. If there's one thing I know, it's that. Whatever the cause of this trouble between you, Rose loves you."

Again, Dave seemed unable to answer. He took a swallow of whisky, squinted in misery down at the table and said: "I'm afraid not, Mrs. Hillyer. I know you mean well, but it isn't any misunderstanding and there's nothing else I can do but shoot her. I love her. . . ." Here Dave's voice almost broke. "I love her even after what she did, that's the worst part . . . I still love her, but I can't live with her any more and that's why I've got no choice but to shoot her, because I can't live without her either. I've got to shoot her and I don't want to, the thought of hurting her makes me sick inside. I'll blow my own brains out the minute I do it, there's no doubt about that. I don't want to live, I don't want to live at all after what happened."

Daddy and I exchanged a glance and I am sure the same thought was in our minds. Dave's young boy, Tom. Who else could it be? Daddy had said he didn't like the idea of the boy being right there under her nose and I myself had been a little worried by the overaffectionate way Rose talked about this boy. It had to be Dave's young son, but Daddy and I had both agreed even Rose wouldn't go that far. Rose wouldn't deliberately do such a thing. If it had happened, then it had to be an accident sort of like the first part of her night with me. That was obviously true: Rose herself at this moment was horrified and stricken with guilt at what she'd done. It was that boy Tom and it was an accident, a thing she had not intended to do—she'd felt no guilt about Buster and the Reverend Jimmy, but they weren't accidents.

Mother was puzzled. "What *was* it, Dave?" she asked. "Why have you got to shoot her even though you love her and don't want to?"

Dave took another swallow of his drink. He seemed to be getting a little tipsy. Evidently, he'd had quite a few already. "Well, Mrs. Hillyer," he said, "you wouldn't want to know about it, a lady like you, it's too awful to talk about."

"But I do want to know," said Mother. "We've got to try to understand Rose, Dave. There's no other hope, no other way, we've got to try the best we can to understand her."

"There's no way to understand her," said Dave.

"Well, Dave, we can *try,* can't we? Isn't that all we can do in life, try and understand the people we love?"

"All right, I'll tell you if you really want to know. But I

hate to, not only because you're the kind of lady you are but because it makes me sick inside even to think about it. You're not going to like it either, Mr. Hillyer, and I got to say I don't think a young boy like Buddy ought to hear such a thing."

I wasn't about to let him get rid of me. Quickly, I said, "I want to hear it. I think I already know what she did, and I bet I know exactly how it happened."

Dave glanced at me with a little frown and so did Daddy, but Mother jumped in at once. "Brother loves Rose," she said. "You'll value his opinion, Dave."

"Well, all right," said Dave, "if you don't mind the boy hearing something pretty awful I don't care myself, nothing matters to me. You said it could be a misunderstanding, Mrs. Hillyer, but Rose was unfaithful, I saw it with my own eyes. Now I'm sorry, I hate to tell decent people such a thing, but do you know what that little bitch did? Do you know what she did? I . . . I . . ."

"Tell us, Dave," said Mother softly.

"I . . . I hate to say this, I do. But . . . well, it was *my boy Tom*, my son, the person I love most in the world next to the little bitch herself. He is seventeen years old, Mrs. Hillyer, that's all, not much more than a child and my own son besides. All right. I got off duty early this evening and came home and found her in bed with the boy, both of them naked as the day they were born. And not to leave any doubt at all in your mind, he was on top of her and her arms and legs were around him when I opened the door, they were *in the act*, her and him. Now what do you think about *that*, Mrs. Hillyer? Am I right to call her a bitch? *Am* I? What would you call her? And what else can I do but shoot her, blow out her damned brains? *My own son*, a boy I love and have raised myself these last years without a mother . . . how could she do that to me, how could she do it? Like I told you, I can't understand her! How could she do such a thing if she loves me at all? How, Mrs. Hillyer?"

Mother and Daddy looked at him in shock and dismay. Dave was definitely tipsy now and the wild look had come back in his eyes. There was still danger in this situation, plenty of it! The thing Rose had done as she herself said was "terrible" and "horrible." By the moral code of the

South of that time, Dave had every right to shoot her, a jury would have acquitted him in ten minutes. And now in the memory of it he was getting wild-eyed again. I could read Daddy's thoughts—maybe the "liquor" had not been such a good idea after all. As Dave gritted his teeth and the muscles of his jaw rippled in his cheek, I said:

"It was an accident, Dave, a complete accident! Rose didn't mean to do that! I'm sure she didn't mean to do it and that she feels as bad about it as you do, maybe worse!"

Slowly as I spoke Dave turned and looked at me and as he listened a little startled frown came on his forehead. Mother jumped in at once.

"I told you Brother loves her, and he's right!" she said. "Rose couldn't have intended to do such a thing, it has got to be a horrible accident. She *never* meant for anything like that to happen, she couldn't have. Rose loves you, Dave, she'd never want to hurt you like that no matter what trouble there was between you. Brother is absolutely right, it was a complete accident!"

"I agree with that a hundred per cent," said Daddy. "Rose is not a cruel or mean girl. She didn't mean to do it, Dave."

"And I'll tell you something else," said Mother. "I'm not saying it isn't terrible, that she hasn't made an awful mistake. But a thing like that could happen to almost any human being, Dave. These feelings nature has given us can be overwhelming. It could happen to nearly anyone, and very easily to a twenty-year-old girl and a seventeen-year-old boy who aren't grown-up. She *didn't* mean to do it, Dave, and if you love her you have got to be brave and somehow find it in your heeart to forgive her."

Mother, Daddy and I had given Dave the reason, the explanation, the excuse he needed *not* to shoot Rose, and Mother's final advice to him was the *coup de grâce*. Dave crumbled, but fought on for a moment. On the verge of breaking down he said:

"That girl doesn't love me. She won't do a thing I tell her. I got an offer to go into the construction business in Savannah, a real good offer and it's a thing I've wanted all my life and she won't go with me. She won't leave Glenville, the girl doesn't love me, Mrs. Hillyer."

"She *does* love you," said Mother. "She told us to tell you she'd go with you to Savannah. She told us she'd do what you said, and if you forgive her she'll never do anything like this again. She said she'd be a good wife to you from now on, and she will, Dave."

"She told you that? She'll go to Savannah, and not act like this no more, she said that?"

"Yes, she did."

Dave was silent for a moment, his jaw clenched. He was obviously at the breaking point. "Well," he said, "about her and Tom, I guess it *was* an accident. That's what she said at the house, she didn't mean to do it. . . ."

"Of course she didn't," said Mother. "Try and forgive her, Dave."

Here Dave gave up. His jaw clenched hard, his eyes shut, he put his head down on his arm on the table and began to weep. It was an awful thing to see, a big strong man choking at sobs. Poor Dave did worship and adore Rose in his way. Surely he had got the message now and he would stop closing Rose in, quit sitting on her head. I felt a real pity for the man, his suffering was genuine and at this moment his effort to "shoot" Rose seemed downright pathetic. It was true Dave was not a man in the sense my father was, there was something boylike about him, but maybe now he would grow up, maybe Dave and Rose both would change.

"I'm sorry!" said Dave. "I'm sorry, I can't help it! It's these drinks, I shouldn't have had this whisky. . . ."

Mother put her hand on Dave's shoulder as he choked, struggling to control himself. "Dave," she said, "you and Rose can have a real marriage now. Suffering can bring people closer together than before."

"What am I going to do about my boy?" asked Dave. "I knocked my boy down, I hurt him pretty bad and threw him out of the house with all his things. That's how she got away, damn her."

"I know," said Mother, "your boy, that's awful. But time heals all wounds, Dave, that's a hackneyed saying but it's true. You haven't lost your son. All kinds of horrible things happen in the world, people endure all kinds of dreadful things. You haven't lost Tom, it'll take a while but you'll have his love again and he'll have yours."

"Well, even if it was sort of an accident with Tom," said Dave, "she's still crazy. What about those other men? *They* wasn't no accident, she done it on purpose."

"I think that was mostly flirtation," said Mother. "Rose is young, Dave. She's not mature yet, but she'll grow up and this experience will help her do it. In the long run it will calm her down and help her find real peace of mind. Painful things often turn out to be the best things, they force us to look at ourselves and see ourselves for what we are. Believe me, Dave, Rose will change. The shock and misery of this experience will make her realize she just can't behave like that, it will force her to become a new and different person. That's what spiritual growth is—*change*, the most painful and difficult thing in life, and the most necessary because when it stops you are dead, even if your body is still living you are dead. Dave, let me tell you that as horrible as this is, what you are going to get out of it is a real wife, and the only thing you have to worry about is smothering her . . . let her live, Dave, and you and Rose will have a beautiful life together."

The oracle had spoken, or as Daddy later put it: "Mother shot her wad." At this point Daddy himself cleared his throat and said: "I think Mrs. Hillyer is absolutely right, Dave. She generally is about such things, philosophy is her specialty. Rose will make you a good wife, now. She can't ever be the same again, not after a mess like this. I can tell you she's in quite a state. She's terrified out of her wits, convinced beyond doubt you're going to shoot her."

"What makes you think I'm not?" asked Dave, but it was a weary question.

"Oh, I think you *will,*" said Daddy. "I'd shoot her myself if it was me. The little bitch deserves to die even if it was an accident like Brother and Mrs. Hillyer say."

"Where is she?" asked Dave.

"If I produce her, are you going to shoot her immediately?"

Here Dave almost broke down again. "I can't," he said. "I can't hurt her no matter what she did, I love her too much. I couldn't shoot her at the house and I'd just seen her in bed with my own boy. A little later on when I grabbed her dress and tore it . . . well, it made me sick. I couldn't hurt her, I really kind of let her go when she run for the car. I could of shot her then and I didn't . . . I can't hurt her, I guess . . . I must be a weak man. . . ."

"That isn't weak," said Mother, "that is strong. Brother, go upstairs and get Rose. Tell her she can come down, Dave won't hurt her."

"Well, if Buddy is leavin' the room, there's *another* thing I want to speak to you about, Mrs. Hillyer, something real important."

"Go on, son," said Daddy, "fetch Rose."

"Okay, sure," I said, and got up and left the kitchen. But naturally I didn't go upstairs at once. I went down the hall then sped on silent tippy-toe cat feet into the living room and the dining room and up to the kitchen door, where I placed an ear at the crack to find out what that "real important" thing was Dave wanted to speak to Mother about that he didn't want me to hear.

"Well, this is a little embarrassin', Mrs. Hillyer, and I hope you don't mind if I speak to you about it. But . . . well, Rose *is* oversexed. It's a problem, and I think she'll always be like that, a leopard don't change its spots completely. To tell you the truth, real frankly, she . . . well, she wants me to . . . she wants me to be a husband to her every night, and that's not natural."

"Well," said Mother, and I could tell from the sound of her voice she was flustered. "I'm not sure that's *unnatural*, Dave, she's a young healthy girl. . . ."

"It's not natural, Mrs. Hillyer," said Dave. "I spoke to Dr. Graves about it and he said once a week was natural."

"Dr. Graves is mistaken about that," said Mother. "Doctors don't necessarily know anything about sex, especially a bitter old man like him. I think for a young woman who loves her husband to want him every night is . . . well, it's a lot, but I don't think it's unnatural."

"Mrs. Hillyer, I'll . . . *take* her, excuse my sayin' it, and then go to sleep and the dern girl will wake me up at three in the mornin' kissin' me. And that ain't all, next mornin' before I'm even woke up she's crawlin' all over me! That girl don't want to do it just once a day, she'd do it three or four times if I was able, and I'm not. A thing like that drains a man's nerves, it ain't healthy. She's oversexed, Mrs. Hillyer."

"Mmm-mm," said Mother, and from the tone of her voice I was sure she was blushing. "Well, three or four times a day . . . that *does* seem a little excessive. Maybe if she took cold showers . . ."

I had to go out of there and fetch Rose. Reluctantly, I tiptoed out of the dining room and back through the living room, then ran up the stairs.

However, "Go fetch Rose" was easy to say but not so easy to do, I had an awful time prying her out of that trunk and it took even more time to get her down to the kitchen. She was crouched down in a fetal position with her hands over her head and still whimpering when I got there. She wouldn't believe at first that Dave wouldn't hurt her, and then she said she couldn't go down there, she couldn't face them, and besides she had to pee something terrible, she was on the very verge of wetting her pants.

"Oh, Buddy, I can't face them!" she whispered as we picked our way through the attic. "I can't face them after what I done, I can't! Do your daddy and momma know what it was?"

"Rose, don't worry about it, it's all right, come on."

"But Buddy, I screwed Tom, his own son! Do they know?"

"Yeah, they know. Come on, Rose."

"Ohhhh-hhh," she groaned. "Ohhh-hh, I can't face them. And on top of everything I got to pee so bad my bladder is bustin'! I dern near pissed all over that trunk! We'll have to stop by the bathroom . . . ohhh-hh, God, I've got to pee so *bad*. . . ."

Rose was in such a nervous state and trembling so badly she could hardly walk and twice she nearly fell down the narrow attic stairs, I had to catch her arm to prevent her from falling. When we got to the bathroom door she grabbed my hand and insisted I come in there with her.

"Oh, *that* don't matter! I got to talk to you, come on in here!"

"But Rose—"

"It won't hurt you to see me pee. Come on—if you don't I'm goin' to do it in my pants right now!"

I had no choice but to let her drag me into the bathroom, then had to stand there while she yanked her white panties down to her knees and sat on the john and peed with a great prolonged tinkling splash. "Ohh, God, what a relief!" she said. "Ohh-hh, Lord . . . Lord . . ." She really had to go. The hissing tinkle went on for quite a while as Rose sat there with her eyes closed and her panties down around her knees, then abruptly it was over.

"We got to get down there," I said. "Are you all through?"

"Yeah, but let me set here a minute," answered Rose. "I got to think." Frankly, I found it slightly embarrassing, this what-difference-does-it-make peeing right in front of me. As she sat there with her dress held around her waist I could actually see part of her behind and the shadow of her pubic hair as well, but Rose didn't give a damn, she couldn't care less. Of course she had other problems on her mind and then I had seen her body before. "Buddy," she said, "they know me and Tom screwed, Dave told 'em. But do they know the important thing, I didn't mean to do it?"

"Yeah, I told them that, Rose. Now pull your dress up, Rose, you're all naked. You shouldn't be like that in front of me and we got to go downstairs, they're waiting."

"Buddy, I got more serious troubles than bein' naked in front of *you*. Now tell me this. Does *Dave* know I didn't mean to?"

"Yes, he knows that."

"Well, I didn't, Buddy. I swear to God I didn't! I didn't even know it was goin' to happen till all of a sudden he stuck it in me! I didn't have no pants on and all of a sudden he stuck it in me and then I couldn't stop! Buddy, I swear to God in heaven I never meant to do it, I never even meant to kiss him! I swear I didn't mean to kiss that boy and I don't know why I did . . . he's cute, I like him a lot and . . . well, God knows the truth, Buddy, it was an accident, I swear it."

"That's exactly what I told them, Rose. Now pull your panties up and let's go downstairs."

"I can't face them," said Rose. "I got to set here a while and think."

I finally got her up off the toilet and out of the bathroom

and down the stairs to the front hall of the house and there she balked again and began to cry. "I can't face them," she said. "After what I done, I just can't go in there."

"Rose, Dave is going to forgive you and Mother and Daddy love you even if you're bad. Now come on."

At the kitchen door, she balked again. Weeping, she held back, and in an irrational tizzy of emotion and fear demanded I go in there and get her a cigarette to calm her nerves. "Get me a cigarette," she said. "I'll wait here, I won't run off."

Daddy and Mother and Dave looked up from the kitchen table as I entered. "She's outside but very frightened to come in," I said. "She wants a cigarette to calm her nerves."

"All right," said Daddy. "Here's a cigarette, son, take it out to her."

"Tell her she don't have to be afraid of me," said Dave.

"She knows that," I said. "She's just ashamed, that's all. And it *was* an accident, by the way."

In the hall outside the kitchen door I struck a match for Rose and watched her take little shallow puffs at the Philip Morris Daddy had given me. She still didn't know how to smoke. "Okay," she said, as her blue eyes again welled with tears. "I guess I gotta go in there."

But she didn't move. Cigarette in hand, shoulders slumped, she just stood there. I took her hand and opened the kitchen door and led her in. Blonde head bowed, she stared down at Dave's shoes and in a trembling voice said:

"Dave, I have got something to tell you and I want you to believe me because it is the truth. I didn't mean to happen what did and I swear it before God. I wouldn't hurt you like that on purpose and I wouldn't hurt your boy like that on purpose, either. It was an accident and I swear it on my soul before God."

"I believe you, honey," said Dave. "I don't want to tell you no lie and say I forgive you right now, but I am going to try to forgive you, honey. I am going to try to forgive you and forget it."

"That's all I ask," said Rose.

"It's all you deserve if I may say so, Rosebud," said

Daddy. "That is a manly statement, Dave. I admire it and I take my hat off to it."

"So do I, it's *more* than I deserve," said Rose. "Now about them other men. Dave, I fooled you. Nothin' really bad happened with Buster, you shouldn't of beat him up. I kissed him a little to make him stay off with me, that was all. And I didn't do nothin' but neck a little with that minister, then tease his wife into gettin' mad. I wanted you to . . . well, I wanted you to stop closin' me in. I was never unfaithful to you until this afternoon and that was an accident."

"Well, as I thought," said Mother, "it was flirtation."

"Well, I'll be damned," said Daddy. "I'll be a monkey's uncle. Rose, you ought to go on the stage. If you're not lying now, you're the greatest actress I ever heard of."

"I'm not lyin', Mr. Hillyer," said Rose quietly. "I never cheated on my husband until today and I didn't mean to do that."

I have often wondered if Rose was telling the truth on this occasion. It seemed to me at the time that she was, but I wonder. In her guilt and shame about young Tom Wilkie, she might merely have been trying to ease up on Dave. How could she get the minister's wife in such a fury if nothing really happened? How could she make the fireman Buster stay out with her over two hours at risk to his life and limb? Why did Buster look so extremely sheepish if all he did was kiss her a couple of times? If she was such a model faithful wife (except for the slip with young Tom), then how could she pay that calm and guiltless "love call" to Daddy? It is impossible to know the truth but I think Rose was *probably* lying about Buster and the minister, although my mother didn't think so and she was seldom wrong.

"Of course she's not lying," said Mother. "It was obvious to me all along that she was just flirting because she wanted for some reason to get back at Dave and that it had nothing really to do with sex at all. And about *that* problem—I think we ought to bring it out in the open, don't you, Dave?"

"Well, I don't know," said Dave. "You mean what we were talking about while Buddy got Rose?"

"Yes," said Mother.

"Sit down, Rose, you and Brother," said Daddy. "You make me nervous standing there like that."

"I think we ought to bring that problem *right out into the open,*" said Mother. "If we let it lurk in a closet it's going to cause trouble. So with your permission, Dave, I'd like to tell Rose what we were talking about."

"All right, Mrs. Hillyer," said Dave. "You're a lot smarter than me, if you think so go ahead."

"Rose, Dave thinks you are oversexed, dear. I don't think so, I think he himself is a little *under*sexed. But whatever the case may be, this could be a problem for you."

"I don't care about that," said Rose.

"I know you don't, but Dave doesn't know you don't. And people are afraid of sex, it terrifies them for some reason, no doubt because the emotions it arouses are so horribly powerful. But sex is just an appetite, like hunger or thirst, it's nothing to fear. I've tried to explain this to Dave, but he has it in his head you have such a *good* appetite for sex you can't control it."

"Well, I can," said Rose. "I never did nothin' with a man I didn't like in my life. Sex don't mean a thing to me by itself, it ain't nothin' but a mosquito bite, it's love I care about."

Mother then, as Daddy later said, shot her wad a second time, and even more powerfully than before. But after she did it a strange thing happened that I did not understand at all. A weirdly disturbing emotion came over me, helpless tears suddenly filled my eyes and I picked up Rose's cigarette from the saucer in which it was resting and took a puff at it and blew smoke at Mother, Daddy, Dave and Rose!

It was a very strange act and I wondered in puzzlement why I should do such a thing—was it pure emotion at Mother's remarks, which affected us all very strongly and caused Daddy himself to wipe his eyes with a handkerchief? Was it sheer relief that Rose and Dave had solved their difficulties and gotten back together? Was it simply a result of unbearable nervous strain caused by fear a girl I loved might get killed? Of course it was my dream to blow smoke at them like the filthy Hollis, but why at this moment? Did I know something they didn't, something I myself was not conscious of, was that why I blew smoke at them?

Well, Mother had said I had "practically no limits," but her remark was cuckoo, outrageous and totally untrue. All human beings have limits, even a freckled redhead in his prime, which fact is revealed plainly by the scope and dimensions of this work itself. Nevertheless, at thirteen I *was* an extremely precocious child and it is possible I had picked up some small part of Mother's own oracular powers. Probably not, most likely it was just pure emotional strain, but maybe it is true, maybe I knew something they didn't, maybe that is why I blew smoke at them and startled Mother and Daddy half to pieces. But let us get back to what Daddy called Mother's great second wad, the extremely emotional advice she gave to Dave Wilkie. Rose had just said sex didn't mean a thing to her, it was just a mosquito bite, that it was love she cared about, and Mother answered:

"I know that, Rose, but *Dave* doesn't know it, so I am going to give him a piece of advice. It's a good idea to imagine the very worst that can happen, because if you can imagine the worst and find an answer to it you are invulnerable, you are like a fortress that can't be taken by fear or shame. Now what is the worst, Dave, what is the worst thing that can happen? You are afraid you have an oversexed wife and she will be unfaithful to you again. You are wrong, she is not oversexed but that is what you fear. You *said* that to me, you asked me how you could stand it if she ever did this again. All right, I'll tell you how you can stand it! If you love her, Dave, and she ever does anything like this again, then turn your back, and look away! Turn your back, Dave, and look away, and let her live! *Turn your back, and look away!*"

19

Rose recalled

THE TALE IS almost told; Rose was nineteen when she came to our house and we have one more chapter to write, one more valentine for her and then we are done. In 1971 early in the month of October, I paid a visit down South to my father, a thing I tried to do as often as possible because he was old and lived alone. He was waiting in the yard when I drove up in an Avis car and greeted me in his usual insulting friendly manner. As I carried my suitcase across the stone patio, he cleared his throat loudly and said to me:

"Er, ah-HEM! Do you recall Rose, son, that big pretty blonde girl with the blue eyes who came to our house way back in 1935 or 1936 and caused such a damnable commotion?"

Daddy was getting very old. How could I not recall Rose? Well, at eighty-one I should have his faculties, if indeed I am in this world at all, which is most unlikely. Writers burn themselves up with whisky and cigarettes and vanity. The profession is not noted for longevity.

"Of *course* I recall Rose," I said with mild exasperation, as I carried my suitcase through the musty kitchen of the little house on Mae Street where Mother and Daddy had spent their declining year down among the sycamores, magnolias and hawthorns and where he himself still held on with an amazing tenacity, although he'd aged a little in the last few years and lived like an old bachelor with crotchets and peculiarities; the house, for example, looked as if it hadn't been dusted since 1966 when Mother died. "How in the world could I forget *Rose,* Daddy? Of course I recall her. Did you hear from her?''

''Well, yes, in a manner of speaking,'' said Daddy. ''You'll have the downstairs bedroom, son, Mother's old art room. I'll hike upstairs, I don't mind, I'm only a hundred and thirty-three. Take your suitcase this way, boy. Come along, son, come along. Watch out for that table, you idiot, you'll fall and break your Yankee neck. How do you stand to live up there, anyway, in all that snow? It's a horrible place, isn't it? Are you a polar bear?''

Something in his tone bothered me. ''What's all this about Rose?'' I asked. ''What do you mean, you heard from her in a manner of speaking?''

''Oh, I heard from her, I heard from her,'' said Daddy. ''I got a letter from her, she's fine. But there is some sad news. Let's get you moored, son. I know you potterack all over the world, but me when I arrive somewhere I like to get moored. Come on in here and I'll moor you.''

He was in a peculiar mood. I'd lost touch with Rose years before, it is sad the way those things happen, but Daddy and Mother through the years had maintained a sporadic but consistent contact with her. Rose kept sending them Christmas cards and Daddy himself cards on his birthday, she rarely forgot it. What was this he was saying . . . sad news? Had something happened to Rose?

''What is it about Rose?'' I asked. ''Did her cancer come back?''

''Oh, no, no,'' said Daddy. ''She got all over that. It's something else. I was going to write you about it, but then since you were coming down anyhow I thought I'd wait till you got here. How, by the way, are your beautiful wife and glorious children?''

''Beautiful and glorious,'' I said, as Daddy led me firmly by the arm down the steps into the ''sunken'' downstairs bedroom, Mother's old art room with the white plaster busts of Indians and the countless doodads and knickknacks she'd collected with a magpie energy in her declining years. The easel was gone, however, the spindly cheap pine easel upon which Mother had painted pictures as arteriosclerosis shut off blood to her brain, bravely painted pictures in order that her gifts not eat her up like cancer—a disease which in actuality had struck our old friend Rose, I hated to think about it, cancer of the breast at forty-nine, from which she had made a complete recovery after having the breast removed six or seven years ago.

It always upset me to go into that room, Mother's old art room. A painful nostalgia came over me as I unpacked my suitcase while Daddy fussed around and nagged at me, telling me how to unpack it.

"*No,* son, don't throw your shirt like *that.* You'll wrinkle it, you fool. Put it down neatly. Give it to me, give me that shirt, give me that shirt!"

I wondered what the difficulty was with Rose. Probably one of her adopted children was in trouble, that youngest boy had been picked up on another drug charge or something. Or was her husband ill? He was older than Rose. Could he be sick, or maybe dead? That would be terrible.

"Is her husband sick or something?" I asked, as Daddy flung my shirts around and criticized my pajamas.

"No, not exactly, Dave is fine," said Daddy. "Did you bring any Yankee whisky with you? I don't see any whisky here. How could a liquor-head like you not bring whisky with him?"

"I am not a liquor-head, you old rat," I said, "I just drink too much. And I wish you'd stop pussyfooting around with this business about Rose. Has that oldest son left his wife again? Or is the daughter laying everybody in San Francisco? Or is there something wrong with Rose herself?"

"Son, Rose is fine. It's another thing. I'll tell you about it when we have a drink out on the patio. Can you unpack this suitcase yourself? I have to piddle. Seems like I piddle constantly these days."

"I think I can unpack it, Daddy," I said. "Go piddle."

"Thank you, son. You always were a goodhearted boy. Insane, but goodhearted. Bring that Yankee whisky with you when you come out, I've developed a taste for it."

I held up a fifth of Teacher's. "It isn't Yankee whisky, Daddy. It's Scots whisky, popularly known or 'knowed' as Scotch."

"To me it's Yankee whisky," said Daddy. "But bring it

along, anyhow, son. I have nothing against Yankees except they're unnatural and can't speak proper English."

This was not too many months ago, about six, in fact. That isn't a very long time, but this book has gone fast. If they are any good at all, most books like bowel movements go fast—like a goose, *splot!*

As I finished unpacking and picked up the mess Daddy had made, once again a painful nostalgia came over me. There on the table beneath a little figurine of a horse was a time-stained piece of paper with handwriting very, very familiar to me. It was my mother's handwriting. The ink was green, faded, and a little Santa Claus was on the paper. How long ago had she written this? Ten years? Twelve? I picked up the paper and read what she'd written on that Christmas day long ago:

"To Dearest Papa—Beloved husband, Father, Grandpa, the life and love of us all. Grandma."

I stared down through a blur at her beautiful tribute. Mother was dead, enfolded at rest in the creative power of the universe. She was gone, the slightly cuckoo lady who although a Southern heiress had had the courage to go to Columbia University and seek a master's degree, who had gone to Emory University to finish her studies, who had taught history at the local women's college for a pathetic salary to pay my tuition for prep school and college, who had appeared to me as an angel in the sky at a boy's camp in North Carolina, who had told me I looked at her at six weeks of age and understood her—she was gone, the slightly cuckoo lady who had given me a large part of whatever gifts or confidence I might possess, she was gone and only the shadows of memory remained, and those shadows too would soon be gone . . . I would be forty-nine years old in another two months, the autumn of my own life had begun and after autumn winter comes.

A painful nostalgia gripped me, not only for Mother but for the South itself, the old South I had known and the people in it, a South that no longer really existed . . . would I never write anything about that South and those people? For years it had been "one of these days," the book about that life and those people. Dear old Southland! What was this hustling and bustling and prosperous Glenville, with traffic all over everywhere? Where was the little sleepy Depression town I had known? Gone, gone like Mother, at rest in the creative universe.

Daddy was waiting in the kitchen, trying to open a can of tiny little Japanese smoked oysters. He loved them. It was what he ate for supper a lot of times. "Love them, son," he said. "You can't beat those Japs when it comes to these tiny little smoked oysters."

"God knows how you keep living," I said. "The things you eat! And the way you live here! Look at that damned refrigerator. It must go all the way back to the hotel."

"Perfectly good, son. Slightly rusty, a little creeping fungus hither and yon, but got another twenty years in it. We aren't all millionaires like you, boy."

"Oh, shut up," I said. Daddy liked to call me a millionaire, and I think in some strange way he believed it. I tried to explain to him it wasn't so, but he wouldn't listen. He'd call up Dolly or Warren and tell them in all solemnity, "Brother is a millionaire." Well, it amused him, I suppose, my son the millionaire.

"Are you *sure* you wouldn't like one of these delicious tiny Japanese smoked oysters, son? It will melt in your mouth. Here on this cracker, that's the way to eat these little babies. Here, boy, eat it right up, it has minerals in it. Here, eat it. Open your mouth, damn you, open your mouth!"

"Daddy, get the hell away!"

"I insist you eat it. Come on, open your mouth."

"I do not *want* the damned thing right at this minute," I said. "I'll just have this drink, then we'll go to the Holiday Inn and get some supper. Put those fucking oysters in that horrible refrigerator, and come on out to the patio."

In deep Dixieland the month of October is almost summery and the stone patio was bathed in a warm yellow afternoon light. What a character Daddy was, what a unique personality. He hadn't changed a bit, he was the same as ever. A feeling of love for the old man came to me as we sat there sipping Teacher's in the golden Dixie twilight . . . well, Mother was gone, but at least he was still here, and in some ways I loved him more.

Comparisons are both odious and idiotic, but in some ways I loved him more. There was an innocence in the man

Mother didn't have, she knew too much. And there was another thing far more important. Despite Mother's screwball brilliance and her great powers of love and affection, she tended to withdraw from life and the cruel world in a way Daddy didn't. Brave as Mother could be at times, he was the more courageous of the two. The old rascal never withdrew, he was always in there. But of course Mother had had severe handicaps: a lonely childhood as a rich orphan, deafness, a terrible shyness and hypersensitivity and bouts of schizophrenia after each child was born and during the menopause. Comparisons are odious and unfair, Mother had her points, but I have got to say the old man was the braver of the two.

Something was wrong with Mother's endocrine balance and postpartum depressions for her were so severe they turned into schizophrenic episodes. The same thing happened to her for a few months during menopause. That was in 1947 and as a matter of fact it was the last time I'd seen Rose, who visited Mother because of her illness. Rose was thirty then and even more beautiful, she looked about twenty-two and I remember she had on an attractive suit and a pretty little velvet hat. Mother, who at this point was *really* in the fourth dimension, took one look at the little velvet hat with its lace and said: "Why, Rose, you have a saucer on your head. And it's got cherries, isn't it pretty?" Rose ran weeping from the room, but Mother got all right; she made about a ninety-five per cent recovery, which was normal for her, she was always slightly cuckoo even at her best.

"Do you know," I said, "it's been *thirty-six years* since Rose came to the house out on Summerton Road?"

"Thirty-six years, my God," said Daddy. "It seems like last week."

"It's funny you would mention Rose. I'm still waiting for you to tell me about her husband's heart attack or Rose's cancer coming back or her adopted son being killed or whatever it is, but do you know I ran into a man today on the plane to Atlanta who was an absolute *double* of Dave Wilkie?"

"He's dead," said Daddy. "Died about five years ago."

"Yeah, I know. But this man was *exactly* like him, a

horrible Southern idiot telling me how the niggers and kikes have taken over Washington, D.C. Do you remember when I ran into Dave Wilkie that exact same way on a plane to Atlanta not long after Mother died?''

''Yes, I remember that, son, I remember it vividly. He called Rose a nymphomaniac. You were quite incensed about it, wanted to get a gun and shoot the poor fellow.''

''You're goddamned right I was incensed,'' I said. ''That miserable son of a bitch, what a pitiful bastard he was.''

''Well, when he lost Rose it ruined the man,'' said Daddy. ''It destroyed him totally when he lost Rose.''

''He didn't lose her,'' I said. ''He threw her away.''

''Yes, I guess he did, son. He threw her away and it was the mistake of his life. It ruined him.''

In 1967, I was out at Kennedy getting on an Eastern Airlines flight to Atlanta when I saw a big, ruddy-faced, almost completely bald man in an expensive, ill-fitting suit. He was waving his ticket in the air and angrily telling some airline representative he had a first-class reservation not tourist, damn it, and what was the matter with that frigging airline, anyhow? The man's voice, if not his appearance, was strangely familiar. I *knew* him from somewhere, but where?

The first thought that came in my mind was Hollywood. My memory association of the man was unpleasant, somehow—had I known him in Cuckooland? Was he a cop at some studio? That couldn't be, most of the cops at the studios were nice guys, the real fuckers and monsters were the producers and the studio executives—and besides, they looked like foxes and this man looked more like a gaunt, balding, half-senile Great Dane than a fox. He'd said angrily he had a ''first-class'' reservation—God forbid, I thought, that I wind up in the seat next to him. Let it be some cute little piece of tail with whom I could exchange philosophical insights, not this Dixieland idiot with grits on his tonsils and muskadine jam between his toes.

The man did not have the seat next to me, but he nevertheless wound up sitting beside me on that flight to Atlanta. I was walking down the aisle looking for my seat and also looking at the cute little ass of a pretty stewardess, when I heard a voice:

''*Buddy!* My God, if it ain't *Buddy!* Well, now, isn't this the derndest thing, I never . . . well, by gosh . . . well, I . . . I just never! *Buddy*, you haven't hardly changed at all! Where are you sittin'?"

Who on earth could he be? Who in the name of God could he be, calling me "Buddy"? Only two people in the world still called me "Buddy"—my sister's best friend of childhood years, Jane Wilcox Smith in Atlanta, and my brother Warren in Palo Alto, California. Who *was* this man? Even my sister didn't call me that any more; she'd made a deal with me, she wouldn't call me Buddy any more if I wouldn't call her Doll or Doll Baby, and I had made that bargain with her. Who was this man calling me *Buddy?*

"Excuse me," I said with a pained smile. "Your voice is very familiar and I'm sure I know you from somewhere. You . . . you ran a liquor store out in Los Angeles, didn't you?—but no, no you're a Southerner, I know you, just give me a minute. . . ."

"Awww-rr-www, Buddy, *come* on," he said with an idiot false-toothed smile, "you know *me!*"

This happens a lot if you get your name in print at all. People think you know them. I had no idea on earth who the jackass was. "You're from Florida," I said. "That's it, Florida . . . or that little town near Florida, Ludohookie or whatever it is where they stop you with that red light that lasts seven seconds. You arrested me once, didn't you?"

"Buddd-eee!" he said in a tone of delighted injury. "It's *Dave Wilkie!* I'm Dave Wilkie, don't you remember *me?"*

"Oh. Oh, God. Of course, Dave, how are you?"

"Great, now where're you sittin'? Are you in first class? Lemme see your ticket."

Seats were exchanged and so it was I wound up in a seat next to Dave Wilkie, right next to the insane son of a bitch for two solid hours. Or maybe it was even more in 1967—did they have whispering jets then? At any rate it seemed like a week however long the flight took. The little stewardess with the pretty ass brought us drinks, thank God, and I had two. I could have used three or four.

"Well, I am in the construction business, Buddy, and without braggin' I have done real good at it. About ready to retire now, I am sixty-five you know, but you can't keep the old fire horse in the station when he hears that bell.

Buildin' a giant motel unit near Alexandria, outside Washington, D.C."

A clammy silence. I didn't know what to say to him. I knew he divorced Rose about a year after they moved to Savannah and she was not exactly a desirable topic of conversation. What to say? He seemed to be waiting for me to make the little conversational ball bounce—an error on my part, it was probably a rumble in his stomach, a fart or something that made him shut up for a moment; the man wasn't interested in anything said to him, he didn't even listen to it.

"Washington is a pretty town, isn't it?" I said. "One of the few American cities that has any beauty to it."

"Oh, it's all right, beats Jew York—" Not a misprint, that is what he said, Jew York. "—but the niggers and the kikes have took it over, just like every other city we got, only worse. The black shitasses will knock you on the head on the street and the kikes will come along and bury you and sue your estate for funeral expenses—ha ha ha ha. Little joke I heard the other day, pretty humorous, huh? Well, I have done real good in the construction field, Buddy. Yes, sir, build all over the Southeast, worked on a motel up in Glenville as a matter of fact, saw your Daddy. I am a kind of *trouble shooter;* what I don't know about construction ain't worth knowin', I knocked off twenty-eight thousand smackaroos last year and how's that for an old Southern boy once up shit creek without even a piss paddle? Of course you make a lot more, ha ha ha. Imagine, sittin' next to a world-famous writer *I* used to know personal! What a thrill. Tell me something, Buddy, how do you dream up all that stuff? Where do you get your ideas? And do you write when you're in the mood or do you just sit and write?"

"Well, actually we have a little black boy named Herbert who lives in the garage," I said. "He writes my books for me."

"Heh heh heh heh, same old Buddy. Always jokin' around. Almost as much of a joker as your daddy."

"Tell me about this job in Alexandria, Dave, this motel you're building."

"*Near* Alexandria," said Dave, and I suddenly remembered a picnic was not a barbecue because one of them had a lot of roast meats and the other didn't. No wonder he drove Rose crazy. I'd risk my life, too, to get away from such a stubborn idiot as this. "It isn't *in* Alexandria, it is *outside* it."

"I see. Outside it."

"That is correct. As for the job, well, the Jewboys give me a lot of trouble, and we use a lot of niggers on the job and they ain't worth a shit. I got to kick their black asses all day long. Oh, I move them, I move them, Buddy, I move those black bastards. I can build anything. You give me the plans and I can build a goddamn staircase to the moon, Buddy. That's right, I can build anything, but *she* never believed that. Doubted my ability all along, the little bitch. You know I never remarried, Buddy, you know that, don't you?"

"Well, no, I didn't, actually."

"I didn't, and that's the reason, she cured me of women once and for all, and I got to thank her for that. Heh! I wouldn't spit on the best part of 'em, let 'em spit on their own goddamn cunts. Who needs them? I don't even bother with 'em no more, but when I did it was once a month just like takin' a shit. Same thing, only it was once a month instead of ever' day. Just like takin' a shit. Once a month, here you are, baby, ten bucks, open your legs, poke it in, bang bang, and that's that, pull your pants up and go home. Why buy a cow when milk is cheap? You know what women used to cost me a year, Buddy? A hundred and twenty dollars, now you can't beat that. Fuck 'em and forget 'em. The little bitch did me a favor even though I didn't know it at the time."

"You are talking about *Rose* I guess?"

"Sure, who else? Oh, I got rid of her, Buddy, I didn't waste no time kickin' that bitch out. About a year, that's all she lasted. Hell, she was fuckin' everybody in Savannah. And don't let her kid you, she screwed the ears off both that preacher and Buster, sucked their pricks and all kinda stuff, just like she done in Savannah. What a liar she was! And what a little bitch—anything in pants, Buddy. If she saw any kind of a prick, Buddy, didn't matter whose it was, she'd suck it and fuck it. Your daddy and momma meant well tryin' to patch it up and I put up with her for about a year before I throwed her out, but it wasn't no good, Buddy, she was a total little bitch, that girl. Hell, I caught her in a motel with this long tall son of a bitch and boy did I beat the everlastin' shit out of *him!* She didn't marry him, though, she later married another poor dumb sucker and went to Winston-Salem with him, he worked for a tobacco company, but it didn't last. *She* couldn't have no lastin' marriage with *no* man, that little bitch, she left him, ran right out on him and married *another* poor sucker. All of this, in a period of ten years, four husbands! Now what kind of a bitch is this? I didn't even know that third one or what his name was, some kind of salesman I believe, he took her out West. But you guessed it, that didn't last neither, hell no. Do you know what she's married to now? A kike! That's right, some kinda kike horse doctor named Schapiro, who's got the nerve to have the same first name as me! Wouldn't you know it, Rose would wind up married to a goddamn kike? She was always crazy, Buddy, out of her friggin' head, and I'll tell you why. I tried to tell your mother, but she couldn't understand me, I'm afraid she was sort of a bleedin' heart that mother of yours. Don't get me wrong, a real nice Southern lady, but sort of a bleedin' heart, Buddy. She couldn't understand Rose, she was too much of a lady to understand her. But the truth is, that girl wanted to fuck all the time, she was sick in her mind and her cunt too. She was a nymphomaniac, Buddy, that's what she was."

I'd had enough. "Dave," I said, "you are as full of shit as a Christmas turkey and you know it. Now if you want to start a fight on this plane and get yourself in jail, go right ahead. But I am telling you, you are full of shit right up to your eyeballs."

With a surprising mildness, almost as if he were pleased, Dave replied: "I don't want to start no fight with you, Buddy. Why do you say I'm full of shit?"

"All right, I know Dave Schapiro, the man Rose married, I met him in 1947 when he and Rose visited my mother who was sick at the time. He is not a horse doctor, he is a heart specialist in Seattle, Washington, and he is a fine and handsome man and Rose has been married to him now for over twenty years, and she has been a faithful wife to him and a good mother to their adopted children. The little girl from the dirt farm has gone a long, long way and to call her a nymphomaniac is the most stupid and pitiful thing I ever heard in my life. Frankly, in my opinion, you ought to have your mouth washed out with Lysol. You know god-damned well that what you say isn't true."

"Well, she did have four husbands," said Dave with a strange little smile.

"Yeah, it took her a while to find Mr. Right, but she found him."

Dave smiled. He was *enjoying* this. "She used to call *me* Mr. Right. You remember that, Buddy?"

"Yeah, I remember it. Rose at twenty was very naïve and very trusting and very childlike. It took her until she was thirty to grow up and find the *real* Mr. Right. But she did it. She grew up and she found him, and you are full of shit."

Dave laughed. "You haven't changed a bit, Buddy," he said. "You're the same as ever, the same old Buddy, heh heh heh heh heh . . ."

For some strange reason it was funny to Dave, but it wasn't funny to me at all. I was appalled and horrified by what Dave Wilkie had turned into. The man was absolutely corroded with hatred. His venomous, slit-eyed talk about niggers and kikes was the least of it. Hate, pure unrestrained hate, had destroyed him. The Dave Wilkie I had known was *nothing* like this jabbering living scarecrow. What had *happened* to him? Dave had never had much upstairs, but I remembered him as an honest and kind man, and this gaunt balding scarecrow didn't have an honest or kind impulse in a single rotten bone of his body.

His talk about monthly visits to prostitutes was bloodcurdling and other things he said were as bad. He told me in all seriousness Hitler had had the right idea and George Wallace was the only hope of this great Southland, except that Old George was too soft on the niggers and the kikes who were trying to "take away our God" and ruin the republic—it was not a democracy, it was a republic and nobody ought to be allowed to vote unless they made twenty thousand dollars a year and paid taxes on property worth fifty thousand. "I am a great patriot," said the scarecrow. "I believe in this country, and our flag. And by God, I would disembowel those bastards that insult our flag and burn it up, and all that shit. I say shoot their goddamned asses off."

It wasn't funny. I had a splitting headache by the time we got to Atlanta. What could I say to the man? He was a maniac. And Dave Wilkie had been a decent, honest man—violent and brutal and Southern, but nothing like this. My headache was so bad and I had taken such punishment listening to him all I could think about was kicking him in his scrawny old-man ass as we walked off the plane.

But I wasn't out of it yet. The miserable creature *insisted* I go into the Dobb's House bar at the Atlanta airport and have a final drink with him. I wasn't about to do it, but then to my amazement he got tears in his scarecrow eyes and said:

"Buddy, there is something I want to ask you. It is a personal favor and it's important to me. I am a sick man, I had a heart attack last year, I wasn't expected to live. Buddy, please have a drink with me, just a quick one in the bar and I'll go on to my Savannah flight and you can get your rental car and head on to Glenville and your daddy. Please. I want to ask you to do something for me. Please, will you, Buddy, for old times' sake?"

How could I refuse? He sounded almost like the old Dave I had known years before. And he sounded in the bar even more like that Dave, a man who was sick in his heart and soul and wanted to be cured.

"Buddy," said Dave, "you get to Glenville quite a bit, don't you, to see your daddy? Well, Rose gets down there to see him, too, don't she?"

"Not in recent years, Dave. She writes Daddy, and sometimes calls him long-distance on his birthday. But she lives in Seattle."

"I know, I know that. But she *does* get to Glenville sometimes and so do you, and it's just possible you are going to see her one of these days."

"Dave, I haven't seen Rose for years and years. She writes me once in a while, a card or something when a movie of mine or a book comes out, but that's all. I'm not going to see Rose in Glenville, it's very unlikely. The truth is, I've lost touch with her, that happens sometimes with old friends."

"You might see her though," said Dave. "I think you probably will sometime." He put his empty glass on the bar. He'd had a double bourbon and had gulped it right down. A look of drawn pain and tension was on his face. "Buddy . . . the favor is, there's something I want you to tell Rose. I . . . I can't write her. I can't, not after what that girl did to me. And I'm not a writer, I can't write letters. There's something I'd like to say to her, and maybe if you see her you could tell her. . . ."

It was incredible. What could Dave Wilkie want to say to Rose after thirty years? The man was in a terrible emotional state, his gaunt hate-lined face was the color of whey, his big man-beating hands now crisscrossed with blue veins were trembling.

"Well, I don't think I'll see her . . . but what was it, Dave?"

He suddenly flinched, shrank, turned with a spasmlike motion and shoved money down on the bar. His back to me, he said, "Oh, fuck it, never mind. Don't tell her anything. Don't even tell her you saw me."

"What did you want me to tell her?"

"Nothing," said Dave, his back still to me. Were tears again in his eyes? His voice sounded that way. "Got to run, Buddy, I'll miss my plane. Give your daddy my best, it was nice to see you."

Dave Wilkie walked away with spasm Frankenstein steps and he didn't look back. I think probably he did have tears again in his eyes and that the thing he'd wanted me to tell Rose was that he still loved her, but he didn't say it.

In the golden twilight with my old father, who almost always would say what was on his mind and reveal what was in his heart, I finally put the question to him direct. Enough pussyfooting and tactful procrastination and abrupt artful changing of the subject—*what was wrong with Rose?*

"All right, Daddy," I said, "we have our drink, I am all unpacked and we are on the patio. You have prepared me for it. Let's have the truth now. Rose's cancer has come back, hasn't it?"

"No, son," said Daddy, "she is dead."

Dead? Rose was dead? The only possible way to put it is to say that literally and truly for quite a few seconds I could not believe my ears. There had to be some mistake. Rose of all people could not be dead, it was impossible, she could not be dead. In dumb shock I stared at my father.

"Rose is dead? You mean . . . she died?"

''I am afraid so, son. About a week ago. Her husband phoned me, she had asked him to call me if anything happened.''

''But . . . but *how?* She was young! Rose wasn't old!''

''She was fifty-six, son. Of course she didn't look it, nowhere near it. But she died the day before her fifty-sixth birthday.''

''But . . . what was the cause? How did she die?''

''Well, the cancer came back, I'm afraid I fibbed about that. But it was very quick, son. A month ago she looked in perfect health. And she didn't suffer, her husband made a point of telling me that. She was in the hospital only two weeks, and the last week she didn't know anything.''

I stared at him in silence for about five seconds, then said, ''Excuse me, I'll be right back.'' I got up, took my glass, went into the kitchen and put the glass by the fifth of Teacher's, then went back to the bathroom.

After a fit of grief in the bathroom, I went back to the kitchen, poured myself a huge slug of Teacher's and rejoined Daddy on the patio. ''Well,'' I said, ''you have knocked me for a hell of a loop, old man. A hell of a loop.''

''I know,'' said Daddy quietly. ''You loved her. So did I. It was an awful shock to me, too. An awful shock. Rose was so alive, it's hard to believe.''

''I *can't* believe it, Daddy. I know it must be true, but I can't believe it.''

''It's true, son. The girl with the cornflower eyes is dead, she is no more. She got cancer of the breast, was operated on and had a seven-year recovery, then the cancer returned. After a brief illness she passed on in her sleep, as the man with whom she'd lived in beautiful love and harmony for twenty-five years held her hand. That is what happened, son, and God rest her lovely soul!''

The story is ended. If the first sentence of this narrative contains its statement, then let the last contain its resolution. The fundamental question about Rose is answered and the final piece of mischief is pulled. *Never* turn you back on love, and look away!